# THE HARBINGER

## INFINITE DARKNESS
### BOOK 1

## H.K. FARRELL

VYREON PRESS

ISBN: 979-8-9899532-0-2 (paperback)

Library of Congress Control Number: 2024901526

Cover design by MiblArt

Formatted with Vellum

For Kelsey Marie, who always helped me weather the storm.

# AUTHOR'S NOTE

When I finally sat down to give voice to the ideas pinballing around my head, I had no comprehension of the journey I was about to undertake. I always enjoyed writing, had even studied photojournalism at one point in my frantic, bumbling quest through academia. At the time, I found journalistic writing uninspiring… perhaps more a statement about myself than the merits or evils of AP styling.

As a fresh-faced graduate of the United States Merchant Marine Academy, I worked as an engineer aboard large, ocean-going cargo ships. Often spending 90-120 days at sea, keeping the boredom and loneliness at bay was a full-time job. When I wasn't on the ship, I had more time on my hands than I knew what to do with. I knew the gaming/binging/sit-on-ass-and-eat-chips trap was an easy one to fall into. What better use of my time than to finally write the novel I'd been talking about for years?

After a couple false starts, tons of bitching, two hard drive crashes, and the subsequent loss of all my work, *The Harbinger* began to take shape. There were times when the words flowed onto paper like water from a tap. Other times, I would go weeks without writing anything that wasn't complete drivel. I've read a lot about people's writing processes; some having complicated, yet meticulous, ways they create characters and plot lines, others claiming to have the entire story detailed in their heads. I envy them.

*The Harbinger* was created through chaos. Pure, unbridled chaos. The ideas laid forth in this book are a galaxy away from the ones I initially sat down with. Chapters were edited, rewritten, thrown out, lost... you name it. If I've gained anything from this process, it's how not to write the next book.

On a more serious note, *The Harbinger* explores the highs and lows of an epic space adventure. Some of the themes contained within are meant for adults. I have struggled with my own demons over the years, and writing has become a way for me to deal with them. We live in a time where our collective mental health is perhaps the worst it's ever been, and this book is meant to entertain, but suicidal ideations and drug/alcohol abuse are no laughing matter. If you need help, please seek it out. No one needs to go it alone.

# PROLOGUE

RHYS KELLY LEANED HEAVILY against the railing of the three-hundred-meter container ship and listened as frigid steel-gray waves swished noisily down the hull. The cry of an osprey greeted his ears, shrieking its solitary farewell as the huge vessel maneuvered slowly from safe harbor and into open ocean. Beyond the breakwater, waves grew steadily in size until the ship pitched gently fore and aft, sending up a cool, misting spray that clung delicately to the vellus hairs on his arms like a web of morning dew.

After a frantically busy port stay, their return to sea brought a certain calming effect, a chance to breathe easy once again. Rhys closed his eyes, bolstering himself against the sense of futility that had begun to manifest over the last few weeks.

For as long as he could remember, Rhys had known the reputation of the *M/V Denebola* and what the senior engineering officers were rumored to be like. 'Incompetent and insufferable' were the first words that came to mind. He had picked up the seventy-five-day job in Seattle and, within a few hours, was steaming up to Dutch Harbor, Alaska. From there, the ship had made its way across the Pacific to the Far East, stopping at ports in Korea, China, and Japan, before heading to Los Angeles and back up the coast to the Emerald City. During his time onboard, they'd made that circuit twice. It felt longer, like a never-ending purgatory of shitty days and worse nights. If the previous eight months unemployment hadn't left him desperate for work, he'd have passed on the *Denebola* gig altogether.

Fishing into his shirt pocket, Rhys removed a carefully rolled joint and flipped it pensively between his fingers. He hadn't indulged such juvenile vices in years, but that was before conditions on the ship had deteriorated to such a miserable state. No one was happy. The Navigator, an aging worm of a man, spent his waking hours lamenting the 'good ol' days' when merchant vessels crewed as many deck officers as engineers, but that time had long since passed. Advances in automation had rendered the position near obsolete, something the Chief Engineer loved to rub in the poor man's face.

*'Ships will always need engineers. It's about time we stopped wasting money on overpaid baristas like you'* he'd say with a malicious smile, breath stinking of week-old coffee and cigarettes. Rhys knew the Chief was fooling himself. It was only a matter of time before the next technological hurdle made their jobs as obsolete as the Navigator's...

Distractedly, he struck a match on a spot of rust peeking from beneath the handrail's flaking white paint and took a long drag on the papery cylinder. Like a creeping vine, numbing tendrils of THC began to ease the tension in his shoulders, and he exhaled with a sigh of relief. Somewhere in the back of his mind, though, Rhys knew he should be careful. Getting caught with drugs, even a legalized substance like marijuana, would result in the suspension of his license at the very least. Regulatory bodies surrounding the maritime industry didn't screw around, harshly punishing infractions of the smallest magnitude.

The odd reality of it, however, was that he didn't care. One way or another, this would be the last time he stepped foot on a ship. He'd been toying with the idea of quitting for years, but the money and time off kept drawing him back... or it had until now. Now, all he wanted was to be back home in Montana with his wife Anne, his dog Sagar, and the solitary, snow-capped peaks of the Beartooth Mountains.

"Stop," he muttered in a moment of self-reprove. "This goddamn trip already feels like an eternity."

Rhys knew it was true. If he started dwelling on everything back home, the final two weeks of the voyage would crawl by at something akin to a snail's pace. His life already seemed to extend no further than the railing he leaned over. Sometimes, after a particularly exhausting day listening to the First Engineer berate everyone, his Montana home felt like nothing more than a dream, a tantalizing fiction that someone else had imagined…

He flicked the butt over the railing and watched it fall nearly twenty meters to the ocean waves. It was a little game he played with himself. How long could he keep track of the tiny white tube before it was no longer visible? Sometimes, he imagined it stayed in sight all the way down, to the point where it disappeared beneath the foaming waves, but probably not.

Rhys blinked and looked forward towards the horizon. Black clouds were gathering, and instead of skirting the storm, the ship appeared to be heading directly into the gale. Wonderful. So much for a good night's rest. He turned to head down to the galley when the radio on his belt crackled.

"Second Engineer Kelly, this is the Chief."

Rhys groaned inwardly and checked his watch – *17:49* – well enough after working hours to warrant a call unless it was an emergency.

"Go ahead Chief."

"I thought I told you to finish rebuilding that bilge pump before knocking off."

The voice was accusatory, and Rhys gritted his teeth to bite back a scathing retort. It had been this same shit, over and over, for the last sixty days. If the First Engineer wasn't publicly riding someone over some perceived infraction, the Chief sure as hell would be. It was one thing to ask him face-to-face, or on a private channel, but sending it out over the airwaves for the entire crew to listen in on was poor form. Rhys didn't require an attaboy for simply doing his job, but he'd been met with hostility since Day One without so much as a nod of acknowledgement from either of them.

"I left a note on your door. Wanted to talk to you at dinner–"

"Well, I don't *eat* dinner," the radio crackled. "That system doesn't have a backup pump, so is it done or not?"

*Two more weeks*, Rhys told himself. He only had to survive two more weeks without blowing his top, and he'd be home free.

"It's done," he said curtly and paused. Rhys knew what he was about to say was a bad idea, but… fuck it. Another fortnight, he'd be out of here for good. "While we're on the subject, Jefe, we do have a backup. Three, if you line up the crossover from our ballast system."

Rhys knew he'd pay later for airing the Boss's ignorance of his own ship. Whether that manifested as a bad evaluation or getting blackballed from the company, he didn't care. It was more satisfying to make a fool of such an unpleasant person than to worry about how this might look to anyone listening. Whatever consequences came his way would be worth it. For a moment, the conversation hung awkwardly over the airwaves before the radio crackled one last time.

"Copy."

Shaking his head at the pointless exchange, Rhys decided against showing his face in the galley and instead trudged back to his stateroom to prepare for the coming squall. Dropping his flashlight on the stained armchair, he tucked his lifejacket and neoprene survival suit beneath the mattress. This 'mariner taco' would keep him from rolling back and forth while the storm buffeted the ship, giving him the best chance at any sleep. He stripped off his dirty work clothes, showered, and climbed into bed.

From the nightstand, he took a battered copy of Robert A. Heinlein's *Starship Troopers* and began to read, the bug-filled worlds and thought-provoking political dialogue displacing some of the resentment he felt. Science fiction had always been his favorite genre. Every couple of years, he found himself rereading timeless classics by Arthur C. Clarke, Frank Herbert, Andy Weir, and James S. A. Corey. No matter how many times he picked up one of their novels, his eyes would remain glued to the page like it was the first time he'd experienced its brilliance. Tonight was no different. Despite overwhelming fatigue, he read page after page until finally drifting to sleep, the book tumbling noiselessly out of his hands.

At two in the morning, an earsplitting scream pulled Rhys from the depths of sleep. Several seconds passed before he realized its source, the stateroom's alarm panel, and he rubbed his face in confusion. He wasn't the Duty Engineer for another two nights, so why were the alarms ringing in his room? It wasn't the first time this had happened. Miguel, the Third Engineer was a good kid, but a bit of a lost puppy. He had forgotten to switch the alarms off Rhys's room and onto his own in the past. Once was a mistake, but three times was treading dangerously close to habit.

Bleary-eyed and annoyed, Rhys flopped out of the folded mattress and nearly toppled over when he stepped onto the floor. A moment passed before he realized why; the ship was listing almost sixteen degrees! Something was terribly wrong.

The panel still shrieked its high-pitched keening as Rhys stumbled toward the display to investigate. What he saw made his heart plummet. The "Assistance Needed" and "Fire in Machinery Space" alarms were displayed at the top, followed by "Main Engine Shutdown" and "Fuel Oil Pressure Low." If their engines had shut down on low fuel, it probably meant one of the high-pressure manifolds had ruptured. Hot fuel spraying over a hot engine… Rhys didn't need an alarm to tell him what that would cause.

Frantically, he threw on his coveralls and boots and sprinted for his fire station. Bounding down the ladder, he took the steps three at a time. When he reached the Damage Control locker, he saw Miguel disappearing through a fire-tight door and into the engine room with a portable extinguisher in tow. Beyond, flickering yellow light and the sound of a raging inferno sent a jolt of fear through Rhys's heart.

"Miguel, wait!" he yelled, pulsating the beam of his flashlight, attempting to catch the younger man's attention. What the hell was he thinking? The kid was going to get himself killed! Rhys knew he should wait for the rest of the fire team. If he acted rashly and went after his shipmate, there was a good chance the crew would have to rescue them both... but dammit, Miguel was right there! He could just go in and get him.

Torn, Rhys hesitated a moment longer before making up his mind. Grabbing the nearest breathing apparatus, he tucked the mask over his face and cranked open the bottle valve. He wrenched open the door, and a blast of hot air nearly knocked him backwards off his feet. Arms flying out to steady himself, he regained his balance and looked around.

Fire had engulfed the engine room. Everywhere Rhys turned, red-hot flames licked the bulkheads and ceiling, transforming the room into a skin-melting oven. A deafening roar filled his ears as fire consumed oxygen as fast as it was replaced. Terrified to move from the door, he searched frantically for Miguel, but the curtain of smoke was too thick to see anything clearly. He'd almost given up when a break in the oily, black shroud revealed a figure stumbling through the haze, heading toward the door. Mouth covered with one hand, Miguel waved at Rhys with the other, motioning for him to get out. Too late. With a scream of rending metal, the ceiling above crumpled, and a torrent of water gushed into the engine space.

Hot, dense steam engulfed the room as cold ocean water doused the blaze. Miguel was swept sideways out of view, and Rhys grabbed for the door, bracing himself against the oncoming wave. In a tangle of limbs, he tumbled out of the engine room, a wall of water slamming him into the far bulkhead. His flashlight flew from his hands, disappearing into the deluge. Dazed, he tried to rise, but couldn't. The air pack had become lodged beneath some unknown obstruction and refused to budge. Wriggling free of the straps, Rhys pulled the mask from his face and sputtered as seawater poured into his mouth. He clawed his way to the surface of the freezing water, but there was no time to catch his breath. It wouldn't be long before the lights went out, once the inrushing water shorted the ship's generators. When that happened, he'd better be somewhere else.

Doggedly, he climbed a ladder to the higher decks and finally heard the alarm he knew must be ringing: several staccato blasts followed by a single prolonged note, the signal to abandon ship. Rhys grabbed his survival suit and lifejacket from under the bed and sprinted toward the lifeboats. Throwing his shoulder into the door, he burst onto the starboard deck and immediately realized his mistake. He had gone to the high side of the ship! The starboard boats were no longer hanging over water. With the severe list, releasing the lifeboats now would only send them crashing down onto the vessel's exposed metal hull.

He turned around and raced back through the passage to the port side. There, cowering in the forward boat, was the rest of the crew. The cook, Jodie, had remained outside, attempting without success to release the wire gripes that held the boat secure in its cradle. Through the open door, the Navigator and remaining engineers shouted angrily for the man to hurry. Only the wizened Steward sat quietly, clutching his chest, and looking very much like he was having a heart attack. Rhys, realizing he was about to be abandoned, was livid.

"Were you just going to leave Miguel and me?" he screamed. Surprise and confusion passed over Jodi's face when he turned to see Rhys sprinting toward them. With a trembling hand, the young man just pointed inside the boat.

"I saw you go after Miguel," the Chief spluttered miserably. "That fire was out of control! I didn't think there was any way you could've survived. Normally, you should've–"

"Does this look normal to you?" Rhys shouted over the howling wind, waving at the devastation behind them.

"Just get in! None of us want to d—"

An explosion rocked the foundering ship, cutting off the man's blustering protestations. Rhys felt the deck beneath his feet undulate violently before searing pain erupted in the back of his skull. A wave of intense heat washed over him, and he felt himself falling… falling…

---

WAVES. Howling wind. Saltwater burning his eyes as he fought to keep his head above water. Fatigue. Such absolute fatigue. He wanted to succumb, to let himself slip beneath the waves. He was tired. So very tired. He felt himself letting go, icy darkness enveloping his body. There were hands. They weren't his, and they were reaching. Always reaching. For him.

---

THE SOUND of lapping water was the first sign his senses were beginning to return. Rhys felt himself rising through the fog of unconsciousness, becoming acutely aware of several pains that hadn't troubled him while he slept. Christ, his body hurt. A dull throb emanated from the back of his head, permeating his skull as if someone had struck him with a hammer. He lay there a moment longer, eyes closed while he tried to assess his injuries. Even the smallest movement sent sharp pain shooting through every fiber of his being.

Deciding he wasn't paralyzed, he opened his eyes. Above him, the canopy of an inflatable raft bathed everything in an orange glow, its brilliance worsening the ache behind his eyes. Squinting, he struggled to sit up, unable to muster enough strength to push against the soft rubbery floor, until he felt a pair of hands lift him from beneath the armpits and prop him against the flexible hull.

"Thanks," he grunted, looking up at whomever had offered help. It was the cook, Jodi. Rhys could tell he'd been crying. The young man's eyes were red and puffy, face streaked in grime. Seeing him, anger flashed in Rhys as the memory of the catastrophe filled his mind. Jodi had been trying to release the boat, an act that would have sealed the fate of anyone left aboard the *Denebola*.

Rhys was about to lash out when he remembered the Chief's words. *'I saw you go after Miguel.'* The old bastard had probably told everyone they were already dead. Jodi couldn't have known otherwise. Everything had happened so quickly, and the kid was just following orders. Slowly, his anger began to abate, and Rhys cast around for something to say.

"You okay?"

Jodi nodded but didn't respond, instead handing over some water from the raft's supply kit.

"Thanks. Did you find the beacon?"

Jodi still didn't answer, just sat trembling, arms wrapped around himself. Rhys tried to collect his thoughts, wondering what he could possibly say to make his companion feel better.

"You're scared. I am too, but there's still a chance we make it through this." He paused, watching the spindly-armed cook, glad the man had mustered enough strength to get him into the raft. "And thanks for pulling me out. I wouldn't have lasted much longer."

A few more moments passed in silence before Jodi seemed to regain some of his wits.

"Explosion threw us inna water. I came up and saw the lifeboat swingin' crazy-like from one hook. People inside… they dead. All dead. Lotta blood everywhere…" Jodi shuddered, a haunted look on his face, and continued in a choked voice. "The raft popped up, and I climbed in and saw you floatin' ways off. Didn't find no beacon or nothin'."

Rhys nodded glumly. He'd been afraid of that. Without the emergency beacon, their chances of survival were significantly diminished. Lost in his own thoughts, he closed his eyes to contemplate their situation. How long could they last with the raft's supplies? A few weeks? A month? He couldn't remember and pressed a hand to his parched throat, wanting desperately to quench the thirst that burned there. He wouldn't though, not yet. Their provisions had to be rationed for as long as possible. Leaning forward, he pulled back the canopy covering the raft and saw nothing but blue sky and sunshine. Bright, hot, burning sunshine. There was no ship, no wreckage, just endless horizon. Rhys tied open the flap, praying it would coax a nonexistent breeze through the sweltering raft. Lying back, he tried to fight the despair growing inside him.

<hr>

TWENTY-SEVEN SEEMINGLY ENDLESS days crawled by before Rhys and Jodi were rescued. By then, more than a week had passed since they'd last spoke, the effort required exacting too great a toll on what little energy they still possessed. The sun had been a brutal overlord during the day and only gave way to freezing cold wind and spray at night. Their rations had run out days before, and nothing but crumbs remained of the tasteless, high-calorie nutrient bars. Luck alone had blown the two men back into the shipping lanes where the *President Fletcher*, a tankship bound for Long Beach, had picked them up.

Emaciated and stinking of death, the delirious castaways were hauled up the *Fletcher's* side and into the infirmary for treatment. Rhys barely noticed an IV inserted into his arm, but as cool liquid coursed through his veins, he began to feel slightly more alert. Attempting to speak, his cracked lips and tongue thick with dehydration refused to form coherent words. The Navigator, who had helped bring the dying men aboard, bent over to listen closely.

"Come again?" he asked, ear trained toward Rhys's mouth.

"Phone," he whispered. "Need to call…"

"You boys've been through a hell of an ordeal," the Navigator said gently, patting him on the shoulder. "Rest. Recuperate. We'll get a message off for you."

Rhys wanted to protest, but the few simple words had left him exhausted. He laid his head back on the pillow and closed his eyes. He was unsure how long he slept, but when he woke, Los Angeles harbor was visible through the infirmary's porthole window. He heard the door open behind him and turned to see a crewmember bringing water and clean clothes. Sitting up, Rhys drank greedily, nearly choking on the cool liquid. His intense thirst finally sated, he asked again for a phone. When it came, he dialed Anne's number, listening to the rings with bated breath as he waited for the sound of her soothing voice. The ringing stopped.

"Hello? This is Anne…"

"Anne, it's Rhys! I've just made it to…" he faltered, heart plummeting, as the voice on the other end of the line kept speaking.

"I can't come to the phone right now, but leave your name…"

He hung up and dialed a second time. Nothing. Again and again, his calls went to voicemail. With nothing but the clothes on his back, he thanked the crew, nodded once to Jodi, and departed as quickly as he could.

Stepping outside the security gate, Rhys felt a sense of unreality. Merely a few days prior, he'd been sure of his own demise, convinced their time in the lifeboat had only delayed the inevitable. He'd begun to feel he might as well have died on the ship with Miguel, for all the difference their escape from the *Denebola* had made… but then, somehow, the inevitable end he'd come to expect never occurred. He and Jodi had survived the unsurvivable. Now, as if departing under normal circumstances, he found himself waiting for a taxi. The Navigator insisted he go to a hospital, but Rhys refused. He would get checked out once he was back in Montana. All he wanted was to go home to his wife and his dog.

Restless, he fished out the phone he'd been given and dialed again. No answer. It wasn't like Anne to ignore calls like this. Rhys knew she'd have been devastated after hearing the news of the *Denebola* and had probably gone back to her childhood home in northern Michigan. Their Montana ranch would have held too many painful reminders of the husband she had lost. Still, it made no sense why he hadn't heard from her. Rhys was sure the news of his survival had spread to the families of the *Denebola's* lost mariners by now. He called once more, waited, then hung up, unwilling to leave another of the countless messages he'd already recorded. Deciding to try something else, Rhys dialed the number for Anne's sister. Ringing. A solemn voice.

"Hello?"

"Kara, it's Rhys."

"Rhys? Oh, *God*, Rhys!" the woman cried. Something that sounded like a dropped phone echoed through the earpiece. "Is it really you? We'd heard someone from your ship had been rescued, but we didn't know..." Her voice trailed off, and Rhys heard muffled crying.

"Kara, is Anne there?" The crying continued, more painful than before.

"Rhys... Rhys, I can't..."

"Please, Kara. If Anne's there, let me speak to her."

"Sh-she... When the news came about your ship..."

Again, the woman faltered, unable to say what was on her mind, and despite everything, Rhys felt a twinge of anger. He'd spent the last month floating on a raft, nearly dead, and now his sister-in-law was stammering stupidly about... what? What was it she couldn't tell him about his own wife?

"Kara, tell me what the hell is going on. Why haven't I heard from Anne?" he demanded into the phone, trying to keep his voice level. "Has something happened?"

"I don't think... Anne couldn't... she's gone."

RHYS SAT ON A RICKETY STOOL, his shoulders hunched and forearms resting on the battered bar top. His head hung limply as a glass of whiskey teetered in his grasp, threatening to spill its amber contents over the stained plywood. In the six months since Anne's suicide, he'd developed a slight shake in his hands from the profuse consumption of grain alcohol. Her death was a tragedy that shouldn't have happened, *wouldn't* have happened if he'd been there. She had begged him not to leave, to find work doing something else, but he had been stubborn, promising like always that he'd return safe and sound. He hadn't, though, not right away. The entire crew of the *Denebola* was believed to have perished for the better part of a month.

In her grief, Anne had swallowed several handfuls of pills and a bottle of vodka, too stricken by his apparent loss to carry on. After receiving the news, Rhys had found the nearest bar and promptly crawled inside a bottle. He hadn't come back up for air since. It was the only way he'd been able to wash away some of the guilt he felt, the gnawing sense that her death was his fault. If only he'd been there for her like he promised...

Now, he was back in Fishtail, Montana, living on the twenty-acre ranchette he and Anne had built for themselves, but the Wrangler Bar was where he spent most of his time. It was a small, dingy establishment. Smoke from Marlboro Red cigarettes hung in the air, choking out what few redeeming qualities the pub had once possessed. Shoved against a far wall, three malfunctioning slot machines chimed feebly whenever their worn levers were pulled. A few frail old women still gambled there, faithfully inserting coins, and praying to the Patron Saint of Gaming to hear the cartoonish jingle that would accompany the machine's meager jackpot. A pair of leather-clad bikers were silently shooting pool, drinking Budweiser beer. Behind them, a poster advertised the establishment's 2076 Fourth of July Celebration, the three-hundredth birthday of the United States of America. Almost a year-and-a-half later, it still hung on the wall, the waitstaff too disinterested to take it down. The Wrangler Bar was lifeless, a quiet haven for drunks looking to forget their worldly troubles... troubles like Rhys's.

He couldn't remember the last time he'd been this drunk. The room had begun to spin, and it was making him nauseous. A small bubble of spit formed at his lips whenever he exhaled, his body swaying slightly with each wobble of the rickety chair. To his right, a homely brunette peeked sideways at him with a less-than-discreet look in her eyes.

Gradually, she edged her chair closer to the point where their knees touched beneath the bar, but Rhys wasn't interested. He gave her a polite smile and shifted his leg away from hers. With a muttered word that sounded suspiciously like "asshole," the woman gave up her pursuit and turned away. He squinted absentmindedly at her back before returning his attention to a television that hung crookedly above the bar. A heavyset woman in a lab coat was featured on the screen.

"...looking for volunteers to take part in a state-of-the-art cryonics study. We've just completed our sixth round of year-long human trials and are ready to undertake–"

The words crackled down at him through failing speakers before ending abruptly when the bartender flipped to a local sports channel. The scientist was replaced with a roaring crowd and fast-paced dialogue of a sports commentator. In Montana, college football reigned supreme. A diehard rivalry split the state, Bobcats versus the Grizzlies, like it was some kind of political statement. If someone asked, 'Cats or Griz' and received the wrong answer, the offending party was likely to be treated with pure, unadulterated loathing... nothing to do with sports really, just classic tribalism... us versus them... that kind of petty shit. Rhys couldn't care less about football, but with nothing else to do besides stare into the bottom of his glass, the game still drew his attention.

A few minutes later, a commotion to his right made him turn back towards the brunette. One of the bikers had returned to replenish his drink and was leaning in close to the woman. He'd taken some of her hair in his hand and was sniffing, leering at her predatorily. Rhys could tell she was uncomfortable.

"C'mon, Sugar. I'll show you how a real man fucks."

The biker's friend joined him at the bar, and they guffawed stupidly at the terrified woman. The burly-faced man sniffed her hair again and grabbed her wrist when she tried to pull away. Without thinking, Rhys pushed back from the bar and stood up, steadying himself on the back of the chair. He still held the glass of whiskey in his hand.

"Why don'choo leave her 'lone?" he demanded. Average in almost every physical characteristic, Rhys wasn't a large man. Scrappy, maybe, but not imposing by any measure. Now, he wished he wasn't so plastered. It was hard to sound tough when he could barely speak. The bikers exchanged an unamused look, then turned toward him.

"Mind your own fucking business," Burly Face replied. Still holding the woman's wrist, he shoved Rhys hard.

Too inebriated to react, Rhys toppled backward and smashed his head on the bar's raised foot support. The glass flew from his hand, shattering on the stained cement floor. As he lay there, the room began to spin more quickly, his nausea growing worse than before. Little white fireflies danced around his vision, and he could feel a knot rising where his head had struck the bar. As if through a wall, he heard the two goons laughing, hurling a string of insults and lewd comments down at him. Well, to hell with that. He wasn't about to give up so easily. Struggling to his feet, Rhys leaned heavily on his chair, bracing this time in case another unexpected shove came his way.

"Leave... her... alone."

His words were clear, but the effort required to muster them left him panting. The bikers' laughter died, and an uncomfortable silence filled the room. Not even the brunette dared make a peep. Without warning, Burly Face rushed forward and pinned him against the bar, shovel-sized hands clamped firmly around his collar. Rhys, reacting by instinct, took a drunken swing at the biker, who easily side-stepped the sluggish attack. A murderous look in his eyes, Burly Face drove a fist into Rhys's stomach. For Rhys, it was the final straw.

With an uncontrollable shudder, the contents of his meager dinner and countless glasses of whiskey came bubbling out of his mouth. Vomit oozed down his chin, running over the biker's hands and onto the front of his shirt. A look of shocked disgust filled Burly Face's features, before turning to pure rage. The next instant, Rhys felt a large fist connect with his jaw, and white-hot agony coursed through his head.

For the second time that night, he was falling, this time splashing into the slippery pool of his own puke. Two pairs of hands lifted him by his wrists and ankles and dragged him out the back door of the bar. They dumped him unceremoniously by a stinking dumpster, one man delivering a sharp kick to his ribs. Rhys doubled up, unable to breathe through the stinging pain, until slowly, darkness enveloped him, and he slept.

---

HE WOKE UP SHIVERING, bags of garbage piled around him. The brisk Montana morning chilled him to the bone, and he was freezing. A throbbing pain beat the inside of his skull, and he pressed his hands to his head, trying to squeeze away the discomfort pulsating there. Dizziness overwhelmed him, and he lay still for a moment, waiting for the sensation to pass.

Several minutes later, he crawled to his knees and stood shakily, slowly making his way back to the pickup he'd purchased with Anne before shipping out on the *Denebola*. Jesus. Even the damn truck reminded him of the sorrow he'd been trying to drown for the last six months. He got in and plucked a hat off the passenger's seat... the one Anne had given him. He tucked it low over his eyes to shield them from the rays of the rising sun. Rhys sat for a moment, not moving too much for the pain in his head.

He fished a hand into the side compartment of the driver's door and retrieved a flask he'd received on his wedding day, Anne's gift to him. Flipping it over, he read the inscription on its burnished metal surface. *Smooth seas never made a skilled sailor.* The proverb was something they'd told each other whenever things got hard, after he'd been gone too long, and it seemed like he would never return. Reading it made his heart hurt. All too clear, this was one storm he couldn't weather on his own. Unscrewing the cap, the spirit's sharp aroma made his nostrils tingle, and he took a long drink, pulling a face as the liquid warmed his insides. Nothing like a little hair of the dog...

TURNING OFF THE DUSTY ROAD, Rhys guided the vehicle down the long driveway of his property. He passed their timber frame cabin and parked next to an adjacent two-story barn. Since Anne's death, he had been living in the upper apartment, seldom setting foot in the main house. Too many painful reminders. He couldn't bring himself to sleep in that big empty bed of theirs. Her fragrance still lingered on the sheets, and it was too much to bear.

Climbing to the top of the frost-covered landing, he kicked off his boots and made a beeline for the shower. The smell of his vomit-soaked clothes was powerful, and the damp shirt clung unpleasantly to his chest as he struggled to pull it over his head. He dropped it wearily in a heap on the floor, then caught a glimpse of his reflection in the bathroom mirror. The unkempt face of a stranger stared back at him.

Matted brown hair hung limply over his ears, and Rhys could see chunks of vomit buried within the bushy rats-nest that was his beard. The punch he'd received the night before had left his face puffy, the skin already showing signs of bruising. A large, purple contusion had formed on his ribs where the assailant had kicked him. Bags hung heavily under his bloodshot eyes, their normally white sclera angry and inflamed. They looked lifeless, devoid of the spark that had once shined there. Staring into those unfamiliar eyes felt strange... Rhys didn't recognize them. Hell, he didn't recognize himself, this train wreck of a human being he'd become.

A warm shower helped lessen a few of the aches covering his body. The pounding in his head had subsided, somewhat, and he no longer felt the urge to vomit. Rhys dressed and checked the messages on his phone. Several texts from Anne's sister and mother... they wouldn't leave him alone. He had never been particularly close with the family he'd married into. His mother-in-law was a recovered (he was generous with the term) opioid addict. Struggling with addiction wasn't something he held against her, but she'd continually bombarded them with dubious requests for cash. It hadn't stopped, even after Anne's death, and Rhys resented the woman for it.

Kara's feelings toward him ranged unpredictably between general apathy, mild dislike, and inexplicable hatred. He'd never figured out what might set her off, but the truth was, he didn't care now. If he was being honest, he'd never liked either of them. His father-in-law had died a few years earlier and was the only one he ever got along with.

Without any close relatives of his own, Rhys had made Anne his world, but that world had crumbled unexpectedly from beneath him. His dog, the one he'd raised from a pup, had been re-homed during the month he'd spent as a castaway. Sagar, his best friend part from Anne, might've saved Rhys a great deal of suffering, but the universe had seen fit to take even that from him. He had a few other friends, sure, but they'd vanished shortly after Anne's death, citing his "drinking problem" as the reason for keeping their distance. Some friends... it had only driven him to seek further solace inside a bottle.

He pondered all this, mindlessly scrolling through texts and emails piling up in his inbox. Union newsletters, Black Friday blowout sales, advertisements for dick enlargement pills... he sighed. No wonder all he wanted to do was drink himself to oblivion. His entire universe had been upended like an antique Port-A-Potty, and all that was left clinging to it were the shit flecks. Sadness welled up inside him, replaced quickly by anger and loneliness. In a grief-stricken rage, he kicked a small end table and sent a lamp crashing to the floor, ceramic shards spreading out in all directions. Rhys drew back and was about to throw the phone as hard as he could against the arched brick wall but stopped when something caught his eye.

On the screen, another advertisement for the study he'd seen the night before glowed brightly. The Denver Institute of Cryotechnology had just completed its first successful human trials. He'd heard something about what they were doing down there... freezing chimpanzees, monitoring their vitals while they were in cryosleep, then reanimating them after a few months. Some spectacular scandals had come out of there in the early days. Several of the first test subjects had developed violent tendencies... lost their marbles while they were under. One of the lead scientists had been killed, a disaster that nearly ended the program altogether. Somehow, though, the Institute had put its tumultuous beginnings in the past. Now, they seemed to have perfected their craft and were proclaiming for the world to hear. They'd just reanimated a dozen human popsicles without a hitch after all...

Now, the research program was looking for someone to volunteer in a ten-year study. Understandably, the people they'd just defrosted weren't jumping at the bit. A year was one thing, but ten? A lot could happen in a decade. Rhys thumbed through some of the specifics… a ten-year study payable under contract while lab-coated scientists monitored the subject's vitals and brain function. He scoffed at the offered sum. A single, three-month voyage at sea paid more than that. Most of the email was full of legalese he didn't understand, but there was enough plain-speak to piece together what it meant. If something went wrong, the Institute couldn't be held liable. Typical.

He couldn't say why, but Rhys had always found the idea of cryogenic preservation intriguing. Well, as an exercise in academic theory, anyway. He would never seriously consider freezing himself. Life in Montana with Anne was a dream come true, and he had no reason to throw it all away… the realization made him pause. Never again would he hold her in his arms. Never again would her laughter fill his ears. Anne was gone forever, and he'd been trying to drown that knowledge for the last half a year. Ten years to sleep, to heal, to forget… what more did he have to lose?

A stab of fear shot through him at the thought, and he reflexively deleted the email. Was he truly that lost, that *stupid* to consider something so rash? Anyway, he'd only be delaying the inevitable. Freezing himself wouldn't magically bring Anne back. Even if Rhys slept for a *hundred* years, he'd still wake up to the same utter devastation. Looking forward, all he saw was loneliness; an infinite downward spiral until he drank himself to death. Why not just end it? Here and now.

With shaking hands and a pounding heart, Rhys picked up his wallet and walked out the door. He keyed the ignition on the dashboard of his truck, and the engine roared to life. The back tires spun when he pressed accelerator, peppering the barn's clapboard siding with flying gravel. Somewhere in the depths of his mind, Rhys knew he wasn't coming back. He hesitated for a moment at the intersection, before turning south and heading into the mountains.

Sᴡᴇᴀᴛ ᴘᴏᴜʀᴇᴅ into Rhys's eyes, blinding him as he clung to the slippery rock. Gusts of wind tugged at his clothes and threatened to pull him from the mountain face. His breath came in ragged, shuddering gasps as he tried to calm his fluttering heart. Daring a glance below, he felt his stomach tighten at the sight of the yawning abyss beneath him. From up here, huge talus boulders appeared no larger than tiny pebbles. The rock-strewn field seemed to stretch on forever, occasionally punctuated by flat plateaus and snowy peaks of the Beartooth Mountains. He took a few more calming breaths and pushed on, feeling his strength waning. There wasn't much left in him.

Pulling hard over a rocky bulge, Rhys shimmied up the last few meters of hard climbing. He wouldn't look down again until he reached the top. If he did, he'd lose his nerve completely. With a final grunting exhale, Rhys pushed himself up to the summit and flopped exhaustedly onto his back.

It was the second time he found himself on this particular mountaintop. The first had been with Anne, nearly four years ago, on the day of their wedding. The climb had been easy then, but recent months of alcohol-soaked excess left Rhys weak, soft. It was here they'd exchanged vows, committing to each other for the rest of their lives... or that's what he'd thought they'd been doing. It had been true for Anne, but her life ended prematurely. No matter. He'd soon be joining her. Pushing wearily to his feet, Rhys walked slowly toward the west-facing bluff. He paused at the edge of the precipice and looked once more into the vast expanse below, empty air beckoning him. Teetering for a moment, doubt welled up inside him, and he stepped back. He couldn't do it. Goddammit. Tears began to leak from his eyes, mixing with the dirt and sweat that covered his face.

THE FIRST TENDRILS of dawn had already begun to stretch across the sky when Rhys reached Denver's city limits. Gently-falling snow blanketed the ground in a peaceful shroud, ushering in the beginnings of what was sure to be a very short autumn. The shift seemed to arrive later each year, summer's oppressive hold refusing to break until cold winter winds forced it out. What would things be like in a decade? Rhys had made up his mind and knew what he was going to do. The prospect scared him... almost as much as throwing himself off the top of a mountain, but he was going to do it before he lost his nerve again. Something in his life had to change, and he couldn't see how else to escape the hole he'd dug for himself. Driving down the interstate, a sign for Downtown Denver loomed from the darkness, and he merged onto the exit ramp. Buildings grew taller as he continued deeper into the heart of the city until arriving at his destination. Lights in the state-of-the-art facility were dark, the Institute still closed for a few more hours. Killing the engine, he leaned back in his seat and closed his eyes.

When Rhys awoke, the full force of daylight streamed into the cab. He squinted and rubbed his face. The parking lot had filled up around him, and the facility now bustled with activity. Men and women, some dressed in business attire and others in white knee-length coats, hurried toward their destinations without sparing so much as a glance in his direction. *So much haste*, he thought, *and for what?* Were their lives so different than his own?

He scoffed humorlessly. The answer to that question was obvious. Mustering the courage for what he was about to do, Rhys stepped out of the vehicle and tossed the keys on the seat. He wouldn't need them. For the last time, he turned away from Anne's truck, and sighed deeply, attempting to let go of the pain he'd been holding onto for so long. His stride was slow, yet determined, as he walked towards the main lobby, pausing only to look up at the sleek block lettering above the door: 'Welcome to the Denver Institute of Cryotechnology.'

# CHAPTER 2
# A NEW THREAT

WARREN O'BRIEN LOOKED through the large bay window of his private stateroom and observed the bustling spaceport where his ship, the *Caspian Explorer*, was docked. Distant, twinkling stars left him longing to be out there, away from the backdoor dealings and criminal politicking that came with selling what he assumed was either stolen or illegal merchandise. The baukken contact through whom he'd acquired the mysterious cargo was a shady character at best, providing no information except the package's destination and the promise of a sizeable commission. Warren had been unable to glean anything else from the alien except its name… Jono or Jeano or Jenco… something like that. He couldn't remember now. It was probably just a nom de guerre anyway. Baukkens were one of those frustratingly cagey species, and no matter how many times he encountered them, Warren always ended up feeling inadequate… like he was too stupid to catch on if they tried pulling one over on him. This time was no different.

At baseline, Warren was distrustful of most everyone, especially new associates. He hadn't dealt with this particular baukken before, but the alien's offer was so lucrative he'd been unable to turn down the contract. He hoped he wouldn't regret that decision. One could never tell when local authorities might raid one of these out-of-the-way ports. Warren had a pretty good idea that he and his crew would be up the proverbial solar slipstream without an antimatter drive if that happened. Nevertheless, he adhered to a strict "don't ask, don't tell" policy, and it had been a long time since that policy failed them. He looked around the room and nodded approvingly, thinking they'd done well for themselves.

It wasn't so long ago, less than a decade in fact, that the crew of the *Caspian Explorer* had survived by scavenging the outlying star systems for scraps. Wreckage from ancient space battles had all too often yielded barely enough money for necessities... food, fuel, maintenance... let alone any extra cash in their pockets.

Warren remembered a particularly difficult period that had nearly resulted in a mutiny against him. Already on hard times and with inadequate fuel to reach the nearest quantum link station, the crew had come dangerously close to starvation. They were about to turn on him when, by a stroke of luck, the *Explorer* stumbled upon a vessel that had ruptured the magnetic exhaust nozzle of its beam-core drive. With no means to direct the high-speed thrust particles generated by proton antiproton annihilation, the ship was left with only maneuvering engines... a sitting duck in an endless expanse. The discovery had been just enough to distract the mutineers from relieving Warren of his mortal coil.

Volunteering to lead the salvage detail himself, he and the last of his loyal crewmen boarded the ship and discovered more high-value cargo than any of them had ever seen, enough to live comfortably for the next several years. It was the good fortune he'd desperately needed. After a collective sigh of relief swept their ranks, they had scanned the payload for homing beacons and discovered only a single, low-quality tracking device per crate. Something about that seemed fishy, however, and Warren had insisted they take a second look. No crew would be reckless enough to risk losing such valuable merchandise just because they were too cheap to properly protect it... and he'd been right. The other beacons were cleverly hidden, but with more scrutiny, the salvage team located the remaining devices and placed them back inside the derelict.

Unwilling to leave evidence of looting, Warren gave the order to plant explosives onboard the abandoned vessel. If the old crew came back for their cargo and found the ship empty, they would probably be inclined to go searching for it. An explosion following a failure of the drive system, on the other hand, would likely be written off as bad luck. What had caused the exhaust nozzle to rupture in the first place was a question Warren couldn't answer, but he wasn't about to complain. Someone else's misfortune had become the vehicle of his crew's salvation. They loaded the cargo and as much byrinium-shielded antimatter as could be safely recovered in their hunger-stricken state and detonated enough charges to cover their tracks.

The atmosphere amongst the crew had instantly changed. Fresh fuel and a promise of wealth breathed life back into his shipmates, replacing the near-starved lethargy that had been present only a few days before. It hadn't been meant to last, however. Two days from the port she'd been limping towards, the *Explorer* was set upon by another group of scavengers. All but three of his crew had been killed, Warren himself severely wounded. The bandits took the salvaged cargo and left them for dead. With a knife wound to his belly, he'd somehow managed to plot their course back to port before falling unconscious. The next thing he knew, he was lying in the medical bay of Vandervol Outpost, his stomach bandaged and head pounding. When the memory of what had happened came flooding back, he vowed to outfit his ship and crew with better weapons and more-efficient engines.

Warren's recovery had been speedy considering the nature of his injury. Following his brush with death, he'd bribed, blackmailed, and threatened his way to several ship upgrades including prototype shielding and a scan-resistant hull coating to camouflage the contents of their cargo bays. So as not to attract unwanted attention, the *Caspian Explorer* kept the outward appearance of a junker. She had been built over thirty years prior, and time had reduced her exterior to something less than remarkable to look at. Housed inside the vessel, several large pieces of decommissioned equipment had been converted into cleverly designed holding areas for high-value cargo. Anyone venturing into the engine spaces would think they were just pieces of broken-down machinery the engineers were too incompetent to fix.

With improved equipment, the scores of the *Caspian Explorer* had grown, and they'd done just enough legitimate business to keep a low profile from the prying eyes of the Galactic Commonwealth. For smuggling jobs, Warren made sure they were also under legal contract. Full crew and cargo manifests were available for inspection by any G.C. authorities. He knew some of the crew thought he was paranoid, but that didn't matter. By preparing for the worst, fortune had since done nothing but favor the *Caspian Explorer*. Now, years later, they had returned to the same godforsaken port he'd nearly died in.

A soft chirping sound pulled Warren from his musings. He blinked and touched the skin beneath his left ear to activate the embedded communicator.

"This is the Captain," he said, speaking aloud to the empty stateroom. Through simple bone conduction, a voice answered that sounded to him as if its owner was in the same room.

"Cap'n, it's Ryan. I'm with Anikar G'hrac naal, the turandian buyer our contact told us to meet. Might need some help on this one."

Ryan Frye was First Officer aboard the *Caspian Explorer* and front man for the ship's business transactions. He was a smart, observant, and generally amicable guy. For whatever reason, people tended to trust him after only one or two brief interactions, which came in handy when securing contracts from skittish clients. If things ever went sideways, Ryan was damn good at covering Warren's ass in a pinch, and he'd gotten them out of more binds than the Captain cared to admit. He was one of the best navigators Warren had ever known, but above all else, the man was like a brother. For as long as either of them could remember, they'd had each other's backs.

At a young age, both had been dumped in Saint Emiliani's Orphanage on Mercury. Even under the best of circumstances, it was a hard place to survive. Abandoned and alone, the two boys had become fast friends. Some of the older orphans, the ones who'd been there long enough to have lost any hope of a better life, took to brutalizing the younger occupants to cope with their own miserable existence. Every few months, a ritualistic beating went too far and one of the broken, defenseless victims ended up dead. Warren and Ryan had fought tooth and nail to protect each other, and at the first opportunity to escape that particular hell, they'd stowed away on an Earth-bound freighter and never looked back.

"Is there a problem?" Warren asked. "The baukken said this was going to be an open and shut deal." There was a long pause while he waited for a response. What in God's name was taking so long?

"Uh, there might be. Hang on a minute." Another pause. "He's unwilling to pay for the cargo. He says he won't take it and that he can't associate with us," Ryan replied, sounding confused. "It took me hours to find this guy in the first place. When he didn't meet me at the rendezvous, I tracked him down and found him fueling up at one of the outbound departure stations. I think the *shaain kah* was trying to skip town on us."

Warren heard the slur and frowned, though not just at the first officer's use of profanity. He already held reservations about the job, and this new complication didn't help. Several red flags had gone up during their negotiations with the baukken, who'd been unconvincing in his assurance that no one would be looking for the cargo. Warren didn't know what it was they were transporting, and he hadn't asked. He'd been blindsided by the size of the proffered commission. They'd received half in advance, a sum far greater than anything they'd scored in a long time, and the other half would be paid upon delivery to the buyer at Vandervol. Unfortunately, that part of the deal now seemed to be in jeopardy.

"Has something happened? We've been running blind since that hot-dogging asshole ran a maintenance skiff into our comms array leaving Merellian Station. Ask the turandian what he's heard," Warren said.

"Will do."

After several painstaking minutes, Ryan reported back.

"He's babbling and frantic. He just keeps saying 'they're coming' and something else regarding the... grool...bar...vock. Grülbarvoc? What the hell is grülbarvoc?"

"Doesn't sound like Common Tongue," Warren said, pausing a moment to think. These new developments were making him uncomfortable. All he wanted was to get rid of the cargo and be on their way. If they offered the turandian a lower price, perhaps the baukken could just take the difference out of what they were still owed. It wasn't the ideal choice, settling for a smaller dividend on this part of the transaction, but it was better than nothing. The remainder of the commission would still leave them much wealthier than they'd been before.

"Tell him we'll go down to seventy percent of the original contract. If he still doesn't bite, we'll have to find another buyer. I'll try to figure out what grülbarvoc means and if we should be worried about it. The repair on the comms array is almost done, so if I hear anything, I'll let you know."

The conversation over, Warren touched his ear and turned away from the window. He walked briskly toward the door, and it snapped open to reveal the passageway beyond. From his quarters, the command deck was still another three levels up. There was a turbolift just outside his room that would take him there, but the car was currently on its way down to the engine room.

Instead of waiting, Warren pushed through a side hatch and pulled himself up several flights of stairs to the bridge. The ship's electrician, a red-faced, foul-mouthed man named Darin, was crammed beneath the communications console where a tangle of multi-colored wires hung in a messy jumble. Several ends had been stripped bare, their conductive innards poking out from beneath insulated sheathes. Grunting, the man groped blindly for a tool and inadvertently touched a wire to the console's metal frame. A small arc and the smell of burning plastic made the electrician yelp.

"Shit! Piss! Goddamn sonofabitch!" He shimmied out from underneath and dropped the tool back into its bag, shaking the hand that had received the jolt.

"Shouldn't do that hot," Warren chided, a half-amused grin creasing the corner of his mouth. He knew the electrician was okay. No charred flesh or missing digits.

"Fuck off," Darin spat. He glanced up at Warren, did a double take, then quickly backpedaled. "Aw, shit. Sorry, Cap. I thought Benji was up here again to see if I was done. He's been buggin' me about every twenty goddamn minutes. You know how pissed he's been about not getting to fondle himself to that weird VR porno shit he loves." The man was apologetic, in a gruff sort of way, but Warren waved it off. He knew there had been no disrespect meant.

"How's it coming?"

"Already installed the new array outside. Was a different manufacturer, so I had to rewire the components in here. We'll still have the same range and data load, but I had to jury-rig the fucker so it'd talk to our system. Once I finish these last couple connections, it should be good to go," Darin replied. There was an air of self-assuredness about him that some would have found off-putting, arrogant even, but Warren knew it came from a deep-seated understanding of all things electrical. He'd never seen Darin fail to diagnose and solve a problem, no matter how elusive. "How'd the exchange go?"

The Captain bobbed his head side-to-side and gave a small shrug. "That's why I'm here. Ryan said the buyer was scared shit-less. Didn't even want to be seen talking to him, and there was something he kept repeating that we couldn't understand; grülbarvoc."

The electrician frowned and mouthed the word silently, picking at a spot on his chin.

"Don't recognize the word, but I'm no xenolinguistics expert."

"What about our translators? Could those be malfunctioning?" Warren asked.

It was unlikely that both his and Ryan's units had failed simultaneously. The translators relied upon an archive of all the known alien dialects in the Galactic Commonwealth. Mostly, everyone just spoke Common Tongue… it was the official language of the G.C. and had been so for nearly a hundred-and-fifty years, but as was the nature of such things, people would often fall back to whatever local parlance they'd grown up with. Being in a line of work that required him to know what they were getting themselves into, Warren had wanted a way to prevent getting conned due to his own incomprehension.

Instead of paying for the exorbitantly expensive and remarkably finicky interpreter units currently on the market, Darin had pirated the software and upgraded their own communicators' processing power to make translations nearly instantaneous. The mere suggestion his brainchild might be malfunctioning had caused the man's face to turn an even deeper shade of red, and he muttered something that sounded suspiciously like 'goddamn-sonofabitchin'-bastard.' The expletive was such an absurd combination of words, Warren found it difficult to keep his face from breaking into a grin. Sometimes, these engineering types were so sensitive.

"No. They're fine," the electrician said through gritted teeth. There was no need to push the issue further. If Darin said the translators weren't the problem, then there had to be another explanation. "Once comms are back online, we'll see what we've missed the last couple of weeks."

"Let me know when it's done," Warren said and turned to leave. He strode slowly back to his room, troubled as to what could have spooked the buyer into abandoning their deal without explanation... but it wasn't just that. Since they'd arrived at Vandervol Outpost, the atmosphere seemed tenser than he remembered. There was an abnormally high concentration of G.C. goons around, and the thoroughness and frequency of inspections had made their arrival more challenging than expected.

Everyone knew Vandervol was a hotbed of black-market activity, but it was so far removed from the rest of the sector that no one really gave a shit. That was the whole point of completing the transaction here in the first place. With luck, a new communications array would shed some light on just what the hell was going on.

THREE HOURS LATER, a soft double-beep chirped in the Captain's ear for the second time that day. He reached up to accept the comms request and heard someone clearing their throat on the other end of the line. The sound made him grimace in disgust. Would it have been so hard to design the communicators so only speech patterns were transmitted, not extraneous noises like sneezing or coughing? Warren didn't need to hear someone hacking up phlegm if he happened to be interrupted during a meal. He guessed Darin could probably work up a software upgrade and made a mental note to mention it next time they spoke. It just so happened, the voice that greeted him belonged to none other than Darin Williams. Speak of the Devil.

"Cap, long-range comms are back online. You need to see what I'm looking at. I'll patch the feed to your stateroom."

"No need. I'm coming up," Warren replied, standing, and walking toward the door. When it opened, he found himself face-to-face with a breathless Ryan Frye, the First Officer's hand outstretched to knock on the previously closed hatch.

"Warren, I need to talk to you. We've got a major problem." The man was gasping as if he'd just run several kilometers.

"Electro's finished his repairs and says there's something I should see. Let's talk on the bridge," Warren said, slipping past Ryan to call the turbolift. A feeling of trepidation had begun to fill his chest, and he feared what the two men might tell him. Something in the way the First Officer fought to regain his breath made him even more anxious... as if the length of time between walking and running had made the difference between... what, exactly? Impatiently, Warren punched the turbolift's call button a few more times, and when it arrived, pushed his way inside before the doors had fully opened. When they reached the bridge, he saw the electrician sitting at the communications console, eyes glued to one of the screens, watching one of the most terrifying things Warren had ever seen.

On the monitor, a fleet of gigantic ships floated before a field of destruction. Fragments of demolished vessels drifted unabated through the rubble. A solar array damaged beyond repair spun slowly, one of the few identifiable remnants of a devastated space station. Beyond, Warren could make out the remains of a half-destroyed moon, debris thrown out in all directions, a charred black gash evidence of an attack harnessing unimaginable power. Without looking up from the screen, the electrician spoke.

"This is all that's left of Merellian Station. According to the report, an unknown alien species showed up only a few days after we left and hijacked the outpost," Darin explained. "The G.C. regiment stationed there tried to put up a fight, but whoever attacked them had some mega fucking firepower. Killed anyone that tried to stop them. One of the survivors thought the aliens were looking for something. Said they ransacked the place but didn't take anything. Described their speech as pretty much incomprehensible, and 'grülbarvoc' was the only distinguishable word anyone could piece together."

"That's what the buyer kept repeating," Ryan said. A worried look creased his brow, wrinkling the skin of his forehead. "Anybody know what they were after?"

"Whatever it was, I'd guess they didn't find it. When they left, they fired off some sort of super weapon that demolished the outpost. Took a chunk out of her moon and trashed the link station, too. That entire sector is essentially stranded from the rest of the Commonwealth now," Darin said. He swiped away from their current view and brought up another window on the display. More images of destruction. "It's the same with Terra Prima, Trimoon Station, and the Veybos Colony."

Hearing the list of ravaged outposts, Warren felt his stomach plummet and the color drain from his face. A wave of dizziness made him grasp the back of Darin's chair, and he swayed unsteadily for a moment as the news sunk in. This couldn't be happening. Not now... he finally understood what had made the buyer so skittish. In barely audible tones, he whispered what the crew must have already pieced together on their own.

"Those are the same ports we stopped for supplies after picking up the cargo on Terra Prima."

The buyer had known the ship's itinerary and route they planned on taking. Warren wasn't happy about providing the information... loose lips sinking ships and all that... but the turandian had insisted, threatening to back out of the deal if they didn't give regular updates. It had been another red flag in an already suspicious transaction. A paranoid thought suddenly hit Warren like a slap to the face. If G'hrac naal suspected these aliens were searching for the *Caspian Explorer*, would he alert the authorities? Was the G.C. already on its way here? Mind reeling, he sat heavily in the chair next to Darin and held his head in his hands. No one spoke for what seemed like hours until he felt a hand on his shoulder.

"I spent the last three hours talking to other interested parties. The minute any of them heard I was from the *Caspian Explorer*, they wanted nothing to do with me. The turandian must've gotten word out to steer clear of us. One of those pricks called Port Security, and it was pure luck I didn't get pinched on the way back," Ryan said, sounding unnerved. He had finally recovered his breath and was no longer gasping, but his voice still quavered slightly. "Captain, we need to get out of here. Now. Before the G.C. or, God forbid, these grül creatures figure out where we are. Let's dump the cargo and get the hell away from Vandervol."

Warren didn't move, blood pounding in his ears and drowning out Ryan's words. How could this be happening? After all they'd been through, all the precautions he'd taken to protect them, how could he be so blinded by the baukken's commission to let this happen? Was it just bad luck, or had they been set up from the start? Lost in his own thoughts, he barely noticed Ryan begin to shake his shoulder.

"Captain, did you hear me? *We need to leave.*"

Slowly, Warren forced his mind away from the despairing thoughts that had begun to take root and focused on what needed to be done. He took one last look at the destruction on the screens, then turned to his second-in-command.

"Recall any crewmen still ashore. We need the stragglers back here ASAP. I'll jettison the cargo once we're well clear of Vandervol." Warren had regained his usual self-assuredness and wanted to kick himself for momentarily losing his composure. Danger was no stranger to him, so why had he let this news affect him like it had? It was a stupid question. He knew why. The firepower required to wreak that kind of havoc scared the living daylights out of him... but that couldn't matter now. Losing his head wouldn't be of help to anyone. They'd gotten themselves into this mess, so they'd better damn well deal with it.

---

Hours later, as the *Caspian Explorer* cleared Vandervol airspace, Warren tried to formulate a plan. Where should they go? He had some serious thinking to do about how they would avoid detection by the grülbarvoc, if that's what he should call them. Their normal routine of hiding in plain sight from the G.C. was no longer an option, not with the kind of firepower this new adversary possessed. Not since their anonymity had been compromised.

"Lay in a course for the Vega system."

"Vega? Are you sure? That's months away, even at max burn. Vandervol's link station is a better–" Ryan began.

"Just do it, dammit!" Warren's voice was clipped and edgy. This wasn't the time for his shipmates, not even his best friend, to question his motives. He was flying by the seat of his pants, with no real plan in mind. He knew he should have followed his instincts, the ones telling him from the start this deal was a bad idea, but he hadn't listened. The money had been too good. Now, all he could think to do was get as far from Vandervol as possible. If someone had tracked their movements through the link stations, then the last thing he was going to do was risk making a jump now. Once they'd burned a good long distance from their current location, they would jettison the cargo, whatever it was. *Whatever it was…*

Now, the wheels were turning in his head. Warren was confident they were screwed unless they came up with a good idea and quick. He had always vowed never to ask what he was carrying. It wasn't his business what his employers wanted moved, he was just an impartial third party. A purveyor of services. Now, though, in a desperate situation, Warren was willing to break that rule. He was going to find out what it was they had onboard.

Ryan held up his hands apologetically. "I didn't mean… I'm sorry. What's the plan?"

"Well, the way I figure, it's only a matter of time before these grül things have a pretty good idea where we're going. Unless we can stay ahead of them indefinitely, I can't begin to fathom how we beat them in a fight. On the other hand, if we had a bargaining chip or a weapon that could get us out of this, then we might stand a chance."

"I don't know what we could…" Ryan trailed off, oblivious to the direction Warren's mind was headed. After a few moments, though, the man's eyes came alight with comprehension. "The cargo?"

"Bingo. We don't know what's inside, but if there's a chance it can help us, I say we take it. That said, I want full containment measures and radiation suits for anyone involved," Warren said, unbuckling from the launch seat. He pushed himself to his feet and tapped Darin on the shoulder. "Meet us down in Cargo Bay Five with an exo-torch… and turn that shit off."

"Yeah. Sure. Okay," the electrician replied distractedly, still ogling the destruction-filled holoscreens.

Warren turned toward the helmsman, a young woman named Natalia whom he'd hired for a single trip after his last pilot contracted a nasty bout of Kaellian measles. She was green as green could get but a real natural when it came to flying. Some of the maneuvers he'd seen her pull off were truly impressive. If Natalia decided to stay on as permanent crew, Warren knew he could shape her into a competent pilot.

"Keep her steady, kid. We'll be back soon."

The Captain and First Officer departed the bridge and began the trek down to the aft cargo bay. From stem to stern, the *Caspian Explorer* was nearly one-hundred and sixty-three meters long and housed five main holds separated by thick titanium alloy bulkheads. In the event of a breach, each bay could be segregated, preventing total atmospheric loss, and maintaining greater integrity of the hull. The aft cargo bay was the smallest of the five, and it was here their mysterious cargo resided. It took them the better part of five minutes to reach the Bay Five airlock, and a few more before Darin jogged up to meet them, his breath coming in ragged gasps.

"Got here… quick… as I could. *HHHOOOO*." The electrician exhaled sharply and lowered a heavy pack from his shoulders. "Ready to pop this bitch open?"

Warren nodded and opened an equipment locker. Inside were eight bulky suits, each equipped with a self-contained breathing system and designed to repel the most-common forms of chemical, biological, and radiological hazards. He handed one to Ryan and another to Darin, then pulled the cumbersome suit over his clothes. Once they were dressed, he moved toward the door's control panel and keyed an alpha numeric code. A faint hiss of escaping air filled the passageway as the outer airlock door opened. When the three men stepped inside, the hatch slid closed behind them. Warren checked the panel for positive pressure (it would prevent the intrusion of any undesirable particulate entering the main area of the ship) and cycled the inner airlock door.

Stepping into the cargo bay, Warren trudged up a loading ramp toward the crate that held their unknown cargo. Its outer surface was perfectly smooth, with no protrusions, panels, or hinges of any kind. He walked in a circle around the container, scratching his head in confusion. Short of cutting into the damn thing, how the hell were they supposed to open it? He stepped back and motioned for Darin to position the torch at the base of the object. The electrician struck an arc with the meter-long electrode and moved forward to begin cutting. As soon as the sparking tip touched the mysterious container, a concussive wave erupted from the point of contact, knocking all three men back in a tangle of limbs. Warren lay on the deck, momentarily stunned. Stupid. *Stupid.* He should have known there might be some kind of protective shielding. Still dazed, he propped himself up on his elbows and saw a molten line where the arc had touched the crate. He motioned for Darin to resume cutting and watched as the electrician traced his sparking electrode along the perimeter of the crate. When the cut was complete, Ryan moved forward, prying open the glowing fissure and flipping the upper half of the container over with a bang.

The object in the middle of the crate was unlike any weapon Warren had ever seen. It sat amid a jumbled mass of tubes and wires, and a compact, albeit powerful, antenna protruded from top. Even with its refrigerated heat sink, the strange device put off a profuse amount of heat. The entire contraption looked as if it had been cobbled together in a hurry, no apparent order in the way the wires and tubes had been routed. Why would the baukken have paid them so much to move a pile of trash? More to the point, why would the aliens pursuing them want it so badly? Warren pushed himself to his feet and approached the device cautiously. Below the antenna, a greenish glow caught his eye, and he leaned in to read a tiny screen. 'TRANSMISSION BURST COMPLETE. COUNTDOWN TO NEXT BURST — 9:23:56:16' blinked on the illuminated display, and it was counting down. What the hell? He reached out and tried to turn it off.

*ACCESS DENIED.*

He tried again.

*ACCESS DENIED. KILL CODE REQUIRED.*

Kill code? Why the fuck would this thing need a kill code? Why was it transmitting in the first place? Had it turned itself on when they opened the crate, or… Warren's heart sank when the realization of what it meant finally set in. Now, he knew how the grül creatures had tracked them all this way… why they would keep tracking them. The crew of the *Caspian Explorer* had been duped, their entire charter nothing more than misdirection. They'd been made an unwitting mule to spew some indeterminate signal amongst the stars. The signal, whatever it was, had probably been designed to send someone down the wrong path for a reason Warren would never know. Now, with nothing to fall back on, he knew their odds of survival had disappeared. An alarm began to sound, reverberating through the cargo bay in an echoing keen, and he turned numbly away from the source of their impending doom.

Back on the bridge, the crew of the *Caspian Explorer* watched helplessly as a fleet of gigantic ships bore down on the small freighter. Without so much as a hail, the lead vessel opened fire sending an unfamiliar energy pulse through their ship. Warren felt a thrumming sensation build within his ribs. It quickly morphed to an uncomfortable vibrating before searing pain emanated deep from within his body. Screaming, he fell to his knees and tore at his chest as the pain surpassed anything he'd ever known.

Madness began to overtake him. He coughed and saw red flecks spray outward. Warren wiped his mouth with the back of his hand and saw skin and nails slough off at the lightest touch, exposing the muscles and sinew below. With a gasp of desperation, he struggled to stand but was unable to find strength to do so. He flopped weakly onto his stomach and lay there drawing ragged breaths, feeling the slow drip of blood from his ears and nose. His eyes met the terrified gaze of the helmsman, who with trembling hands, tried to staunch the flow of her own bloody end. To die so young and with such a bright future ahead of her... the thought filled him with a final pang of guilt, but a moment later, Captain Warren O'Brien felt no more.

# CHAPTER 3
# AWAKE

DARKNESS. An overwhelming sense of fatigue. Fragments of memory the man did not understand. A brilliant flash of light... intense heat... screams. Thousands of screams. A *world* of screams. As if through a fog, his brain fought to claw its way out of an unfamiliar gloom. He slowly became aware of his body. It felt sluggish, like a long-neglected machine. Sensation began to return to his fingertips, little pinpricks of discomfort shooting upwards. Sight and hearing still eluded him. He was perturbed, unable to recall where or even who he was. More feeling in his hands and feet. Something was pushed into the crook of his elbow, and he felt a small pinch. Icy tendrils began to creep through his arm, diluting the haze that clouded his brain. *Rhys*, he remembered finally. His name was Rhys. Beyond that, his memories were a blur... nothing more than a jumbled, disjointed cache of images that made no sense, as if they belonged to someone else.

Through the gloom, an image swam into view, putting his fears of blindness at ease. It was the face of a woman, but no ordinary woman. She was fierce and exotic and... alien. *Alien?* More quickly now, Rhys's senses began to kick in. She certainly didn't appear human, but how was that possible? Her ears were just a little too pointed, her face a little too long. Dark hair, darker than the blackest night, accentuated the curve of her high cheekbones.

The woman's skin reminded him of the greenish-gray color of mountain sage, but most striking were her eyes; violet, full of penetrating intelligence, and, to Rhys's dismay, brimming with fear.

"Wake up! You need to *wake up!*"

She grabbed him, shaking him by the shoulders. Still unable to control his limbs, Rhys flopped like a ragdoll, his head rolling backward no longer able to see her. When the shaking subsided, he felt another uncomfortable pinch in the crook of his arm. An injection of some kind. Its effect was instantaneous. He could move his arms and legs, unsteadily at first, but quickly regaining motor function before turning his head to dry heave toward the floor. Whatever had just been injected into him was strong.

"Get up! We can't stay here!"

She was shouting at him again, tugging frantically on his arm. Groggily, he tried to take stock of his surroundings. They were in a circular white room, empty except for a gleaming console that stood erect in the middle of the space. He was half sitting, half lying in the cryostasis pod... the last thing he had seen before darkness enveloped him. On the far side of the room stood an open door, the passageway outside dark and ominous. Amber lights strobed rhythmically, pulsating every few seconds to illuminate what lay beyond. The sound of an alarm told Rhys something was wrong.

"What's happening? Where am I?" he asked. "What... who are *you?*"

"My name is Doctor Sekami Ryele. I'll explain more later, but right now, we can't stay here," she said again, continuing to pull at his arm. "The station is under attack!"

Station? Attack? What did she mean? He was supposed to wake up... somewhere... only he couldn't remember. Still confused and slow to react, Rhys lifted himself out of the cryo chamber. His limbs hadn't fully recovered, his legs still shaky, but he tried to hurry all the same. The woman's fear was infectious. In his haste, he toppled out of the tube, falling painfully in an untidy heap at her feet.

Not waiting for him to recover, Sekami began dragging him towards the door. Her breath came in ragged gasps, but she kept pulling, frantic in her efforts to move them forward. They were almost to the exit, when she stopped, giving Rhys time to push himself onto his hands and knees. She pulled a tube-shaped object from the bag slung over her shoulders and gripped his elbow, pressing the device roughly against his skin. Instinctively, he jerked away, suspicious of what exactly she kept shooting into him.

"No more!"

Rhys was stern. He'd already been given two injections, and his heart was pounding. He didn't know if that was an effect of the serum or the woman's terrified manner. Clambering to his feet, he saw her sprinting away, shouting for him to move. He hurried after her, following sluggishly through the maze of passages. Nothing seemed familiar. Some of the details from before had begun to return, and their surroundings seemed wrong. Foreign. Were they even still in Denver? The walls around him looked weathered, like they'd seen years, *decades* even, of neglect. The facility he remembered was state-of-the-art, sleek and bright and new. Where were the scientists, the businessmen, all hurrying toward whatever tasks held their attention? Could so much have changed in only ten years?

Rounding a corner, he pulled up short, his guide stopped dead in her tracks. Once again, Sekami was digging inside the bag, looking for something. After a frenzied search, she pulled out two thin, metallic circlets, each fitted with a clasp... collars of some sort. She placed a long finger against the first device, and its inner diameter began to emit a subtle yellow glow. Fastening this around her neck, Sekami extended the second toward Rhys. He reached out questioningly, baffled as to the collar's purpose, but before he could accept it, a shudder ran through the walls as if a great blow had been dealt to the station. Both were thrown to the floor, the second collar falling from the woman's grasp and skittering noisily away over metal deck plates. Terror flashed across her face.

"They're here." She was frozen for an instant longer before scrambling to retrieve the collar. "Put this on. It should give you some protection."

"Protection?" Rhys asked perplexedly. "From what? Just tell me what's going on! *Who* is here?"

He watched Sekami power up the collar, saw the same yellowish glow and felt the touch of cool metal when she fastened it around his neck. She gave him an anxious look but didn't reply. Disoriented as he was, Rhys found the lack of information maddening. It seemed as though this strange person couldn't, or wouldn't, give him any reason for their current predicament. Without further explanation, she turned away, and his anxiety got the better of him. He reached out and grabbed her arm, pulling her back more forcibly than intended.

"Give me some damn answers!"

Before he could react, she whirled out of his grasp, twisting his wrist and elbow behind his back and slamming him to one side of the passage. Her forearm pressed against his neck, pinning his face against the wall. Rhys was stunned by the efficiency with which she had just disabled him. Even with her slight frame, the woman was much stronger than she appeared.

"I was sent here to get you, to find you before *they* did," Sekami explained quickly, still holding his arm. Another impact shuddered through the station, but her grip remained firm. "There are things you don't yet understand, but I'll explain everything once we're away from here. Just do as I say!"

Rhys nodded in agreement, clenching his teeth against the pain. Thankfully, Sekami released him a moment later and stepped back. She turned and bolted down the passageway, and Rhys tried his best to keep pace. Up ahead, there was pandemonium. Overhead lamps cast flickering shadows as if somewhere, a dying generator threatened to plunge them into darkness. With barely enough light to guide their path, the way forward had turned into a nightmare. Strange creatures, *inhuman* creatures, crawled over each other as they tried to escape the attack. In another violent quake, a structural beam crashed down from above, trapping several aliens underneath. Some were killed instantly by the crushing force. Others weren't so lucky. They lay pinned beneath the debris, moaning pitifully and reaching out for assistance. Rhys, torn between an innate desire to help and reflexive xenophobia, hesitated a moment, but Sekami never slowed her headlong tilt down the corridor. He ran on.

They hurried through another door into a tubular passageway whose walls were made of some transparent material. Expecting to see the Denver city skyline, Rhys was thunderstruck by what lay beyond. Stretching out in infinite directions was the vast expanse of space. He skidded to a halt, gaping in astonishment, until an angry yell from Sekami spurred him forward.

As he ran, Rhys stole another glance outside, still unable to believe his eyes. Against the backdrop of an icy, cloudy haze floated a ship that dwarfed any man-made structure he could recall. The gigantic craft resembled nothing he'd ever seen, its construction strangely bird-like. Beneath its curving, hawkish bridge was a spherical aperture that revealed a glowing core. An ethereal shimmer emanated from within, blurring the lines between the craft's rigid hull and the substance housed inside. The ship was a menacing goliath, ready to obliterate everything in its path. In the distance, dozens of tiny vessels began to detach from the cryostation, attempting to flee their impending destruction. *Too late*, Rhys thought, as a flash of incandescent energy pulsed from the ship's glowing core.

Momentarily blinded, he tripped over something lying in his path. Still too weak to cushion the fall, his chin struck the deck when his arms folded uselessly beneath him. Images he didn't recognize came barreling to the forefront of his mind as if jogged loose by the blunt impact. Another blinding light, then something burning... something huge and frightening and incomprehensible. A deafening cacophony of disembodied screams pierced his ears, as though countless, tortured souls had simultaneously forced themselves into his brain. Rhys was filled with inexplicable anguish, wanted nothing more than for it to stop, to die if that's what it took… when he felt Sekami hauling him to his feet. The terrible apparition was gone as quickly as it had arrived but left him trembling and, if possible, more weak-kneed than before. Steadying himself, Rhys shook his head and looked back outside. On the battlefield, the fleeing ships were gone. Nothing but mangled debris and an eerie blue-green aura remained.

*Chunk-chunk-chunk.*

In rapid succession, a barrage of artillery from the cryostation fired at the massive ship, the weapons emitting a white-hot blaze as their propellant drove them forward. Striking their intended target, an explosion burned across empty blackness and spread out in all directions. The enemy ship momentarily hidden from view, Rhys held his breath and waited for the inferno to dissipate. From behind the fiery veil, their attacker reemerged unharmed. Volley after volley, the goliath remained intact, each round of missiles failing to destroy its target. Rhys, stunned by the seemingly invincible enemy, heard Sekami shouting at him, urging him once again to move.

Turn after turn, he sprinted down the corridor until they reached a heavy-looking door with the words *HANGAR 8* emblazoned in large white lettering. His guide slammed her palm against a glowing scanner, desperation evident in her every move, and the hatch snapped open. At the end of the hangar sat a solitary ship, different than the ones that had just been obliterated. Sleek and black, the craft looked as though it had been built for speed. Winded but fueled by adrenaline, Rhys ran hard, his footsteps echoing through the otherwise empty hangar.

It was unnoticeable at first, but a strange sensation, beginning as nothing more than imperceptible thrumming, was building in his chest. The ship was only a dozen paces away now, and he saw Sekami open the exterior door. When he reached her, he was shocked to see her nose bloody, a dark green rivulet oozing from one of her nostrils. Had she hit her head? Been struck by falling debris? As Rhys fought to recover his breath, he became acutely aware of something else… an unnatural pain burning in his chest… something that wasn't from all the running.

"What's happening to me?!" His fear was back, fresh as the waves of terror he'd experienced earlier.

"It's their weapon," she cried. "Our collars are absorbing some of the energy, but… agh!"

She let a strangled cry, grasping her head in both hands. Blood leaked from her other nostril, flowing much greater than before.

"We have to get away… before it's… too late."

Sekami's words were forced as she pulled herself through the open airlock then fell to the deck in a heap. Clambering after her, Rhys crashed against the far wall, his teeth clenched in a silent grimace. Pain like he'd never felt consumed him, but he fought to stay conscious. He *had* to stay conscious. They *had* to get out of here, but now, the woman seemed too beaten to go any farther. It was his turn to help. Mustering what little strength he had left, Rhys bent down and slung Sekami's arm over his shoulder, supporting her waist with one hand and using the other to pull them to their feet. She pointed feebly in the direction they needed to go, and he began to grope his way forward.

Rhys had nearly reached his limit when they stumbled into the cockpit. He deposited Sekami in front of a blinking console then collapsed into a nearby padded chair. She fumbled weakly with the controls until the exterior hangar door opened in a hiss of escaping air. Their exit loomed like a yawning mouth, taunting them with its nearness. Cursing under her breath, Sekami's hands trembled frantically over the switches, but still the ship remained motionless. As Rhys sat there, watching her struggle, something else begin to rise through the fog of pain. An itch at the base of his skull… like a scab that needed picked.

Suddenly, as if through someone else's will, he lurched to his feet and pushed her away from the controls. She didn't resist and struck the floor hard, lacking the energy to soften her fall. His fingers worked fast, a trance-like glaze covering his eyes. Abruptly, the ship began to move. It rocketed out of the hanger, speeding away from the station and the attacking vessel. Knocked backward by the sudden g-force, Rhys felt himself falling, light from a blue-green aura filling the inside of the cockpit, before his head struck the hard metal deck. Darkness enveloped him.

------

HE AWOKE TO BLINDING LIGHT. A mere pinpoint of dazzling white, it bored into his brain like a drill. Rhys tried to close his eyelid but found he couldn't, that something held it open. The light remained for only a moment longer before it disappeared, and his other eye was unceremoniously pried open. The dazzling pinpoint returned. When it finally clicked off, he blinked rapidly to clear the spots lingering in his vision and found himself looking into the face of the mysterious alien woman.

"How are you feeling?" she asked, leaning back to give him room.

Cautiously, Rhys sat up, gasping with a sharp intake of breath. Everything, down to the small muscles in his hands and feet, seemed to hurt. Pressing his palms to his face, he tried to suppress the tide of pain that washed over him. The pressure helped a little, and he pushed deeper into his eye sockets, praying for more discomfort to abate. As he held his aching head, something else floated up through the veil of pain; the memory of an alien space station... of strange, inhuman creatures... of a menacing ship... and agony... red, searing agony that thrummed from deep within his chest, blocking out everything else. Beyond that, only a few disjointed images he couldn't interpret. Only the memory of pain seemed clear, as if he'd been the victim of a vicious beating.

"Terrible," Rhys reported. He dropped his hands and looked up into Sekami's face. "Absolutely awful."

"You've been unresponsive for almost forty-eight hours.

Between the attack and the lingering effects of cryosleep, I was beginning to worry you'd sustained more severe injuries than I thought."

"Have I?"

"No," Sekami replied, shaking her head. "It may not seem like it now, but your injuries are superficial."

"My insides felt like they were melting," Rhys grunted, his expression drawn. The thrumming sensation had been the most awful experience of his life, and he never wanted to repeat the encounter. "Did they leave? Whoever attacked us?"

"You don't remember?"

There was surprise in her voice, but that wasn't all. Rhys thought he detected a hint of something else, something like… relief? But why? Because he couldn't remember? *No*, he told himself. That didn't make sense. He felt scrambled, unable to interpret even her smallest emotional cues. Of course, that wasn't the reason. They had just survived an attack of a magnitude he still had trouble comprehending. If she was relieved about anything, it was probably that they were both still breathing. Hell, he was relieved of that, but it didn't change the fact he had no idea where they were or how they'd gotten here.

"The last thing I remember is running down the hangar toward a ship. Your nose was bleeding."

He trailed off, unsure of what had happened after that. The small, cramped room in which they now sat couldn't be on the cryostation, not after what he'd seen waiting outside and the fervor with which Sekami had ushered him along. At what point had he passed out? Had she carried him to safety? Sekami was strong, that much he remembered.

"We boarded the *Erebus* shortly before the station was destroyed. If we'd taken much longer, our fate would have been the same."

Rhys felt a guilty squirm in his guts. He'd been lagging behind from the start and not just because he was still defrosting from cryosleep. She'd urged him forward half a dozen times, but he'd been slow at every step to comply. What could she expect? Everything had been so overwhelming, was still overwhelming…

"I'm sorry. This is all just…" he trailed off. Just what, exactly? Terrifying? Confusing? Nightmarish? Was any of it even happening? Was he actually still in the cryotube, waiting to be thawed? Or would he wake up in his own bed, frightened but relieved it had been nothing more than a bad dream. He reached down and pinched the skin of his forearm, grimly aware of such a morbidly cliché reality check. It hurt, dashing any hopes that he might be dreaming. Shit.

"My name is Rhys."

"Neither of us would be here if I didn't already know that," Sekami replied cryptically.

It was a strange thing to say, but he suddenly remembered one of the first things she'd said to him: *I was sent here to find you before they did.* The memory caused a knot to tighten in his stomach, and for the first time, he understood the gravity of her words. It had to be a mistake. He was nothing, a nobody. Why would anyone be looking for him? He fell silent, at a loss for words, filled with confusion and worry.

"This must all be very alarming for you," Sekami consoled. Cautiously, she reached out one of her long-fingered hands to lay on his arm, before changing her mind and placing it back in her lap. "I apologize for the abruptness you were brought out of cryosleep. Normally, rehabilitation should've taken place very slowly. The implant you received during stasis would've guided you through a gradual assimilation period, but our situation was dire. There wasn't time to follow established procedures."

"I have an implant?"

"Yes. You were given a cerebral interfacing module while you slept," the woman explained. "Not only does it translate speech to your native language but also allows your eye to interpret and understand written word. Its development was crucial in the formation of our interspecies government, the Galactic Commonwealth. Imagine it like an integrated smart device. Everyone has one, so it's a means of communication as well. Just touch the area below your left ear to activate the interface."

Several questions formed in Rhys's mind all at once. Still sitting, he swung his legs over the side of the examination table and tried to gather his thoughts. They were erratic at best, and he had difficulty organizing them into any useful timeline. He had killed his wife... no, that wasn't what had happened. His wife had killed herself because he went to sea... again, that didn't seem right. Rhys pushed his fingertips to his temples and tried to remember. A sinking ship... empty ocean... the rescue... his wife Anne. Memories were fleeting at best.

"I'm having a hard time remembering much from before I went into stasis. There are big empty spots where I can't really recall..." Rhys fell silent, hands still holding the sides of his head. He willed himself to concentrate on the one person that had brought him happiness, but something was wrong. He couldn't remember her eyes, the shape of her nose, not even her smile. Anne, the wife he'd loved so dearly, had become nothing more than a faceless memory. A pang of despair shot through him.

"Memory fragmentation is a common side effect of cryogenic freezing, especially for someone who was in stasis as long as you were."

"As long as I was? What's that supposed to mean? How long was I frozen for?"

The timbre of his voice trembled slightly, and Rhys fought the apprehension beginning to build in his chest. Spaceships, aliens, superweapons... these were just a few of the glaring clues that more than a decade had passed since he'd gone to sleep. A lot more. Sekami shifted uncomfortably, and he could tell she was unaccustomed to breaking this type of news. Instead of answering directly, she attempted to sidestep the question.

"At this point, it would be difficult for you to understand the interstellar time and date format used by your species, along with the other alien races they interact with."

"Okay. Fine. Earth years then." Why was she being so evasive? An uncomfortable pause followed before Sekami replied.

"The current Terran year is 2687."

Stunned silence filled the room as the news came crashing down on him like a ton of bricks. With the clinical detachment of someone reporting the weather, she was telling him that he'd been frozen *centuries* longer than expected. Rhys gaped at her.

*"2687? It's been over six hundred years since I went to sleep?"* He'd been expecting something else, some kind of reassurance that what he'd seen could be explained away. That hadn't happened. Now, he was unsure how to react. Was he angry? Frightened? Did he believe her? Rhys wanted nothing more than to ignore what his eyes and ears were telling him and pinched his skin a second time. The futile gesture served only to send another jolt of pain down his arm. "I don't understand how this could've happened. I was only supposed to be frozen ten years!"

Sekami waved her hand over the console, and a hologram appeared. 'Kelly, Rhys F' was displayed in the upper left-hand corner, and she began to flip through the file, frowning.

"According to these records, six hundred ten years is the length of time you agreed to." She swiped her hand midair, turning over the holographic document and showing it to him. There was his name, scribbled in his untidy scrawl. In the box next to his signature, a line of text read 'Patient: Kelly, Rhys F. – Age: 31 – Length of Cryostasis Period: 610 years. – Witness: (No next-of-kin provided) Dr. Keri Martins, MD, CS.'

Keri Martins? Who the hell was Keri Martins? Rhys had memory of no one by that name, let alone even talking to anyone at the Denver Institute. At some point along the way, something had gone wrong. Had someone mistaken a zero for a six, or perhaps, changed his record while he slept? If so, why? Nothing made sense, and everything Sekami told and showed him was at odds with whatever broken memories he could scrape together. His thoughts were erratic, a jumble of nonsense the recently dormant synapses in his brain tried to process.

"You should've just left me. Why risk your life for a six-hundred-year-old nobody from the past?" His questions were coming quickly now.

"I'm sorry," she said, frowning. "Are you questioning the decision to rescue you?"

Rhys spread out his hands and raised his eyebrows as if the answer were obvious.

"That's exactly what I'm doing. You haven't told me a damn thing, except that anything I remember is either wrong or directly contrary to where I currently find myself. Who the hell was attacking us? And how am I in space right now? When I went to sleep, there wasn't even any such things as aliens!" he demanded. His anxiety was ramping up, and Sekami's perceived calm wasn't helping. When he brought up the attack, however, a spasm of fear passed over the woman's face, and her hand made an involuntary twitch on her knee. The crack in her façade vanished quickly.

"I was sent to find you, like I said." A generic response.

"Yeah, okay, but why? And by who?" he snapped, tired of the evasive answers.

"The person I represent can give you a much more satisfactory answer than me," Sekami said, her tone placating. "You were due to be woken up in another few months. If the circumstances of your revival had been otherwise, the effects of the news I've given you would have been lessened. As it was, I had to wake you up without the assimilation program... for both our sakes."

"So, who are they, the people who attacked us?" Rhys was trying his best to stay calm. He was exhausted and frightened... and hungry now that he thought about it. God, he was starving! When was the last time he'd had anything to eat? If there was any truth to what Sekami was telling him, his last proper meal had been over six hundred years ago. Rhys could kill for a steak and a beer, but his host appeared oblivious to his plight.

"The race of beings who destroyed the cryostation are known as the grülbarvoc. Most of us just call them 'the grül.' They first appeared over thirty-four years ago and brought unimaginable weaponry with them," she explained solemnly. "Of the dozens of sentient alien species populating our small corner of the galaxy, none has been able to withstand their might. Our weapons do not damage them. Our shields do not repel them. All we can do is run and hide."

A faraway look filled her eyes as she spoke, a familiar emptiness behind them. Rhys knew those eyes. They were the same eyes that had stared back at him in the mirror in the months after Anne's death. They were the eyes of someone who had seen true horrors and experienced terrible loss. He watched Sekami turn away and busy herself at the workstation but wanted nothing more than to demand why such creatures might be looking for him. As if sensing the unspoken question, Sekami turned back toward him.

"I know you have more questions, but I need to work. There are bunks and a galley in the aft compartments. You must be hungry. Try to get some sleep if you can. I'll wake you when we arrive."

"Where are we going?" Rhys asked, thinking the woman wasn't so oblivious after all.

"Someplace safe."

# CHAPTER 4
# PROXIMA STATION

THERE WAS no knob on the door, and it opened automatically as Rhys approached. The passage beyond was brightly lit, and he tried to orient himself. The corridor looked the same in either direction, featureless gray walls that ended in a closed hatch. Sekami had directed him to the aft compartments, but which way was aft? She hadn't exactly given him a map... he shrugged. The ship wasn't large. If he went the wrong direction, he could just turn around and go the other way. Eventually, he would find what he was looking for. About to take a step to the right, a green path appeared at his feet, leading from where he stood and down the corridor to the left. He hesitated, turned, and followed it, intrigued. Looking over his shoulder, Rhys expected to see the route back the way he had come, but it had disappeared, its terminus remaining always at his own two feet. He continued along the illuminated track until it ended at another closed hatch. When it snapped open, the room beyond was clearly a galley. Interesting. How had the ship known to bring him here?

Pushing the question aside, he opened every compartment, frantic in his quest to satiate his hunger. Strange foods he'd never heard of sat neatly organized, their containers labeled with things like 'uulgar eggs' and 'otochokes' and 'iokuri juice.' He picked up the container of eggs, inspecting their jet-black shells flecked with yellow. Was any of this safe for him to eat? While he pondered how best not to poison himself, a voice spoke out, making him jump and almost knock over a container of bulbous red fruit.

"All foodstuffs are safe for your consumption."

Rhys looked around, sure he'd been the only person in the room, and verified that there was indeed no one else.

"Um, hello? Is someone there?"

"I am BAIN, the Baukken Artificial Intelligence Network onboard this vessel."

The voice was coming from the ship itself, and Rhys gave his head a little shake, trying to wrap his mind around yet another unexpected piece of technological advancement. First alien super-weapons, now this. He was less surprised by the A.I. After all, the late twenty-first century had been near enough to its own functional application of such technology.

"What's a baukken?"

"A race similar to humans but superior in strength and intelligence. Dr. Ryele is a baukken female."

"Oh," Rhys replied blandly. He was impressed by the seamlessness of the voice. It was like speaking to another living, breathing person. "Did you lead me here? How'd you know I was hungry?"

"Your body exhibits a physiological response to hunger, and I have been monitoring your vitals since you arrived onboard. When you awoke, I assumed you would perform the enduring human tradition of 'breaking fast' and projected a path to your implant to guide you here."

"So, you weren't reading my mind?" he asked, thinking the last thing he needed was a computer probing his every thought.

"I am sorry to disappoint you, Mr. Kelly. As advanced as my programming is, I have yet to elevate myself to the capacity of 'mind reader.' Interpretation of biological functions is the best I can do. If you require anything, I am paired with your CIM and can be prompted by verbal commands or at any of the holoscreens onboard."

"I'll remember that," Rhys said, turning his attention back to the food.

He reached out and picked up a container of pale blue Hanekaarian flaakas covered in green fuzz. Green fuzz was usually a bad sign for food, but after a hesitant sniff, he was surprised to find no rancid smell of decay. With the first tentative bite, sticky yellow liquid dripped over Rhys's fingers, and peach-like sweetness engulfed his taste buds. Grunting in delight, he finished the flaaka and picked up a second, greedily devouring it more quickly than the first. He wiped the sticky nectar from his fingers and dug through other compartments, ravenous hunger gnawing his innards.

Inside one of the cold storage units, a large bin contained a butchered animal carcass, the label declaring it 'roast goah.' Rhys dislocated one of the attached limbs and hesitated. White, chalky veins of fat ran through the reddish-purple flesh. It would be better warm. He looked around for something that might resemble a microwave, but no such luck. About to tear into the strange-looking meat, Rhys remembered the A.I. monitoring every beat of his heart. It could certainly direct him to a heat source.

"Uh, BAIN?"

"Yes, Mr. Kelly?"

"Where's the microwave?"

"We are currently traveling through space. There is microwave radiation everywhere. If you would like to know more about the Cosmic Microwave Background, I can–"

"No. Sorry," Rhys interrupted. "I meant something I can use to heat this, er, goah."

A green line appeared on the deck and led to an open-ended cylindrical tube. It was strange to think this was nothing more than a projection, that only he could see the glowing path now leading to his desired endpoint. He wasn't sure he liked the fact an A.I. could project images into his eyes. Had anyone's implant ever been hijacked? Was that even possible or were there safeguards against such things? The thoughts were unsettling, but they were thoughts to be considered at a different time. A loud rumble from his stomach reminded Rhys he was still starving.

Placing the roast inside, he waited for something to happen. Before his eyes, the runnels of fat began to turn translucent, then ran clear. He pulled the steaming meat from the tube and dug in, chewing more slowly this time. Now, he savored the meat's unique flavor. It was like nothing he'd ever tasted. On and on, Rhys continued his culinary exploration, sampling everything he could lay hands on. When he could eat no more, he felt bloated, the mass of food a heavy weight in his stomach. He wiped his mouth and pulled at the tight waistband of the thin synthetic pants he'd been wearing in the cryotube. It was the first time since waking up he felt satisfied… or at least, no longer hungry. Satisfaction was a different story. Everything Sekami had told him had served only to uncover more questions… questions she couldn't, or wouldn't, answer. Despite this, his eyelids drooped heavy, as if the weight of the food were pulling them down. He needed sleep. Real sleep. In a real bed. Pushing slowly to his feet, Rhys left the galley, found the nearest unoccupied bunk, and promptly fell into a deep, food-induced slumber.

———

HE AWOKE SEVERAL HOURS LATER. The darkened room was cold, making the covers of his bed a comfortable cocoon. *Just a few more minutes*, he thought. Rolling over, Rhys reached out, searching for Anne, but his fingers scratched at nothing but empty sheets. Her absence puzzled him. Of the two of them, she'd never been the early riser. His confusion lasted for only a moment longer before the truth of where he really was hit him like a speeding train; the green-skinned woman, endless black space, and pain… terrible pain. He clenched his eyes shut, hoping desperately to remain in the dream that was quickly fading from memory. Anywhere but here… there was no reprieve. Sleep did not return, and he was left with a growing sense of desperation.

Rhys rubbed the lingering weariness from his eyes and stood on unsteady legs. Grunting in discomfort, he tried to massage life back into them before lurching awkwardly toward the door. He needed a distraction. Simply lying in bed hoping for more sleep while his mind spiraled out of control wasn't a good option.

"BAIN, where's Sekami?" he asked aloud.

"Dr. Ryele is sleeping in her quarters."

Not wanting to disturb her but in need of something to occupy his thoughts, Rhys began to wander aimlessly through the cramped ship. Despite the vessel's featureless gray walls, its spartan design held a sort of familiarity. There was elegance in its simplicity. It reminded him of other ships he'd been on. They, too, had lacked needless extravagance. Purpose-built. Utilitarian. Huge, floating fortresses used to move cargo from one place to another. Their goals had been clear, the way forward well-defined. Rhys had understood those things in his life and had excelled at them. It felt good to have some shred of familiarity to grasp onto. He wanted more.

"How do I get to the engine room?"

"Dr. Ryele has designated the engine room as 'off limits,'" the computer replied.

Rhys grunted in protest. He had a knack for understanding machines and was curious to learn how they'd changed in the twenty-seventh century. Fixing them had always helped take his mind off his troubles… not that he was about to tinker with complex alien technology unsupervised. Making a mental note to petition Sekami for access to the machinery space, he asked where he was allowed to go.

"The observation area, galley, and your quarters are the spaces approved for access."

"Take me to the observation area," Rhys said, somewhat dejectedly.

For the third time, a green path appeared at his feet and led him toward the forward part of the ship. He followed them up a ladder to the deck above and stepped into a tiny, windowless room. From the chamber's rounded contours, Rhys guessed its location was just aft of the cockpit, at the outermost skin of the ship. The room itself was bare, but before he could ask BAIN what exactly he was supposed to observe, the lamps above dimmed, then plunged him into darkness. A different light began to fill the room, its source seeming to originate from *outside* the ship. Awestruck, Rhys watched as the walls and ceiling began to disappear, fading from opaque to translucent to clear until nothing seemed to stand between him and the boundless expanse that lay beyond.

Glowing celestial bodies zoomed by in a dazzling blur of multi-colored light. Struck by the vastness of the galaxy, Rhys felt, for the first time, the true insignificance of his being. The things that troubled him seemed laughable... nothing he'd done or would ever do could affect the cosmos in any meaningful way. He was a mite, a tiny indistinguishable speck in an infinite ocean. Attempting to wrap his head around the mere scope of outer space, he felt the ship begin to slow and watched as distant objects took shape. The most prominent formation was a nebula of cloud and dust, a stunning coalescence of reds and blues and yellows.

Rhys heard the door of the observation deck open and turned to see Sekami striding through the hatch, her figure lit by the brightly glowing marvel outside. The woman's hair hung loosely around her shoulders, framing her face in a way that reminded him of Anne and accentuating her high cheekbones and penetrating eyes. It was disconcerting. Sekami possessed an exotic beauty, there was no doubt about that, but that wasn't what he found unsettling. How, after all they had been through in their short time together, did she manage to look so... vibrant.

"Beautiful, isn't it?"

Her voice held no trace of the fatigue Rhys felt. He nodded, a lump in his throat, and forced himself to look back out the window.

"'Overwhelming' is the word I would choose," he said when he found his voice. "I don't know what I expected to find when I woke up, but it wasn't this. I still don't understand why I wasn't revived earlier."

"I'm sorry. I don't have a good explanation. Cryonics was in its infancy at the turn of the twenty-second century. If what you say is true, about how long you were supposed to be frozen, then there are only a few plausible reasons for your circumstance. In the early stages of commercialized cryogenics, regulations around the technology were lacking at best. There were documented reports of fraud, most often involving a patient with no next-of-kin. Skilled coders could forge an extended revival date for a patient in stasis, and payment the cryonics lab thought they were getting would be funneled into a private account. Eventually, the patient's funds would run out, and the lab would have no choice but to wake them up."

Sekami paused and brushed a strand of hair away from her face with a long finger. "It was particularly detrimental to the patient. They'd be thrust into a vastly different society with no resources and no one to help them. Many of them died or ended up in worse condition than before their stasis period. That's why the assimilation program became standard procedure."

"Are you saying that's what happened to me?" Rhys was flabbergasted. If he had truly known the risks he was taking when he decided to freeze himself… it made his head swim.

"Not with any certainty. If you participated in one of the original studies, all that would've been years after you went into stasis. In my opinion, I'd guess you were the victim of someone's innocent, yet very damning, mistake." She fell silent, not saying anymore. Still preoccupied with the decisions he'd made, Rhys didn't press the issue. None of it mattered. He was here now, and there was no going back. They were quiet for a time, watching the exquisite colors of the nebula pass by. Finally, Rhys broke the silence.

"These grül things… does anyone know what they want?"

"No one knows what initially brought them to our galaxy, but we do know what keeps them here. Years ago, a piece of their technology was stolen, and they've been trying to recover it ever since," Sekami explained in a detached voice. The same distant look he'd seen during their last conversation had returned to her eyes at the mention of the grül. "Major settlements, cities, even entire planets have been devastated in their search. Survivors are spread throughout the Commonwealth, hiding as best they can and running when they need to."

"And us?" Rhys questioned. "Where are we running?"

"To the man they're searching for."

For a moment, he thought she was joking. By the look on her face, however, he quickly decided she wasn't. He felt his heart plummet at the thought of another altercation with their terrifying foe.

"I thought you said we were going someplace safe!"

"Where we're going *is* safe… safer than anywhere else," Sekami countered. Resignation replaced the detached stare that had been present on her face just moments before. Rhys opened his mouth to argue but faltered at the sight of the ever-changing vistas outside. Where before, the nebula had been the most eye-catching feature, he now saw a sprawling asteroid field, chunks of rock ranging in size from that of a small bus to near mountain-sized proportions. The ship was heading directly into the debris, correcting course to avoid collision.

"There's a settlement hidden deep within this asteroid belt dedicated to finding a way to fight the grül. That's where we're going," she explained, nodding toward the horizon. "So far, the grül haven't located the outpost here. We suspect the field's magnetic properties have kept it concealed, along with the diligence of those who know the location of Proxima Station.

Everyone who's taken refuge here takes great care in covering their tracks."

Before Rhys could demand more details about the crusade he was involuntarily being made a part of, the ship banked gently left and began heading for a particularly large asteroid. Sekami turned to leave and beckoned for him to follow. They departed the observation deck and made their way down to the cockpit. Taking a seat in the copilot's chair, he watched Sekami make adjustments to the ship's systems on the holographic console in front of her. Something about the cockpit felt familiar, but he couldn't put his finger on it. Had he been here when they escaped the cryostation? A strong sense of déjà vu filled him as the asteroid in front of them grew larger.

"Where's this colony supposed to be?" he asked, giving Sekami a quizzical look.

"You're looking at it."

As she spoke, a flurry of sparking electrical interference surrounded the ship and obscured the looming rock from view. Alarmed, Rhys gripped the armrests of his chair, his knuckles white.

"Relax. We're passing through a layer of optical cloaking. It shields the colony from any unwanted reconnaissance imaging. Almost through."

Sekami was calm and unreactive. Clearly, she'd done this before. Moments later, the disturbance outside the ship ceased. Rhys hadn't realized in the moment, but he'd been holding his breath and let out a long, slow exhale. Surprise filled him at what was concealed behind the sparking veil. Before, there had been nothing, just a featureless asteroid pockmarked with craters. Now, a gaping hole loomed in the surface of the rock like a gigantic mouth. They moved closer, heading straight for the chasm. When the vessel was still several kilometers away, Sekami reached up and gripped the flight controls, pulling back on the throttle until their forward momentum slowed to a stop. Her fingers flew across the holographic display, and a face materialized on the screen.

"Proxima Station, this is the *Space Vessel Erebus*. Requesting permission to land."

"*S/V Erebus*, transmit your credentials and docking code," the face replied, unsmiling.

Sekami pressed a button on the console. After a momentary pause, the holographic face nodded.

"Verified. Welcome back, Dr. Ryele. Please proceed to LZ Two."

The transmission clicked off and Sekami eased forward on the throttle. Rhys felt the ship begin to move as she expertly guided the vessel into the mouth of the tunnel. Several minutes passed in darkness, the only light coming from the softly glowing controls. When the tunnel ended, the ship drifted silently into a gigantic, well-lit cavern. Held in position by some unseen force, eight spherical structures floated in the center of the cave nearly filling the massive space. Like electrons positioned around a huge white nucleus, seven smaller pods encircled the primary structure. From the main sphere, a network of enclosed passages connected it to the secondary modules. To Rhys, the entire nexus resembled a huge, macroscopic depiction of a chain molecule.

Directly ahead and attached to the central edifice was a landing area where five other ships sat unattended. Flashing navigational beacons lit the way for their approach, and Sekami touched down gently on a pad in front of the huge white sphere. Rhys heard a clunk from somewhere aft of the cockpit and felt his ears pop. He gave Sekami a questioning look, and she pointed at a flashing orange light on the display console. Leaning forward, he peered at the description and read '*Airlock Pressure Stabilizing.*' A moment later, the light blinked to steady green. '*Airlock Pressure Equalized.*' Sekami unstrapped from the seat and strode purposefully from the cockpit.

Rhys unclasped his restraints and followed her, catching up when she stopped at the inner door to a double-hatched airlock.

Again, he felt an unsettling sense of déjà vu, but it shouldn't have come as a surprise. They must have boarded the ship from here. Rhys willed himself to remember what had happened, but the expression on Sekami's face distracted him from his introspection.

"It's best if the general populace doesn't know why you're here," she said.

"I wish *I* knew why I was here," he replied grudgingly.

"You will soon, I promise. I know this must be frustrating, but it would be better to receive answers directly from the man who sent me to get you," Sekami replied, a note of consolation in her tone. Rhys felt anything but consoled. "That said, Proxima Station's security hangs in a delicate balance. The people here are distrustful of outsiders, so don't be surprised if you're met with some hostility."

"Great."

She ignored his sarcastic tone and cycled the airlock doors. When the outer hatch opened, Rhys took a step backwards in surprise. A towering creature stood on the other side, red and scaly and menacing. Muscles bulged under the lizard-like skin protruding from beneath battle-scarred armor covering its torso. The alien's powerful legs were wrapped in the same protective plating, and its clawed feet clicked noisily on the metal floor. When it saw them, the creature's lips pulled back to reveal several rows of worn yellow teeth, and a croaking sound rose from its throat. Rhys couldn't tell if it was growling menacingly or if the unintelligible noises were supposed to be speech. He began to wonder if his translator had already malfunctioned, but a moment later, the snarling ceased.

"I am pleased by your safe return, Dr. Ryele, but your companion is not cleared for entry," the colossus croaked. The beady eyes inset into the creature's squashed face were fixed on Rhys, studying him. Its nostrils flared as if it was sniffing him.

"Thank you, for your concern, Captain. Mr. Kelly has been granted beta-level clearance. Hopefully, he'll prove an asset to our research team," Sekami said, turning slightly to include Rhys in the conversation. "This is Captain Rynnavek. He's our security chief."

Rhys stuck out his hand, and the creature looked at him quizzically. Its nostrils were still flared.

"Human?" Rynnavek asked, inspecting him from head to toe, then at his outstretched hand. "Stinks of old meat…"

His hand still suspended in midair, Rhys began to feel foolish. Of course, they didn't shake hands in the twenty-seventh century. He was about to drop it when, to his surprise, Rynnavek stuck out a shovel-sized fist and gave Rhys's entire arm a brisk shake. Again, its lips pulled back to expose rounded fangs, and he realized it was smiling… or, at least, doing its version of a smile.

"I need to report in," Sekami said, speaking to Rhys. "In the meantime, the Captain will show you to your quarters."

"Come," the creature said. "You are in need of cleaning."

Sekami walked away, and Rhys followed Rynnavek down the passage to another door. Emblazoned on its surface was a symbol, a box with figures inside and two arrows on top, one facing up and one facing down. Its meaning was instantly recognizable. Next to the door was a glowing screen, and Rynnavek placed one of his scaly hands against its surface and ushered Rhys inside. Squeezing its bulk next to him, the creature grunted, then spoke aloud.

"Bunk Pod One. Level Six. Hold on Mr. Rhys."

The door closed and the lift began to move, quickly picking up speed. A short ride later, they stepped into a vestibule with rounded, white walls. Rhys saw five doors situated in a half circle, all facing toward the center of the room.

"You will be in Room Five," Rynnavek said, motioning to the right as he spoke. "The others are occupied by Dr. Ryele and her research team. Introductions will be made when she comes to fetch you."

With that, the alien climbed back into the lift and departed. Rhys, now alone, walked to the door marked *FIVE*. When it didn't open immediately, he hesitated, noticing a scanner like the one

Rynnavek had used to activate the lift. He pressed his palm to the reader, and it glowed brightly, the hatch sliding open a moment later. *Strange,* he thought, wondering how the door had already been coded to his print. Inside, the room contained only the most basic amenities, but he was no stranger to sparse accommodations. He'd lived with less during his sailing days. At least, this was clean. All the same, he found it difficult to make himself at home. Everything he'd seen was so foreign, so alien, in a very literal sense. He felt drained and unable to focus. His mind was saturated with the terrifying new realities of a futuristic universe he knew nothing about. Who the hell were these people? Why had he been on that space station? More to the point, when had interstellar travel even become possible? The questions kept coming, and the more he learned, the more confused he ultimately became. Rhys just wanted to go home, back to Earth and to some shred of familiarity.

Tired, dirty, and not knowing what else to do, he decided to take Rynnavek's advice. Either way, he'd feel better after a shower. Stripping off the grubby cryotube garments, he wandered into the bathroom but was confused by the contraption that stood before him. Instead of an overhead nozzle, Rhys saw a cylindrical booth with dozens of vertical slats, all running up from the floor and curving at the top to meet in an enclosed arch. It was open at the front, and as he approached, the slats slid back smoothly to reveal thousands of tiny electronic eyes, all directed inward. Unsure of what to do, he voiced a question aloud.

"BAIN, where's the shower?"

"Water conservation is imperative in space. All fluids are recycled and processed for reclamation. Moisture showers have been replaced by the ultrasonic photosterilizer you see here. You will find the process superior to an antiquated 'shower.'"

Shrugging, Rhys stepped into the cubicle and felt a strange sensation as countless bright blue lasers fired around his body. Vibrating turned into pinching and back into vibrating again. A blast of air blew his hair back before it all abruptly stopped. Less than two minutes had elapsed. Rubbing his hands over his arms, Rhys supposed he felt clean, but it was certainly no substitute for a hot shower. He walked naked back to the bedroom and stood in front of the dresser. There were no handles to open the drawers. He groped around, feeling for a hidden lip to pull on, when his fingers passed over the upper righthand corner of one of the drawers. It slid open unexpectedly, and he touched the spot again. This time, the bin closed.

Familiar with its operation, he began to peruse the contents of each drawer. Identical sets of shirts, pants, and undergarments sat neatly folded, the color of each the only noticeable variation. He selected a tan, wool-like shirt and dark blue-gray pants. Surprisingly, each article of clothing fit him perfectly. He pulled a pair of sturdy boots onto his feet and heard a knock at the door.

"Come in," he said, adjusting the tightness of the straps.

The door opened and in strode Sekami. She had changed clothes and pulled her hair into a loose knot. Often, Anne had worn her hair the exact same way. Jesus, it was unsettling, to keep being reminded of what he'd lost in this way. Seeming oblivious to how flustered he'd become, she looked him up and down, and a small smile creased the corner of her mouth.

"You've at least remembered how to dress yourself."

Distracted by her resemblance to Anne, he was taken aback by the woman's playful behavior. He wasn't sure he appreciated the jab at his amnesia. It was slightly off-putting to have someone he barely knew tease him like they were old friends… if Rhys had been a lesser man, he might have replied with an abrasive comment but instead decided to let it slide. She hadn't meant anything by it. Like him, she was probably just relieved to be alive.

"Like riding a bike, I guess… once BAIN helped me figure out the sterilizer-thing," he replied.

Frankly, the few things he could still remember were becoming less and less detailed, like dreams fading into the ether. He'd expected a good night's sleep and a belly full of food to awaken some of the dormant memories buried within the depths of his mind. Now, though, it seemed as if the opposite was happening. Worry began to creep back into his chest and brought blood pounding to his ears with every heartbeat.

"Come with me," he heard Sekami say, her voice muffled as if speaking through a wall. "I want to introduce you to our team."

# CHAPTER 5
# THE MACHINE

RHYS FOLLOWED Sekami through a series of decontamination locks into a spacious, well-lit laboratory. Like everything else in the station, its walls were brilliant white. Holographic screens displayed complex mathematical formulas and schematics of unfamiliar machinery. The center of the room was isolated from the rest of the lab by two humming force fields, one inside the other. Encircled within the transparent barriers was a sphere.

Roughly a meter in diameter, its surface was textured like hammered iron; jet black as if exposed to extreme heat... and unless his eyes were deceiving him, it was floating unsuspended behind the shields. An image of the sphere was visible on one of the displays nearest to Rhys. Hunched over it, he saw three figures deep in heated discussion. Two of them, a man and a woman, appeared human, but the third was equipped with four powerful-looking arms, its entire body covered in thick black hair. Sekami strode in their direction, ignored until nearly abreast of them. When they finally noticed her, one of the strangers cried out in relief.

"Dr. Ryele, you're alright! We'd heard there'd been an attack."

The woman who'd spoken was average height, with curly red hair and a full figure. From across the room, she'd appeared human, but as Rhys drew nearer, the less true that seemed to become. Her pointed ears were the first indication she had descended from something other than a shared Cro-Magnon lineage. The next, and more noticeable clue were her large eyes that possessed a second set of membrane-like lids. Each time she blinked, Rhys saw a transparent film slide across the surface of her corneas at a fraction slower than the fleshy outer skin. Smiling at Sekami, the woman inclined her head and touched the fingertips of her right hand to her lips and then forehead.

"We're okay. It's good to see you Marasa," Sekami replied and repeated the gesture, leaving Rhys to wonder if the entire spectacle was the equivalent of a handshake. "This is Marasa Bok naal. She's one of the research scientists here at Proxima Station."

"Nice to meet you. I'm Rhys." He leaned his head forward and imitated the greeting he had seen the two women use. A look of surprise passed over Marasa's face, before an embarrassed smile formed on her lips.

"You're familiar with turandian customs?" she asked.

"Um, not exactly. I've sorta been in cryosleep for a while..."

This time, Marasa blushed deep red, and Sekami cleared her throat uncomfortably. A half-smile twisted the corner of her mouth, and she bit her bottom lip in a feeble attempt to hide her amusement. Rhys, oblivious as to what was so comical, stared at the pair of them with a baffled look on his face.

"Did I say something funny?" he asked bewilderedly. Sekami coughed again then recovered her composure, the poorly veiled smile disappearing from her lips.

"The greeting Marasa and I exchanged is a turandian custom reserved for females bound by blood or trauma. Woman to woman. When a male extends this salutation, he's initiating a complex connubial ritual, and if the female accepts, a lifelong bond is forged. In other words, you just propositioned Marasa for marriage... and sex," Sekami explained, amusement creeping back onto her face. "Only death can sever the bond. Seeing as she hasn't clawed your eyes out, I presume she accepts."

"I didn't... I just... Jesus. Sorry," Rhys stammered. How could he have been so foolish as to thoughtlessly imitate an alien custom he didn't understand? Hoping to divert attention away from the blunder, he tried to change the subject. "If I can ask without sounding offensive, what's a turandian?"

"There's no need to apologize, but to be clear, I do *not* accept. I understand you were just trying to be polite. It may be wise, however, to refrain from parroting any other alien customs until you fully understand what you're conveying. If you'd done that to a pureblooded turandian, the consequences could have been more serious," Marasa replied. She had finally stopped blushing. "To answer your question, though, I'm a turandian. Well, half turandian. From my father. My mother was human."

"You mean, *our* mother was human," a voice called.

It came from a dark-haired man, the other human, no longer hunched over the display. Standing upright, Rhys was easily a head taller than the scientist now striding toward them across the room. What the man lacked in stature, however, he made up for in build. Broad-shouldered and fit, Marasa's brother swaggered over with an almost comical spring in his step.

"Remember, Little Sis, as hard as you might try to forget, we're still related," he said, slinging an arm around Marasa and mussing her hair with his free hand. A sour look passed over the woman's face as she quietly endured the undignified display of affection. When it was over, he grinned like a Cheshire cat and stuck out his hand to Rhys, who shook it.

"Kieron Adara. You've already met my darling sister...though, she's not in the habit of telling people *that* bit of embarrassing trivia. Can't figure out why," he said, his brow furrowed with mock perplexity. "Anyway, in a pitiful attempt to distance herself from a remarkable brother, Marasa uses her father's name, Bok naal. Naal means 'child of' in the turandian language."

"Bok naal... so, Child of Bok?" Rhys clarified. He was pretty sure he understood but wanted to make certain after his last misstep.

"Well, waddaya know? Seems like you've thawed some ice off that frozen brain of yours."

A smile crinkled the corners of Kieron's eyes, and Rhys felt the color rising in his cheeks. Clearly, the man had overheard his uncomfortable exchange with Marasa or enough of it to be aware of his time in cryosleep. He already felt foolish for having made the blunder, but now, he'd probably have to endure constant reminder of it. Kieron didn't seem like the type to let go of such easy pickings. Rhys would just need to nip this in the bud. Before his 'frozen brain' could make a retort, however, Marasa spoke up in his defense.

"Just ignore my… brother," she said, grimacing as if the mere use of the word was painful to utter. "I'm not entirely convinced he isn't descended from some other less-evolved species… like an uulgar or something."

Rhys recognized the word from the carton of eggs on Sekami's ship, had even eaten one, but still the insult held no meaning to him. Seeing the blank look on his face, Marasa explained further.

"Uulgars are small, six-legged creatures that root around in their own feces looking for nutrients. To use an old Earth vernacular Kieron was kind enough to teach me; he's a shithead."

She blushed when she said it, like a little kid trying a swearword for the first time. Her brother held up his hands, a feigned look of hurt on his face. Rhys felt his stomach turn over and made a mental note to never again eat anything that came from an uulgar. If that was the creature's most defining characteristic, why the hell had BAIN let him eat one? Admittedly, it had been delicious, but he wouldn't have tried alien shit eggs if he'd known.

"Better an uulgar than that *shaain kah* father of yours… and anyway, Mother would've beaten you around those pointy, half-breed ears if she'd heard you speak to me that way," Kieron replied with a sneer. There was a stinging edge to his voice, and Marasa's smile gave way to a crestfallen look. Rhys didn't know what *shaain kah* meant but was willing to bet Marasa's sudden dejectedness might be attributed to the half-breed comment. Her brother ignored this, however, and directed his attention back to Rhys.

"So, ah, Sleeping Beauty... where'd you say you're from?"

"Montana... Earth, if you don't know what that is."

"I know what Montana is, Cowboy. So, what? Get tired of being a rodeo clown or something? Needed a fresh start? Must've been frozen a long time if you don't know what turandians are."

Kieron smiled again, clearly entertained by his own deplorable wit. Rhys ignored the crack about being a rodeo clown. He knew people like this were just after a reaction, and he'd be damned if he was going to oblige. Kieron was a dick, but Rhys wasn't going to give him the satisfaction of saying so.

"A lot longer than I was supposed to be, yeah. I was an engineer before going into stasis back in '77."

"That's barely a decade. We've been allies with the turandians for—"

"Sorry. Not 2677... 2077."

At this, Kieron laughed aloud.

"2077? Well, that's great. Really, just... classic," he said, then turned to Sekami. "We were under the impression you'd brought back someone useful. Are you sure you thawed out the right person? Seems like this guy should've found his way into a museum, not a deep-space research station. I guess a few years on ice makes someone forget where they belong."

Hearing Kieron voice the very thing Rhys was most afraid of struck a nerve. He wasn't stupid... he knew how out-of-place he really was, but hearing these people talk to him as if he were just some idiot tourist was pissing him off. They didn't understand the things he'd done, the things he'd seen, or the sadness he'd endured. This station was the last place he wanted to be and so far, hadn't even been told what he was doing here. If he was anything more than an interesting relic to be ogled and joked about, someone had better tell him soon.

"My wife ended her life because of mistakes I made," Rhys

retorted, no longer able to keep the anger out of his voice. "You're damn right I wanted to forget!"

"Well, boo-fucking-hoo. You're not the only person around here who's lost someone," Kieron bit back, no longer smiling. "While you were cozied up in a cryotube, our galaxy has been fighting to survive, and let me tell you, *partner*, it's not going so well. If your reaction is to run away and freeze yourself when things get hard, there's no place for you here."

"That's enough!" Marasa, having found her voice again, placed herself between them and fixed her brother with an icy glare. "Why do you always have to do this? If you weren't so busy abusing everyone, we might be closer to understanding *that*."

She pointed angrily toward the humming containment fields. The two men ignored her, however, their eyes locked in a simmering battle of unspoken machismo. Rhys hated it. These introductions weren't going the way he'd imagined. First, he'd embarrassed himself by unwittingly propositioning an alien for sex, and then had somehow managed to get himself into a pissing match with her brother... all within the first few minutes of being here. There was nothing he could do about it, though. Not now. If Rhys was the one to back down, he knew Kieron would use that as license to walk all over him. To hell with that. He'd stare down this prick for as long as it took. When the tension in the room seemed about to boil over, Kieron scoffed with derision and shook his head. He walked away, pretending to busy himself at an isolated workstation, before delivering one final jab over his shoulder.

"If that walking popsicle thinks he gets to go on a little pleasure cruise, meet some aliens, and then go home, he's in for a rude awakening."

Rhys sensed Marasa stiffen, perhaps expecting him to retaliate, but she needn't have worried. He'd won the pointless dick-measuring contest. Still though, it felt like a hollow victory. What had Kieron meant by that last taunt? Had it just been one more attempt to get under his skin? Marasa, looking exasperated, tried to diffuse some of the tension.

"I'm sorry for my brother. He... *we*, are all under a lot of stress. We've made almost no headway in our work here," she said, a tired look in her large eyes. "You're an engineer?"

Rhys let out a short, humorless laugh.

"I'm not sure my fragmented, six-hundred-year-old-marine-engineering knowledge is going to help you crack some state-of-the-art alien tech... if that's what you're asking," he said gloomily.

She smiled.

"Of course not, no. I just thought it might be interesting to learn how things have changed."

Rhys recognized Marasa's effort to break the ice, but if truth be told, teaching 'Antiquated Engineering Principles 101' to an overeager half-alien seemed pointless. Besides, with how little of his past he could remember, it would be a short lesson anyway. These scientists weren't the ones in over their heads. If he was interested in anything, it would be to glean as much information from *them* as he could. Not the other way around.

"Your brother. What did he mean about being on a pleasure cruise, meeting some aliens, and then going home? What was that all about?" Rhys was wondering what Kieron had meant. "This has been anything but pleasurable."

Marasa gave Sekami a worried look, then dropped her gaze and refused to look him in the eye.

"Rhys," Sekami began, "I don't know if now's the best time for this conversation."

"What conversation? What aren't you telling me?" Something didn't feel right. He could tell by Sekami's tone there was something she wanted to say, but for whatever reason, she was hesitant to do so. He looked between the two women, an awkward silence filling the laboratory. Finally, Sekami spoke up.

"I didn't intend for you to find out this way, but there's no easy way to put this. Earth is... no longer habitable."

Ice-cold shock drenched him like a plunge into a frozen lake.

"I don't understand," he choked, barely able to force the words past a lump that had formed in his throat.

"The grül. One of their weapons set off an atmospheric chain reaction a few years ago," she explained in a soft voice. "Nobody on the surface survived. Even ships in a near-Earth orbit didn't make it."

With memory-like clarity, he imagined a brilliant flash of reddish light crawling across the sky, the screams of billions of people, and something else... something unexpected; two figures locked in mortal struggle. Their features were indistinct, but he felt a strong sense of familiarity intertwined with overwhelming anguish. It sent him reeling, his mind spinning uncontrollably from the immense gravity of Sekami's news.

In desperate need of a means to ground himself, he gaped at her in disbelief. She couldn't be telling the truth. Was this some kind of sick joke? He wanted to believe that, but the look on her face told him it wasn't. Like the fist of some inevitable reality closing around his heart, Rhys realized he truly had nothing left. No wife, no direction, no home... nothing. Here stood this *alien*, telling him it was all gone, like they were discussing the weather. Burying his face in his hands, he slumped heavily onto a nearby stool. An involuntary spasm gripped his body, the turmoil inside him bursting forth like water through a ruptured dam.

"Rhys?"

He felt a gentle touch on his shoulder, but didn't answer, instead taking several deep, steadying breaths. For a time, no one spoke, the only sound coming from soft electronic beeps and frustrated grunts of the hairy figure still hunched over the far display. Rhys felt a hollow spot forming in his chest, an ache where his sense of self and home used to be.

"Why?" he asked finally, head still cradled in his hands. "Why are they doing this?"

"Since they first emerged, the grül have murdered countless people," she explained somberly. "Our military forces tried to oppose them, but nothing they possessed could stand against the grül's weaponry."

"That wasn't what I asked," Rhys replied, lifting his head to meet Sekami's gaze. When their eyes met, she shifted uncomfortably, once again hesitant to give a straight answer.

"Several years ago, we acquired a piece of their technology and have been trying to find a way to harness its power." She pointed toward the far end of the lab, at the strange black orb floating behind the containment shields. "Somehow, the grül discovered we possessed one of their machines and began a tenacious pursuit to recover it. Four years ago, a ship in their fleet tracked us to Earth and..."

*Laid waste to my home.* Silently, he finished the sentence for her. He knew that's what she'd been thinking, even if she was unwilling to say it. Sekami cleared her throat and continued.

"We spent the next eight months in search of refuge, but nothing felt safe from their reach. Eventually, we stumbled upon this asteroid belt and its abandoned military outpost. Much of the infrastructure was already here; the field's magnetic properties, the optical defenses, the eight modular superstructures... all we had to do was convert the facilities to our specific need and rebuild the resources we'd lost."

A look of sadness filled her eyes. It was the same faraway look he'd seen during their conversation on the *Erebus*. She'd lost someone back on Earth, he realized. A friend, maybe? Or a lover? He opened his mouth to ask, thought better of it, then closed it again. If Sekami noticed this backpedaling, she ignored it and nodded toward the hairy, four-armed creature still pouring over schematics.

"That's Otaan Yabar, a Hanekaarian engineer recruited from Merellian II, one of the G.C.'s deep-space imaging facilities. His species possesses expert knowledge of all things mechanical. Marasa and Kieron are leaders in the field of xenotechnology, but even since they joined the team, we've made no real headway in operating the machine's most basic functions... powering it on, for example. For two years, they've worked doggedly, but unsuccessfully, to make any progress."

"So, this person you keep referring to, the one who brought you all here... the grül are looking for a machine he stole? And that's why they destroyed Earth? You don't see the problem with that?" Rhys asked in a strangled voice. The news about Earth had made his voice thick with grief, and the more Sekami explained, the more upsetting the situation became. It was beginning to sound as if these refugees or exiles or whatever they were had bitten off more than they could chew. They'd stolen something from an advanced alien species, were attempting to weaponize it, and in doing so, had drawn the wrath of said aliens. No matter how someone framed it, these people were, in a way, responsible for the desolation of his home. A storm of emotion swirling inside him, he saw the two women exchange an embarrassed glance, but only Sekami would meet his gaze.

"I know how this must sound, but there are good reasons he took the machine–"

"Does this *savior* have a name?" Rhys interrupted, spitting the word. How? How could she stand there so calm, so detached and try to make excuses for the loss of his... everything! Why did it always feel like she was side-stepping his questions? Since his revival, Sekami had given multiple long-winded speeches, while telling him as little as possible... or she had, until dropping that last proverbial bomb about Earth's destruction on him. Now, he saw kindness and understanding in her penetrating eyes. He didn't care. *Fuck understanding*, he thought, gazing back defiantly.

"His name is Marcus Volkerson, and if you need time to process this, take however long you need," she replied, her voice pacifying. "When you meet him, he's going to ask something important of you, and it's critical you consider his request in a clear state of mind."

"Because having this shitstorm land on top of my head is really giving me clarity!" he barked angrily, unable to keep his emotions in check any longer.

Rhys turned away, exhausted from the emotional roller-coaster he'd been riding. Fear, anger, sadness, then fear again. It was fear and sadness he felt now more than anger, and he was ashamed. Ashamed for how he'd reacted. Ashamed for leaving Anne to cope alone. Ashamed for running away to an unknowable future. Ashamed for *surviving* when so many had perished... he felt a watery itch behind his eyes and knew he needed a distraction. Anything he might use to bury the pain and anger welling up inside him. Blinking back tears, he walked to where Otaan Yabar studied a diagram of the mysterious sphere.

When he drew close, he saw four alien hands working furiously over the holographic display. The creature didn't look at Rhys as he approached and seemed quite adept at ignoring him, completely focused on its work. Its pointed face contained an unblinking set of jet-black eyes that were fixed on the three-dimensional image. Other than the strange texturing on its surface, the sphere appeared featureless, nothing more than a ball of ugly black metal. There were no hinges, no buttons, no hoses... the entire surface was one continuous unbroken piece. Beneath its exterior, the schematic showed nothing but empty space. Whatever scanning equipment had been used to create the image seemed unable to penetrate the machine's outer shell... if there was even anything inside to be seen.

An error message blinked on the screen, and Otaan Yabar pressed a button to clear it. A few seconds later, the message returned, and once again, he cleared the alarm. The process repeated itself several more times, and the creature snorted in frustration. Obviously, something wasn't going the way it was supposed to, but the engineer looked quite capable of inflicting serious bodily harm if trifled with. Rhys wasn't about to interrupt. Otaan Yabar flicked through screens on the workstation, pausing only when the words *'Diffusion Scan'* were emblazoned on the display. He touched one of his hairy fingers to a button marked *'Position,'* and soft whir filled the room as a robotic arm inside the containment detached itself from the ceiling, then poised motionless above the floating orb.

Rhys walked toward the machine until he was less than a meter from the humming outer barrier. For reasons he couldn't explain, he was strangely drawn to the contraption. It reminded him of his days as a marine engineer, where he'd experienced similar feelings toward unfamiliar equipment. He had always been good with machines. They were easy, their needs were simple. When they malfunctioned, there was usually a clearly defined problem, however small it may be. Once it was resolved, the machine would work again... the same was probably true of this one. Rhys realized he was aching to learn about the device. What was it made of? How did it work? What secrets of the grülbarvoc could it reveal?

Momentarily distracted from his troubles, he heard the soft whirring again and watched as a long, thin object extended from the head of the robotic arm and began to spin at high speed, moving toward the skin of the floating sphere. Something began to itch at the back of Rhys's mind, like he'd forgotten to do something important. Suddenly, like an alarm going off in his head, he had the feeling this was a terrible idea.

"Wait!"

Unthinking, he reached out as the spinning head touched the machine's rough, black surface. His hand connected with the containment field, and the repellant force tossed him violently backwards. Rhys skidded to a halt at the feet of Otaan Yabar, who had begun to yell in distress. Dazed, he shook his head and tried to make sense of what had happened and why the Hanekaarian was still shouting. When he regained his bearings, he understood what had upset the engineer. The machine on the other side of the field had sprung to life.

## CHAPTER 6
# A CLOSE CALL

THE SPHERE BEGAN to emit an almost imperceptible vibration, and Rhys watched in astonishment as its surface began to separate at a single point, disappearing into itself like molten steel. A strange, mirage-like shimmer emanated from the aperture that was quickly growing in size. The hole was now large enough to see what was housed inside, and he saw a silvery fluid-like core, shimmering and pulsating as the machine discharged its indeterminate contents into the room. Immediately, a claxon began to ring, and Rhys heard BAIN's voice broadcast throughout the lab.

"Warning! Therleon particles detected. Primary containment field failure. Secondary field at sixty percent and falling. Evacuate all personnel from the immediate vicinity." The message began to repeat, over and over. Rhys had not thought it possible, but Otaan Yabar now worked faster than before, his hairy fingers flying over the console. He listened as BAIN continued to relay the message, now including an estimated countdown to when the breach would occur. Less than five minutes.

"What did you do!?"

Rhys, still sitting on the floor, saw Sekami, Marasa, and Kieron barreling down on him. Before he could answer, they rushed past and crowded around the console. The four-armed alien gestured at the machine and then back to the display.

"I was about to initiate a scan, when the human fell into the containment field," Otaan Yabar explained, pointing at Rhys who had pushed himself up onto hands and knees. "The next thing I knew, the machine turned on. Ryak!" The alien swore loudly, the implant in Rhys's ear failing to translate the word into something comprehensible. He was about to protest the seemingly accusatory gesture but stopped when he saw alarm in the others' faces. Rhys felt a knot form in the pit of his stomach.

"Does someone mind telling me what's going on? What are therleon particles, and why can't your containment fields hold them?" Rhys asked, clambering to his feet. Kieron waved off the question and gave him a look that said, 'not now.' Sekami, on the other hand, spoke without taking her eyes from the display.

"It's *their* technology! The grül's. It's what they use to power everything from propulsion engines to the weapons we encountered earlier. Therleon particles make it all possible. If enough of that stuff gets out..." Sekami trailed off for a moment, at a loss for words to explain. "An uncontrolled release has the potential to wipe out this entire station!"

*Three minutes to secondary containment failure.*

"How did it turn on?" Kieron exclaimed. "Seriously, how the *fuck* did it turn on?"

The Hanekaarian uttered another string of profanities but could only gesticulate wildly, unable to explain the machine's sudden change of state. Sekami, looking frightened, glanced furtively at Rhys before turning away and hurrying back into the decontamination chamber from which they'd entered. She stepped through a series of locks into the adjacent room where, through a thick plate glass window, Rhys saw a line of bulky suits hanging from the bulkhead. Sekami ran to the nearest suit and began pulling it over herself. When she returned a few moments later, Kieron stepped to block her path.

"What're you doing?"

"Preparing," she said, her voice muffled through the plastic hood. "We need more power to the containment fields, and I want some protection if the secondary goes down before I figure out how."

"That's insane! If you screw it up and those shields fail, we're dead," he yelled, grabbing her by the wrist. "You don't even know how to turn off the machine!"

She yanked her arm forcibly away and glared at him.

"We could die anyway if those particles escape the lab. We don't know what'll happen if we can't keep them inside. If I fail, the tertiary backup may hold long enough for everyone to evacuate," she spat. "If you want to stay and help, then by all means do so. Otherwise, get out of my way."

Kieron looked like he wanted to argue, but Marasa pulled desperately on his arm, and the three scientists hurried toward the door. Otaan Yabar rammed his fist against a large red button, and BAIN began to repeat a new message: *Report to stations. Standby for evacuation protocol.* Rhys stood rooted to the spot, his mind and heart racing. Seeing he had remained, Sekami's eyes narrowed.

"There's no leaving the lab once they raise the tertiary field," she said, a hard look on her face. "Go with the others."

"I'm staying. Two sets of hands are better than one. Let me help," he replied. His decision to stay had been impulsive and unplanned. He hoped he wouldn't regret it. Sekami opened her mouth to protest, but no words came out. Instead, she just stepped aside to let him through.

An eternity seemed to pass as Rhys stood in the airlock, trembling as he followed the instructions BAIN gave him while his mind tried to process what was happening. The others' fear had been infectious, and his hands shook as he grabbed the nearest suit. He balled it in his arms, slinging the air supply over his shoulder and hurrying back through the airlock. With Sekami's help, he donned the suit and watched as she retraced its heavy zipper with a pistol-shaped applicator. The substance inside the device began to spread over top of the seam, creating what he guessed to be a perfectly air-tight seal. She handed the applicator to him, and he hurriedly repeated the process on her suit. He gave one last glance toward the exit and saw Kieron looking back at him through the glass. The man gave a curt nod, then pulled a lever to energize a third field around the lab's perimeter.

*Thirty seconds to secondary containment failure.*

Rhys looked at Sekami, worry etched in his face.

"Any hope of surviving if that stuff gets released in here?"

She shook her head. "From a concentrated dose like that? I don't know. I'm sorry if you didn't understand that before you volunteered to stay."

Working furiously, she typed at one of the consoles before pointing across the room to a large electrical panel, where several dials and holoscreens illuminated the surrounding area.

"When I say, open the far-left lever on that workstation. The one *all the way* to the left. Wait for my signal, then close the one next to it. That will isolate the primary field onto battery backups. Our grid's already operating at max load, so that should strip enough power off the board to give the secondary more juice. It's not a great solution, but it's what I've got."

Rhys lumbered over to the workstation as quickly as he could. The heavy suit was cumbersome to move in, and his heart was racing in overdrive. Reaching the panel, he rested his hand on the lever and waited for her signal.

"Now!" Sekami roared.

He pulled down hard, the switch taking most of his weight to open. Out of the corner of his eye, Rhys sensed the secondary field brighten. Sekami motioned again, and he closed the other lever. The glow from the inner containment field flashed back into existence, and he was filled with elation. It had worked! He let out a whoop of triumph, then froze, feeling his stomach plummet. The primary containment had already started to destabilize. It dimmed, brightened, then dimmed again. The field held for a moment longer before dissipating into nothing. To his horror, the secondary field began to flicker.

"It wasn't enough!"

*Containment failure imminent. Inadequate power to sustain tertiary field.*

Rhys watched in trepidation as the glow from the secondary field went out, allowing the invisible particles to spill into the room around them. *No, no, no,* he thought as his fingers began to twitch. He watched Sekami's hands move furiously over the holo-screen and felt a wave of dizziness wash over him. Was he about to die? For sure this time? He didn't know what made him do it, but he began to stumble in the direction of the machine, hands outstretched toward the shimmering core as his vision blurred. The countdown echoed in his ears.

*Two seconds to tertiary failure.*

His fingers twitched, and he heard Sekami scream.

THE POWERFUL ALIEN STOOD SILENTLY, only half-listening to the squabbling holographic figures in front of him. His arms were crossed defiantly over his once-muscled chest as the members of the grülbarvoc High Council argued over one another, attempting to tell *him*, Fleet Captain Xorin, how best to do his job. *One might consider it amusing*, he thought as a particularly shriveled-looking member of the council jabbed a bony finger down at him. That was, if Xorin possessed a sense of humor. Instead, he found the formality infuriating, the idea these politicians thought he should answer to them.

"We demand an explanation, Xorin! Why, after so long, have you been unsuccessful in recovering a single machine?" the shriveled councilmember demanded. "This 'Marcus Volkerson' has evaded you for thirty-three cycles, and there has been no sign of him the last four! You have accomplished nothing since the desolation of his world."

"*Fleet Captain Xorin*," he replied coolly. The councilmember was caught off guard. He vacillated inanely before puffing himself up in an attempt to present himself as Xorin's superior.

"Insolence will not be tolerat–"

"Let me remind you, Councilmembers, I do not answer to you. Exalted Leader Küddar has tasked me with recovering our stolen technology, and his authority eclipses your own. I have been instructed to use whatever means necessary to complete my mission. Informing you of *any* of my decisions is merely a professional courtesy, and one I am currently reconsidering."

An awkward silence filled the room as the Council shifted uncomfortably in their seats. *Fools*, Xorin thought, disgust welling up inside him. He wished for a return to the days when the High Council did not exist, when military strength ruled above all, but times were different now. True, he'd been granted the authority to do whatever necessary to recover the machine, but as soon as he succeeded, he would be bridled once again by the Council's recently-founded rules of engagement. The thought grated on his nerves. Xorin took a deep breath and tried to keep the contemptuousness out of his voice.

"After the devastation of the Interloper's home world, we tracked his ship to a remote cryostation at the farthest reaches of their Solar System, within what they call the Oort Cloud, before losing the trail. In case he ever returned, I thought it prudent to place constant surveillance over the system to keep watch for this... *Volkerson*," Xorin explained, the name feeling foreign on his tongue. "A few days ago, that very ship returned to the system, and I could not forego the opportunity to capture or destroy it. The reappearance of his ship after nearly four cycles seemed significant. I dispatched the nearest vessel in my fleet, only to have him escape once more. The warriors responsible for this loss have been punished accordingly, and they will not make the same mistake a second time. Under threat of Duoranath, they will not rest until they have found the Interloper and his missing ship."

The shriveled councilmember snorted derisively, unconvinced of the Fleet Captain's resolve.

"The Duoranath is an archaic and barbaric tradition. Its use on your own soldiers is a heinous violation of the progress we grülbarvoc have made over the last hundred cycles. There will soon come a time when your beloved Exalted Leader will succumb to the Sickness, and your outmoded methods will no longer be tolerated. Clearly, you were *not* the correct choice for this mission… regardless of your reputation."

At this, the last of Xorin's patience was consumed, and he seemed to visibly grow before the council as he raised himself to his full stature.

"I am the last Captain of the Küddarian Brotherhood, from a time when the grülbarvoc followed strength, not the whims of sniveling bureaucrats! I will complete the task set before me by any means necessary," Xorin thundered. He was forceful in his constitution, and not one of the Councilmembers dared interrupt him. "If you wish to replace me, then, by all means, send someone worthy to challenge my authority. Until that time, however, this task remains my own, and I will proceed as I see fit."

While the Captain shamed the Council, a figure approached him stealthily from behind, but Xorin's keen sense of hearing alerted him to the presence of another warrior. He braced slightly, suspicious of anyone lurking in the shadows, and readied himself for an attack. This was how he had reached Fleet Captain, after all, by forever preparing for the worst and striking first if needed. Xorin sniffed the air and recognized the scent of the young warrior. It was Commander Feyt, his second-in-command. In terms of size and strength, Feyt was little better than average, but what he lacked in these attributes, the Commander far exceeded with speed and intelligence. He possessed a sharp mind for strategy, and Xorin had personally seen him best dozens of bigger, stronger warriors in ritualistic combat for the position of his Executive Officer. Now, Feyt leaned close to whisper in the Captain's ear.

"Sir, we have just detected a burst of therleon energy near the Alpha Centauri star cluster. A few lightcycles from Proxima Centauri."

Xorin held up a hand to silence the bureaucrat now apologizing for the shriveled Councilmember's insults and turned his head slightly toward Feyt. He frowned, brow furrowed in concentration, and gave the Commander his undivided attention.

"It was nothing more than a blip. The signature appeared on our instruments for only a moment," the warrior explained. "We have pinpointed the location, but there is nothing else coming out of that sector. Long-range imaging shows only rocky debris."

"Do we have any ships operating near there?"

"No. Nothing of ours could have generated the burst, and it was not sustained. Merely a fraction of a second," Feyt replied. "Sir, there is more. It matches the signature of the machine we are looking for."

Xorin smiled inwardly. Finally, after four cycles of searching, the trail was no longer cold. He breathed deeply through his nose and turned back to face the High Council.

"Councilmembers," he addressed, "you will be pleased to hear we have just detected a surge of therleon energy matching the signature of the machine stolen by the Interloper. As all my ships are accounted for, there is little doubt as to what this means. My ship and crew will be investigating the disturbance post-haste. However, after this disgraceful spectacle you call 'progress,' we will not speak again until I deem it necessary."

Xorin ended the transmission, and the shimmering projections of the grülbarvoc High Council faded to black. He turned and walked quickly past Feyt, heading for the ship's command deck. He gestured for the Commander to follow, and Felt fell into step behind.

"Chart a course to the origin point and issue a fleet-wide order," he instructed, speaking to Feyt as they hurried toward the bridge. "I want to rendezvous with them on our way to find the Interloper."

"Captain, with even such a small release, do you think there will be anything left to find? The debris from our imaging scans–" Feyt began, but Xorin interrupted.

"Forget the scans. The Interloper has evaded us for many cycles, hiding himself with technology far inferior to ours, which leads me to believe he possesses a brilliant mind," the Captain explained. "I do not know what he hopes to accomplish with the machine, but the fact he has once again activated it, even momentarily, means he is nearer to his goal. If the device has not destroyed him, then our mission is more urgent than ever."

Commander Feyt nodded in understanding and hurried ahead to give orders to the bridge, leaving Xorin to ponder his elusive prey. What had the Interloper been doing all this time? What was he planning? There was a strange sensation in the pit of Xorin's stomach, one he was unfamiliar with, and with a growing sense of disgust, he realized it was apprehension. Before all this began, Xorin was aware of the so-called Galactic Commonwealth and the species it embodied, the way he was aware of the existence of insects, but the idea of such a primitive civilization in possession of *their* technology... he could find little comfort in the thought.

When he arrived on the bridge, the soldiers snapped to attention before returning to their assigned duties. Xorin settled himself in front of the window, hands clasped behind his back, and watched as the galaxy folded in upon itself, over and over, propelling them through the void at a speed faster than light. It had been a lengthy campaign, but with any luck, they would finally recover what they'd been searching for so long to find.

"AAAAH!" Rhys sat bolt upright, the scream dragging him suddenly from the depths of unconsciousness. It was pitch-black all around. Disoriented, he peered through the darkness, hoping to identify something that might indicate his current location. Was he still in the lab? Where was the machine? His eyes ached and a godawful pounding resonated inside his skull. Unable to see, panic rose quickly in his chest. He was blind, he was sure of it. His eyes had been burned away… he remembered Sekami's scream… the overwhelming fear… a shimmering, pulsating orb… knew that he would never see again, oh Christ!

"Where is everyone?" he shouted, praying for someone to respond. No one answered. "Hey!"

He held a hand in front of his face, and although he could sense its proximity, it remained invisible to his sightless eyes. Straining his ears for even the smallest noise, he hoped desperately that they too had not been rendered useless.

*GRIIIIIIIIIND BUMP.*

Rhys heard a faint sound of overworked gears and metal striking against polymer. Taking stock of his surroundings, he felt something soft and groped blindly in the dark, his hands finding a large, fluffy object. A pillow. He was in a bed he realized, the soft material beneath him a blanket. So, not the lab. Swinging his legs over the side, Rhys grunted at the stiffness in his back.

*GRIIIIIIIIIIND BUMP.*

There it was again. He stood unsteadily and fumbled his way in the dark towards the sound. Creeping forward, he noticed a feeble light coming from the right side of the room and felt foolish at his undignified fear of blindness. Whoever had put him here had probably extinguished the lamps as well. When he reached its source, Rhys saw a small screen, information for temperature, humidity, oxygen content, and ambient light displayed on the glowing surface.

"Hey, BAIN? You there?" Rhys asked aloud. He hadn't thought to prompt the A.I. in his blindness-fueled panic.

"I am, Mr. Kelly."

"How do I turn on the lights?"

"The interface in front of you can be used to adjust the room's environmental controls," the computer replied. "While you were unconscious, I analyzed your sleep patterns and regulated the settings to an optimal condition. You may adjust them as desired. I must caution against further increases in humidity, however. Any higher, and the moisture content in the air will begin to exceed what the reclamation units can process, resulting in waste. I will gradually lower the percentage as you acclimate to the dryness of space."

Rhys could tell it was already very dry. His throat was parched, and the inside of his nose felt cracked and inflamed. Grimacing at the thought of further reductions in humidity, he declined a reply and continued to study the screen. *Sleep Mode* was the current lighting condition he noted and scrolled through the available choices. He selected *Normal* and adjusted the brilliance setting to fifty percent. From above, light slowly intensified until the room was filled with a soft glow. Now that his sore eyes could see reasonably well, he glanced around his quarters in search of the rhythmic scraping noise.

*GRIIIIIIIIIIND BUMP.*

The sound seemed to be coming from the head. When he entered, its source was immediately apparent. Part of the photo-sterilizer had malfunctioned, and as he watched, one of the protective shrouds ground against a set of protruding lasers before slamming noisily back into the open position. *GRIIIIIIII-IIND BUMP.* Rhys approached the machine and leaned in for a closer look. It wasn't hard to spot the problem.

A pair of mechanical linkages, one at the top and one at the bottom, pushed the entire set of lasers forward when the slat retracted. The top linkage had loosened somehow, and the entire apparatus was now askew, preventing the cover from closing. There was a slight delay between each *GRIIIIIIIIIIND BUMP,* and if he was quick enough, he would be able to reach in and recon-nect the arm. Tapping out the rhythm with his foot, Rhys waited until he was sure of the timing and darted in, slipping the linkage back into place. He pulled his fingers back just in time as the realigned lasers retracted, and the cover slid quietly closed. Finally, the obtrusive *GRIIIIIIIIIIND BUMP* had ceased.

He left the bathroom and approached a window that faced the cavernous expanse of the asteroid in which Proxima Station was nestled. From here, he could see the colony's seven other pods. A network of walkways and trams spider-webbed between them, connecting back to the central edifice where the research lab was located. In the distance, he saw a second landing area, different than the one where they'd docked the *Erebus*. As he watched, the doors of a large hanger bay opened to reveal several pieces of mechanized equipment moving between the moored vessels. From this vantage, he had a clear view of truck-sized shuttles loaded with supplies and sent to other pods. If he didn't know better, Rhys would have guessed Proxima Station was an active spaceport. Just how many people knew about this place? He stood there, contemplating this strange new reality, still in disbelief he was on the run, more than six hundred years in the future. It wasn't long before his thoughts turned to Anne.

Rhys wondered if she would have liked to see some of the

things he had. He doubted it. Anne hated the idea of outer space. There was no reason for it, just an inexplicable fear she'd always harbored. Now that he'd experienced it for himself, though, he supposed he couldn't blame her. Space was a terrifying reality; an infinite darkness where nothing but thin walls of metal separated living tissue from hard vacuum. He wanted nothing more than to rewind the clock, to go back and forgo that fateful voyage onboard the *Denebola*.

At this, he felt a strong sense of regret, of missed opportunities that could have been spent with Anne. If only he'd made different decisions, he might've relived those happier times... times he could barely remember now. It was distressing to feel their memories together fading away into abstractness, as if someone had told him they'd been happy, and he was expected to take their word for it. All he felt, the only things that truly seemed his own, was the pain and anguish that had followed the *Denebola's* fire, a disaster that had brought his life crashing down...

Unwilling to relive the difficult months after Anne's death, Rhys forced himself to think about something else. He gazed out the window, peering absent-mindedly at the spectacle before him. Several minutes later, a knock at his door made him jerk, ending the few peaceful moments he'd experienced since arriving at Proxima Station.

"Come in," Rhys called to the closed door. He heard the hatch slide open and turned to see Marasa outside holding a tray of food and looking in on him timidly.

"Marasa! Thank God! Is everyone alright?" He hurried over to the door, glad to see someone who might answer his questions. The woman waited patiently as he shot off rapid-fire questions, and only when he paused to take a breath was she able to speak.

"May I come in?" she asked politely. She gestured at him with the tray in her hands. "Dr. Ryele thought you might like some food. It's better than the stuff in the galley."

"Of course. Please," he said and beckoned her in. "With everything that's happened, a meal's been the last thing on my mind. I've only eaten once since we left the cryostation... couldn't even say when that was."

"I understand. Dr. Ryele was kind enough to give you some of her personal stores. Mostly, we just get nutrient rations, but every now and then a shipment of fresh provisions comes in and gets divided amongst the team," she explained and handed him the tray. "Make this last as long as you can, otherwise it's just the goop from the messroom."

Rhys walked to where a small chiller stood in the corner and placed the items inside, making a mental note to thank Sekami the next time they were together. While he put away the food, his mind ran wild with more questions about the events in the lab. His memories were clear, right up to the point where the containment failure was about to occur, and then... nothing but a jumbled blur. With the food stowed, Rhys turned back to Marasa.

"Did someone deactivate—"

"Are you feeling—"

Each of them had begun to speak, then paused to let the other person ask their respective question. Rhys smiled awkwardly and raised his hand.

"Sorry. You first."

"I just wanted to ask if you're feeling alright. That whole ordeal must've been terrifying. We've never seen the machine do that... turn on, I mean."

"Do you know what happened?"

Marasa shook her head.

"Kieron thinks it was some kind of defense mechanism. That was the first time we tried to physically breach its shell," she explained. "For obvious reasons, none of us were thrilled about the idea of drilling into it."

"So why do it?"

"Desperation, I suppose. You can't know how frustrating our time here has been," she explained, a tired expression filling her large eyes. *"Two years!* Two years we've spent, going 'round and 'round, stalling our reactors, and accomplishing absolutely nothing. Kieron and I came here expecting to achieve something, to contribute in some meaningful way. If we figured out how to defend ourselves against the grül, we'd be heroes of the Commonwealth! But you know what we are? Nothing but a troop of shrieking kyrianths playing with a fusion device."

It was as if his question had been the key to unlocking her internal floodgates. The woman brimmed with disappointment and uncertainty, and Rhys doubted whether she had anyone but Sekami to vent her concerns. Breath heavy with frustration, she seemed to be reaching out to him for some sort of reassurance. He didn't know what to say. Eventually, her breathing slowed as she began to reel back in.

"Sorry for unloading that," she said abashedly. "It's not like telling you is going to change anything."

"It's okay. Waking up to all this... it's been hard to keep perspective for anyone else's problems but my own."

She nodded, seeming to understand.

"Thank you for listening. Sekami's usually so busy with other things, and Kieron... he's not exactly the person I go to for emotional support. Not since Mother died," she said. It struck Rhys as only somewhat odd she'd chosen a total stranger to confide in, but everything in her demeanor indicated she desperately wanted someone to talk to... or just someone to listen.

"When did she pass?"

"A long time ago," she began, seeming relieved, yet sad, he'd chosen to humor her. "Kieron and I had just finished university. After she and Father separated, Mother took a security job at Vandervol right before... before the grül..."

"I'm sorry," Rhys replied. He didn't know where or what Vandervol was, but that probably didn't matter. It was easy to guess what had happened... and anyway, what else was he supposed to say? He didn't know this woman.

"It's the only reason Kieron convinced me to come here. I'm usually one to run away from confrontation, but this was something tangible I could contribute to. I just wish we could make more progress. Right now, it feels like I'm failing Mother... failing everyone. Sekami's been supportive through all this, despite everything."

"I'm sure Dr. Volkerson understands," Rhys said.

When he mentioned the man's name, Marasa's expression turned grave as if a switch inside her head had flipped. She had been polite and friendly before, a little timid maybe, but that was all gone. The familiar air with which she'd acted evaporated into the room's thin, dry air, and Rhys could tell she was uncomfortable. Now, the only thing he sensed from her was apprehension.

"Is something wrong?" he asked, probing for some hint behind the unexpected change in her behavior. In the same way she'd done in the lab, however, she refused to meet his gaze and simply pointed toward the bathroom.

"Dr. Ryele wanted me to tell you he's ready to meet. If you haven't already found them, the facilities are in there. You may want to clean up beforehand," Marasa said, wrinkling her nose. There was no longer any trace of the person who'd confided in him a moment ago. "Let her know when you're ready, and she'll accompany you to meet Dr. Volkerson."

With that, Marasa turned and left, leaving Rhys alone in his room and more confused than when she'd arrived.

AFTER GLIMPSING his own disheveled reflection and deciding to endure another unremarkable bout in the photosterilizer, Rhys donned a fresh set of clothes from the dresser near the bed. He was still amazed Sekami had managed to size him up perfectly, let alone inform the station in time for their arrival. It felt good to be clean. He'd been sweating profusely inside the protective suit, and whoever brought him back here had, for obvious reasons, declined to remove his soiled garments. It was understandable, preferable even to the idea of a stranger undressing him, but nonetheless, he'd woken up feeling grimy. Sitting on the edge of the bed, he pulled on the stiff boots, wincing slightly as he pushed each aching foot inside.

Now, he needed to find Sekami. He remembered the implant, the 'CIM' as BAIN had called it, embedded beneath his left ear. Touching the skin, an interface suddenly appeared in front of him, projected through his optic nerve overtop of the room around him. Disoriented, his eyes darted around in search of a familiar landmark as menus, dropdown lists, and a dozen other images flitted across his view. Hastily, he touched the skin over the implant, and the interface disappeared. Rhys groaned, his head spinning.

"BAIN, how do I navigate my CIM?"

"Your implant projects a false image through your optic nerve. Retinal tracking is used to navigate the various menu items. The current sensitivity setting is eighty percent."

"Is there any way you can turn it down? Maybe to thirty?"

"I have done as requested," BAIN replied after a momentary pause. "Might I suggest avoiding any unnecessary eye movement while you access the interface?"

"Figured that one out on my own. Thanks."

Rhys braced himself and touched the skin beneath his left ear once again. This time when the interface appeared, he was ready. With small, deliberate movements, he began to familiarize himself with the implant's operation. After a few minutes of searching, he found a catalog of registered users and inside, a listing for Sekami Ryele. He selected the entry and heard a series of double beeps as the implant attempted to connect. When it did, Sekami's face appeared before his eyes, her image remaining fixed no matter where he turned his head.

"I'm glad to see you're awake," she greeted. "You seem to be learning how to use the CIM."

"Had a little trouble at first, but BAIN helped me out. I'm ready whenever you are."

"I'm in the common area below Dr. Volkerson's private pod. BAIN can guide you here."

"Right. See you soon," he said and terminated the connection.

When he stepped into the vestibule outside his room, a familiar green path appeared at his feet. He walked to the lift and felt it move downward when the doors slid closed. A short ride later, he disembarked and turned left, following the illuminated track as it twisted and turned through the passageways until ending at a closed door. When he entered, he saw a collection of soft chairs arranged around a tiny room. A window overlooked the spiderwebbing maze that made up Proxima Station. Seated in front of the glass was Sekami who glanced over at his arrival and stood to greet him.

"Hello," she said. Rhys heard a heavy note in her voice and thought she looked tired. Finally, after all they'd been through, she was beginning to show signs of fatigue. Foolishly, he caught himself thinking *she's human after all,* but no, Dr. Sekami Ryele was nothing of the sort. "Are you feeling alright?"

He shrugged his shoulders noncommittally.

"Sure, I guess. Been better."

"What you did in the lab... the station might've been destroyed if not for your actions. Thank you."

"Except it didn't work," he replied, confused by the look she was giving him. "I flipped the switches, but the containment fields still failed."

"Don't you remember?"

"Remember *what*? I heard the countdown, heard you scream, but after that..." he trailed off, scratching the back of his head while he tried to drag the memories from beneath the haze filling his brain. "Is this normal? After cryosleep, I mean. It's like I have some sort of episode or blackout whenever things get out of hand. I've never had this problem before."

Frustration had edged into his voice again.

"And now, for whatever reason, you're looking at me like I did something miraculous."

He took a few deep breaths and tried to calm the emotions swirling in his chest. They were a blend of frustration toward the amnesia, worry there was something seriously wrong with him, and an indefinable fear of what the future might hold. Sekami must have sensed this because she laid a soothing hand on his arm. Normally, Rhys disliked being touched by strangers, but he found hers oddly comforting.

"I know I haven't been entirely forthcoming, but it's time you were given some answers. Dr. Volkerson has much to show you. It should explain quite a lot," Sekami replied, turning towards the door.

They left the cramped room and continued down an unfamiliar passage to another turbolift. Sekami pressed her hand against its scanner, and there was a brief pause while BAIN verified her identity. When the surface of the device turned green, the door slid open, and they stepped inside. Rhys felt a slight downward pressure as the lift began to rise, quickly picking up speed as it propelled them toward another pod. When the car came to a stop, they stepped out into another vestibule, home to a single closed door. Instead of entering, however, Sekami turned to face him.

"This pod is where Dr. Volkerson conducts his research. No one, not even me, has free access to this area. If any unauthorized personnel try to use the turbolift, they typically receive an unpleasant visit from Captain Rynnavek," Sekami explained. "I must warn you, in the time we've been hiding here, Dr. Volkerson has developed a kind of bluntness. Some of what he has to say might be upsetting, but please consider his request before making any hasty decisions."

With that, Sekami turned and knocked on the closed door, leaving Rhys to ponder the exact nature of the decisions she referred to. The hatch opened noiselessly, and they entered a sparsely decorated abode. The room was much larger than Rhys's but still did not contain any superfluous creature comforts. From what he could see, the space was devoted to researching the mysterious grülbarvoc machine. A large workstation sat directly ahead of them, with five separate holographic displays. Each appeared dedicated to a singular function, and on one, Rhys saw a video feed of the main laboratory where the other scientists worked. Another showed the same image of the machine Otaan Yabar had been pouring over, while a third displayed a series of repeating letters and sets of vertical columns, all varying in length and color. Written next to the columns were hundreds of alpha-numeric codes, all of which was lost on him. Not finding an immediate answer, his gaze moved to the last two screens filled with complex formulas, the strings of numbers looking more like a foreign language than mathematical equations.

The wall of the room was not a wall at all but another gigantic window overlooking the station. The view was breathtaking, and Rhys guessed this must be the highest point inside the asteroid. Looking out, he could see the central pod hundreds of meters below their current position. The landing area he had seen before was farther away now, the lights from incoming and outgoing ships winking at him like tiny blinking orbs. Far in the distance, the most striking feature was the cave's gaping entrance and the asteroid field beyond.

Movement inside the room reminded Rhys why he was there. At the workstation, a gray-haired man stood and strode purpose-fully toward their place inside the room. Rhys noticed the man's imposing stature, and although older, he was clearly strong. Sinewy arms swung easily at his sides, his rolled-up sleeves revealing chiseled forearms and powerful-looking hands. When he finally reached the door, the gray-haired figure towered over them.

"Rhys, this is Dr. Marcus Volkerson," Sekami announced, introducing them. He extended his hand, and Rhys felt the crushing pressure of a vice as the man grasped his outstretched fingers. Unsure of what he'd expected from his introduction with

Volkerson, he knew it wasn't this. Considering everything Sekami had told him, he'd imagined someone very, very different.

"I'm glad to see you and Dr. Ryele have arrived safely, though the recent malfunction in the lab would have been catastrophic."

Volkerson's voice was deep and although he did not speak loudly, the words seemed to rumble from his chest like a distant storm. Rhys found the man's demeanor unnerving, full of a self-possessed air that exuded brilliance. Here was someone who was probably good at most everything. Although easily into his sixties, Volkerson was in excellent physical condition. Rhys guessed the man could probably hold his own in a scrap, but the most unsettling feature, however, was the shrewd intelligence that burned in his gray-flecked eyes.

"It's been a rude awakening to say the least," Rhys replied, feeling somewhat daunted by such an imposing nature. "I'm certainly grateful to Sekami for saving my... me. For saving me."

"It seems as though without you, our time on Proxima Station might've been terminated prematurely. It's us who should be thanking you," Volkerson said, motioning toward the display that showed the main lab. It was the second time someone had alluded to the events of the previous day, and Rhys shifted uncomfortably. They couldn't be referring to his decision to help Sekami. That hadn't mattered in the end. The fields had still failed... hadn't they? What the hell had actually happened?

"And yet, I've already observed your confrontation with one of my scientists."

The abrupt declaration caught Rhys off guard, once again pushing aside his preoccupation with the events in the lab as he remembered what Sekami had said about Volkerson's bluntness.

"In my defense, I was provoked," he began, keeping his voice level. Volkerson waved off his words.

"We aren't here to discuss your temperament, though rest assured, you must gain better control of your emotions, especially in light of what I'm about to propose."

"No offense, but the only things I'm interested in gaining right now are answers. No one's told me a damn thing about what I'm even doing here," Rhys countered. *No more deliberation*, he thought. He would dig his heels in here and now if that's what it took to get some well-deserved information.

"And you'll have them. Come with me, Mr. Kelly."

# CHAPTER 9
# FIRST CONTACT

"IT'S CALLED an Immersive Holographic Record. An IHR."

They were standing in a darkened room, empty except for a single computer terminal near the entrance. The walls were muted gray, matching the tint and texture of the floor. The whole room was unremarkable, containing no clues as to what it was supposed to be.

"Okay. An IHR. So, what's it do?"

"See for yourself," Volkerson said, walking over to the terminal.

A keyboard materialized in front of him, and he typed a command. Suddenly, in a rush of sound and color, the room transformed. Rhys threw up his arms reflexively to protect his face as the chamber swirled around them. He experienced a moment of intense disorientation before a soft beeping replaced the thunderous tumult. Slowly, he opened his eyes and lowered his arms, mouth agape with awe.

They were standing inside the cockpit of a small ship, looking out into a dark void. Through the window, Rhys saw the tail of a comet stretching as far as the eye could see. Sunlight reflected from a nearby planet glinted off billions of icy particles forming the debris trail of the celestial body. Sekami and Volkerson stood quietly beside him as he stared, captivated, at the spectacle in front of them. Reaching out, he touched the pilot's chair and felt the cracked fabric flex beneath his fingertips.

"We're still on the station?"

"Correct," Volkerson replied, his tone devoid of the same excitement and disbelief.

"Incredible!" Rhys exclaimed. "It's like we're actually here. Is it possible to…"

His voice trailed off, and he pushed the chair, spinning it around. For a moment, the seat rotated freely before the image flickered and snapped back to its original position. He gave it another push, with the same result. Interesting.

"Sounds, touch, smell… it's all here. The IHR allows us to interact with objects inside the recording, but any disturbance will reset to its normal position after a few seconds. You just witnessed this function with the pilot's chair," Sekami explained. "Major events, a person's trajectory for example, can't be influenced, but it's a useful tool for data analysis."

"Is it possible to get hurt in here? Like from an explosion?"

"No. In the case of flying debris or something similar, the IHR's safety system will kick in. Whatever the danger, it'll just dissociate for a moment as it passes around you."

As if on que, the cockpit door opened and in walked a much younger-looking Marcus Volkerson. The holographic man walked right through the real Volkerson before taking its seat in the pilot's chair. Rhys poked its shoulder with his finger and felt muscle beneath the scratchy fabric of the hologram's shirt. He shook his head in disbelief, utterly impressed by the IHR technology.

"How much detail is recorded?" he asked.

"Anything within the scope of BAIN's sensor range. Here, it's the inside of the ship and the immediate vicinity," Dr. Volkerson told him. "This recording is from a mining operation over thirty-four years ago. Before the grül arrived, I was an expert in propulsion sciences. My partner, Jenco Ryele, was a biochemical engineer, and we were attempting to develop a new kind of prime mover. The research was so revolutionary, no one had the raw material we needed, which was why we'd come to this comet in the first place."

While Volkerson spoke, Rhys wandered around the cockpit, marveling at the level of detail displayed in virtual reality. It really was like being there, in the moment. The texture of the chair felt exactly as he would have expected, soft beeps emanated from the flight control console, and the faint metallic smell of an oxygen-rich environment tricked his olfactory receptors. The only evidence his surroundings weren't real was when he tried to permanently move an object... or if one inadvertently walked right through him.

Rhys paused to stand behind Volkerson's younger holographic version and peered over the man's shoulder. The area in front of him was cluttered, surrounded by complicated controls, haphazard stacks of annotated core scans, and a pair of large indicators displaying time and a set of quickly decreasing numbers. According to the labels posted underneath, the dials showed an elapsed drill period and a countdown to target depth. Two video monitors were mounted above the gauge panel, and Rhys peered at them intently. One feed showed a close-up of some sort of high-powered laser punching through rock and ice, while the other showed a different area of the ship. There, he saw a second figure, this one with pale-green skin. Hadn't Volkerson said he was with someone named Jenco Ryele? Did the figure in the feed have some connection to Sekami?

He watched the depth indicator reach zero, and a soft beep emanated from the drill console. Holographic Volkerson looked up from his instruments and cursed softly under his breath at something on the screen. Reaching over, he pressed a button on the console.

"Jenco, Site Twelve failed. Moving to the next set of coordinates. Brace for drill and anchor retraction."

The man in the lab gave an affirmative gesture, and Rhys felt a slight bump as the virtual drill retracted to its stowed position. Deftly working the controls with the touch of someone who'd done it every day of his life, the holographic Volkerson withdrew the ship's anchoring system and engaged the maneuvering thrusters. The comet began to drop away, and for a moment, it felt like they were actually flying. As Rhys peered down at the comet's icy surface, the cockpit around them flickered, and the crater he'd been staring into disappeared. He looked questioningly at Sekami.

"Excess footage has been scrubbed," she explained, pointing to a clock on the gauge panel. Rhys nodded in understanding when he realized it had skipped ahead several hours.

Except for the terrain outside, the recording hadn't changed much. A few more seconds passed uneventfully before the cockpit shook violently, and Rhys heard a shriek of alarm bells. He gripped the back of the pilot's chair, knuckles white, all too familiar with the panic their holographic companions must have experienced. Looking down, he saw the younger Volkerson had fallen out of the chair and was picking himself up off the deck. The man jumped back to his seat and fastened his restraints before steadying up on the controls. Judging by the view outside, they were still gliding silently over the comet's surface. There didn't seem to be anything out of the ordinary, but as the ship turned on its axis, the source of the disturbance came into view.

A huge, undulating *something* filled the cockpit window, and Rhys tried to wrap his mind around what he was seeing. Was it a hole? In space? He was sure his eyes were tricking him. Whatever it was lay in stark contrast to the void around it. The twinkling stars that should have been there were distorted, their pinpoints of light stretched and swirled. Seeing it formed a knot in the pit of Rhys's stomach, and their virtual chaperone seemed to freeze as the sight of the anomaly. An inadvertent twitch of the man's hand on the stick made the ship lurch nauseatingly. For a second time, Rhys heard the earsplitting shriek of alarms and the computer broadcasting its message.

"Proximity Warning – aft port quarter thruster."

It came a moment too late. The ship brushed the surface of the comet and entered a spin, the view outside spiraling. Volkerson struggled to control the damaged ship, cursing as it spun out of control. They hurtled toward the nearby planet with ever increasing speed, the mysterious anomaly only visible through the window when the ship made a full rotation. With each dizzying glimpse, the object looked more and more like the mouth of a gigantic celestial beast ready to devour anything that came too near. The virtual man let out a low growl that built to a full-fledged roar before the room went black. Rhys and the others were engulfed darkness.

A few moments of ear-ringing silence passed before the hologram returned. It flickered intermittently, cutting in and out. The cockpit was a smoldering wreckage, dust and debris filling the cabin. Rhys looked around, waving at the smoke without effect, before regaining his bearings. He saw Volkerson splay-legged in his seat, a deep cut on his forehead. The young man groaned and smacked the release button on his restraints, tumbling to the floor like a ragdoll. He coughed violently, choking on the dust and smoke, before crawling to his knees and peering out of the cockpit window. There hadn't been time to warn Jenco before the crash, and he called out, only to be overtaken by another fit of coughing. A full minute passed before he was able to stop long enough to shout for his partner a second time. There was no reply. In what must have taken great effort, the younger Volkerson pulled himself to his feet.

"BAIN," his voice was cracked and scratchy. "Are you operational?"

"Ye– Marcus. I am he–"

"Is Jenco alright? Report his vitals."

"Unab– comply. Sen– offli–"

"Check environmental readouts. Do we have air?" Volkerson rasped, clutching his throat.

"Unable t– –ply."

"Switch to your backup processor."

"Unab– comply."

Another fit of coughing overtook Volkerson before the hologram froze again, the man's rasping protracted into one long, mechanical din. When the fit subsided, the picture jumped, and the virtual man now stood in the rear of the cockpit. Rhys picked his way through the debris to follow. Near the aft hatch, his guide donned an environment suit equipped with a hard, full-faced mask and an air pack. The erratic, disjointed recording made his movements appear robotic, and Volkerson raised his left arm on which a small, flexible interface was built. Light from its screen cast a strange glow as it cut through the smoky air. Rhys moved to stand beside him while he poked at the display. A moment later, a pair of small disk-shaped objects approximately ten centimeters in diameter detached themselves from Volkerson's suit. A glowing red lens shone on the face of each as they hovered at eye level.

"Transfer IHR acquisition to drone units."

The red lenses blinked to green, and the view of the cockpit shifted slightly. The image was no longer choppy but smooth as before the crash. Their group moved to the next compartment and came to another closed hatch. Around its perimeter, Rhys saw crumpled steel, the metal jamb gouged deeply into the material of the door. It didn't look good. With a grunt, Volkerson braced one foot against the frame and wrenched hard, but the door wouldn't budge. He tried again. Still, nothing. Standing unsteadily on the surrounding debris, he peeked into the next room through a hole that had been torn between the deformed frame and the rest of the bulkhead. Whatever he saw, his body tensed, and Rhys heard a sharp intake of breath.

"Jenco!" Volkerson shouted. "Jenco, can you hear me?"

There was no answer at first, but a moment later, a feeble moan escaped the other side of the door. Jenco was still alive. In a frenzy, Volkerson searched for something to pry open the damaged hatch. Rhys watched as he jammed a wedge of jagged metal between the door and the frame, then pulled heavily with a long section of broken pipe. A lot of grunting and swearing, but nothing would budge the sealed door.

Volkerson paused for a moment, then turned and ran back to the cockpit. He heaved debris out of a corner of the room, uncovering a hidden compartment. When he ripped open the cover, Rhys saw what the man was looking for. Inside was a heavy-looking backpack device. A shielded hose ran from the bottom of the pack and terminated in a pistol-shaped tool at the end. Grabbing the pack and a second air mask, Volkerson returned to the mangled door. He squeezed the tool's trigger, and the head ignited in a powerful beam of green energy. Guiding the arc over the crumpled metal door, a thin black line appeared around its periphery. He set the cutter aside and heaved on the makeshift wedge, pushing with his feet and leveraging his body with the pipe. The door broke free with a screech of metal, and he jumped clear when it came crashing down. Working furiously, Volkerson tore away the wreckage piled on top of the green-skinned man and placed the spare mask onto his face. Wheezing and coughing, Jenco's eyes fluttered open and reached out feebly toward his companion.

"Who gave you a license to fly?" he asked, lips curling into a pained smile.

"I told you... saw an ad for it on one of those kiddie shows. Came with rocket boots and a tinfoil hat," Volkerson replied, voice wavering with relief. "Are you alright?"

Tentatively, Jenco began to move his arms and hands, all which seemed to be working. He moved his right leg and rotated his ankle. When he moved his left, however, the baukken grimaced in pain.

"Leg's broken, I think," he said, his face contorted as he struggled to make himself more comfortable. "What was that thing? Got a glimpse of the exterior camera after the proximity alarm went off."

"Don't know. Sensors were going haywire. Showed massive g's and magnetic inversions all over the place. I don't understand why the alarm didn't... it should've gone off sooner," Volkerson finished. His voice sounded hollow, and Rhys wondered if it was an artifact of the recording. Judging by the crestfallen look on the hologram's face, though, it probably had more to do with their current predicament.

"Did we crash on the comet?"

"The nearby planet," Volkerson stated with a shake of his head. "AZ-one-six-something-or-other. It's the turandian terraforming colony we were warned to steer clear of, so we'd better get moving if we don't want to end up in one of their work camps."

"And do what?" Jenco grimaced, shifting again to find a less painful position. "There's no guarantee we're anywhere near the colony or of getting a warm reception if the turandians find us. They certainly aren't going to give us another ship."

"All the more reason to get going. For now, I'm betting they're preoccupied with that anomaly and where it came from."

"And be looking for someone to pin it on," Jenco muttered under his breath. Volkerson ignored this and helped the injured man struggle into the rest of his environment suit.

"Let's get you someplace more comfortable. We can stabilize your leg with the suit's medical–"

"I'm fine, Marcus," Jenco snapped, irritable from the pain, but raised his arm and flicked through the menu all the same. A faint hydraulic whine filled the room when the suit's lower left leg shrank, stiffening to administer a splint around his broken appendage. Gritting his teeth, Jenco flicked through the interface once again.

After a moment, the baukken's eyes turned glassy, his battered features beginning to soften. Drugs, Rhys realized. Powerful ones, apparently. Volkerson slung Jenco's arm over his shoulder, and the two men stumbled from the wreckage and onto the alien world. Mist rolled over their boots as dense fog enveloped them, limiting visibility to less than fifty meters. Volkerson limped with the injured man to a large boulder and helped him sit against it.

"Will you be okay?"

Jenco nodded, his eyes closed.

"I'll keep my comm line open. As soon as I find something, I'll come right back for you."

Volkerson gripped his partner on the shoulder, and after a moment, stood and walked away. Rhys bent down to grab a fistful of dirt, letting the grains slip between his fingers and tumble back to the ground. He brushed the dust from his hands, fascinated by the realism of the alien planet, and stepped to where his guide stood looking at his arm display. No sound could be heard except the crunch beneath his boots and a gentle breeze that swirled the fog eerily around them.

"Relay topographic and lifeform data to suit interface," he heard Volkerson tell one of the drones. Its green eye blinked once, and the disk shot off to begin reconnaissance. After a few seconds, a glowing dot appeared on the arm display, pinpointing their location. Around it, a map began to materialize, gaining detail as the drone covered more ground.

"Show me planetary coordinates."

There was a short pause while the second drone accessed its database, and a blinking message appeared.

*Turandian Terraforming Colony, AZ-16781. Caution: Planetary designation - "RESTRICTED." Trespassers subject to extrajudicial punishment. High likelihood of violence if discovered.*

"It's a risk we'll have to take," Volkerson replied. "Drone One, modify search parameters. Prioritize antimatter drives or byrinium shielding. Anything indicating a ship."

*Byrinium signature detected. Bearing one-three-three degrees. Distance 42.9 kilometers.*

The hologram groaned, and Rhys hoped they weren't about to walk the distance of a marathon. Setting off, they carefully picked their way through the thickening fog. The landscape held sparse vegetation, but a prolific blue-black moss covered the ground and many of the large boulders they passed. The sun lurked behind dense fog, never truly shining on them. Infrequently, Rhys saw towering cliffs stabbing into the sky whenever gusting wind made a break in the misty shroud. Volkerson made intermittent checks on the suit's readout, looking toward the sky whenever the first drone zoomed overhead. Without warning, everything around Rhys froze. He was slow on the uptake and walked right through his holographic guide. Feeling a hand fall heavily on his shoulder, he jumped and craned his neck around at Sekami and the real Marcus Volkerson standing behind him.

"I'd almost forgotten you were here," Rhys exclaimed, realizing how silly that must sound. "I was so taken up with… what's wrong? Why'd everything freeze?"

"It's another function of the IHR," Sekami explained, seeming amused by his enthusiasm. "It allows us to pause the feed and inspect items of interest. We can also perform high or low-speed scrubbing with the computer."

Rhys watched as the feed quickly backtracked, then played ahead in slow motion.

"There's so much detail. The file sizes must be enormous. How do you prevent lag in the feed?"

"It's the twenty-seventh century, Mr. Kelly. Quantum computing became commonplace centuries ago," Volkerson replied, seeming annoyed by yet another interruption. Rhys was about to ask a second question, but his host waved it away. "There'll be time for questions later. Please, we must continue."

The shapes around them dissolved in a rush of sound, then faded to silence as the image reformed. When the room stabilized, their environment hadn't changed much. They were still standing on empty rock-strewn ground enveloped in heavy fog. The holographic Volkerson appeared mid step, his visage one of utter exhaustion. He was frozen a moment longer before beginning to move once more. Rhys caught a glimpse of suit's interface and saw the elapsed counter now showed the man had covered nearly forty-two kilometers. When a second blip appeared on the display, Volkerson paused to view the message.

*Multiple contacts. Bearing one-three-seven degrees. Distance 1.2 kilometers.*

"Turandians?"

*Forty-six of forty-eight contacts confirmed turandian.*

"And the others?" Volkerson asked. There was a pause while the computer processed the query.

*Species unknown. Proceed with caution.*

"Continue high-altitude scanning," Volkerson commanded. "Activate thermal camouflage."

Cautiously, he adjusted his heading and continued on. The ground began to slope upward until Volkerson was scrambling over broken scree, using his hands to prevent himself from toppling backwards down the mountain. Rhys clambered over the rocks, surprised by the effortlessness of what should have been a laborious climb. By the time they reached the summit, the sound of the hologram's ragged breathing resonated in their ears. The fog lifted slightly, and Rhys suddenly found himself at the edge of a high cliff. He swore in surprise and jumped back. One more step and... he didn't know what might have happened in the holographic environment. His guide, however, stood at the precipice and surveyed what lay below.

"Half a kilometer... and right over the damn cliff," the hologram muttered to itself. "BAIN, display alternate routes."

They waited for the drone to find a way around the cliff. When it returned, however, Volkerson's face didn't express good news. He unslung the pack from his shoulders and pulled out a small bundle. Unfolded, Rhys noted two items; a canister of filament wire and a small, complicated-looking device. Volkerson placed the contraption against the surface of the rock, before standing up and stomping down hard.

A staccato *BANG* resonated through the air, and a puff of dust rose around the gadget. The hologram bent over and pulled hard on the end nearest the cliff. When it didn't budge, he clipped the eyelet of wire to the fixed piece and the canister to a loop on his suit's integrated harness. With sudden understanding, Rhys realized the man had just built himself a bomb-proof anchor. He watched, impressed, as Volkerson eased himself over the edge. Slowly, after a few calming breaths, the hologram began to descend, masterfully controlling the speed of his descent until disappearing into the swirling white fog.

Once again, the scene around them jumped, and Rhys found himself standing at the base of the cliff. He looked up in time to see Volkerson descending smoothly down the face of the mountain. The fog had lifted slightly, revealing more of their surroundings. Touching down, the man detached his harness from the wire canister and left it hanging, leaning back to take one final look at the sheer, overhanging buttress. Rhys followed his gaze, the towering face enough to make his heart flutter. Volkerson turned away and consulted the map on his arm.

"Dead ahead."

Somewhere in the talus field beyond would be the lifeforms the drone had warned them about. Volkerson crept forward silently, occasionally checking his suit for information as Rhys and the others followed behind. Coming to a break in the boulders, their guide crouched down to stay out of sight. A strong wind whipped through the rocks, and as they watched, the last of the swirling fog cleared away.

In the middle of the clearing stood a ship, and Rhys felt his breath catch in his throat. Although much smaller, it had the unmistakable hawkish profile of a grülbarvoc craft, like the one he'd seen attacking the cryostation. The outer door was open, and two towering creatures guided an ugly black sphere down the gangway. One of them pressed its hands against the surface of the object, and the rough exterior began to open, exposing a silver, shimmering core.

"Jesus," Rhys breathed in recognition. It was the same machine, or one just like it, that resided in the lab on Proxima Station. He turned questioning eyes toward Sekami, but she pressed a finger to her lips and pointed back toward the clearing. In front of the device was a large pen, and a knot tightened in Rhys's stomach when he saw it was filled with dozens of people. They weren't human. Their overlarge eyes and pointed ears told him that much.

"Terraforming colonists," Sekami told him solemnly.

A horrific braying filled the air as the turandians pleaded with their captors. One prisoner held a child in her arms, begging the gray-skinned aliens to let them go. Others sat quietly, looks of terror and disbelief etched in their faces. Revulsion washed over Rhys, but he seemed unable to avert his eyes. He stepped out from behind the boulder and walked into the clearing toward the ship, intent on getting a closer look at the creatures responsible for such atrocity.

Huge and imposing, the grül were a sight to behold. Their powerful bodies were mottled gray, dull red streaks running in deep striations throughout their leathery skin. Eyes that burned with vicious intelligence were set deep into their unsmiling faces, and their six-fingered hands looked as if they could rip a man's arms from his body. Rhys knew they couldn't hurt him in the IHR, but the menacing figures were so fearsome, so lifelike, he found their presence formidable.

Positioning the sphere in front of the doomed turandians, an argument broke out between the two warriors. The bigger grül gesticulated toward the caged prisoners while the other shook its head. Without warning, the large alien rushed its companion, grabbing the smaller by the throat while it struggled to break free. The big grül slammed its fist into the side of its companion's head, who immediately dropped to the ground, one hand raised in surrender. Slowly, it stepped back and allowed the fallen warrior to stand. The struggle for some indeterminate meaning resolved, the big grül inserted its arms into a pair of holes that had appeared on the opposite side of the machine, away from the aperture facing the pen. A moment later, the air between the device and the prisoners seemed to shimmer, the cage's metal bars humming as if through high-resonance vibration. The captives' cries for mercy grew louder, transforming into blood-curdling howls as the scene descended into madness.

Writhing in pain, blood began to leak from the turandians' eyes and noses and ears. Rhys watched, horrified, as the caged victims clawed at their own bodies, skin and nails sloughing to the ground in bloody sheets. As the massacre continued, the dull red streaks in the big grül's skin burned brightly. Incredibly, *terribly*, the beast began to change, its wrinkled skin growing smooth as the battle-worn tunic stretched tightly across its back.

Unnoticed by its companion, the smaller grül suddenly rushed forward, pure malice burning in its eyes. With the skill of an assassin, it drove a metal spike through the back of the big grül's head. The creature slumped forward, its arms falling limply from the holes in the machine. The assailant grabbed the lifeless body by its shoulders and unceremoniously dumped its carcass on the ground, kicking it out of the way. It placed its arms inside the machine and continued what the big grül had started, slowly draining the lifeblood from their helpless victims.

Rhys heard a grunt behind him and tore his eyes away from the macabre scene. While he'd been distracted by the carnage, the holographic Volkerson had hefted a large boulder and held it perched on his shoulder. Lumbering forward, the man lifted the rock high above his head when he neared the back of the unsuspecting alien. At the last moment, the creature sensed danger, but it was too late. Volkerson brought the boulder crashing down, smashing a fist-sized dent in its skull. The grül slumped and fell to the ground next to its dead companion. Rhys could hear Volkerson's ragged breath as the man heaved the beast onto its back before leaping away in surprise. The alien, although incapacitated, was still alive.

"What...? Why...?" Volkerson panted, his voice trembling with fear and adrenaline.

An unintelligible rasp escaped the creature's lips as a trickle of blood ran down its chin. With its last, dying breath, only a single word was left to reverberate throughout the room.

"Grülbarvoc."

# CHAPTER 10
# A PART TO PLAY

THE FEED PAUSED. Volkerson's frozen gaze was locked on the dead aliens, until a moment later, the images dissolved back into the drab gray of the IHR. Rhys stood immobile, stunned by what he had just seen. Such casual slaughter left him feeling sick to his stomach. The bleeding eyes, the sloughing nails... would he and Sekami have met the same excruciating end if not for their narrow escape from the cryostation? Had that been what happened to those unable to flee? The gravity of his decision to help in the lab suddenly dawned on him, making his entire body tremble. When he finally found his voice, the words stuck in his throat.

"Was that..." he began, swallowing hard against the lump. He tasted bile. "Is that what they do? Just... go from place to place feeding on other lifeforms?"

The real Volkerson regarded him for a moment as he weighed the question.

"Beyond the obvious regenerative effects, we aren't entirely sure of their motivations," he said, "but do the reasons truly matter? You saw what these monsters are capable of. Since that first encounter thirty-four years ago, I've had very few face-to-face confrontations. To risk further engagement with the grül is to risk our lives, our research, and in essence, our entire civilization. We've lost nearly everything once before."

"You make it sound like you're some lone warrior in all this," Rhys replied, still fighting back the urge to vomit. He understood the loss to which Volkerson referred was directed toward whatever had happened on Earth, even if the man didn't say it outright. "What about your government? Why not ask them for help?"

"We did. They condemned our actions and labeled us provocateurs. Under charges of incitement, we were stripped of funding and cast from the professional societies to which we belonged," Volkerson explained, disdain in his voice. "We were left to fend for ourselves, and it wasn't long before an entire fleet of grül ships appeared, but by then, it was too late. The Commonwealth possessed nothing that could stand against such weaponry, and the attack on Earth was the final nail in their own coffins."

Rhys mulled over this new information. With as many resources as an interspecies government must have possessed, even they hadn't been able to stop the grül. Would that outcome have been different if they'd listened to Volkerson? How much could have been learned about the machine in the time he tried to give them? Based on what he'd seen, Rhys doubted it would've made much difference. Now, the G.C. was in ruins, and he found himself in the company of the very people a fleet of murderous aliens were looking for. If things began to spiral out of control, it meant no one was coming to save them. That was a sobering thought.

"What happened after you killed it?" Rhys asked. Volkerson's story seemed half-finished, a mere drop in the bucket of questions on his mind. Even despite such grim new realities, he yearned to hear more.

"The grül ship was beyond my comprehension, but there was a turandian-built vessel near where I'd found them. The trip back to Jenco was much faster, minutes as opposed to nearly a day, and we returned to the sight of the massacre to... give the victims rest." Volkerson paused, seeming haunted by the terrible memory. It wasn't a reaction Rhys expected given Sekami's description of the man's callousness. "We burned the turandians, in part because of the smell. Jenco was fascinated by the grül ship, and I half expected him to work out how to operate it. He was an excellent pilot and much more mechanically intuitive than me. Before we left, I showed him the IHR footage collected by the drones, so he too could understand the danger these creatures posed. We both agreed. If their presence was the harbinger to some greater threat, then we needed to learn how to defend ourselves. What better way than to have a piece of their own technology to study?"

"And you don't think taking their machine is the reason they're hunting you?" Rhys asked. At his question, anger flashed in Volkerson's eyes.

"The grülbarvoc are monsters," the man growled, his nostrils blooming wide. "With that kind of power at their disposal, what chance do you think our galaxy stands against them? What chance do you think Earth stood?"

Rhys knew he'd overstepped an invisible boundary. He hadn't meant to ask the question, even if such thoughts were on his mind. It had just popped out, unbidden. Now, Volkerson looked at him with the same disdain he'd heard earlier in the man's voice. *Great start, dipshit*, Rhys thought to himself. An awkward silence filled the room, and he cast around for something to distract from his recurring case of foot-in-mouth. Another question had been nagging at him for some time.

"Your partner. Does he have any connection to–"

"Jenco Ryele was my father. He was killed in the attack on Earth."

It was Sekami who spoke, and Rhys glanced at her. There was a hard look in her eyes, but he saw thinly veiled sadness behind them. Now, he understood her stake in this fight, and another realization dawned on him. Her pained reaction in the lab hadn't been due to the loss of some lover... it was because of her murdered father. Rhys had no distinct memories of his own parents. They too had vanished in the abyss that had swallowed the rest of his life before the *Denebola*. He was surprised that didn't bother him more. Still, as he observed the anger on Sekami's face, he couldn't image what it must be like to lose someone to such horrific circumstances. He hoped for her sake she hadn't seen it happen.

"I'm sorry. I won't pretend to know what that's like," he said, unsure of what words to offer her. She opened her mouth to reply but closed it again when Volkerson laid a hand on her shoulder. The gesture appeared an attempt at comfort, but she seemed to take little solace in his touch.

"It's true," Volkerson said. "It's been a difficult four years without him. Not just as a fellow researcher but as a friend. My only friend. I owe it to him to look after Sekami."

Rhys looked from one to the other, beginning to understand the relationship between them. Volkerson was her guardian. A stand-in father figure, so to speak. They must have gone through a lot together. Nevertheless, something seemed strained between them. He couldn't put his finger on it. Something in the way Sekami had reacted to the man's touch... like it had been a warning of some kind... but a warning against what? Breaking the silence that had fallen over them, Volkerson began to steer the conversation in a direction Rhys didn't yet comprehend.

"Our first real discovery came when Jenco tried to move one of the dead grül. He'd propped its corpse against the therleon machine, unwittingly causing the device to energize. I heard him yell and saw him yank the body away, at which time the machine promptly fell dormant," Volkerson explained. "After our initial shock had worn off, we placed the body back in contact with the device to observe what might happen. It began to vibrate, but nothing more. There was no shimmering core, no powerful death ray... the machine just seemed to sense it was being handled. We repeated the experiment several times, always with the same result. There appeared to be a tactile relationship between the grül and their technology, so we each tried it ourselves. Neither of us could elicit any response from the device, however. It was as lifeless as the rocks around us. Something in the grül's genetic code is designed into their equipment and acts a kind of safety mechanism. Without this marker, their machines won't even turn on."

Rhys, listening to all this, was confused. He thought back to the lab where he had seen with his own eyes a piece of alien technology nearly wipeout the entire station. The fear he had felt was still fresh in his mind.

"I'm sorry," he protested, "but are you sure about that? Didn't we just see that, *thing*, almost destroy your whole operation here? No one touched it, and it still turned on."

An image of the drill floated to the forefront of his mind, and he remembered what Marasa had said about Kieron's theory, that the machine's response was a defense mechanism of some kind. Volkerson and Sekami exchanged a look, but its meaning was lost on Rhys. It was just another piece in a growing puzzle that surrounded Proxima Station and its scientists. So far, all he had heard was a mind-boggling story about one man's crusade, none of which answered any of the questions he'd been asking. Maybe he needed to be more direct. Before he could ask a more pointed question, however, Volkerson spoke.

"BAIN, please display my blood profile. Show us a grülbarvoc genome as well."

The IHR's drab gray was bathed in colorful light when the files appeared, floating at eye level. Rhys recognized the same vertical lines and alpha-numeric codes that had been displayed on Volkerson's personal workstation. A moment later, the computer displayed a second image showing a more complex set of lines and codes. The block lettering across the top told him to whom it belonged: *Sequenced Grülbarvoc Genome, Beta Specimen*. Still fuzzy on the direction they were heading, Rhys struggled to understand.

"What's the point of all this?" he asked, frowning.

"I'll spare you some of the details, but after we began our research into the grül, the first thing we did was map the differences between baukken, human, and grül genomes. Along with his proficiency in biology and chemistry, Jenco had an extensive background in xenogenetics. Through much painstaking work, we isolated the gene that allows the grül to operate their machines," Volkerson said. While he spoke, the computer highlighted a tiny section of the alien genome and enlarged it for a better view. "We dug deeper into our own DNA, hoping to devise some sort of therapy we might use on ourselves. All the samples we took from baukken and human specimens, however, failed to have the genetic marker we needed."

"After we lost my father, I began to work more closely with Dr. Volkerson," Sekami explained. "With no real success developing an effective therapy, I suggested a new approach. We began to investigate the evolutionary progress of our respective species, and what do you think we found?"

Rhys shrugged, still oblivious as to what they were getting at. He found Volkerson's expression disturbing, an almost manic look in his eyes. It made Rhys uncomfortable, and he shifted uneasily, feeling a sudden chill in the empty room as goosebumps rose on his bare skin. Volkerson swiped away the first hologram, and a third appeared. Another sequenced genome.

"Over the last six hundred years, humanity has, through tiny, nearly imperceptible mutations, evolved. During that time, certain changes took place within our genome. Some of them occurred naturally, while others happened artificially with the advent of germline engineering. There was only one change, however, that we were interested in, and that was the disappearance of a single, vestigial marker. One so similar to the grül's, their own technology might not differentiate between the two..."

Volkerson stopped speaking, and Rhys felt the cold room grip his spine like an icy hand. He gaped at the scientist in disbelief. It was impossible... absolutely impossible what the man was alluding to.

"We searched, Mr. Kelly," Volkerson continued, his deep voice resonating throughout the room, "for nearly three years. Every cryonics registry... every lab archive... everywhere we could possibly think to look that wasn't under the watchful eyes of our enemy."

"I don't... this doesn't..." Rhys stammered. "What are you saying?"

Sekami laid a hand on his arm, and he looked at her, eyes wide in disbelief.

"I told you I'd been sent to find you. This is why. You're the one person we've found with the genetic marker we need," she said gently and motioned to the third hologram. "This genome is yours."

For a second time, the computer highlighted a tiny fragment of the new image and overlaid it atop the enlarged section of grül-barvoc code. It was a perfect match. Rhys felt a wave of dizziness wash over him, and he swayed where he stood. This couldn't be true. It had to be another lie to convince him of some indeterminate falsehood. Why couldn't they have just let him sleep? Why had he ever frozen himself in the first place?

"I don't believe you."

A moment later, the IHR's transformative roar filled his ears, and he found himself back inside the main laboratory. A holographic version of himself, suited and standing at the electrical panel, put its entire weight behind a switch. Rhys saw the flickering containment fields, heard Sekami's terrified voice. BAIN's countdown reverberated in his ears. *Three, two, one...* he watched himself stumble toward the machine, ripping the attached gloves from his hands and falling blindly forward as the fields sputtered out of existence. When his bare hands touched the machine, his hologram's body tensed for a moment, and a silent scream etched his features. A moment later, though, his figure slumped to the floor, and the machine fell silent. Numbness gripped Rhys's body as the IHR returned to its usual featureless gray.

"Do you see?" Volkerson asked, quiet triumph in his voice. "This proves your compatibility with the machine. *You* prevented the lab's destruction."

"I don't think I can be what you want me to be," Rhys spluttered. He wasn't angry. Hell, he certainly wasn't happy. He didn't know what to feel. The knowledge they had just given him didn't exactly change the stakes of his situation, only his role. Now, he understood their interest in him from the start. Why else drag a six-hundred-year-old man around the galaxy instead of just leaving him to die on a cryostation with thousands of other frozen, nameless people? The first few pieces of a seemingly infinite puzzle rattling around his head had finally fallen into place.

"You're the only person we've found from your time, the only human in the known galaxy who carries a genetic marker that has long since disappeared," Volkerson admonished. His tone was sharp. "We aren't asking you to become a weapon, only to energize the machine long enough for us to gather sufficient data to develop our own. The grül have left the survivors of our galaxy two choices; fight or die. There's nowhere safer to face this conflict than Proxima Station. Haven't we shown you enough evidence of their brutality to warrant your cooperation?"

As loathe as he was to admit it, Rhys saw the truth of the scientist's words. There really was nowhere else for him to go. He no longer had a home. The grül had seen to that. Now, the only people he knew in the entire universe were right here on Proxima Station. Whether he liked them or not, their company was better than facing whatever danger lurked beyond the safety of the research facility alone. If he had somehow been given the tools to fight the monsters that had decimated billions of lives, he would do it. He *had* to do it. Anne would have wanted him to.

"I'll help you," he said finally. "God knows, I don't have much choice."

Rhys couldn't keep the reluctance out of his voice nor shake the feeling he'd just resigned himself to some terrible fate. Nevertheless, his words seemed to please Sekami, and she gave him a small, albeit sad, smile. Despite his hesitancy, he felt a sense of responsibility toward her. She had saved his life, after all, and he felt indebted to her for doing so. If his help brought vengeance for her father, he supposed he couldn't deny her that. Perhaps justice would be enough to repay his debt.

"I'm happy of your decision, Mr. Kelly," Volkerson answered. The emotion didn't extend beyond the man's words as he turned away. "But now, if you'll excuse me, I have other business to attend. I suggest you get some rest. In the morning, our work begins."

"One last question before you go," Rhys replied, frowning at the man's back. "If you haven't been able to activate the machine for the past thirty-four years, how could you develop containment fields for its therleon particles?"

Volkerson halted in his tracks and stiffened. Rhys saw a red splotch bloom on the back of the man's neck as the question hung in the air. A moment later, though, the scientist strode from the room without ever looking back.

# CHAPTER 11
# DUORANATH

XORIN WATCHED the young warrior let out a noiseless scream, a look of intense suffering stretched across his swollen features. At least, the scream carried no noise through the airlock's thick membranous window. He knew the solider must be shrieking at the top of his lungs. His show of will had been laudable at first, carrying with it a determined impudence toward punishment, but that hadn't lasted long. The Duoranath was too much for even the strongest grülbarvoc to bear stoically.

"Lower the pressure five more tarrons," the Captain commanded.

A sergeant to his left obeyed, reaching a hand into the fluidlike interface near the door. Outside, a puff of gas escaped into vacuum, and the warrior's already-distorted features seemed to stretch even more, if that was possible. His eyes bulged grotesquely in their sockets; gums bleeding freely as delicate capillaries began to burst. Staring detachedly at the writhing body on the other side of the window, Xorin knew that if the warrior survived the Duoranath, he would not make the same mistake again. Any future blunders would carry a much heavier penance. A few more moments passed in silence before he signaled an end to the punishment.

"Enough!"

The sergeant obeyed, bringing the airlock back up to match the ship's internal pressure. Xorin opened the inner door and released the shackled prisoner, who crumpled face-down on the deck. He turned the limp form over with the toe of his boot. Blood dripped from the warrior's nose and ears as the Captain bent low over his subordinate.

"I trust you will not disappoint me a third time," he hissed, awaiting the soldier's reply.

"By my oath, Fleet Captain Xorin."

The words were barely audible but satisfied him all the same. Failure came at a heavy cost, and his warriors knew that. Only a few needed reminding at times, but the ones who did, never forgot again. With his punishment administered, Xorin straightened and turned to leave. He had business with Commander Feyt. Brushing past, he barked an order to the sergeant, who nodded and hurried in to scrape the dishonored warrior off the deck.

When he arrived on the bridge, Xorin's officers snapped to attention and rendered a salute before returning to their assigned duties. He smiled inwardly. These were *his* men, hand-picked with the assistance of Commander Feyt, and he took pride in knowing they were the fiercest, most dangerous fighters in the entire grülbarvoc legion. There was the occasional exception, but for the most part, these warriors had accepted the subtle teachings he'd bestowed upon them. They were loyal to *him*, not to the diluted High Council. Looking around, he spotted the Commander walking in his direction and beckoned for him to follow. In the privacy of his room, Xorin sat while Feyt stood at attention. The young warrior was all business, and that pleased his Captain.

"Per our previous discussion, the offender has been punished accordingly," Xorin growled. He watched Feyt for a reaction, but the Executive Officer was stoic.

"With respect, Captain, I would have preferred to administer the Duoranath myself. It was I who recommended the sentence, after all."

"Have you ever experienced the Duoranath?" Xorin asked. It was a rhetorical question. He already knew the answer, and Feyt shifted uncomfortably.

"No, but I–"

"You have risen quickly through the ranks, and although that is a credit to your ambitious nature, there are still things you have yet to learn," the Captain interjected. Feyt stood stock still, not daring to interrupt. "As a young warrior, I too was extremely driven, but unlike you, I *have* been subjected to the Duoranath. You cannot truly know what it is without first having endured it."

"Then if it is knowledge I lack, let me experience the Duoranath for myself," Feyt replied.

Xorin heard a touch of pride in the warrior's voice and saw him stiffen. He was unaccustomed to having his decisions questioned by subordinate officers. If the circumstances had been different, Feyt would have come dangerously close to overstepping his bounds. Judging by the rigidness in how he now held his body, the Executive Officer understood this. He needn't have worried, though. Xorin liked this hunger the young warrior displayed. He was willing to subject himself to indescribable pain to better command his men. Someday, Feyt would make a formidable leader.

"An admirable request, but I will not have my Executive Officer chance needless death when we are this close to attaining our goal," the Captain replied. There was a note of finality in his voice. "The Interloper is almost within our grasp, and we cannot risk losing the machine again."

"I will honor your decision, but I would one day beg you to reconsider... perhaps after we apprehend the Interloper and return to Vyreon triumphant," Feyt answered. He paused for a moment, as if weighing something else that was on his mind but unsure where the invisible boundary of the Captain's patience lay. Xorin looked at the Executive Officer expectantly and nodded to indicate he would entertain further discussion on the matter. Feyt's rigid posture relaxed.

"With regards to our quarry... I have never fully understood what allowed the Interloper to acquire one of our therleon generators in the first place."

Xorin reminded himself of the Commander's youth. Feyt was capable, the best Executive Officer he'd ever had, but he was still born in the time of the Enlightenment. He had not lived the Old Ways, the Küddish teachings Xorin still secretly supported. Feyt had risen through the ranks in a time of grülbarvoc 'illumination,' as the High Council would describe it. Xorin saw it only as a weakening of the species, and it disgusted him. He was careful, though, always keeping his true beliefs hidden just below the surface. To do otherwise would risk his position as Fleet Captain and imprisonment on his home world. Needless to say, Xorin had been cunning in his indoctrination of the crew, subtly steering them back toward the Old Ways. It was his duty, he felt, to save at least some of his species from self-annihilation.

"How much do you know of the Küddarian Brotherhood, Commander?" Xorin probed, attempting to gauge the depth of the warrior's knowledge. Feyt's continued silence told him what he needed to know.

"The Interloper appeared after a transformation in grülbarvoc ethos. The populist ideals with which our people are now saddled resulted in the condemnation of thousands who clung to the Küddish teachings. Most were imprisoned or executed, but not all. Three such warriors defied the weak-minded bureaucrats and were to be made an example of," Xorin explained. "They did not meekly submit for punishment, however. After fighting their way to freedom, they disappeared without trace. Nearly a full cycle later, their ships were tracked to an unexplored galaxy by one of the High Council's assassins."

"And the warriors?" Feyt asked. "Were they located as well?"

"Two of them were found murdered with their ship," Xorin said, nodding.

"The Interloper?"

"Evidence recovered from their vessel conveys exactly what happened. The assassin's message to the High Council described the warriors' bodies as fuller, stronger... revitalized from the Sickness. Clear signs they had continued the Rhonath's forbidden practice," Xorin explained, darkness creeping into his voice.

An ancient fury smoldered inside him as he remembered the fall of the Küddarian Brotherhood one hundred cycles before. Blinded by their own sense of infallibility and a dwindling supply of life-sustaining resources, they had allowed the subversive ideals of the Enlightenment to take root. Like fools, the Brotherhood had dismissed such flaccid, open-minded philosophy as anything but threatening. Their enemy had wielded a weapon that was foreign to him, to the others, and one of unexpected power; political ideology. It had given birth to the High Council, a body of hypocrites and tricksters who had seduced many grülbarvoc into believing science alone could alleviate the horrors of the Sickness... so many, in fact, the Brotherhood had unwittingly found itself outnumbered and outmoded; a relic of a near-forgotten past. Now, too few of them were left, and that served only to compound the tragedy of the outcasts' deaths... Xorin had fallen silent and saw Feyt peering curiously back at him. Careful to avoid betraying his true feelings, he forced his thoughts back to the Commander's question.

"Most noteworthy, the assassin's message showed the Interloper murdering the condemned warriors and stealing their therleon generator."

Silence filled the room when the Captain finished telling his story. He had embellished it somewhat, of course. He knew the Interloper had not killed both warriors, that in fact the weaker of the two had murdered its companion. Feyt did not need to know this. It would serve no purpose. The lowest a grülbarvoc could sink was to kill one of his own brethren while his back was turned. He doubted it would have happened if the Old Ways had not fallen out of favor, and the warriors had not been driven to desperation. A heaviness began to settle in his chest, and he no longer felt willing to entertain Feyt's questions. He dismissed the Commander with a wave of his hand, and the young warrior gave a crisp salute before marching toward the door. When the hatch opened, however, Feyt hesitated a moment and turned back.

"Something else?" Xorin asked.

"You said three fugitives escaped. What happened to the third?" Feyt asked.

The Captain felt a twinge of annoyance at his Executive Officer's lingering presence. The young warrior knew better than to remain once dismissed, but something had emboldened him. Xorin would entertain this final question, but if the Commander pressed further, he would be treading on dangerous ground.

"Presumed dead. After erasing any evidence of the exiles' presence, the High Council's assassin detected traces of an explosion in the atmosphere of a nearby planet, matching the therleon signature of the third warrior's propulsor," the Captain explained. Then, his voice grew sharp. "But that is a story for another time. You are dismissed, Commander."

"I know how you feel about the Old Ways," Feyt blurted out. Xorin didn't move. Had he given away too much? Would Feyt report him? His mind began forming a plan to deal with this new complication, but the young warrior had more to say. "... and despite anything the Council decrees, I fully support your decisions. Although the Küddish teachings died before my time, I too see the path our species has taken, and I fear where it leads. My loyalty to you is more unwavering than ever."

With that, the Executive Officer turned and left Xorin to his thoughts. That final declaration certainly hadn't been what he'd expected to hear. He felt a swell of hubris and pushed up from his chair, stepping toward the window to gaze out on the gathered fleet. They had rendezvoused with his six remaining warships and would now begin their search for the mysterious therleon signature. It *had* to be from the Interloper. There was just no other possibility. Xorin felt the hum of the engine and watched as an interstellar bridge formed in front of the fleet, bending the light of countless stars around it. It grew larger when he felt gentle forward motion, until the ship entered the anomaly, and space began to fold over itself, speeding them toward their distant destination.

**CHAPTER 12**
# THE PILOT

RHYS HAD WANDERED AIMLESSLY the last twenty minutes, lost in thought over the things Volkerson and Sekami had told him. They had answered a few of his many questions, but the new information had been unsatisfying. In a way he hadn't thought possible, their answers weighed more heavily on him than the questions themselves. His own genetic makeup was the key to unlocking the grül machine. At least, that's what the scientists were hoping for. They couldn't be sure at this point... or could they? Hadn't Volkerson shown him what really happened in the lab, and hadn't Rhys seen himself deactivate the machine? But why couldn't he remember doing it? The thought of interacting with the device summoned a memory of the caged turandians, and it made his skin crawl. How was he supposed to control the dangerous substance inside? It's not like they'd given him a damn manual to study.

His rumination was interrupted when the corridor ended abruptly at a turbolift. Blinking, he looked around at the unfamiliar surroundings and realized he must be in a completely different part of the station. Sekami had stayed with Volkerson, leaving Rhys to find his own way back, but now, his feet had led him somewhere other than his quarters. In front of him, the turbolift door slid open and out stepped a short, fleshy-faced alien. It scampered toward him on a pair of spindly legs, and he opened his mouth to ask for directions.

"Excuse me," Rhys began.

The alien cast him a suspicious glance and declined to answer, only scurried further down the passage. He frowned, remembering what Sekami had said about the residents of Proxima Station being mistrustful. It made him feel even more alone. Yearning to hear a friendly voice, Rhys reached out to the one entity he knew couldn't ignore his presence.

"BAIN, are you there?" His query echoed in the empty corridor.

"At your service, Mr. Kelly," the computer replied.

"Please, call me Rhys," he said, amused on some level by how familiar the artificial intelligence had become. In his tiny, isolated universe, BAIN was one of the few beings Rhys felt at ease with. The computer had, after all, given him one of his first real conversations since waking up.

"What can I do for you Rhys?"

"I seem to have gotten a little turned around," he admitted sheepishly. "Was trying to get back to my quarters."

"Bunk Pod One is on the other side of Proxima Station. From this location, the fastest route would be to transit the maintenance corridor through Hangar Three."

Hearing he was so close to one of the hangars, Rhys reconsidered his decision to return to his quarters. His interest had first been piqued when he spied the ships coming and going from the station and wondered what sort of characters he might find there. How different could a starship's crew really be? Sure, this was *space*, not an ocean, but that shouldn't matter. Each respective crew spent a long time in close quarters with only themselves as company. Rhys wanted to see what a spaceport was like, and it would be refreshing to be around those who understood an iota of where he'd come from.

"Since I'm already here, can I see the hangar?"

"You are authorized to visit the hangar deck. I will guide you there."

Rhys followed the green track back down the brightly lit passageway until he faced a hatch with *BAY THREE ACCESS* stenciled on its surface. BAIN opened the door, and he stepped into a long, windowless corridor. Muted light from overhead lamps illuminated the path in front of him, their brilliance swallowed by the dull gray of unpainted metal walls. His footsteps echoed noisily down the tubular corridor, reverberating back to him in a chorus of taps and clicks. The maintenance tunnel seemed to stretch on forever, before the green path at his feet terminated at another door. It slid open with a hiss, and Rhys stepped through.

Inside, the hangar was huge, nearly eight stories high and two hundred meters long. Its width was easily a third the overall length. The hatch through which Rhys had entered deposited him in the bay's rear port-side corner, out of the way of the bustling activity inside the hangar. To his right, dozens of crates were stacked against the back wall, where workers checked over their contents with hand-held scanners before an autonomous gantry crane moved them to another location. Looking outward, Rhys saw the hangar opened onto a landing area outside. The scope of the pad was impressive. Three ships, two of them bigger than the one he'd arrived on, sat quietly moored as men in streamlined vacuum suits guided crates into and out of their cargo holds.

As he watched, one of the hovering gantries lifted a crate outside and flew back toward the hangar where he stood. When it reached the entrance, a momentary distortion illuminated the hangar when the crane passed through some invisible barrier before setting its load gently on the deck. The machine promptly turned around and flew back the way it had come. Once again, Rhys saw the flash of light as it exited. He walked forward, stopping only when a conspicuous message on the deck caught his eye.

*DANGER – TEN METERS TO ATMOSPHERIC BARRIER*

The bright yellow words were painted in large block letters, creating a thick yellow line running the length of the bay. Closer to the entrance and parallel to this was a second stripe, red, marking where the hangar ended and the landing pad began. There were breaks in the line approximately two meters apart, between which were words painted in the same ostentatious color.

*ATMOSPHERIC BARRIER – EVA SUIT REQUIRED BEYOND THIS POINT*

Rhys backed up a few paces and made a mental note to stay well-clear of the red line. Not wanting to be underfoot, he kept to the side, behind the yellow-stenciled words and observed the activity around him. At first glance, there seemed no obvious system in the way the cranes distributed cargo to and from the ships. Looking closer, however, he began to see a pattern. There was a method to the hangar's apparent disorder, not so unlike a swarm of bees. This spaceport, if that's what it should be called, wasn't so different than the seaports he vaguely remembered... and yet, it was all so very, *very* different. About halfway down the hangar, something had caused a breakdown in the systematic flow of cargo. A commotion had broken out, and he squinted toward an amassed group of people, all looking outward and pointing in confusion. In the distance, another ship approached the landing area. Rhys could see nothing out of the ordinary until, looking closer, he saw the smoke.

It billowed from a gash in the hull, propelled forcibly outward by the pressurized atmosphere contained inside. In a fiery display, a final burst of flame escaped through the hole before vacuum quickly extinguished the blaze. Although the fire had gone out, the ship was still in trouble. It continued its precipitous approach, the nose of the vessel at a sickening angle to the deck. Without slowing, it smashed into the landing pad, debris spinning wildly in all directions as the mechanical carcass crunched its way forward. The entire spectacle was eerily silent, the pad outside devoid of any medium to transmit sound, until the ship passed through the atmospheric barrier. A deafening, metallic scream suddenly pierced the air, and Rhys clamped his hands over his ears.

Finally realizing the danger, people inside the hangar scrambled to get out of the way of the wreckage barreling down on them. Though safely outside the crash trajectory, Rhys dove behind a crate as the ship scraped its way into the bay. A cacophony of shrieks and booms assaulted his senses when the vessel collided with several gantries, crushing them as if made of paper, before grinding to a halt only meters from the aft bulkhead. Heart pounding, Rhys hauled himself off the deck to survey the damage. Acrid smoke filled the bay. Three of the autonomous cranes were smoldering heaps of misshapen debris, while a fourth was engulfed in flames. Those workers who hadn't escaped the carnage lay unmoving on the deck. Some were crouched, frantically moving debris from atop their friends, while others fought to dowse the blaze.

"Hey! *HEY!*"

Rhys heard someone shout and searched through the haze for the voice's owner. By now, visibility had deteriorated to less than ten meters, and it was only getting worse. He began to cough, gagging on the toxic fumes spewing from the inferno. Peering into the miasma, he could just make out a silver-clad figure waving its arms above its head, clearly trying to attract his attention. The figure shouted again.

"Get over here and help me!"

Running to assist, he made for the ethereal stranger, tripping over debris now littering the deck. When Rhys reached him, the stranger thrust a second silver suit into his hands.

"Put this on. Hurry."

He stepped into the loose-fitting pants and pulled a pair of oversized galoshes over his boots. As he shrugged into the heavy silver jacket, the stranger helped him don the hood and mask, jamming the darkened shield roughly down over Rhys's head. He felt his heart rate begin to climb when he faced the wrecked ship. Although hard vacuum had extinguished the flames, there had been nothing to cool the scorching-hot metal. With a fresh supply of oxygen, the vessel had reignited and even through the suit, he could feel its heat. The stranger was already running toward the blaze, shouting for him to follow. Feeling like a potato about to be thrust into an oven, Rhys experienced a moment of panic, thoughts inevitably returning to the fire onboard the *Denebola*. He forced himself to think of something else. *I'll be okay. I'll be okay*, he kept repeating in his head. He raced after the stranger, adrenaline coursing through his veins.

Rhys's companion hadn't waited for him to catch up and thrust a rectangular device against the skin of the cockpit, slamming a silver-clad palm into its center. The object telescoped open, elongating vertically to nearly two meters. With a *POP* that sounded like the release of massive amounts of hydraulic pressure, the device pierced the cockpit, creating a vertical slit in the plating as it forced its way through. By some internal mechanism Rhys couldn't see, it pushed against the edges of the incision, compressing the metal hull until a man-sized hole appeared.

Scrambling through, the heat inside the cockpit was almost unbearable. The pilots had sealed the door to the rest of the ship, which now burned ferociously. Rhys pressed a gloved hand against the closed hatch but quickly pulled it away, the silver fabric smoking. The faceless stranger wagged a finger as if to say, 'not that way,' then motioned for him to follow. They cleared a path through the cockpit to the pilots still strapped into their chairs. Both were unconscious. The stranger quickly cut away their restraints and pointed at one, motioning for Rhys to carry her. With a grunt, he tried to heave the unresponsive woman over his shoulder but soon realized her rag doll body was too awkward, the cramped space too confined.

Grabbing her wrists instead, he dragged her through the cockpit, pausing only to help the stranger lift each victim through the forced entryway. Safely outside the burning ship, a medic ran to meet them, bending down to place something under the head of each pilot. The mysterious objects transformed, expanding beneath their unconscious occupants into a pair of fully autonomous stretchers. A strange sight to behold, the gurneys levitated off the hangar deck before whisking the injured women out of sight.

"Sickbay will take care of them," the medic said to no one in particular, then hurried off to assist elsewhere.

Rhys collapsed to his knees, utterly exhausted, and pulled the mask from his face. Sweat-drenched hair plastered his head, falling into his eyes that already stung with smoke and dust. He felt a hand beneath his arm and someone pulling him back to his feet. It was the silver-clad stranger. He had removed the hood, revealing his face for the first time. Eyes crinkled from a life of ironic humor gazed back at him, and a look of relief etched the man's rugged features. A head of disheveled black hair framed his tanned face, though his complexion might have been from the layer of dirt caking his skin. From beneath his collar, bird wing tattoos climbed up the man's neck, terminating below either side of his jaw.

"Can't stay. They're about to purge atmo," the stranger explained, pulling off the rest of his proximity gear.

Rhys followed him into the passageway, the bay door sliding closed behind them. While his companion grabbed a passerby and shot off several rapid-fire questions, Rhys removed the bulky suit and looked through a window into the hangar. Fires still burned inside, but he no longer saw anyone bothering to fight them. Everyone left alive had already evacuated. Some milled around the corridor, while others watched through more windows. Beyond the glass, a warning light began to flash, and he heard a slamming sound as the doors locked closed. No one was getting back in while the hangar was under vacuum.

"They're purging now."

The man had returned to stand behind Rhys, peering over his shoulder as he watched what took place inside. Slowly, the fire began to dwindle, transforming from an angry blaze, to a muted flicker, and finally to a dying smolder as air inside the hangar vented to space.

"Lockdown will last a few hours until everything's cooled off. Then, a team will go in and overhaul the wreckage."

They watched the last of the smoke leave the room, nothing but charred remains left inside. Rhys was giddy, the memory of the *Denebola* catastrophe once again fresh in his mind. He'd never wanted to go near another fire again, but he didn't think the stranger would've taken 'no' for an answer. In the moment, he'd worried he would just clam up, useless with fear. He hadn't, though, managing to hold the pyrophobia at bay long enough to assist in a way he'd failed Miguel, the young engineer whose life had been prematurely snuffed out all those years ago.

"Rhys Kelly," he said finally, introducing himself.

"Conrad Silas."

They shook hands. Now that he wasn't hidden beneath a proximity suit, Rhys could see the man had a good ten years on him. His weathered face had stubble from several days growth on his chin, and a shock of wavy black hair sat atop his head. There was a softness around Conrad's middle and a reddish tint to the tip of his nose, like someone who enjoyed just a little too much beer. He was dressed in a heavy jacket, a pair of dirty leather gloves stuffed into one of its pockets. His pants were tucked into a pair of battered, calf-high boots that looked as if they'd seen better days. There was an air of casual nonchalance about him, like a man who lived and died by his own rules, and it completed the appearance of some kind of cowboy... a space cowboy. Rhys snorted, amused by the juxtaposition.

"Somethin' funny?" Conrad asked, lifting an eyebrow questioningly.

"Just relieved to be out of there is all."

"Makes two of us," the man replied with a nod. "For a second, though, I thought you were gonna turn batty on me. Glad that didn't happen. At least one of those pilots would've died if I'd been on my own."

"Yeah, sorry. Just had a bad moment. Fire a few years back," Rhys told him, neglecting to specify exactly how long 'a few years back' actually was.

"I get it. That sorta thing messes with you. Had one onboard my own ship a couple years ago while we were dockside. Ain't like it mattered. After that, I was a fuckin' liability for longer than I care to admit," Conrad said solemnly. "When you've been up close and personal with a big fire, it takes cojones to do it again. Don't know about you, but I could use a drink. Hell, I owe you one just for stickin' around."

Rhys waved away the man's thanks, feeling slightly ashamed he'd considered running for the exit instead of staying to help. His instincts had been screaming for him to head for safety, and he'd very nearly listened. Remaining in the burning hangar had taken all his willpower, but in the end, he hadn't deserted Conrad. He felt bolstered by the realization that he could keep a level head under pressure, knowing full well he'd succumbed to moments of weakness with far less on the line after Anne's death. Considering what they'd just been through, though, a drink sounded like the perfect way to calm his overworked nerves.

"I'll take you up on that," Rhys said. "God knows I need one after the past few days."

Had it only been days since he'd woken up to this nightmare? Yes, he supposed, it had. So much had happened since first meeting Sekami, seeing that look of sheer terror on her face as she urged him out of his centuries-long stupor, that it felt like weeks had passed. The cryostation attack, their journey to Proxima Station, the malfunction with the machine, and his meeting with Volkerson... it had all happened in a short, six or seven-day span. Something in his expression must've given away his thoughts because Conrad let out a long, low whistle.

"I've seen those haunted, you-don't-know-the-shit-I've-been-through eyes before... but I'll wager you ain't looking to drudge up old war stories at the moment. Maybe someday, if we get too drunk, you can tell me about 'em."

Conrad led them through the station's twisting maze of corridors to an unfamiliar pod. Inside, the light was low, and it took a moment for Rhys's eyes to adjust. The place was small, home to only a few tattered chairs and tables scattered haphazardly around. Along the back wall, a single metal-topped bar ran the length of the room. Based on the characters he'd met so far, Rhys didn't expect to see many customers. He wasn't wrong.

Aside from the two of them, the place was empty except for a single patron who sat hunched, facing away from the pod's entrance. They approached the counter, and Conrad waved companionably to the barman as they sat down. Rhys stole a glance at the other customer, about to say hello, when he realized whose face was peering back at him. Goddammit. Kieron Adara leered moodily over a half-empty glass of amber liquid. By the defined sag in his shoulders, Rhys guessed the scientist was already several glasses in.

"Well, if it ain't my good buddy Kieron," Conrad oozed. Rhys didn't miss the sarcastic tone. "Say, how's that eye doing? Seem to remember you ran it into my fist last time we crossed paths..."

Kieron didn't respond. Without so much as another glance in their direction, he lifted the glass to his lips and threw back the rest of its contents. He turned away, stood, and left the pod. Conrad grinned like a hyena.

"Don't think he likes me. Get us a couple rounds will you, Tybur?" he chortled at the bartender, then lowered his voice conspiratorially. "Of the good stuff."

The barman, Tybur, nodded and dropped the rag he'd been holding. He produced two clean glasses and placed a round, walnut-sized ball of ice into each. From an unmarked jug, he poured some murky liquid and slid the glasses across the bar.

Conrad picked one up and downed its contents in a single gulp, pulling a face and slamming the cup down noisily.

"Hit me again… and ditch the ice."

Tybur dumped the ice from the empty glass and refilled it, pouring more than before. Rhys took a tentative sniff, hesitant of the liquid's sludge-like appearance. The smell alone was enough to make his eyes water.

"What the hell am I about to drink?" he asked, lifting the cup to take a sip, but Conrad stopped him.

"Better to just take it all at once. No good pussyfootin' around with that stuff."

Against his better judgement, Rhys took the man's advice. He downed the noxious substance, and the ball of ice knocked painfully into his teeth as fire engulfed his chest. Several uncomfortable seconds passed while the liquid burned like roiling pitch, gripping his throat in an iron fist that prevented him even from coughing. When the pain finally subsided, he began to hack uncontrollably until he was red in the face. Conrad laughed jovially and smacked him on the back.

"Well, can't say that's the saddest first experience I've seen with bacca," he said gleefully.

"Where in God's name did you find this crap?" Rhys choked. Conrad glanced furtively around, then lowered his voice.

"See, there's this place… might call it an off-the-books mining colony… but they're the only ones who make this particular distillation. Kind of a local favorite, you know? Sometimes, if a run takes me out to that sector, I'll make a little unscheduled stop. Gets a little hairy if I'm not careful. The people there are serious about keepin' the location of their assets a secret. I have to scrub my nav computer and do a little creative fuel accounting before they clear me for departure," he explained, keeping his words low. "I'd do it anyway 'cause I don't think the Boss Man would appreciate me risking a supply run on account of a little hooch… but, hey, there's only so long a man can go without a proper drink, and the shit here tastes like watered-down uulgar piss. Gets you about as drunk, too."

"You aren't seriously suggesting something tastes worse than this."

"Hey, at least bacca does the trick," Conrad replied, feigning offense. "Anyway, whatever I bring back, I split with Tybur here since he runs the bar as a side gig to his logistics duties. Kind of pro bono deal. He stashes the bacca and keeps it away from any of them unscrupulous types. I know we just met and all, but I couldn't ask you to face death and not trust you enough to have a discretionary drink."

"Well, thanks for the sentiment," Rhys replied, his voice still hoarse, "but maybe warn the next fool you plan to force that on."

The man laughed again and pushed the empty glass towards the bartender, who dutifully filled it with a more generous amount. Steeling himself, Rhys took another gulp. It still burned worse than anything he'd tasted but not nearly as bad as the first glass. He could already feel a pleasant tingling sensation he'd not felt in, well, years.

"Strong stuff," he declared, pushing on the tip of his quickly numbing nose. "So, you're a pilot?"

"Yep. Proud owner-operator of the *Kestrel*. She's small and fast and can make a quick getaway if she needs to. Drive compensators will absorb an acceleration jump to eighty-nine-point-six percent lightspeed baby! Ain't like the other lumbering P.O.S.'s you see coming in here. About once every other rotation, I make a run for some high-value items. You know that baukken gal, Ryele? She sets everything up. The rendezvous point, the contact, the goods... it's all pretty hush-hush. Even I don't know what I'm moving, just that it's important to whatever work Volkerson's doing."

"You mean, you don't know?" Rhys asked, frowning.

"Know what?"

"What he's working on."

"Well, I know it's got to do with the grül," Conrad replied facetiously.

"Worked that one out for myself."

"Listen, only a very tight-knit circle of people knows what's really going on around here," Conrad said in hushed tones. "Remember the guy sitting here when we first arrived?"

"We've met," Rhys replied. "Real charmer."

"He's an asshole, but that ain't my point," the pilot continued. "He's one of the scientists Volkerson brought in to help. I guess they're a little more in-the-know than I am, but even those guys don't have the whole story. Basically, it's the Big Cochise and the baukken gal runnin' the show, and they keep their chits pretty close to the chest."

Rhys wondered about this new information. If it was true, it painted a very different picture of the atmosphere within Proxima Station than the one portrayed by Sekami and the others. Until now, he hadn't really given any thought to how the support network for the hidden base must function.

"I thought this whole operation was to find a way to fight the grül?" he asked hesitantly.

"You ain't been here long, have you?" Conrad probed. "Well, yeah, that's why we're all here. I guess. Volkerson and the girl hand-picked everyone that knows anything about this place. Kinda makes you feel like you're gonna be part of some spectacular resistance at first. You're brought here to do a specific job, so you do it. It's good for a while, but then the monotony sets in. You start askin' questions that go unanswered... that, or their *lizard* of a Security Chief pays you an unwanted visit. Eventually, you just give up tryin' to figure it all out, shut your mouth, and feel happy the grül ain't found this place yet."

"Hmm," Rhys grunted noncommittally, looking into the bottom his empty glass. "And how does all that explain why you keep drinking this caustic pigswill?"

The skin around Conrad's eyes crinkled as his secretive demeanor vanished in a bout of laughter. A few tears of mirth formed at their corners, and he wiped them away with the back of his hand. When the fit subsided, he took another long pull from his cup.

"You like it, I can tell," he replied, smacking his lips. "Guess I got off on a tangent there, didn't I? Well, if we sit here long enough and keep drinkin' this pigswill, as you call it, I might just tell you."

He motioned for Tybur to fill their glasses once more, then lifted the refreshed drink into the air.

"To all the pretty baukken gals, who are bow legged and oft pegged," Conrad toasted, making Rhys squirm uncomfortably as an image of Sekami floated into his mind.

The two men clinked glasses and downed the liquid in a single gulp. They joked and drank, swapping stories late into the night and proceeded to get very, very drunk.

# CHAPTER 13
# A SUDDEN DEPARTURE

WHEN RHYS AWOKE the next morning, his head ached worse than he could have imagined. Six hundred years without a drop of booze, and he'd tied one on like a professional alcoholic... or a wet-behind-the-ears teen at his first bender. His actions probably aligned more closely with the latter. Sitting up in bed, he felt the room begin to spin and promptly lay back down. It had only been a few hours since he'd gone to bed.

The night had grown late, and each godawful glass of bacca went down easier than the one before. Lying there, he remembered the taste... oh god, the *taste*. Just thinking of Conrad's foul distillation was enough to make him lose the battle raging inside his stomach. He struggled to his feet and stumbled into the bathroom, only moments before he retched. Ejecting the previous night's liquid dinner, he heard BAIN's voice impose unwelcomely upon his pounding ears.

"Rhys, Dr. Ryele is at the door. Should I invite her in?"

"No. For chrissake, don't invite her in," he groaned between bouts of heaving. "Her silent disapproval is the last thing I need."

"I will tell her you are unavailable."

Rhys laid his head on his arm, the one resting on the rim of the toilet, and took a few shuddering breaths. The powerful retching had magnified the pain in his head, but for now, his nausea had abated to a subdued roil. Exhausted and trembling, he wiped spit and bile from his lips with the back of his hand.

"Thank you, BAIN. You're a true friend," he mumbled, too tired to muster enough strength to move from the bathroom.

He sat on the floor for several minutes, his head down and eyes closed. When the dizziness subsided, he stood shakily and walked stiff-legged into the other room. He fumbled inside the set of drawers, looking for anything that might lessen the excruciating pain that threatened to explode out of his skull. Sensing his distress, the computer spoke again.

"If you're searching for a Veisalgia remedy, I suggest you look in the medicine cabinet. You'll find an auto-injector and two-hundred milligram cartridges of Proniacam."

Distracted by the discomfort in his head, Rhys failed to understand.

"Sorry… what?"

"Veisalgia. An alcohol-induced state with symptoms of nausea, headaches, vomiting…"

"Ah," he said, finally understanding. "Just call it a hangover. Not Vays-a-lag-a-whatever."

"My apologies."

"What's the drug again?"

"Proniacam. It's a blend of non-steroidal anti-inflammatory and targeted neuroinhibitors. One cartridge should be sufficient."

Rhys grunted. Another string of words his brain couldn't easily process. He stumbled back to the bathroom and opened the cabinet, taking out the auto-injector and one of the small green capsules. He read the instructions on the side of the tube, comprehension slow to work itself into his impaired mind. Fumbling with the injector, he cursed under his breath at the breakdown in communication between his head and his fingers. They felt like fat, bloated sausages, devoid of structure and dexterity. When the cartridge finally clicked home, he held it poised above his thigh then faltered. Rhys hated needles. In all forms. During his shipping days, there had always been some requisite vaccination before he was allowed to report. He'd had his fair share of needle sticks, but they never got easier.

Gritting his teeth, he pressed the injector against his leg and felt a small pinch as the cartridge automatically dispensed its contents. In a matter of seconds, the wonder drug brought a significant improvement to his overall constitution, its speed and efficacy nothing short of amazing. The pounding in his head diminished from a brain-splitting fissure to a near-imperceptible throb. Relief flooded him, washing away the urge to vomit in a glorious, drug-induced swell of reprieve. The medicine didn't make him feel addled, just alert and pain-free. Unfortunately, it had done nothing to remove the taste of bile still coating the inside of his mouth. He brushed his teeth fervently for a few minutes, swished something from the cabinet that tasted only marginally better than his own vomit, then spat into the sink.

"BAIN, is Sekami still outside?" Rhys asked, rubbing at a new sensation that had begun to plague his stomach. Without the unpleasant effects of the hangover, his hunger had returned.

"She is."

"You can let her in."

He heard the hatch slide open, and when he walked back into the main room, he found Sekami waiting patiently, looking like something out of a dream. Her midnight-black hair was tied in a loose knot at the back of her head, a few strands hanging freely near her temples. The fatigue he'd seen the day before had all but disappeared, her violet eyes as bright as ever. She smiled warmly at him, and Rhys felt a flutter in his chest. How was it possible, that every time he saw her, she looked more striking than before?

"Morning," he said stiffly, perturbed by how off-guard the alien woman always seemed to make him.

"Feeling better?" she asked. There was nothing accusatory in her tone, but Rhys had the distinct sense she knew he'd gone on a bender. BAIN must have told her about his hangover, and he didn't feel inclined to lie about it.

"Better than when I woke up," he replied with a shrug. "Pretty hungry... like I'm catching up on six hundred years worth of calories."

"Did you receive the food I sent you?"

Rhys had forgotten about the items Marasa had brought him and about his mental note to thank Sekami.

"I did. Meant to say it earlier, but a lot's happened," he said apologetically. "So, thanks."

They were standing just inside the door, and he kicked himself for not offering her a seat. He motioned toward the chairs to her right, and she accepted with a smile. Sitting next to her, Rhys caught a faint whiff of her perfume, and it made the hairs on the back of his neck stand up. He couldn't put his finger on it, but something about its fragrance was strangely familiar, like a forgotten scent remembered anew. It made him feel hopeful, almost euphoric. Maybe the hangover drugs had made him more addled than he'd thought... either way, Sekami's effect on him was unnerving, the slightest bit of concentration made difficult by her presence. For a moment, their eyes met, and he held her gaze just a little too long before glancing embarrassedly away.

"I heard you helped during the fire yesterday," she said, seeming almost as flustered as him. Rhys was thankful for the diversion. "On behalf of the pilots you and Mr. Silas rescued, I wanted to thank you. You'll be pleased to know they'll survive without lasting injury."

He was glad to hear their efforts hadn't been in vain. Nothing in his recent, disjointed memory had been positive. Everything, all the way back to the fire onboard the *Denebola*, to Anne's death, and to the drunken misery he'd fallen into, had been nothing but a constant stream of bad news. Even since waking up, it seemed as though that depressing trend would continue. Now, though, it was a relief to finally hear something good. Perhaps this was a turning point. Maybe, just *maybe*, things would start looking up.

"Will I still be meeting with Dr. Volkerson?" he asked.

"We're gathering at the main lab in an hour. I spoke with him after the fire, and he wants our experiments to begin today," she replied, nodding. "I don't know how the machine will affect you, especially with a lingering hangover, but I suggest you try eating something in the meantime."

———————

RHYS ENTERED the messroom ten minutes later after devouring one of the flaakas in his refrigerator. The fuzzy blue fruit had served only to further arouse the hunger gnawing at his stomach, but Marasa had warned him to ration it out. Even that had seriously tested his self-control. Looking around, he found no familiar face in the cramped cafeteria. There was a queue to his left, and he fell in with the others in search of something to eat.

The line moved forward steadily, but there didn't seem to be anyone serving food. Instead, several tube-like receptacles were built into the bulkhead next to neat stacks of plastic dishes. Each diner would grab a tray and a bowl, then place the empty vessel inside one of the tubes. Rhys craned his neck around the people in front of him, unable to get a good look at what took place, only that steaming food suddenly filled the previously-empty containers. When it was his turn, he picked up some plasticware and placed the bowl inside the receptacle. Nothing happened. He began to hear grumblings and half-muttered obscenities in the line behind him, their annoyance evident at the delay he caused. Rhys turned to the stern-looking man next to him.

"I'm not sure what I'm–"

The man brushed past to another open dispensary before pointing wordlessly at a scanner next to the tube. It was an impersonal gesture, annoyance permeating the stranger's mannerism. Was no one on this station, save Conrad, going to give Rhys the time of day? Put off by the hostile encounter, he turned back to his own machine and pressed his palm against the scanner. The device emitted a happy chime and, through a descending nozzle, dispensed a steaming ration of... something... into his bowl.

Grimacing, he picked up the tray and made his way to find an open seat.

He scanned the small groups of people huddled together over their bowls of mush. Spotting an empty table, Rhys picked his way through the room and was about to sit down when a familiar voice called out. Turning, he saw Conrad waving at him, gesturing to an empty seat at his table. Changing course, he circled around and sat down next to the pilot.

"Someone's beaten you with the ugly stick this morning," the man greeted, squinting at him through puffy, blood-shot eyes.

"Says the pot to the kettle. You look about as good as… whatever this crap is supposed to be," Rhys replied, looking down into the bowl of slop. "If I have to eat or drink something terrible every time I see you, then I'm not gonna like being your friend."

The pilot laughed and nodded toward the slime-filled contents of the bowl.

"You don't know how bad that stuff really is. Rhys, my boy, you think you've seen hard times? Just wait. The contents of that dish will show you the true horrors of the universe," he quipped, making slurping noises as he sucked a spoonful of goo into his mouth.

The sound made Rhys cringe as he scooped some up and let it splash back into the bowl with a wet, slapping *plop. Here goes nothing,* he thought and took a bite. Its runny texture landed somewhere between tapioca pudding and overcooked oatmeal, both of which he disliked. The flavor was about the same, and despite his hunger, Rhys had a hard time stomaching it. He held his breath and ate quickly, doing his best not to gag as the sludge slid disgustingly down his throat. Conrad, a look of revulsed amusement on his face, watched him force it down like it was the last meal he would ever eat.

"I have to admit," he said, grinning and pushing a glass of water toward Rhys, "you look worse than before."

"Ugh… I feel worse too. Where can a guy get some coffee around here?"

Conrad shuddered and made a face.

"If you thought the food was bad, the coffee's worse. I suggest you kick that particular habit for your own good."

"That bad huh? So much for a new and improved future," Rhys replied glumly. The pilot gave him a questioning look, his visage one of confusion.

"You lost me."

Rhys hesitated. Should he tell Conrad about where he'd come from? Pondering the question, he failed to come up with any good reasons why not. Neither Sekami nor Volkerson had directed him not to tell people his story. The man sitting across from him, the one slowly spooning personal torture into his mouth, had trusted Rhys enough to keep his security-violating quest for liquor a secret. He'd known the pilot for less than a day, but together, they'd already faced down death and come out the other side intact. Perhaps he was naïve for doing so, but he trusted Conrad.

"I'm over six-hundred-and-forty years old," Rhys declared. The confused look on the pilot's face changed into one of skepticism.

"Come again?"

"I'm over six-hundred-and-forty years old," he repeated. "I froze myself in 2077, and because of certain events my frigid ass couldn't control, I was kept in stasis for six hundred some-odd years."

"Well... shit," Conrad said after a while, sitting back and frowning. He was looking at Rhys with newfound curiosity. "So, that fire a few years back..."

"On a sailing ship, the last one I ever stepped foot on, over six centuries ago," Rhys explained. "I've only been awake about a week."

"Huh... can't say I've ever met anyone that's froze themselves," the pilot said simply. "Cryonics was somethin' I learned about growin' up, but people just don't do it anymore. Ain't really worth it. With the grül out there terrorizing the galaxy, nobody believed they'd get woken up again if they went into stasis. It'd be

like committing suicide. Better to just off yourself the old-fashioned way than drag it out for eternity."

"I was only supposed to be frozen for a decade. Human trials
were only approved a few years before, and I was part of one of
the first longevity studies," he explained, pausing to drink some
water. His mouth was parched from the previous night's binging.
"I still don't understand why they let me go so long…"

His voice trailed off as he thought about the file Sekami had
shown him after their narrow escape from the cryostation. Its
contents were vastly different than the contract he imagined he
would've signed. The worst part of it all, though, was that he
couldn't even remember enough to say for sure that he hadn't
agreed to such terms. Six hundred ten years… it was upsetting,
knowing he was so far removed from his own past it meant basically nothing to anyone. The present was so vastly different from
the future he had expected to find, and no one, except for this
pilot, seemed able to relate to anything he was experiencing.
Through his vacant introspection, he felt Conrad tap him on the
arm with the back of his hand. Rhys looked up and saw raised
eyebrows on the man's face.

"Did you hear me?" he asked, holding Rhys's attention once
again. "I'm scheduled to depart in an hour. Super-secret squirrel
stuff. Be gone a couple weeks, but when I get back, we'll polish off
more of that pigswill you like so much."

Rhys made a face.

"Only if I've forgotten what it did to my insides…"

Conrad laughed and stood, extending a hand to Rhys, who
gave it a brisk shake. Parting ways, he watched the pilot round a
corner out of sight, wondering how different things might be the
next time they crossed paths. He didn't know what Volkerson had
in store for him, and he felt apprehension building in his gut.
Tapping the implant to check the time, he still had twenty-five
minutes before their rendezvous at the lab. Having no one else to
converse with, he decided to make his way there anyway.

He arrived at the lab with fifteen minutes to spare. Stepping through the decontamination locks, he saw the only other occupant was Otaan Yabar, already hunched over a workstation and poring over the machine's strange schematics. When Rhys entered the room, the alien's hairy ears quivered, flicking back toward the door, and he turned to see who had arrived. With an interest that had not been present before, Otaan Yabar beckoned Rhys over.

"There's more to you than first meets the eye. Much more," the creature said, continuing to fix him with its inquisitive gaze. "I don't understand the contribution you're expected to make, but I'm beginning to suspect our work here might have been in vain without it."

"I have a hard time believing that's the case."

"This station shouldn't exist, not after what happened on the day of your arrival... and yet, here we stand. I tried reviewing the footage from the event, to perhaps discover some mistake I might've made, only to find the file's access has been restricted. Why do you think that might be?"

Rhys shrugged, unsure of what he should and shouldn't say.

"Whatever the reason, you aren't, as Kieron suggests, some straggler enjoying Marcus Volkerson's glowing hospitality. No one is granted asylum on Proxima Station without fulfilling a specific purpose." The Hanekaarian's voice was suddenly thick with resentment. "My own family was delayed joining me because their presence wasn't considered a priority. A year I begged Dr. Volkerson to bring them here, but by the time arrangements were made, it was too late."

Otaan Yabar's ears had begun to tremble once again, only this time the cause seemed to be overwhelming emotion. The alien had become agitated, each shuddering lungful of air exhaled in an angry snort. All four of his hands were balled into fists the size of watermelons and were flexing and unflexing in time with the creature's heaving breaths. Rhys didn't know how to respond and decided that silence was his safest option.

"Do you know what happened when the grül found Merellian II, the outpost my wives and children should've left months before?" Otaan Yabar continued, still visibly distressed. "They were slaughtered, like animals, with the rest of station... all because they'd been judged to possess no useful attributes."

Rhys felt a pang of sadness for the Hanekaarian. He couldn't imagine what it must have been like to leave his family, to aid in the effort to stop a murderous alien race, only to see his loved ones killed anyway. Shame began to fill him... shame at how selfish he'd acted. He'd been so centered on his own plight, he'd barely considered what those around him must have gone through. While wallowing in self-pity, he'd ignored the fact that everyone, it seemed, had suffered unimaginable loss at the hands of the grül. Far more than he. Otaan Yabar let out a final, heavy sigh and pointed at the ugly black sphere behind the containment fields.

"Do you know what that is, Rhys Kelly?"

"I do now," he replied, glancing toward the machine. As before, it hovered silently, a seemingly docile piece of metal, but now he understood the destructive force contained within.

"Considerable mystery surrounds this machine. We've labored for years to make it work, to understand it, to *learn from it*. The day you arrived was the day I chose to test a different scanning method. Was that an unfortunate coincidence or a stroke of good luck? None of our team knows how to activate the device or even what to do with it if we'd succeeded, but you... there is more to you than any of us yet understand," Otaan Yabar declared.

Before Rhys could reply, he heard the door open and glanced over his shoulder. Marasa and Sekami stepped out of the decontamination chamber and took a seat at one of the tables. Behind them, Kieron distractedly scribbled notes on a handheld. He glanced up from what he was doing, a half-smile on his face as if ready to make some ill-conceived wisecrack. When he caught sight of Rhys, however, his expression grew sour.

"What's Father Time doing here?" Kieron demanded, scowling up at him. "Hasn't he caused enough trouble?"

Sekami, it seemed, was not in the mood.

"Sit down and refrain from your usual tripe, or Dr. Volkerson will be made aware of this behavior when he arrives."

Her tone was menacing, but Rhys hadn't expected it to curb Kieron's bullshit. To his surprise, however, the threat was enough to shut him up. He closed his mouth and sat heavily in one of the chairs, returning sulkily to the notes on his device. Rhys and Otaan Yabar joined the others at the table and waited for Dr. Volkerson's arrival, the group sitting quietly until Marasa broke the uncomfortable silence.

"Do you know why he wants to see us?" she inquired, shifting uneasily.

Sekami gave Rhys a look that told him to keep quiet for now.

"It's nothing to worry about Marasa," she reassured. "He just wants to inform you of certain developments himself."

"What developments? Have the grül done something? I know you said not to worry, but it's not like him to meet us face-to-face. I've only seen him a handful of times since Kieron and I got here."

"It's important, that much I'll say, but he wants you to hear it directly from him..." Sekami spared a glance at Kieron "... so there's no question as to his intent."

Annoyance flashed across the scientist's face. He opened his mouth to speak, thought better of it, then closed it again. Sekami nodded in approval at this display of restraint, and a hush filled the room once more. It didn't last long. Marasa, seeming uncomfortable with such pregnant pauses, began to tap a fingernail nervously on the table, desperately looking like she wanted to say anything at all to fill the muted silence. Volkerson entered a few minutes later and stood before them. The atmosphere in the room was already strained, but his arrival seemed to compound the tension. He glanced around the table at each of them, his eyes lingering a moment longer on Rhys, before turning to address the xenotechnologists.

"Have you succeeded in boosting power to the containment fields?" he probed in his deep, resonating voice. He gave no greeting, just launched into the matter at hand. Shifting uneasily, the siblings looked at each other then back at Volkerson.

"Sir, we aren't sure if... um, yes," Kieron began, faltering under the man's unyielding gaze. "Nonessential loads have been stripped off the grid, and we've isolated each field onto its own dedicated power supply. The best improvement we could get is about two-hundred eighty percent of the original field strength."

"Good. Have you tested them?"

"No. You can understand why we've been hesitant to repeat–"

"What I understand, Mr. Adara, is that this station was nearly obliterated by your incompetence powering them in the first place," Volkerson replied, venomous accusation in his words. A vein had begun to pulse at his temple, and he directed his attention toward Marasa, leaving a humiliated Kieron to look very much like a deflated balloon. "Why would the machine activate on its own?"

Rhys found this line of questioning to be confusing. What was the point of all this? If Volkerson already knew what had activated the machine, or more importantly, who had turned it off, why was he pressing the scientists for unattainable answers? Why embarrass Kieron in front of everyone? It seemed like a pointless show of authority and reminded him of pulling the legs off a fly. Cruel, malicious, and most of all, unnecessary. He tuned back into the conversation as Marasa explained the progression their research had taken.

"... process by which it was activated," she was saying, still tapping nervously on the table. "Our working theory is that its response to the diffusion scan was a defense mechanism, though none of us can guess what turned it off. Dr. Volkerson, we've all seen the IHR footage from when you and Jenco Ryele recovered the machine. Short of obtaining a grül specimen, how do you expect us to–"

When Volkerson raised a hand, Marasa immediately fell silent.

"There's something you haven't considered," he said to the room. "I've kept this between myself and Dr. Ryele, for fear of the information falling into the wrong hands. Over the past two years, I've tasked you with finding a way to control this machine, to gather enough data to develop weapons and defenses that would be effective against the grül. Without their DNA, I knew that might prove to be fruitless, but I needed to know if there was another way. During that time, Dr. Ryele and I conducted our own research, and what we've discovered may be the key to our success."

Volkerson pointed at Rhys, and the siblings exchanged a confused look.

"I'm sorry," Kieron interrupted, "but I don't follow. What can this... tourist... possibly contribute with his centuries-out-of-date knowledge?"

"Not his knowledge, Mr. Adara, his genetic code," Volkerson explained, fixing Kieron with a piercing stare. Kieron glared back defiantly, some of his pompousness having returned. "You're all aware Rhys Kelly didn't fall into our company by accident, that we sought him out. The genome of twenty-first century humans contained a genetic marker that Dr. Ryele and I theorize is similar enough to the grül's that there may be a possibility he can activate and control the machine."

At these words, Marasa fixed Rhys with her wide-eyed gaze, distracted enough to even stop her incessant nail tapping. Pure skepticism replaced the defiance on Kieron's face, and Otaan Yabar made a sound that could only be interpreted as all his suspicions being confirmed at once. Regardless of what they thought of Volkerson's news, the scientists were now all looking at Rhys with fervent curiosity. Unsure of what to say, he stayed quiet, letting the the man speak on his behalf.

"Mr. Kelly has agreed to assist us," Volkerson continued. "Your duties will change slightly to accommodate these new developments, but rest assured, each of you remains an asset to this team. That said, it's more important than ever to be discretionary in what you choose to speak of beyond the walls of this room. Considering their attack on the cryostation, we can only assume the grül have intensified their search for us. Any clues that lead back to this station could very well be–"

"So, let me get this straight," Kieron cut in, his tone insolent. "You let us stumble around in the dark while you took resources that might've helped and went off in a completely different direction? Was there ever a time in the last two years the research you had us doing was part of your master plan?"

Volkerson eyed the man, clearly unimpressed with the multitude of interruptions. In a voice that was terse and to the point, he addressed Kieron directly.

"The goals were always the same, but I wasn't about to risk the entirety of this operation on a single postulate," he replied dismissively before turning his attention back to the others. "Preventing any more potential leaks to the outsi–"

"You're a goddamn liar!"

Once again, the outburst had come from a red-faced Kieron. He was on his feet, hands balled into fists as he hunched over the table. The man was so angry he was shaking.

"This was your plan from the beginning, wasn't it? Do whatever it is you've been doing while the rest of us just waste our time jerking off? I didn't know I'd agreed to be duped for the past two years. You've kept us here, living in fear of the grül, all the while scheming behind our backs. I'll bet *he's* in on this whole thing!" Kieron spat, pointing at Rhys.

"Haven't you been listening?" Marasa pleaded, placing a pacifying hand on her brother's arm. "They *had* to keep it a secret! It still almost got Sekami killed. Do you think she and Rhys would've survived if anyone else knew?"

"You don't get it. They've been lying to us, and they're going to keep lying to us. Why can't you see that? You think he's telling the truth now? You're a naïve idiot if you believe that!"

Without uttering a word, Volkerson took one step toward the table. He was head and shoulders taller than Kieron and looked down into the man's face as he towered above. The intent was menacing, but Kieron didn't back down... not at first. Like a snorting bull, his breaths were heavy and his shoulders taut. Tension inside the lab was now so thick it could be cut with a knife. The two scientists squared off, face-to-face, and no one dared speak. Eventually, Kieron's conviction began to waver, the thought of a physical altercation with Volkerson playing out across his face. He forced his hands open and placed them flat on the table.

"Fuck this. Fuck *you*. We're leaving."

"Leaving?" Marasa's upper lip quivered.

"Leaving," Kieron said again. "This room. These people. This station. All of it. Let's go, Marasa."

She didn't move and looked at her brother with begging eyes.

"Please, don't do this," she said in a small voice. "We can't. I can't."

Kieron shook his head in disgust and made for the airlock. At the first hatch, he stopped and turned back to look only at Marasa. There was still anger in his expression, but Rhys saw something else in his eyes. Sadness maybe, or apprehension. Of what? Losing his sister? Or what leaving Proxima Station might mean? He couldn't tell.

"There's a personnel transport heading for the Proxima link station in a few days. I'm going to be on it. I hope you are too, Little Sis," Kieron said. The nickname caught in his throat. Although barely above a whisper, Marasa's voice rang out like a bell in the silent room.

"I'm staying. They need our help Kieron."

There was no more anger in the man's face. Sorrow at the prospect of parting ways with his sibling had replaced his rage. He opened his mouth, perhaps to utter some final, heartfelt plea, but no words came out. Kieron Adara bowed his head and stepped into the airlock, turning his back on the others for the last time.

# CHAPTER 14

# THE TASK AT HAND

WATCHING her brother leave the laboratory, Marasa's whole body began to shake uncontrollably. She covered her face with her hands to stifle a few choking sobs, succeeding only to make them sound more grating. Sekami tried to ease the woman's grief, whispering some indistinct words into her ear. Glancing up at Volkerson, Rhys saw his expression had turned to one of exasperation. He doubted this was going the way the scientist had imagined. The conversation had been inundated with constant interruptions, then Kieron's abrupt departure, and now, this... the man's teeth were clenched, masseter flexed, in a clear sign his patience had waned.

"Enough!" Volkerson warned. His tone was sharp. "If you need time to grieve your brother's departure, then do so in your own quarters. You're still a valued member of this team, but unless you regain some semblance of professional bearing, we'll make do without you."

Wiping the tears from her eyes, Marasa shook her head.

"I'm fine Dr. Volkerson, really. I want to help. Kieron said the shuttle leaves in a few days. Maybe he'll change his mind before then."

"Your brother," Volkerson said icily, "is no longer welcome on this station."

Marasa looked as if the man had just murdered her pet cat. Sekami placed a reassuring arm around her shoulders, but she seemed anything but comforted by the gesture. Nonetheless, she sat quietly, holding back tears, and not daring to challenge Volkerson's decision. By what little he knew of Marasa, Rhys wasn't surprised by her reluctance to confront him. He knew the type of person she was, one to quietly take whatever abuse got dished her way, but it was disheartening to see a brother and sister split up under such circumstances. The last thing they should be doing is dividing amongst themselves... and at such a dangerous, chaotic time.

"Your duties will remain mostly unchanged. With BAIN's assistance, Dr. Ryele will monitor Mr. Kelly's health during contact with the machine, including any lasting effects that may manifest from prolonged exposure," Volkerson explained, interrupting Rhys's thoughts. He motioned toward Marasa and Otaan Yabar. "Your jobs will be to collect and record as much data as possible. Anything that might aid in building effective defenses against these weapons. Seeing the machine in operation should expedite this process."

The apprehension in Rhys's gut had twisted itself into a squirming mass of worms. All this talk about his health and lasting effects... what had he gotten himself into? He looked around, attempting to gauge the others' reactions to this new assignment, to see if they were as nervous as he was. The looks on their faces, however, were implacable, outwardly showing a perceived calm he didn't share. Of course, they were calm. They weren't the ones being asked to handle a deadly alien machine.

"Going forward, the lab will operate with all three containment fields at full power whenever the machine is energized. Even on dedicated power supplies, we may need to restrict how long the machine is allowed to run," Volkerson continued. "Anyone working inside the lab will be required to wear protective equipment in the event of another containment failure. Mr.

Kelly, unfortunately, cannot be afforded this protection, as this would prevent direct interfacing with the machine."

"Wait a minute. I don't get anything?" Rhys asked, taken aback. He heard the waver in his voice. "I'm sorry, but none of this sounds particularly safe. From where I'm sitting, it feels like I'm the one taking all the risk. I mean, *Jesus*, you don't even know how this thing's gonna react when I touch it! At least give me one of those collars, or a gloveless suit, or *something*. Back on the cryo-station, my insides felt like they were boiling, so who knows how long I'll last with nothing."

"You won't be on the receiving end of the machine. If its operation relies purely on extrasensory inputs from the user, then a device that inhibits the pathway between mind and machine could make it more dangerous to control. The grül we observed on the turandian colony didn't seem to suffer any ill effects. Quite the contrary."

"It probably affects them differently! We don't know, that's what I'm saying," Rhys protested, remembering the awful burning sensation that had eaten at his insides.

"What were you expecting?" Volkerson demanded, irritation returning to his voice. "A tidy, risk-free science experiment? In case you've forgotten, an uncontrolled therleon release almost destroyed this entire station a few days ago. So, no, Mr. Kelly, you aren't assuming all the risk. That's the point. This is dangerous ground we tread, but what choice do you think we have? Even with the care we've taken to remain hidden here, it still may only be a matter of time before the grül find us, especially considering our newest security risk."

Rhys was silent as he weighed his options. He wanted to help, but the idea of voluntarily subjecting himself to excruciating pain frightened him more than he cared to admit. Or suppose, if he did succeed in energizing the machine, and there was no discomfort, how would he control it? Were there little levers inside he would feel? Did he use his mind, as Volkerson suggested? What happened when he got in over his head, lost control, and someone got hurt... or worse. His thoughts cascaded downward, each more fatalistic than the last. This was all far beyond anything he'd ever faced before.

"We'll be here to guide you. If, at any point, the risks become too great, we'll abort the operation and reevaluate our approach," Volkerson told him. "Nevertheless, we're still dealing with advanced alien technology. It's important to take whatever precautions we can, but at the end of the day, we need this weapon... whatever the cost."

Those last words filled Rhys with a sense of foreboding, amplifying the doubt that had begun to grow at the back of his mind. Something in the man's tone cast a pall over the reassurances he offered. How far was he willing to go in pursuit of vigilante justice? Judging by the look in his eyes, as far as was necessary. Pushing the thought aside, Rhys tried to ignore what his instincts were telling him. After all, Volkerson was probably right. What choice did they have? The grül were a terrible enemy, and risks would need to be taken to fight them. *Please don't let me kill everyone*, he thought. That wasn't a sacrifice he was willing to make. He took a deep, calming breath and nodded, steeling himself for what they were about to do.

"I can't promise to be what you hope."

"Do not doubt your abilities before we've even begun, Mr. Kelly. Each of you is more valuable than you know," Volkerson replied, looking pointedly at each member of the group. He turned from the table and walked to stand in front of the machine, his hands behind his back. Staring through the containment field, the man seemed pensive.

"I've waited many years for this. What we do in the coming days could very well be the turning point in our fight against the grül. Make whatever preparations you need. I want to start right away."

The other scientists around the table stood, and Rhys pushed up to join them. Sekami beckoned for him to follow, and they stepped back into the airlock. Over the last few days, he'd passed through the decontamination chamber several times, and its use had become second nature. Thinking back to the day of his arrival, though, when the machine had nearly wiped out the entire station, his trips through the airlock were a blur. He'd been so scared they were about to die, that now, he barely remembered going back for one of the suits.

"Raise your arms and maintain position," Rhys heard BAIN say. He complied, and a blinding red light shone into his eyes. After a moment, the light vanished.

"Scan complete. No therleon contamination detected," the computer informed them.

Ahead, the far side of the airlock slid open, and they stepped into the lab's prep room to join Marasa and Otaan Yabar. The sinister-looking suits had been returned to their support brackets on the bulkhead. Seeing them reminded Rhys of sickness and disease, the kind of gear scientists from his time might wear while fighting a pandemic. Large semi-flexible hoods gave the wearer a wide field of view, and a heavy-duty zipper ran from the left knee to the right shoulder around the periphery of the mask.

Marasa approached the far bulkhead and pulled a suit down from its bracket. With the ease of a professional, she stepped her legs inside and slipped her arms through the straps of the internal air pack, hefting its load onto her back. She slid her hands through the sleeves and into the attached gloves, flexing and unflexing her hands to work the material between the web of her fingers. Standing with her arms outstretched, she waited while Otaan Yabar worked the zipper closed and sealed its seam with one of the handheld applicators. Airtight, she moved away from the wall and bounced the pack up and down until its straps were comfortable on her shoulders. Otaan Yabar had donned a suit designed to accommodate his four arms, and Marasa assisted him with the final seal.

"Rhys, would you help me?"

He heard Sekami's muffled voice and turned to see her already dressed, looking back at him through the transparent hood. She raised her arms to her sides, and he grasped the zipper in his sweaty fingers. They shook slightly as he slid the tab upwards, trembling in anticipation at the task that lay ahead. It stuck a few centimeters below the hood, the suit's material catching in the metal teeth. He struggled to free it, his brow furrowed in concentration.

Rhys was so close to Sekami he could hear her breath inside the hood as he worked to free the zipper. He tried to focus on his task, but it was the second time that day he'd been distracted by the faint scent surrounding her. Feeling her eyes on him, he stole a sideways glance in her direction. There was something there, something in Sekami's expression he'd not seen before, something like… it reminded him of the way Anne used to look at him. He felt color rising in his face, until thankfully, the zipper broke free. Smiling abashedly, he closed the hood around her and retraced the seam with the sealing device. He turned away, only to feel Sekami's hand on his arm, pulling him back.

"Everything will be alright. Just trust him."

Rhys gave a single nod but didn't reply. The worms squirming inside his stomach told him that opening his mouth was a bad idea.

"BAIN and I will be monitoring your vitals, so if there are any problems, we'll know right away," Sekami told him. "Try to stay calm and follow Dr. Volkerson's instructions."

Rhys followed her back through the airlock to rejoin the others. Stepping out, he saw Volkerson suited, waiting for them to return while Marasa finished sealing him inside. Otaan Yabar took up his position at the main console and activated the tertiary containment, encircling the lab in a powerful, humming field. Sekami double-checked her suit, then sat down at another display. She typed at the holographic keys and brought up a set of chirping, spiking graphs on the screen.

"Your blood pressure and heart rate are elevated," she stated, her voice clinical.

*No shit*, Rhys thought. Blood pounded in his ears, and the skin beneath his right eye had begun to twitch in a nervous tic. He felt cold sweat everywhere on his body, a few drops breaking free and trickling down his spine. Volkerson approached him. Beneath the clear hood, the man looked calm and collected. No sweat, no visible signs of anxiety.

"Are you alright Mr. Kelly?" he asked.

"Just feel like I'm going to my own execution is all."

"Do exactly what I tell you, when I tell you to do it," Volkerson said. "If I say to stop, immediately extricate yourself from the device and wait for us to lower the containment fields. Pay close attention to how the machine makes you feel. This will be valuable information for later."

He walked to where Marasa and Otaan Yabar were seated and reached over them to key a command. The outer containment field around the machine disappeared, and Rhys stepped inside. It re-energized, briefly trapping him between the inner and outer barriers. A moment later, the primary field dropped, and for what must've been the second time, Rhys saw the machine without the bluish tint cast by its protective barriers. With nothing standing between him and the deadly machine, he felt his heart rate spike.

"Whenever you're ready," he heard Volkerson say. He took a deep breath and stepped forward. As soon as he entered, the inner containment field rematerialized around him. Now, everything except the machine was tinged in blue. Approaching the device, Rhys wiped his sweaty palms on his pants, only to have the dampness return an instant later. He walked slowly around the machine, taking in every millimeter of its textured skin. The rough surface was uniform, not a single crack or hinge visible on its blackened exterior. Unsure of what to do, he stood facing the others and waited for a command.

"Do I just..." he asked tentatively, reaching out toward the device.

Volkerson nodded visibly through his suit, and for a moment, Rhys held his trembling hand a few centimeters above the machine's surface. With the hesitance of someone caressing a sleeping tiger, he ignored every inhibition screaming in his mind and let his fingers rest gently on top of the strange device. A feeling unlike anything he'd ever experienced flooded his body. It was electric and terrifying at the same time. He felt joy and desire, loneliness and pain, as all the synapses in his brain seemed to fire simultaneously.

In vivid detail, he saw the same scorching red flash crawl across the sky of a familiar blue-green planet... his planet... *Earth.* The screams of billions of people filled his ears as he imagined their bleeding, thrashing bodies consumed with the same pain he'd suffered escaping the cryostation. Beneath their chorus of agony was another voice, repeating the same word over and over. *Failure, failure, failure.* It echoed in his ears against the backdrop of a maddening din. The struggling, indistinct figures from before had returned, the hands of one gripping the throat of the other, squeezing the life from its body. *Failure, failure. The price of failure.* Their bodies morphed, melting into each other like lovers in the throes of passion, and then, after what felt like an eternity, they were gone. Rhys felt himself coming back, clawing his way out of the muddied waters of his subconscious. He had a task to perform. He tried to concentrate, to will his mind back to some sense of clarity. Somewhere, an alarm was ringing, forcing the screaming, echoing voices back down from wherever they'd come.

"BAIN, disregard all non-containment therleon alarms!" someone shouted over the ear-splitting wail. A moment later, all was quiet as the claxon and flashing lights faded to silence. Rhys strained to open his eyes, then peered at the people beyond the containment fields. Their faces were pale and scared.

"Rhys, are you alright?" Sekami demanded, her tone urgent.

"It's-s-s," he tried to speak, his words stuttering and broken. "It's l-like... I c-can't..."

"Like you can't what? Do you need to stop?"

"N-no," he replied through clenched teeth. Even just a few words took every bit of his concentration. "I'm o-k-kay."

"What do you see? Has the machine physically changed? Remember what you saw in the IHR." Volkerson's voice was strained, full of ardent anticipation. With difficult, jerking motions, Rhys forced his gaze down toward the device. In front of him, two openings had appeared in its textured skin.

"Armholes," he forced out, keeping his palm pressed firmly against its surface. "T-two armholes ha-have a-p-p-p-ppeared."

Rhys mustered the strength to look up and saw Volkerson staring back at him through the containment field, his expression impossible to read.

"Should I p-put m-my hands in?"

The scientist didn't answer right away. Instead, he bent low toward Marasa and Otaan Yabar and spoke softly to them as they worked. Rhys couldn't hear what was said, but that didn't matter. With his brain feeling like it was on the brink of overload, merely keeping himself upright required all his concentration. Terrible images kept trying to force themselves into his mind, and it was all he could do to keep them at bay. Every now and then, one would slip through, and he'd be bombarded with a firestorm of different, conflicting emotions. Every sensation in his body had increased a hundredfold. The tic beneath his eye had transformed into a jackhammer, the trembling so great he feared it must be shaking loose his eyeball. Somehow, through it all, he became aware of Volkerson coming back to stand in front of the barrier.

"That's enough for now. Deactivate the machine, and we'll lower the containment fields."

*No!* Rhys thought, inexplicable reluctance filling his mind. He needed to keep going, to see more, to learn *more*. The others didn't know, couldn't possibly understand the almost-magnetic pull radiating from the machine. How could they? For a moment, he felt a strong urge to stick his hands inside the holes that had appeared. The scientists couldn't stop him, not in the time it took to lower the containment fields. It was what they wanted him to do, after all… he hesitated, his scrambled neurons on the verge of hurling him into the unknown.

After grappling indecisively for an unknowable length of time, Rhys forced himself to break with the machine. Its blackened exterior crawled back together, hiding each of the shimmering armholes beneath its unremarkable surface. Silent once more, the device resembled only an ugly sphere of lifeless metal. The images and emotions bombarding his synapses were suddenly stripped away, leaving his mind a blank void.

Like air filling a vacuum, everything he'd felt before touching the machine, all his anger, his sorrow, his fear, came flooding back in a wave of stomach-churning reality. Someone had already lowered the inner barrier, and he stumbled into the space between the fields. The first containment energized behind him, and he felt a blast of wind and heat as the air inside was forcibly exchanged. Breathless and dizzy, he waited anxiously for the scientists to let him out. His nausea had returned in force, and vomiting into a repellant forcefield was the last thing he wanted to do.

"Lower the damn shield!" he choked.

The outer barrier fell away, and Sekami rushed forward to help. Rhys pushed past her, however, and stumbled to his knees as the last of his strength disappeared. With a shuddering heave, he found himself staring into a pile of the meager breakfast he'd eaten that morning. The sight of it, not looking much different than it had in the bowl, brought on another bout of retching. Blood rushed to his head, and the room around him blurred. When there was nothing left in his stomach to evacuate, he flopped backward and curled into a ball, waiting for the terrible sensation to pass. Sekami knelt beside him and shined something into his face. The device emitted a strange kind of luminescence his overwrought brain didn't recognize. It wasn't light, not in any traditional sense, but it made his eyes hurt all the same. Reflexively, he squeezed them shut and felt a hand gently turn his chin back toward her.

"Rhys, please," she coaxed, the device still poised. He forced his eyes open, the effort required making them water. "Your vitals are erratic."

She hurried back to the monitor where she'd been stationed. Momentarily consulting the display, Sekami rummaged through several drawers before coming back to where he lie.

"Hold still."

There was an audible *click*, and Rhys felt a sharp pinch in the crook of his arm. Something cold crept through his veins, forcing the tumultuous upheaval in his gut into a chemically induced calm. Sekami's scope was in his eyes again.

"Vitals are normalizing." Her voice was less strained than before. "Are you feeling better?"

"I'll be okay. Just need a second."

A few minutes later, she helped him up, and his body groaned in protest. He still felt terrible, but at least the urge to vomit had passed. They stepped into the airlock, Sekami supporting him as best she could, and waited while BAIN began the decontamination procedure. Doing his best to follow the computer's instructions, Rhys's mind slipped back to his brief interaction with the machine. If he was being honest with himself, he didn't know what to make of the experience. It had been terrible, yes, the brain-melting explosion in his synapses, the awful images that had flooded his mind, but beneath it all, there had been something else, something he'd only understood abstractly until now. The device contained unimaginable power, like nothing he'd ever felt... a near-infinite source of raw energy there for the taking. Rhys didn't know if he felt worse than before interfacing with the machine. Perhaps now, everything just seemed more abysmal because he'd been momentarily distracted. Unsure of much else, he was surprised to discover one irrefutable truth. Despite whatever consequences the machine might wreak on his mind and his body, he would try again. He *ached* to try again.

Red light scanned over them, and they were suddenly drenched in a spray of cold liquid. Without a suit, Rhys began to shiver uncontrollably before a blast of hot air filled the chamber, warming and drying him until the cleansing solution had evaporated. Stepping out of the airlock, Sekami helped him to a bench and began removing her rubbery hazard suit. Rhys watched the others pause in the decontamination chamber, red light and spray washing over them. Free of contaminants, the hatch slid open, and the scientists removed their suits, hanging them back on the wall-mounted brackets. Volkerson walked to where Rhys sat and stood over him, a hungry look in his eyes.

"A promising first step."

Something in his demeanor was unnerving. There was a kind of wild fanaticism hidden just below the surface, visible only for a moment through cracks in the man's steely façade. It was gone as quickly as it had arrived. Rhys wondered if anyone else had noticed or if he'd merely imagined it in his addled state.

"Is it always going to make me feel so…" Rhys began, casting around for the words to describe the experience, "… awful?"

"An unexpected side effect, though not surprising given your first real interaction with the machine," Volkerson replied. "Marasa and Otaan Yabar collected more data in the short time it was active than in the last two years."

"I expected it to be, I dunno, more like the grül attack I guess," Rhys explained. "It was, sort of, but then again, not. My brain felt like it was about to explode… like I was reliving every emotion and memory I've ever had…"

Volkerson nodded, seeming unsurprised, as if already knowing how the machine would affect him. Without another word, he turned away and walked to Marasa and Otaan Yabar, engaging them in hushed conversation. Rhys, unable to hear their discussion, closed his eyes and leaned his head against the cool metal bulkhead. He was exhausted. The brief interaction with the machine had drained him in a way he hadn't expected. He felt like he could sleep for days if someone let him. Maybe he'd just stay right here, on this bench, until they needed him again…

"I'd like to review the data we've collected before our next session." Volkerson had returned and his words pulled Rhys back from the edge of unconsciousness. "We should continue as soon as possible, zero eight hundred tomorrow, if you're able Mr. Kelly."

Rhys didn't reply but nodded, silently swallowing his disappointment at not being allowed to sleep for the rest of eternity. Without another word, Volkerson turned on his heel and left. Rhys closed his eyes once more, about to return to the near-comatose state he'd been working toward, when he sensed someone else nearby. It was Sekami.

"There are clean clothes and a photosterilizer through there," she told him, pointing at a side door within the prep room. "Once you've cleaned up, there's something I need to show you."

# CHAPTER 15
# JENCO RYELE

RHYS PEELED the vomit-stained shirt off his back, trying his best to keep the leftovers away from his face. Most had come off in the decontamination chamber, but it had done little to dampen the smell. Grimacing at the ripe odor, he searched the room for a place to dispose of the soiled clothes and found a chute marked 'WASTE' mounted into one of the bulkheads. Dropping the clothes inside, he walked to the photosterilizer and stepped inside. The door closed behind him with a soft hiss, and a few seconds later, the cleansing process began. It was still strange, the sensation of thousands of tiny lasers probing every crevice of his body, eliminating the corporal filth with light and sound. While efficient, Rhys found the experience to be utterly lacking. Nothing would ever beat a good old-fashioned shower.

Finished, he pulled open a locker in search of the clothes Sekami had promised were there. The pants and shirt were baggier than his own garments, but they fit well enough. If nothing else, they weren't covered in vomit. He was about to leave when he heard hushed murmurs coming from the other room. Pausing in his tracks, he strained to hear what the voices were saying. They belonged to Sekami and Marasa, and the two women spoke in whispered tones as if they didn't want to be overheard. Rhys didn't know what prompted him to do it, but he crept stealthily toward the hatch and stood to one side, eaves-dropping on the unsuspecting pair.

"I'm just worried what he might do," Marasa's muffled voice said through the closed metal door. "I mean, didn't you see him? He was angry. I'm scared he might do something terrible."

"Nothing's going to happen." Sekami's voice.

"You don't think... Dr. Volkerson wouldn't... he wouldn't... have him killed, would he?" Marasa asked, her voice full of fear.

"Listen to yourself!" Sekami hissed. "I know Marcus frightens you, but he's trying to *defeat* the grül, not make things easier for them."

"But you heard what he called Kieron. A security risk! He won't just let him leave. Not with what he knows about the project. About this place." More indistinct whispering. "Okay, maybe he doesn't physically harm Kieron, but would he, I dunno, alter his memories or something? God, Sekami, if he did and it went wrong! Meeting my brother and seeing no recognition in his eyes would be unbearable!"

"No. He wouldn't do that. You know cognitive reconstruction was banned almost eighty years ago." Sekami's voice was firm, but there was something missing from her tone that left the words unconvincing. Was it a lack of conviction? "The moral and ethical implications aside, tampering with someone's mind is incredibly dangerous. Why would Dr. Volkerson bother trying to save the Commonwealth if he was just going to ignore the tenets on which it was built?"

"I still have a bad feeling about this, even if you're convinced there's nothing to worry about. Will you at least talk to Dr. Volkerson? Make him see reason? If I can convince Kieron to stay, maybe let him return to the team?" Marasa's whispers were becoming more frantic.

"Make him?" Sekami repeated, her voice full of skepticism. "Marasa, I think you overestimate the influence I have with Dr. Volkerson... but I'll try. Not for Kieron. He's never done anything for the team you couldn't have done yourself, but you've been like a sister to me these last few years. I'll do what I can."

Marasa didn't answer, but Rhys could hear muffled crying. Something had convinced her Kieron was in danger, but what? If she thought Volkerson was capable of killing or lobotomizing her brother, she clearly didn't have a very high opinion of the man. An accusation like that must have a damn good reason behind it… that, or she was just overreacting. It had been a difficult day for everyone. Still though, what had she seen or heard to make her think any of that was possible? He strained his ears to hear more, but the whispered conversation had come to an end. Stepping out from his hiding spot, Rhys entered the room in time to see Marasa disappear through the exit. She didn't notice him as the hatch slid closed behind her. Now, the prep room was empty except for Sekami. Abashedly rubbing the back of his neck, he brought up the conversation on which he'd just eavesdropped.

"Um… couldn't help but overhear, but Marasa seems pretty upset," he said. Sekami's eyes narrowed in suspicion, and Rhys gave her a guilty look, spreading his hands apologetically. She didn't offer a rebuke, however, and her expression grew heavy.

"Marasa's worried about Kieron. She knows how reactive her brother can be. You've seen for yourself."

"No offense, but it sounds like she's more worried about what Volkerson might do."

At this, Sekami began to fidget, twisting each finger and cracking the knuckle joints with an audible CRACK. It was a strangely human eccentricity that seemed out of place in the alien woman's demeanor. Then again, Rhys reminded himself, she had spent at least some of her life in the company of one. Still, he couldn't begin to guess what was going on in her head, and it was clear the subject had made her uneasy. The allegation Marasa had leveled against her mentor, or whatever Volkerson was supposed to be, carried weight. Was that what had made Sekami so uncomfortable, or was something else bothering her? He hadn't meant to upset her, but if there was any truth behind Marasa's suspicions, he deserved to know.

"You can tell me," he said, gently pressing for more information. "I just want to know if I should... tread carefully. It doesn't change what we're doing here. Puts things in perspective, really."

Sekami ceased cracking her knuckles and folded her arms across her chest, remaining silent for a long time. Something like fatigue, or maybe loneliness, crept into her eyes. It reminded him how he'd felt climbing back down the mountain after failing to fling himself from its summit, all those forgotten centuries ago. She looked absolutely lost. Rhys had the sudden urge to reach out, to take her into his embrace and offer the comfort she seemed so desperately to need. He resisted though, knowing that in their short time as acquaintances, it would be inappropriate. When Sekami found her voice again, it was devoid of the clinical tone it so often held.

"There are things about Dr. Volkerson, about this whole project, I can't tell you. Even the others don't know, but he's the one person who's given us a chance to survive. Everything he's done in the past year has been for you. To find you. To bring you into this fight. With your help, we might be able to save the Commonwealth from..." she trailed off in search of the appropriate words. When her face darkened, her voice was filled with forced conviction. "...from monsters! Do you think that comes without certain sacrifices? Isn't that *worth* those sacrifices?"

A deep-seated sense of unease formed in Rhys's belly at her words. Perhaps Marasa's fears hadn't been so unfounded after all. Could Volkerson really be capable of murdering her brother, only to prevent a loose end from escaping his sphere of control on Proxima Station? He hadn't thought so. Pondering this for a moment, he remembered what he'd seen in the IHR; an unsuspecting alien, the young scientist's snarling face, and the bloodied rock... the man was clearly capable of killing... but, then again, that had been a completely different circumstance. Volkerson's, and ultimately Jenco's, survival had been on the line. He'd just watched one of the grül kill its companion over... over what? Which of them got to drain the life from a cage of defenseless turandians? The creature wouldn't have thought twice about killing the shipwrecked men if given the chance. Still, though...

The thing Rhys found most unsettling was Sekami's apparent lack of opposition toward Volkerson's methods. Had she really bought into his lecture about saving the Commonwealth, at 'whatever the cost?' *Do you think that comes without certain sacrifices?* Those had been her words, after all, but how much of that did she actually believe? From what little he'd seen, he couldn't identify any ulterior motives behind Volkerson's or Sekami's actions. At least, no clear ones. The operation on Proxima Station did indeed seem dedicated toward fighting the grül. He himself wanted to aid in that effort, but if protecting what was left of his species from an advanced alien race meant abandoning... hell, willingly sacrificing... innocent friends and family, then what was the point in saving any of it? What in God's name had he become involved in?

"Rhys, I promise Dr. Volkerson won't harm Kieron. We're all free to leave at any point, regardless of what rumors might circulate around someone's departure," she said gently, seeming to sense his confliction. Her words were meant to reassure, but to him, they only felt pacifying. "Don't let Marasa's misplaced fears for her brother cloud your judgement. She's as close to family as I have now, but she's always been naïve. Her brother made a point to take advantage of that whenever he could."

Rhys wanted more than anything to believe her, to know he hadn't been woken up only to be thrust into a conflict between a murderous alien species and a crusading madman. Looking into her eyes, he decided he believed Sekami, or at least, that she believed her own words. He nodded and smiled, showing he understood. This seemed to satisfy her, but he still felt troubled. Rhys realized he would need to be very careful about who he chose to trust on Proxima Station, and he wasn't sure it was Volkerson. Nevertheless, the way things were going, Rhys could think of no better place to be. The hidden colony was safe, relatively speaking. At least here, he could help fight against the creatures responsible for destroying everything he'd ever known. And anyway, what choice did he have? The only thing he maintained any control over was how much of the gelatinous nutrient ration he ate each morning. Feeling his stomach turn over, he decided not to think about that particular unpleasantness. Not right now.

"What did you want to show me?" he asked, changing the subject.

Her furrowed brow eased somewhat at his diversion.

"I was going to take you back to the IHR... if you're interested."

"That's not just for Volkerson's use?"

"Each pod has a dedicated terminal," she explained. "You're free to access it whenever you like. We'll go to the one nearest our quarters."

Despite the lingering queasiness Rhys still felt, the offer piqued his interest. After witnessing Volkerson's initial discovery of the grül, he'd burned with fascination at such a detailed means of data collection. It had felt like something from one of the novels he used to find himself engrossed in, tales of adventure, danger, and cutting-edge technology. The irony wasn't lost on him. His own experiences since waking up had been more akin to a horror story. Nevertheless, he nodded eagerly at the prospect of another venture into the IHR.

"I've been wondering," he mused, following Sekami out of the lab, "what type of data gets recorded? Is it just what we can hear and touch and see? Or is temperature and pressure and stuff like that logged as well?"

"Depends on the input conditions," she said. "If, for example, the parameters were set to monitor heart rate, blood pressure, and neurologic impulses of a patient, then all that data could be recorded. That's a very specific utilization of an IHR, though. For the most part, it's an event reel, to be played back later. In shipboard application, it's often used as a black box data recorder to document missteps leading up to an accident."

"That's a huge amount of data to sift through if it's running constantly."

"Again, it depends on the application. Holograms have been commonplace for hundreds of years. The idea's the same today as when it was first developed, but there have been significant advances in resolution and data acquisition," Sekami explained. "At first, it was a true hologram; laser light manipulated to display a three-dimensional image. There was no physical substance behind the images, but you see what it's evolved into. Now, an IHR can generate tangible objects that look, sound, feel, and smell exactly as they would in the real world. They're no longer true holograms, in the original sense of the word, but no one thought it was necessary to redefine what IHR technology meant."

"How long has it been around?" Rhys asked, glad to be momentarily distracted from his own troubling thoughts. "In its current form, I mean."

"Forty years at least. I'm not sure exactly," she replied. "After the grül showed up, merely surviving was all anyone cared about. Technological advancements came to a screeching halt, but it was common practice to record in IHR when I was a child. Let me show you."

Without realizing, Rhys had followed her into an empty gray room identical to the one in Volkerson's private pod. He'd been listening so intently, he hadn't noticed their arrival. Sekami walked to the computer terminal and plugged a small memory drive into the interface. This time, he knew to expect the train-like rush of sound and color and closed his eyes against the disorienting flurry. When the images in the room stabilized, he looked around.

They were standing in an open meadow, up to their knees in leafy green ferns swaying gently in the breeze. A turquoise sea reached as far as the eye could see, reflecting warm sunlight off its surface onto rocky islets dotting the horizon. Brilliant blue colored the sky overhead, punctuated only by dark clouds far in the distance, their bellies swollen with rain. Parked in the clearing next to them was a ship, the foliage around it flattened and trampled. Its loading ramp was down, but there seemed to be little activity happening inside. He saw Sekami heading away from the craft, toward the summit of a small hill, and he jogged to catch up. When they got closer, he noticed two people sitting on the ground, a man and a little girl, both of whom had pale green skin. The girl's hair was deepest black, and Rhys recognized the piercing eyes of a very young Sekami Ryele. He knew the man next to her, too, from the feed he'd seen in Volkerson's IHR; her father, Jenco.

"It's you," Rhys murmured. Sekami nodded.

"I was eight. We'd returned to Lyterea, my father's home world, attempting to hide from the grül. We never stayed in one place for long. This was one of the few instances where life seemed almost normal... when my father wasn't buried in his work or talking about the machine. This IHR feed... it's not exactly a happy memory, but it's best one I have of him. I wasn't even born when he and Dr. Volkerson found that infernal machine, and running from the grül is all I've ever known."

Rhys heard the bitterness in her voice as she told her story. He couldn't blame her. To be so young and thrust into an endless nightmare, always on the run. He couldn't imagine what that must've been like.

"What about your mother?"

"Died... in childbirth. I have no memory of her. Papa was always too sad to talk about it much."

"I'm sorry," he replied somberly.

They fell silent and watched the two figures sitting on the ground. The girl's head rested on her father's shoulder, one of his arms slung around her. They stared off toward the distant rain clouds before the girl, fidgeting restlessly, stood up and tried to wrestle. Jenco laughed and took her into his arms before gently pulling her back to the ground to tickle her ribs. She squirmed and giggled, breathlessly kicking her legs as she struggled against his grasp. Breaking free, she stood up and ran a few paces away before turning around to face him. With a child's war cry, she sprinted back in a headlong tilt, windmilling her arms overhead. Jenco smiled warmly as she fell into his waiting embrace, and the two of them rolled partway down the hill, giggling happily until tears streamed down their cheeks.

Breaking apart, the young girl stood up and walked circles around her father, patting him softly on the head several times before sitting down heavily at his side.

"Are we ever going to stay here, Papa?" she asked. "I don't want to leave anymore."

"Someday, maybe. With luck," Jenco told her. He regarded his daughter for a moment, sadness in his eyes. "But for now, we keep moving. You understand why, don't you?"

The girl nodded, gazing off into the distance. She picked at the ferns, pulling off leaves in a childish display of boredom and tossing them into the air. Rhys watched as the pieces blew away, lost in the eddying wind. When she looked back at her father, her bright eyes were full of pity.

"I feel bad for him," she said, changing the subject. "He seems so lonely. He used to be my friend, but now he's always too tired. Too sad. You still find time to play with me, so why can't he?"

A pained look appeared on Jenco's face, and he seemed to struggle, searching for the words to comfort his daughter. She gazed at him expectantly, waiting for his response. Shifting uncomfortably on the ground, he wrapped an arm around her, pulling her close and giving her a little squeeze.

"We've been working day and night, Mimi. I know you don't understand the toll it's taking on him, but he's very tired," Jenco replied. "The work we're doing is critical to our survival. I wish things were different for us, for you. I haven't given you the life I should have."

His last words were choked, and he turned away from his

daughter's gaze. She blinked, and her lip began to tremble when she saw how upset her father had become. The girl wrapped her arms around him and buried her face in his chest. They sat there awhile, comforted by each other's presence, until a faint call drifted up to them, carried on the wind. Disentangling themselves, they stood and gazed back at the distant ship. A man approached, waving as he came. Even from here, Rhys recognized the purposeful stride of Marcus Volkerson.

The girl sprinted down the hill toward the approaching figure and latched onto his arm when she reached him. The man lifted her playfully, swinging her around like a discus thrower until both were thoroughly dizzy. Jenco let out an exasperated sigh and began trudging toward the new arrival. Rhys and Sekami followed him, walking a few paces behind the holographic representation of her father.

"Marcus," Jenco said stiffly, inclining his head in greeting.

"I know you wanted time with Sekami, but there's something I need to show you," Volkerson said and gave the girl a sideways glance. "Just you."

The baukken fixed his partner with an irritated glare, then knelt to speak with his daughter. From his pocket, he pulled a round disk and handed it to her. Rhys recognized the object as a BAIN drone. The girl clasped it in both hands and gave her father a stricken look.

"Mimi, Dr. Volkerson and I have to get back to work. You can stay out here as long as BAIN is watching," Jenco told her. He reached out and pressed a finger to the center of the drone. It sprang to life and hovered a few meters off the ground, awaiting instructions. "Keep an eye on her."

The two men turned and walked up the loading ramp, disappearing into the ship. The young Sekami lingered for a moment before sitting down to rip up more ferns, a disheartened look on her face. When her hand stopped in midair, the leaves suspended in space, Rhys knew the recording was over. The room dissolved around them and when he turned toward Sekami, he saw her face was as sad it had been all those years ago. Rhys didn't know what to say. She had shown him this for a reason, but what was it? He grasped at straws, feeling as though he should say something… anything.

"You've been involved in this a long time, haven't you?" he asked. God, it sounded stupid, but he couldn't think of what else to say. Thankfully, it seemed Sekami didn't require him to say much of anything. She nodded and massaged her face, as if to rub away the sense of loss she must be feeling.

"I was six the first time the grül found us. Twenty-five years ago, now… it was difficult. Wanting a friend and suffering from childish impulses, all the while trying to be strong for Papa. The reason I brought you…" her voice trailed off as she struggled to keep her emotions in check. "It seemed important for you to understand what he was like; the reason I keep going. What we're doing here… I'm not doing it for the Commonwealth. It's too big, and I'm too tired. What I'm trying to say; find whatever is worth fighting for, and never give up."

Rhys nodded thoughtfully as he considered her words. He understood what she meant, and he agreed. Trying to defend an interstellar civilization was more than overwhelming. It was inconceivable. Something of that scope was beyond anything anyone should be asked to do, but that's exactly what Volkerson had done. Sekami, though, was telling him something different. Like Marasa, she fought, day after day, for only one person; her father. Trouble was, everyone Rhys had ever known had died hundreds of years ago, long before the grül were discovered. The only people he knew were the ones he'd met since arriving at Proxima Station. The scientists, Conrad, Sekami… all strangers in a strange time. He didn't know them well, but he hoped it was enough. It *had* to be enough.

"I know what's worth fighting for," he replied quietly, meeting her eyes.

When she didn't glance away, Rhys felt his pulse quicken as he gazed into her violet irises. A deep-seated sense of longing flooded his body, filling him once again with the desire to reach out, to embrace her... to kiss her. More than the others, he felt a connection with Sekami, but he couldn't say why. Though he'd just met this woman, it felt like he'd known her for a very long time. Was the machine still affecting him somehow? Had his sense of self and time become scrambled in a way he didn't yet understand? Through this, he was aware of her stepping toward him and lightly grasping the back of his neck. He didn't pull away, and they moved closer, the warmth of their bodies coming together as she pressed herself to him. Like static before a storm, he felt the hairs on the back of his neck stand up when her lips brushed softly over his.

# CHAPTER 16
# THE FIRST OF MANY

RHYS AWOKE the next morning feeling conflicted. After repeated brushes with death, his moment with Sekami had made him feel more alive than he had in a very long time. It hadn't gone anywhere. They'd shared a single, passionate kiss before his inhibitions caused him to offer up reasons of exhaustion and fatigue. He grimaced inwardly at the lame excuse, but he'd been so caught off guard by his sudden, inexplicable desires that he'd gotten cold feet. Nothing more intimate had transpired, so why did he feel like such a cheat now? The reason was obvious. He'd be lying to himself if he claimed ignorance... Anne. His insides twisted into a guilty knot at the thought of his dead wife. He knew she'd been gone for hundreds of years, but to him, her death still felt like only a few months before. Between the shame of betraying his wife's memory and the stirrings of affection toward Sekami, he was now caught in an emotional stew that made his head spin.

Thinking back, Rhys realized the entire thing had probably been inevitable. Confronted with her vulnerability, the strange aftereffects of the machine, and his wildly out-of-balance six-hundred-year-old libido, it had happened through an unpredictable and perhaps unrepeatable set of conditions. Either way, he feared he may have complicated the situation. There had been few words spoken between them afterwards, but Sekami hadn't seemed regretful… at least, not then. Would she see things differently this morning? Did he?

Regardless of whatever else he might be feeling, his thoughts kept returning to Anne. He knew he had to let her go, but it just wasn't that easy. Hell, he'd contemplated suicide *and* somehow gotten himself into the middle of an intergalactic struggle because he couldn't let Anne's memory rest. Of course, it wasn't easy. Still, none of that changed the fact he had no idea what to say when he saw Sekami. Would she want him to say anything at all? It was probably best not to bring it up, and Rhys decided to let her broach the subject if she so desired.

Glancing at the clock next to his bunk, he realized there were only ten minutes to get to the lab by the agreed upon start time. Swearing, he kicked off the covers and hurried to get dressed. He ran down the passageway and, for what was perhaps the first time, did not require BAIN's direction. He burst into the lab's prep room a few minutes later and glimpsed the others through the glass, dressed and waiting. Hurrying through the airlock as quickly as the automation would allow, he muttered an apology when he stepped out to join them. His gaze fell on Sekami, and an anxious flutter filled his chest.

"Morning," he said, cautiously testing the waters.

"Good morning, Rhys," she replied. Her face was impassive, as if having totally forgotten their intimacy the previous night. Jesus, she could be hard to read.

As before, Marasa and Otaan Yabar powered up their monitoring equipment and waited for the experiment to begin. There was an eagerness in the Hanekaarian's demeanor that hadn't been present before, as if thrilled by the chance to finally witness something that had eluded them for years. Sekami positioned herself in front of the screen displaying his vitals and consulted its readout for a moment. Apparently satisfied with what she saw, she nodded to Volkerson then gave Rhys a little, reassuring smile. It didn't help. Nervous anticipation had begun to force itself in beside the misgivings he felt over their affectionate moment, and by the time the outer field was lowered, a familiar trepidation had all but consumed his thoughts.

The first barrier de-energized, he stepped forward, followed by the second, until once again, nothing stood between him and the ugly machine. Only now, he wasn't the containment's sole occupant. A cage had been placed directly in front of the device, and seeing it filled him with confusion. Inside was a furry, six-legged creature. The small rodent scampered around its confines in obvious distress, fear evident in both sets of beady eyes.

"What the hell is this?" Rhys asked, horrified, when comprehension finally smacked him in the face.

"Your first test," Volkerson replied with a steely voice. Disbelief welled up inside Rhys, but when he opened his mouth to protest, the scientist cut him off. "What did you think was the point of learning to use the machine? To further academic theory? Wake up, Mr. Kelly. This is a weapon, and if we can't study its characteristics when used as such, how can we develop effective defenses against it?"

Rhys didn't answer, afraid of what he might say if he failed to hold his tongue. Looking into the creature's eyes, he tried to tell himself it was no different than what mankind had done in the wild for eons... except, this *wasn't* the wild. At least there, the hexapod would've been given the opportunity to fight or flee. Instead, it had been given a cage... a prison in which to die horrifically. It just felt wrong. Inhuman.

"I'm not in the habit of slaughtering penned animals," Rhys replied through clenched teeth.

He closed his eyes and tried to justify what they were doing. *Remember what Sekami said about sacrifices*, he told himself. If killing this creature allowed them to discover a means to defeat the grül, then it barely qualified. For chrissake, they weren't even offering up a child, as the timeless dilemma went. This had to be done, and it was going to be done without any real ethical quandaries. Mustering what little detachment he could, Rhys took a deep breath and directed his attention back toward the machine. His scalp began to tingle with unease when he pressed his palms against its surface. Once again, he felt an overwhelming rush of sensation course through his body, filling him with oppositional feedback. Death and life, pain and pleasure, failure and triumph. Through it all, his brain managed to comprehend the two familiar holes that had appeared in front of him.

"Time to find out what's inside," he heard Volkerson say as if through a pane of thick glass. Jerkily, and at what seemed like a snail's pace, he reached forward and slid his arms into the shimmering holes.

"What do you feel?"

"N-not… sure," Rhys stammered. He felt detached, disembodied, like his voice was not his own. "Fluid of some… k-kind. It forms ar-ar-around… fingers… noth-nothing else."

Groping around, he felt the material morph around the contours of his hands. He pulled an arm partway out, expecting it to be covered in something wet, but no. Whatever the substance, it stayed within the confines of the machine. Pushing both arms in as far as they would go, his fingers grasped at nothing but more of the strange material enveloping them.

"Visualize opening the aperture," Volkerson commanded.

Even through Rhys's machine-addled state, something seemed off in the scientist's manner. He was almost too calm, too certain that thoughts alone would be enough to elicit a response from the machine. Did he already know it would work? If this truly was the furthest his research had progressed, how could he be so sure? Forcing himself to focus, Rhys fought to bury the images bombarding his brain long enough to remember what he'd seen in the IHR. He imagined the surface peeling back to reveal a pulsating nucleus. When nothing happened, he concentrated harder, willing with all his might for the machine to open. The jackhammering tic beneath his right eye had returned, and beads of sweat from intense mental exertion trickled down his forehead. Suddenly, without any warning, the device parted at its invisible seams to reveal the shimmering core. Somehow, in some inexplicable way, it had worked as Volkerson seemed to know it would. Now, the caged beast scampered around its tiny prison squeaking noisily, terrified by what occurred in front of it.

"Good. *Good*," Volkerson urged, no longer seeming the calm, detached scientist. Instead, an almost manic urgency had come over him as he stared through the humming fields. "Focus your thoughts on the uulgar."

An overwhelming sense of self-loathing filled Rhys at what he was about to do, churning to the surface of the storm boiling inside him. His thoughts turned grim as he imagined killing the creature, its twitching nose a conduit through which he could sense its fear and confusion. The uulgar continued its frantic scurrying, but although clearly frightened, the hexapod remained unharmed. No matter what he thought, no matter how hard he concentrated, Rhys was unable to inflict any harm through the device. *Remember why you're here*, he told himself, conjuring images of six twisting legs... of a bleeding corpse... of death.

Despite such gruesome imagery or perhaps because of it, tendrils of doubt began creeping into his mind, and the shimmering light from the machine's deadly core started to fade. The aperture was closing! He willed himself to concentrate, to refocus, to *succeed*, but nothing seemed able to displace the revulsion that had taken root in his brain. A moment later, the machine fell dormant once more. He ripped his arms free of the holes, unwilling to maintain the stream of venomous thoughts toward the simpleminded creature. Shame filled him, coupled with the nauseating aftereffects of the machine, as his would-be victim squeaked defiantly from its prison.

"I couldn't do it," he said quietly, directing his blank, thousand-meter stare to a spot on the floor. "I tried. God knows I tried. The things that crossed my mind trying to kill it..."

No one spoke. Not a single word.

# CHAPTER 17

# PROXIMA FOUND

"CAPTAIN, we are approaching the location of the therleon burst."

Xorin heard the Commander's call, and a thrill of anticipation coursed through him. At last. At long last, they could recover the machine and deliver retribution upon the Interloper. His fleet was assembled, his warriors thirsting for a fight. He, too, could almost taste long-sought victory, but the implications of impending success were not lost on him. The High Council would expect him to relinquish the authority bestowed by the Exalted Leader and return meekly into the fold of their neutered dominion. *No,* he told himself. No longer would he deny his training, his way of life, or the teachings of the Küddarian Brotherhood. For too long had he been led on a wild hunt, evaded by so simple a creature as the Interloper, that the thought alone made his blood boil with hate. His search was almost at an end, and when it was, Xorin would personally subject Marcus Volkerson to the Rhonath. The Council's laws be damned.

Outside the bridge window, a distorted sky snapped into clarity as the ship emerged from its wormhole. A massive asteroid field materialized against the backdrop of a colorful, gaseous nebula, and Xorin motioned for the pilot to hold position. Immediately, the huge vessel began to slow until finally coming to a stop a few moments later. Rocky debris stretched on as far as the eye could see. He glanced at the ship's sensor readouts, making little sense of the erratically jumping numbers. Some variability was to be expected, but their values swung wildly, never settling into a normalized range. He frowned and leaned forward in his seat.

Directly in front of his chair was a rounded console that looked as if it had grown from the ship itself. Supported from the bottom, its base swept up from the deck in a curving arc. The device it held was unremarkable, its rough, black surface broken only by two shimmering holes that appeared upon contact with Xorin's skin. He inserted his hands and closed his eyes to concentrate. *Show me the fleet's sensor readouts.* Forming the words in his head, information began to fill his mind as the knowledge he sought passed through the therleon network, an organic grid of signals and connections, that linked his fleet. It was a perfect system, immune to miscommunication or errors in transcription. His commands were both instantaneous and flawlessly executed.

Merely an instant passed before the knowledge Xorin desired was fresh in his mind. *The fleet's instruments are as erratic as mine,* he knew. No matter. They would just need to look the old-fashioned way. *Cloak your ships and move into the field toward the origin point.* Without delay, he felt engine thrust once again. Several painstaking minutes passed as they maneuvered their way through the debris. It wasn't long before the coordinates of the therleon disturbance lay dead ahead, but there was nothing visible but more huge chunks of shattered rock. Perhaps Commander Feyt had been correct. Perhaps there was nothing left of the Interloper to find. Xorin leaned forward to order the fleet's probes deployed but paused when an excited shout filled his ears. One of his crew had raised the alarm and was now pointing at something in the field beyond.

In the distance, a strange electrical storm had formed just above the surface of a particularly large asteroid. The disturbance was small at first, a mere pinpoint of light, but continued to grow until the rock was entirely veiled in a flurry of sparking interference. Without warning, the nose of a ship seemed to appear out of nowhere, coming directly out of the storm. They all watched as the mysterious apparition emerged. As soon as the vessel was through, the disturbance vanished as if it had never existed. Xorin smiled and understood why their deep-space scans had yielded no evidence of a settlement here. The Interloper was even cleverer than suspected.

"Disrupt communications and target their engines!" he commanded.

An energy pulse sped toward the lone ship, extinguishing the glow of its propulsion drive upon slamming home. The effect of its impact left the vessel helpless, drifting in space with no means to escape the grülbarvoc's grasp. Xorin dispatched a team of warriors and watched the boarding craft speed toward the hamstrung transport ship. Resistance would be met with extreme prejudice. Those who surrendered would become hostages... for now. Any prisoners would be bled for whatever valuable information they possessed until they were no longer useful.

# CHAPTER 18
# ROCK BOTTOM

TWENTY-SEVEN DAYS... it had been twenty-seven horrific days since first attempting to kill the uulgar, and twenty-seven days of abysmal failure. Rhys stood in front of the mirror and looked at his unkempt reflection, the heavy bags beneath his eyes evidence of sleepless nights. Interfacing with the machine wasn't just taking a mental toll on him but a physical one as well, and its effects were beginning to show. Dull eyes peered back at him, empty and lifeless in a face grown gaunt with hunger, but thoughts of food were the furthest thing from his mind. When he did eat, each meal was more depressing than the last, and he'd be forced to endure the nutrient rations under Sekami's watchful gaze. Rhys felt himself slipping away, despair taking hold with every glutinous bite.

He'd realized a week ago what Volkerson was driving him to do was poison to his mind and his sanity. His own newfound willingness to kill the animal made his insides squirm with shame. At first, his thoughts had been half-hearted, but as Rhys grew more frustrated and more desperate to succeed, they'd turned frighteningly darker. It was disturbing, the depths to which the human mind could sink when faced with its own survival. The images he'd conjured plagued his dreams, nightmarish visions of twisting legs, bleeding corpses, and shattered planets.

During one particularly bad night, he'd relived the scientist's discovery of the grül, but instead of large, gray-skinned aliens slaughtering the turandians, it had been *him*. He'd awoken violently, covered in sweat, and tangled in the bedsheets. Since then, he'd begged to stop several times, but Volkerson's displeasure had been evident as he drove them relentlessly forward. More than anything, Rhys wanted the experiments to end, but no one seemed to understand what he was going through.

As they had countless times over the past month, his thoughts turned toward Sekami. That was what hurt the most. Did she understand how much he'd suffered? Did she even care? Since their intimate moment in the IHR, he'd been careful not to broach the subject. She hadn't uttered a word about it and had avoided any physical contact with him, though he wasn't sure if that was intentional or just incidental. Either way, even the smallest gesture of sympathy would've gone a long way. He felt isolated and alone, like he had after the *Denebola*, and it was tearing him apart.

Rhys knew he'd have a better chance of controlling the machine if his misgivings over Sekami were one less thing on his mind, but dammit! He couldn't get her out of his head. Staring blankly into the mirror, he wished for nothing more than a reprieve from the toxic existence he'd become trapped in. He couldn't have said how much time passed, standing there in front of the mirror, grasping to retain the humanity he felt slipping through his fingers. Very soon, something was going to give, and he feared it would be his sanity.

Rhys left his room ten minutes later looking more disheveled than ever. He'd been wearing the same clothes for the last three days, too tired and depressed to give a shit about personal hygiene. The trek down to the lab occurred on autopilot, having become so familiar he could've done it with his eyes closed. When he arrived, he stepped through the hatch and into the lab's brightly lit prep room. There, waiting patiently, was Sekami. As she had every day of the past few weeks, she appeared well-rested... as well as someone could under the circumstances. He trudged toward her, looking like the weight of the world rested upon his shoulders.

"Are you alright?"

He heard the concern in her voice but found it unmoving. Coming back to the lab always intensified his feelings of despair. Declining a response, he sat down heavily at the table and accidentally knocked a steaming bowl of nutrient ration to the floor; the same, godawful breakfast Sekami had been bringing him each morning. It clattered to the deck in an explosion of sticky brown protein paste, but Rhys didn't move, only stared detachedly at the mush now smeared across the steel plating. Sekami stepped forward with a handful of rags.

"Let me help."

Bending down, her hand found his shoulder. It was a simple, innocent touch, but he felt his body tense nonetheless. *Not now*, he wanted to plead. *Don't do this now*. Any unexpected empathy from her would be too much for him to bear. It would only send his brain careening down a path it shouldn't go when he was preparing to use the machine.

"I'm fine, Sekami. I just didn't sleep well," he said, too drained even to register how pathetic his excuse sounded. It had the desired effect, though, and she gave him room to gather the contents of the spilled bowl.

While he scooped up the sticky mess, Sekami slipped into her rubbery suit and waited silently for him to finish. He helped her with the final seal, then trudged heavily through the airlock to where the other scientists waited. Otaan Yabar had already taken up position at the control console and was scrolling aimlessly through the screens. Marasa sat quietly next to him, eyes red and puffy, as if she'd been up all night crying. That came as no surprise. Kieron had promised to leave nearly a month ago, but the transport ship had been delayed. His sister had spent much of that gifted time trying desperately to convince him to stay, but her efforts had been in vain. Once its maintenance issues were resolved, the ship had finally departed, less than a day ago, and Marasa had been thoroughly miserable ever since.

When his gaze fell on Volkerson, Rhys saw only apathy in the man's face. Few words had been spoken between them over the last several days. With each failed attempt to control the machine, the scientist had become more aloof, until finally providing no direction whatsoever. Rhys remembered the last thing the sanctimonious prick had said to him... some useless shit about having been given the tools, but it was up to him to use them. Now, Volkerson's expression was devoid of any expectation. There was no reassuring nod, no word of suggestion... just an icy stare.

Otaan Yabar lowered the containment fields, one after the other, and Rhys stepped inside, placing his palms on top of the machine. Interfacing with the device was now almost too much for his weakened mind to handle. He was at the end of his rope, and the intense rush of sensation nearly floored him. Struggling to stay on his feet, he stuck his arms inside and tried to focus. *Kill it,* he thought, too miserable to truly muster the manufactured hate he'd used over the past weeks. If he could just kill it, all of this would be over.

The animal watched him with beady eyes and squeaked placidly from its cage, no longer frightened by its potentially lethal habitat. Rhys's concentration wavered, the familiar doubt slithering into his brain, until he was no longer able to keep the aperture open. When the shimmering light disappeared, he pulled his arms from the device and stared absentmindedly at the penned hexapod. It chirped timidly at him, and he wondered what it thought of this strange relationship they'd come to share... if its new existence was better or worse than from wherever it had come. He wished he could convey to the strange little beast that he was sorry.

Rhys heard the hum of the containment fields grow quiet and the footfalls of someone approaching. Looking up, he saw Volkerson's face behind one of the clear hoods, anger evident in the scientist's eyes. Without a word, he opened the cage and removed the uulgar. No longer in the relative safety of its prison, the creature squirmed madly in the man's grasp. He set the hexapod on the ground, and it made a frantic bid for freedom. It hadn't taken more than two steps, however, before Volkerson brought his boot down on its head. An agonized squeak was cut short, and blood squirted out from beneath the man's foot. Rhys, thunderstruck, couldn't tear his eyes away from the twitching corpse and the bloody pool blooming around it.

"*That* is what awaits us at the hands of the grül!" Volkerson bellowed. The man's face was red, spittle flying from his mouth and landing on the inside of the plastic hood. "The price of failure!"

Rhys couldn't move. He was frozen by the casual way the uulgar had been slaughtered. No hesitation, no remorse. The killing had been effortless. Anger welled inside him, quickly replacing the dismay he'd felt moments before.

"You bastard!"

He balled his fists and lunged forward to punish Volkerson. To hurt him. To expel all his repressed frustration and rage pummeling the man who'd led him down this path. His attack was easily side-stepped, however, the scientist surprisingly agile in the bulky suit. Rhys turned back but nearly lost his footing in the slippery, pooling blood. Before he could lunge again, he felt four strong hands clamp around his arms and chest, crushing the air from his lungs. Otaan Yabar had grabbed him, and the alien's strength easily overcame his feeble attempts to struggle free.

"Rhys, please! You need to stop!"

Sekami had joined the fray and inserted herself between the two men. Her face was pleading, a wordless appeal for him to come to his senses, but anger like he'd never known had consumed his entire being. Seconds passed like hours, until finally, after what felt like an eternity, he stopped struggling. The tension in the room was palpable. No one spoke, not daring to upset the delicate calm that had settled over them. Rhys couldn't bring himself to look anyone in the eye. He knew attacking Volkerson had been a grievous error. The only reason he'd been brought here was in the hope he might control the machine. If he couldn't do that, would he still be granted asylum, or would he be expelled from Proxima Station like Kieron? He stole a glance at Volkerson, and when he peered into the man's cold, gray-flecked eyes, Rhys felt his heart plummet.

"Call Captain Rynnavek," Volkerson snarled, a thick vein pulsating at his temple, "and get this coward out of my sight."

Otaan Yabar tugged on Rhys's arm, leading him away from the containment area and back through the decontamination chamber. Numbly, he gazed through the airlock's thick glass window at the three figures who'd remained in the lab. Someone, Marasa perhaps, had raised the containment around the machine so that once again, it was tinged by the humming blue fields. He wondered if this would be the last time he ever saw it. A moment later, he was drenched in cold spray before being hit by a powerful blast of warm air. When the decontamination process finished, the Hanekaarian accompanied him out of the prep room and into the corridor where Rynnavek waited. The security chief dismissed Otaan Yabar, and saying nothing to Rhys, escorted him back to his room. When they arrived, the Captain steered him firmly through the door but did not enter.

"Restricted to quarters until further notice," he said before the hatch snapped closed.

Rhys heard a mechanical *click* as it was locked from the outside. Walking over, he sat heavily on the bed and ran his fingers through his hair. What the hell had he been thinking? Attacking Volkerson? Getting himself restricted to quarters? Almost immediately, he'd regretted the decision to engage in a physical altercation. It was just more proof the machine was poison to his very soul. He knew he should have kept his emotions in check, but that had proved too difficult. His exhaustion from the last twenty-seven days, coupled with a stunning display of cruelty toward the uulgar had been too much for his fragile mind to handle, and he'd snapped. He doubted he would be given a second chance. Volkerson had made it abundantly clear that Kieron was no longer welcome on Proxima Station. Even if Marasa had somehow convinced her brother to stay, the man wouldn't have allowed it. Now, Rhys would pay the price... whatever that might be.

Hours crawled by feeling more like days. For a while, he paced back and forth, occasionally prompting BAIN with requests for information. Even the A.I. seemed to be giving him the cold shoulder as its replies felt more terse than usual. Eventually, his apprehension gave way to frustration at being unceremoniously locked away. Rhys picked up the nearest heavy object and advanced on the bolted door, intending to bang incessantly until someone came to give him answers. Even if whatever they told him was bad news, it would be better than waiting here in suspense. Before he could enact his plan, however, the computer warned him against such action.

"Mr. Kelly, I will be forced to take further measures if you proceed on your present course," BAIN told him. Rhys didn't know what those measures might be, and BAIN would not elaborate, but the threat of additional restrictions was enough to discourage him from beating on the door.

An hour later, he heard another *click* from outside his room. When the hatch opened, Sekami stood in the doorway, a grim look on her face.

"May I come in?"

He stood aside and allowed her to enter, thankful it was Sekami and not Captain Rynnavek who'd come to see him. Maybe it meant she didn't blame him... well, not too much, anyway. When the door closed behind her, she turned to face him, observing his unkempt appearance before closing her eyes and pinching the bridge of her nose.

"What were you thinking?" she asked, unable to disguise her frustration. "Do you know how close you came to..."

Sekami's voice trailed off, and when she finally looked at him, Rhys was unable hold her gaze. Her expression was a strange mix of anger and bewilderment, but beneath it all he saw real concern. There had been several moments over the last month where he'd questioned what he meant to her. Did she actually give a shit about him or was he just some tool to manipulate, so he would do what was asked of him? Those feelings had been more pronounced on the worst of his days. Now though, he saw none of that had been true, and it made the guilty knot in his stomach twist even tighter.

"So, will I be left in here to rot?" he asked tentatively. She shook her head and let out a heavy sigh.

"After you were escorted out, Dr. Volkerson was..." Sekami paused, once again at a loss for words. "I've never seen him like that. It was the first time I've ever been frightened of him. Of what he seemed capable."

"What did he say?"

"It wasn't anything he said. There was just... a look."

Seeing Sekami so perturbed was unnerving. Even though Rhys had sometimes doubted the nature of their relationship, she was the one steadfast thing in his life, a rock to cling to in an ocean of madness and unknown. Now, it was like watching the rock crumble from beneath him, the edge of a dark abyss creeping ever closer. Despite his press for information, though, she refused to tell him anything else, just shook her head as if the motion would make her forget the things that had upset her.

"He wants to continue our experiments, but if something like this happens again, the repercussions will be much more severe."

"I understand... and I'm sorry. I screwed up, but you don't know what the last month has been like. I feel sick. Like I've been poisoned or something. Well, not literally," Rhys said, once again sinking onto the bed and running his hands through greasy hair. "Every time I tried killing the uulgar, I wished it was me on the other side of that thing... so it could all be over. I just... I don't think I'm capable of what Volkerson wants me to do. This was all just a guess anyway. A long-lost genetic marker? C'mon. There was no guarantee that would work."

"But Rhys, it *does* work. You've seen it. We've collected more data in a month than the last *two years* we've been here, and that's all thanks to you. This was never about making you the sole defender of the galaxy. Your role was always to activate the machine long enough for us to gather enough information to develop our own therleon-based defenses... something that doesn't rely on genetic material," Sekami insisted. Some of her conviction had returned. "Please. If you walk away from this, everything we've done will have been for nothing. Take a few days to rest. We all need it... especially you."

Looking into her pleading eyes, Rhys felt his heart sink when he knew he'd comply with her request. Even fearing the consequences of his error, he'd been half-relieved at the thought of being done with the machine. He wouldn't miss the toll it took on his humanity. Now though, he realized that reprieve had been doomed to a fleeting existence. He would take the time to rest, but when he returned, he would succeed in controlling the machine, or he would die trying. Either way, there was an end in sight to his suffering.

XORIN'S DISAPPOINTMENT peaked after the twelfth prisoner failed to provide any useful information. Over the last two days, Commander Feyt had extracted intel regarding the Interloper's defenses but nothing more. None of them seemed to know anything about the stolen machine; where it was, who possessed it, or how they'd managed to energize it, however briefly. Now, only a single survivor remained, and the Captain felt nothing but disdain as the human male cowered in the corner of the holding cell, its fleshy white face betraying the terror it felt. *Such a weak species*, Xorin thought with disgust. He motioned for Feyt to bring the prisoner, and the Commander pulled the creature roughly to its feet. The human let out a shriek of pain.

"No, please! Don't kill me!" it pleaded, stumbling forward reluctantly as they marched down the corridor.

It continued its pitiful braying as the Commander pushed it unceremoniously into the interrogation room before turning to leave. Xorin watched their quarry whimper piteously, wet tears leaking from its eyes. Feyt returned a moment later, guiding one of their therleon generators in front of him. The sight of the floating black sphere made the prisoner's eyes go wide, and a sound escaped its trembling lips that made Xorin's skin crawl. Feyt positioned the device in front of the hostage and stuck his hands inside, closing his eyes to concentrate. The skin of the machine peeled back to reveal its shimmering core, and the human stiffened, bound immobile by the invisible therleon force that held him.

"Do you recognize this machine?" Xorin asked quietly, stepping close to his prisoner. "A man named Marcus Volkerson stole one just like it many cycles ago."

The human's lips quivered in terror.

"I c-c-can't... I d-don't... I don't know w-what you want," it pleaded. "P-please don't use that thing on me."

"Tell me what I want to know!" Xorin roared.

His patience had run out, and rage filled him by how dim-witted the thirteen prisoners appeared to be. Did they value their lives so little as to brazenly defy his will? Why wouldn't they just give him what he needed? Taking matters into his own hands, he pushed Commander Feyt away from the machine and inserted his own arms into the device. *Tell me what I want to know,* he demanded again, this time in his head. The human gasped at the foreign presence in its mind, and its eyes rolled back to reveal white sclera. It began to struggle against the invisible bonds, but its attempts to oppose him were feeble. Before long, Xorin had broken through the creature's mental defenses, and flashes of memory that were not his own filled his mind.

Every memory the human possessed was now free to be accessed. All Xorin had to do was ask. He knew the human's name. It was a strange name, an alien name: Kieron. He saw the stolen machine sitting behind a humming containment field. He saw the Interloper, older now, but unmistakable from the man he'd first gazed upon in the footage collected by the High Council's assassin. He saw the newcomer, Rhys Kelly, and sensed Kieron's dislike of the stranger. Now, he saw the machine... saw it energize, its power momentarily held at bay by a rudimentary shield, felt the human's fear during the event, and watched as if from his own memory as the man fled in search of safety.

Xorin had seen everything he needed. The machine was here,

along with the Interloper and his accomplices, and they had no idea who was closing in on them. The long hunt was coming to an end, his elusive prey unaware of its impending doom. A hunger he'd resisted for many cycles stirred inside him, and having no further use of the sniveling human, he decided to indulge it. Without so much as a warning to Feyt, Xorin initiated the Rhonath. The creature cried out in pain, its body twisting grotesquely in front of them.

Draining the lifeblood from the shrieking human, Xorin's symptoms of the grülbarvoc's genetic Sickness were burned away. He felt himself grow stronger, his once-atrophied muscles now bulging against the confines of his battle garb. His mind was sharper, his body more agile, his faculties deadlier. It had been too long since his last Rhonath, and he remembered something he'd known long ago. *This* was what the Küddarian Brotherhood had used to make the grülbarvoc strong, to make them fearless, to make them near *immortal.*

He knew the effects wouldn't last... a few months, a cycle maybe, before the wasting disease began to rob him of his strength once again. That didn't matter anymore. He knew what had to be done. His kind had allowed themselves to succumb to a path of weakness and disease. The High Council had chosen to deny the very things that made them what they were, to the detriment of their species. If they were to survive, the grülbarvoc must return to the Old Ways, the hallowed path preordained by the Divine Leader.

When the last of the human's vitality drained away, the Captain removed his arms from the machine, and his victim's lifeless, bloody carcass collapsed to the floor. He inhaled deeply through his nose. He'd forgotten how everything seemed brighter after the ritual. Colors were more vivid, smells more intense, and sounds richer than before. Feyt looked at him with a mixture of fear and awe at what had just occurred. For a moment, something else flashed in the Commander's eyes, something that could have been doubt... it wasn't concerning. Xorin remembered the first time he'd seen a Rhonath, and he too had been alarmed by its apparent brutality.

"Dispose of this mess," he said, tilting his head toward the decimated corpse, "and do not speak of what happened here."

Xorin returned to the bridge and settled into his chair, activating the command module to deliver orders to the fleet. *Prepare your ships for attack. I will personally lead a boarding party to recover the machine and capture the Interloper. If he slips through our grasp, he must not be allowed to escape the blockade.* Their instructions understood, the fleet moved toward the hidden station. Through the membranous bridge window, the Captain caught one final glimpse of the barren asteroid field before it was obscured by a sparking, crackling shroud.

RHYS HAD SLEPT MOST of the previous day. His entire being felt drained and aching, and the apprehension he'd endured over his unknown fate left him profoundly exhausted. Thankfully, Sekami had given him a generous dose of sleep aid, and as soon as his eyes were closed, he'd fallen into the first dreamless slumber in weeks. Now, twenty-two hours later, the much-needed rest had eased some of the despair he'd felt a day ago. He still suffered from a lingering sense of guilt at the dark places his mind had gone while using the machine, but it was less gut-wrenching than before.

Lying on the thin mattress, he stared at the ceiling in his darkened room and allowed his mind to wander. The prospect of a few days away from that goddamn machine was the best gift anyone had ever given him. He couldn't have imagined his actions in the lab would result in such a welcome reprieve. He knew his moment of relief would be short-lived, once Volkerson's soul-sucking experiments resumed, and he felt his insides twist with dread. Even the thought of what lay ahead threatened to send him back down a road he didn't want to travel. Perhaps they could try something else, something that didn't involve slaughtering a defenseless creature.

Needing to piss, he kicked off the covers and crossed to the bathroom, catching a glimpse of his reflection in the mirror as he walked by. He still looked like hammered dog shit, but the bags beneath his tired eyes seemed less pronounced. A hint of their old spark had returned, a change from the emptiness that had manifested over the last few weeks. He knew that wouldn't last for long, not once they returned to the task at hand... it was a depressing thought, and he didn't want to spoil the time he'd been given to recuperate. Forcing the notion from his mind, he turned to leave, hearing the toilet gurgle softly as the reclamation process began.

For a while, Rhys milled around his quarters, enjoying uninterrupted solitude. There were no humming force fields, no terrified squeaks, just a near-imperceptible whisper of the air recyclers. It was the first time in nearly a month nothing terrible was being asked of him. He settled into one of the cushioned chairs and tapped his jaw to activate the implant.

In the early days of using the machine, he'd still possessed enough resilience to ignore its unpleasant effects and investigate what had happened over the last six hundred years. BAIN had helped him access the station's library, a massive virtual database filled with everything from entertainment feeds to historical records to complicated engineering theories.

The latter were of most interest to him, particularly regarding the progression of space exploration: the advent of nuclear fusion as it came and went, the first, very-limited application of a fusion-antimatter engine, and finally, the beam-core drive now prolific aboard long-range spacecraft. Most noteworthy was the G.C.'s slow but continuous expansion into a vastly unexplored galaxy.

Long before the Commonwealth had formed, Hanekaar had tasked its science vessels with building a network of quantum link stations; facilities capable of transporting matter across vast swaths of space almost instantaneously. Proof of concept came in the form of one brave volunteer who had been the first sentient creature to travel between two prototype stations. Having proved the theory, the first real test came nearly five years later, after sending a ship on a two-year voyage to the nearest celestial body. Three years on-station to build the massive receiving facility, and suddenly, faster-than-light travel had become reality.

The network had its limitations, however. Not only were the link stations prohibitively expensive to build, but they also required sometimes decades-long transits to the coordinates of any proposed station. The Hanekaarians had worked on the network for centuries, but it still accessed only a microscopic area of the galaxy. Nevertheless, it had given mankind (and other members of the G.C.) the stars. During his initial investigations, Rhys had found much of the information beyond his comprehension, filled with technical jargon and groundbreaking concepts that should have been lost on him, but the more he read, the more surprised he was by how easily he came to understand. Even then, he'd only begun to scratch the surface of the available material. There was so much to know.

Scrolling through the menu, he found his most recent text and began to read, picking up where he'd left off in *The Rise and Fall of the Sahmian Empire*. It was a fascinating account of a hundred-year period in Earth's history, during a time when the entire planet had been unified beneath a single, technologically minded dictator, Phineas Sahm. Although attributed with mankind's successful expansion to the edges of the Solar System, the despot had led an incredibly violent regime. Those who willingly followed his cult-of-personality were so rabid in their support, that any dissent was often punished with severe vigilante justice. For a long time, the men and women who might've stood against such tyranny instead turned a blind eye to the atrocities committed in Phineas' name.

When Rhys first discovered the mighty tome, he had often read late into the night, whittling away countless hours until falling asleep in the chair. Now, though, after several torturous weeks with the machine, it wasn't long before his thoughts turned inward. He tried to focus on the spark that had finally led to Sahm's overthrow, but it was no use. When given the chance, his mind inevitably went to the darkest place possible, and sitting alone brooding seemed like a detrimental use of his time.

All he wanted at this moment was a strong drink in his hand. He smirked humorlessly at the irony. That sort of behavior had been what landed him here in the first place. Swiping away the text with a quick sideways glance, he scrolled through the menu once more to access the station directory. A few double beeps chimed in his ear, and a moment later, a smiling face appeared in front of him.

"I was wonderin' if you were still among the living," Conrad greeted.

"Barely," Rhys replied grimly. "It's been a rough couple of weeks."

"Rhys Kelly, ladies and gentlemen. The galaxy's oldest broken record," the pilot needled.

"Yeah, yeah. Can it, would you?" he fired back, glad of some good-natured banter.

"Sensitive this morning. Nothing a stiff drink can't fix."

"That," Rhys said, his voice growing heavy, "is exactly what I need."

There was an awkward moment of silence.

"Everything okay? You sound a little out of it."

"It's... complicated," Rhys began, wondering how much he could, or *should*, say. Sekami and Volkerson had been adamant about not discussing what they were doing with anyone. Conrad was trustworthy, he was sure, but if Volkerson caught wind of him blabbing to a near-stranger... Rhys was on thin ice already.

"Ain't tryin' to be nosey. Just seems like you need to get whatever it is off your chest," Conrad said. "Gimme some time. We're finishing up some repairs on the *Kestrel*, and the Maintenance Chief's a real ballbuster. I can meet you in... an hour?"

"See you then."

Rhys ended the transmission. Looking around his cramped quarters, he suddenly felt an overpowering sense of claustrophobia. He couldn't stay cooped up any longer and left his room without a particular destination in mind. Anywhere but here. Try as he might, he couldn't keep his thoughts from the unpleasant memories in the lab, and sitting around on his own didn't help. Now, with even Phineas Sahm unable to distract him, the scene of the uulgar's brutal execution kept replaying in his head; its twitching legs, the squirting blood, Volkerson's manic eyes. His mind felt like a ticking bomb, as if it were only a matter of time before it began to cannibalize itself. *Something about the devil and idle minds... or hands*, he thought, unable to remember rest of the old proverb.

A few minutes later, Rhys found himself facing the door to the IHR. This too, he'd been using regularly during his downtime for the first several days of their experiments. As was true with the virtual library, however, things had gotten so bad in the last two weeks that all he'd wanted to do after leaving the lab was curl up in the relative comfort of his bed. Now, for whatever reason, his subconscious had brought him back. The hatch slid open, and he entered the darkened room.

When he stepped inside, the lights brightened to a soft glow and revealed the featureless gray walls. They were a blank canvas, patiently waiting for someone to paint a vibrant picture on their unremarkable surface. Pausing in front of the control module, he considered what recording to view. So much had happened in the past six hundred years, and he'd barely scratched the surface of it. Fingers poised over the keypad, the gears in his brain ground forward until, finally, he settled on an event that had changed his life forever, something he'd been avoiding. He didn't know what made him do it, didn't know why he chose now of all times to see it, but keyed a command into the computer and waited as the room transformed.

In a tornado of color and sound, the molecules of the IHR rearranged themselves into a new configuration. Rhys was standing inside a cockpit looking out across a star-dotted void. Directly ahead was a blue-green planet, white clouds swirling through the atmosphere in a slowly churning display of turbulent beauty. It was a breathtaking scene. He knew it was just a recording, a false image, but it was more glorious than he could have imagined; Earth, as he remembered it from images in his past. It seemed little had changed over the six hundred years he'd been frozen. He gazed longingly at his old home as the ship continued its trajectory, circling the planet until the sun seemed to melt into the horizon. Hearing a sudden commotion behind him, Rhys turned and saw a familiar holographic figure hunched over a panel, frantically spinning knobs and dials on the console. Volkerson.

"Jenco! Can you still hear me? They've targeted the African Territories! Where the hell are you?" the scientist demanded, his voice panicked. The holoscreen in front of him hissed with static. Intermittently, Jenco's green-skinned face appeared through the interference, his speech garbled and broken. Even though Rhys couldn't make out his words, he could see the baukken was terrified.

"Breaking orbit– somewh– Nepal," he replied before the monitor was once again consumed by static.

"Jenco. *Jenco!*"

There was no reply.

Volkerson hurried to the pilot's chair and took manual control. The view outside the cockpit window lurched wildly as he nosed the vessel into a lower orbital path around the Earth. A thump reverberated through the false cockpit as the ship engaged its maneuvering thrusters and sped toward an unknown destination. Rhys watched intently as the Earth's curvature revealed more of the planet's surface. Then, from behind the horizon, appeared a massive ship. It was identical to the one Rhys had glimpsed while escaping the cryostation. Seeing it made the hairs on the back of his neck stand up.

The assault had already begun. From below, the planet's

defenses unleashed an onslaught of firepower that rained down on the attacking vessel, yet it remained unharmed, not even bothering to return fire. Rhys was hit with the sudden mental image of angry gnats, bouncing harmlessly off the hide of an elephant. It was a disconcerting analogy. The bombardment from Earth's defenses amounted to less than a minor inconvenience to the grül incursion. Beneath the ship's bridge, a huge, spherical aperture peeled open to reveal its shimmering innards. With renewed vigor, Volkerson tried again to contact his partner.

"Jenco, are you there? They're going to fire!"

"I hear you! Sending my position!"

The response was much clearer than before, whatever previous interference no longer disrupting their communications. They must be getting close. A moment later, a tiny red ring blinked into existence on the cockpit window, tracking something moving toward them at breakneck speed. As the halo grew larger, Rhys saw it encircled a fast-moving craft, tracking the vessel's movement as it sped away from the planet's surface.

"Coming up on your shuttle," Volkerson called out. He peered intently at the glowing ring, chewing his lip in anticipation. In the background, something pulsed from grül ship's aperture, and the scientist's expression changed from one of hope to one of horror. "Jenco, you're too close! You need to get–"

Blinding red light filled the cockpit, and Rhys squeezed his eyes shut against the glare. When darkness returned, he blinked away spots that filled his vision. Outside, he only saw fire... an inferno crawling across the sky in a wave of unspeakable annihilation. The destructive surge moved outward from its epicenter, consuming Earth's atmosphere and anything nearby in fiery conflagration. As the shockwave built, Rhys saw Jenco's shuttle trying feebly to escape its path, and the baukken's face appeared once more on the view screen.

"Marcus, tell Sekami-mi-mi-mi..."

The craft was overtaken, and Jenco's voice hung in a stuttering, mechanical loop before cutting short in a burst of static. The tracking circle on the cockpit window made several erratic attempts to stay on target before it too disappeared. There was nothing left for it to track. A strangled cry escaped Volkerson's lips before he jerked the ship away from the oncoming tide of destruction. Rhys heard the drive spool up and took one final look outside. The therleon attack had burned everything within their view, and what it left behind wasn't Earth... not really. The scorched surface was devoid of blue oceans, of lush green forests, of swirling white clouds. All that was left was a lifeless rock, the skeletal remains of what had been.

A moment later, the cockpit dissolved around him, and he clenched his eyes shut against the disorienting wave. When he opened them, the IHR's dormant state had reappeared. Its very existence seemed to mock him, the drab gray walls hiding unspeakable horrors as if nothing had happened. What the hell had he been thinking? He'd wanted to know what occurred on the day the Earth was attacked... to see the event with his own eyes. It seemed important, to truly understand why he would never return home. He hadn't thought Sekami and the others were lying, but the news had felt abstract... surreal. Now that he'd seen it for himself, though, the recording struck a nerve. Rhys had known it would be difficult to watch, but he hadn't thought he'd feel worse after witnessing it. He'd been wrong.

He left the room in a daze, blindly following his feet for the second time that day. The things he had seen kept replaying in his head, the unhesitating destruction of an entire planet making his skin crawl. Despite everything the man had done, Rhys finally understood why Sekami still stood by Volkerson's side. She must have seen the same recording, and although it wasn't her planet that had been annihilated, her father had been blinked out of existence along with the rest of humanity. He knew the anger and sadness it sparked in him and couldn't begin to imagine what Sekami must have gone through... forever wondering what Jenco's final words to her would have been. What could Rhys ever say to console her, to let her know he understood? Nothing, probably. He wasn't good at expressing words of comfort for someone's loss. To him, they always sounded forced and insincere. A few gratuitous words wouldn't make everything alright. Better to say nothing at all than give lip service to a few awkward untruths like 'I understand' or 'things will be okay.' Nobody wanted to hear that shit.

By the time he noticed where he was going, Rhys found himself at the bar. He checked the time, saw he was early to meet Conrad, but decided to go for a drink anyway. *A lot of drinks*, he thought. He stepped into the room and glanced around, noting two other patrons at one of the tables, quietly engaged in some version of chess he didn't recognize. He chose a seat at the darkest end of the bar, away from the other two occupants, and offered a greeting to the barkeep.

"Hello Tybur. Pour me something strong."

Tybur nodded once and returned with the same unmarked jug as before. He poured some into a glass and left the bottle on the bar. Rhys swirled its contents, noting how, even when it spread thin against the sides of the glass, no light penetrated the murky liquid. Knowing better than to sniff, he tipped his head back and downed it in a single gulp. A harsh burn of ethyl alcohol filled his chest when the bacca slid down his throat.

He immediately filled and drained his cup twice more before letting its effects begin to take hold. He knew this was dangerous, remembered only too well where it had landed him after Anne's death, but right now, all he wanted was to forget the image of a desolate Earth now seared into his brain. By the time he felt a hand on his shoulder and heard Conrad's familiar voice, his head was swimming. The pilot looked down at him and shook his head, an amused look of concern creasing his brow.

"You look like you're fast approaching one-too-many, my friend."

"Eh, whadda you know anyway?" Rhys replied with a faint slur. He raised a hand for Tybur to bring another glass and motioned to the seat next to him. Conrad sat and reached for the jug, but Rhys grabbed it first, pouring its contents to the brim. "S'bad luck to fill your own cup."

"To forgetting our troubles, then," the pilot toasted, leaning forward to sip the top off the overfilled cup, then raising it into the air. Clinking them together, they drank and refilled each other's glasses. "You look like hell. Worse than the last time I saw you."

Rhys stared into his cup, contemplating what exactly he should say, before deciding to throw caution to the wind.

"What do you think happens here?" he asked, still looking into the depths of his half-empty glass.

"You 'n' me get a little too drunk?"

"No, smart ass, I mean here on the station."

"I've got my theories."

"Which are?"

"Everyone knows Volkerson's working on a way to fight the grül," Conrad replied tentatively, tipping his head from side-to-side, forming his thoughts into words. "I think that's what's going on, but I also think there's a lot that goes unsaid 'round here. People assume they're an asset to his team, but I have a gut feelin' most of us aren't as indispensable as we think. Once that man succeeds with whatever he's working on, I think he's going to cut and run, leavin' the rest of us out to dry."

Rhys was silent while he contemplated Conrad's theory. He hadn't truly given any thought to what would come after their experiments with the machine succeeded. What was Volkerson's end game? How did he plan to harness the weapon's power, and what did he plan to do with it? That was all food for thought but not quite the question he'd been asking.

"Sure, but what do you think he's *working* on?" Rhys pressed. Conrad gave him a blank stare.

"How the hell should I know? I told you last time how much information gets passed to the pissants 'round here," he replied. "You know something I don't?"

Rhys needed an outlet, an impartial third party with whom

he could commiserate. He filled Conrad's glass for a third time and looked around to see if they would be overheard. Tybur was occupied at the far end of the bar, dutifully wiping some already-clean glasses, and the chess players had since departed. Now, they were the only two people remaining. In a hushed voice, he launched into an explanation of everything he knew; the research team, the grül technology they were hiding, the true reasons he'd been tracked down, and the setbacks they'd encountered. The more he divulged, the wider the pilot's eyes grew, until shock and disbelief were written in his face. When Rhys finished, Conrad reached for his glass and drained it in a single gulp.

"And here I was thinkin' you were just some lost stray who happened to be in the right place at the right time," the man joked feebly.

"I think you mean the wrong place at the wrong time," Rhys muttered back. At these words, Conrad placed his cup forcefully down on the bar. The resulting bang startled Rhys, and he looked up to meet his friend's gaze.

"Jettison that shit from your head. Trust me, the last place you want to be is anywhere but here." Humor had left the pilot's eyes, and his expression was dead serious. "You don't know how bad it is out there. I know how I come off, but I'm scared *shitless* every time I make a run. Don't ever forg–"

The alarm's ear-splitting shriek shattered the muted ambiance within the room. Startled, Rhys dropped his drink and clapped his hands over his ears. The metal cup clattered to the deck, sticky liquid splattering over their feet. Conrad pushed away from the bar and sprinted toward a glowing holoscreen near the door, one hand clapped over an ear, the other typing furiously at the screen. Rhys's heart pounded as he stumbled over to join him. Was it the machine? Had something happened? The thought sent a sudden jolt of fear coursing through him.

"What's going on?" he shouted, leaning close to Conrad's ear so he could be heard over the wailing claxon. The pilot's face was ghostly white, whatever information on the screen draining the color from his skin.

"They've found us," he croaked, still white as a sheet. Rhys felt another stab of fear shoot through him, and an unpleasant queasiness began to churn his stomach. He couldn't tell if it was from all booze or the news he'd just been given. With frantic urgency, Conrad grabbed him by the arm and began pulling. "We need to get out of here. My ship–"

Rhys wrenched his arm free of the man's grasp and ran for the door. "Sekami will know what to do!"

"Goddammit, we don't have time for that!"

"I'm not leaving without them!" Rhys shouted, running the opposite direction of where Conrad wanted to go. He heard a groan and glanced back to see the pilot hurtling after him.

Rhys had been on Proxima Station long enough to finally learn the network of connecting passageways. Unsure of where he might find the scientists, he tried to access BAIN's network but to no avail. Something kept disrupting his connection. Not knowing where else to go, he headed toward the lab, trailed closely by Conrad. Rounding a corner at full speed, he smashed headlong into Sekami. The impact knocked her to the floor as Rhys staggered drunkenly into the bulkhead. All the running had quickly metabolized the bacca, and the room spun like a merry-go-round. Unsteadily, he reached out a hand and pulled Sekami to her feet.

"We were coming to find everyone," Rhys told her, jabbing his thumb over his shoulder toward Conrad. "How'd the grül know where to find us?"

"We'll talk about it later." Her voice was urgent as she waved for them to follow her back the way she'd come. "The others are evacuating the machine."

They sprinted after her, and when they passed a window, Rhys saw the central lab far in the distance. A flashback of their escape from the cryostation twisted its way into his brain, the memory of strange, thrumming pain as fresh as if it had happened yesterday. *Not again,* he thought pleadingly. *For chrissake, not again.*

Without warning, the walls around them shuddered, and the passageway imploded. Debris flew inward as the corridor ahead crumpled in on itself. Rhys felt his ears pop as pressurized air inside the walkway escaped into hard vacuum. Somewhere in the back of his mind, he knew it was only a matter of time before BAIN's safety system took steps to mitigate the damage, isolating the ruptured section from the rest of the station. When that happened, their fate would be sealed. The remainder of their air would leak out of the passageway, and they would be trapped inside to suffocate.

Clinging desperately to one of the crumpled stanchions, Rhys heard the rush of escaping air suddenly cease. Something had sealed the breach. He gasped a lungful of sweet, life-giving air, only to choke on a fog of dust and smoke sucked in from some other part of the station. Now, it was nearly impossible to make out his surroundings, and he squinted through the haze in search of his companions. A few meters away, Conrad struggled to his feet, a dazed look on his face. Sekami, however, was nowhere to be seen.

"Where's Sekami?" Rhys demanded, frantically searching through the rubble filling the corridor. "Sekami!"

He heard a cough to his left and stumbled forward, tripping in his haste. She was piled under loose debris, and he pushed it away to free her. Hauling her up, he saw a cut above her eye, a knot beginning to form over her brow. She clutched his arm and coughed forcefully, hacking on the particulate filling her lungs.

"Are you alright?" he asked, seeing her wince each time she tried to weight her left foot.

Sekami didn't answer. She was staring straight ahead, and he felt her body tense. Rhys followed her gaze through the fog, toward the crumpled end of the corridor, and froze. The twisted metal framework of the damaged hull was gone. As the dust settled, a sight far more terrifying met his eyes.

The crushed end of the passageway had disappeared. It had been cut cleanly away but did not open into the bowels of the asteroid. Instead, something had attached itself to the end, sealing around the circumference of the damaged corridor. Through the clearing air, Rhys saw figures… tall, powerful figures, with red-streaked gray skin, and a fresh pang of terror coursed through him. The grül. At the head of the group stood a particularly large alien, older and stronger than the rest… and it was staring right at them.

# CHAPTER 21
# BOARDING PARTY

VISIBILITY WAS poor as Captain Xorin stepped off the boarding craft and into the alien compound. He could sense his warriors' anticipation, their yearning for battle. His own blood ran high at being so close to their goal, to the end of a cycles-long campaign, that he could almost taste victory. Only the sudden appearance of a mysterious transport ship had alerted him to the station's unseen presence. If the timing of their arrival had been different, they may never have discovered the Interloper's hiding place.

Xorin had gleaned what little information he could from the wretched prisoners, then promptly taken his flotilla through the optical defenses to find the secret base within. Although nothing more than a cluster of interconnected spherical structures, the station had been cleverly hidden inside an asteroid's yawning belly. He'd ordered the fleet to guard the cave's entrance, while he led a boarding party of his fiercest warriors to capture their elusive prey. So far, their arrival had been met with little resistance, the facility's paltry defenses abandoned as its occupants scurried to flee imminent doom. Now, they were inside, and the dust of their incursion had begun to settle. Dead ahead, he saw three figures extricating themselves from a pile of rubble and felt a thrill of excitement course through him. Two of them he recognized from the Kieron creature's memories; a baukken woman (the Interloper's most-trusted colleague), and the newcomer, Rhys Kelly. He did not recognize the third. For what could have been a moment or an endless eternity, Xorin stood stock-still, eyes locked together with the baukken, before she turned and fled with her companions.

"Do not let them escape!" Xorin roared, pointing toward the backs of the fleeing aliens. If their raid somehow failed to recover the machine, the baukken may yet provide some useful information. If not, then perhaps her capture might be used as leverage.

Three of his warriors sprinted after them, bounding effortlessly over debris that littered the passageway. With the remainder of his party, Xorin hurried down a different branch in the corridor. He would leave the pursuit of the Interloper's compatriots in his warriors' capable hands. There was still the machine to find and the primary fugitive to capture... those objectives he would see to personally. Consulting a hand-held detector, he pointed the way toward a faint therleon signature.

Moving deeper into the station, the scanner's chirps and clicks grew more frequent as the signal grew stronger. Xorin rounded a corner and found their way impeded. The first defenders to stand against them, a group of cowering aliens had formed a phalanx across the breadth of the corridor. By the looks of their weapons and armor, these were the station's security personnel. Nevertheless, they proved only weak, pathetic excuses for warriors. Several volleys from their primitive rifles merely grazed his thick grül-barvoc hide. Only their leader, a red, scaly creature nearly as tall as Xorin, put up a respectable fight. It had discarded its ineffective weapon and ripped open the belly of his nearest warrior with its clawed feet. The beast advanced on a second before Xorin grew tired of the delay and grasped the snarling creature by the throat. It began to struggle, eyes bulging against the crushing force over its windpipe, but it was no match for his rejuvenated strength. With a final twist of his wrist, a loud *SNAP* echoed down the corridor, and the creature went limp.

The rest of the security contingent was quickly neutralized, and the boarding party continued unhindered to the lab he'd seen in Kieron's memory. To Xorin's displeasure, there was nothing to be found. No Interloper, no machine... only a faint trace of its therleon signature. Roaring in frustration, he upended one of the cluttered tables, equipment raining down onto the hard floor in a shower of broken glass and polymer. The Interloper had slipped away yet again, and he, Xorin, the last Captain of the Küddarian Brotherhood, had been unable to prevent it. The thought only enraged him further, and he proceeded to systematically destroy the contents of the lab. No tool would be left for the Interloper to continue whatever meddling in which he'd been engaged.

"Fleet Captain Xorin," a tentative voice said behind him.

He twisted amongst the shattered instruments and saw one of the warriors he'd sent in pursuit of the baukken. At the soldier's return, Xorin reminded himself that all may not yet be lost. If his compatriots were still on the station, then so too must be the Interloper. If he'd escaped, however, the baukken would unquestionably know where he'd gone. She would give him the information he needed to track down his objective, once and for all.

"We were unable to apprehend the Interloper's companions," the warrior explained, clearly hesitant to be the one to relay bad news. "They... disappeared."

Xorin's moment of hopeful expectation was quickly extinguished by blind rage. He rounded on the warrior, grabbing him with lightning-quick speed and slamming his head against the wall. His unsuspecting victim dropped to the ground, dead, the side of its skull crushed in the vicious attack. The two remaining soldiers backed away, attempting to remove themselves from the incensed Captain's reach, only to find their paths blocked by the rest of the boarding party. Xorin breathed heavily, reining in the murderous intent that had filled him at the news of their lost quarry.

"Escort them back to the ship," he growled, nodding toward

the disgraced warriors. "The Duoranath is too kind a punishment for their failure. Let their deaths serve as warning to the crew."

Turning away, he consulted the scanner but failed to detect any stronger therleon presence. The further from the lab he moved in any direction, the weaker the signal became. The machine had been moved in its dormant state, and until it was activated again, they would be unable to trace its location. No other option remained but to return to the fleet. Their mission hadn't resulted in total failure, not yet. The instruments onboard his ship had far greater range than the hand-held detector. He pushed through the group of warriors, and they fell into step behind him, meeting no other adversaries as they returned the way they had come.

When they reached the boarding craft, the place where he'd first seen the baukken, Xorin took one last glance at the scanner in his hand before flicking it off and hurrying aboard. The small vessel detached itself from the corridor's mangled structure and flew quickly back to the rest of the fleet. Once onboard, he hurried to the command deck, acutely aware that every second's delay only increased the Interloper's chance of escape. Bursting onto the bridge, he was met by Commander Feyt, who'd been left in charge during his absence. The Captain did not offer a greeting, and to his benefit, Feyt was astute enough not to ask if their mission had been successful.

"Have any ships passed through our blockade?" Xorin demanded, striding intently to the command module in front of his chair. *All ships resume scanning for any unidentified therleon presence,* he ordered, his arms inside the shimmering interface.

"No, Captain," Feyt replied. "A few small transports appeared at the cave's entrance but retreated as soon as they spotted our fleet. Under your original instructions, we commenced suppression protocols as soon as we detected your shuttle returning."

"Then, the machine must still be here," Xorin mused, examining his instruments intently.

If the Interloper was allowed to slip away, what would he tell the High Council? Even the thought of it enraged him. He was loath to give them the satisfaction of his failure. Never in his life had he been unable to accomplish a mission... and to have been eluded by a mere human? Xorin knew that if he failed, the Exalted Leader, the last vestige of the Küddarian Brotherhood and the authority that granted him the power to spurn the High Council, would hand him over to those weak-minded bureaucrats. Then, he would have no choice but to submit to their will. If he refused, he would be stripped of rank and condemned for the crimes he'd committed in the name of the Old Ways... in the name of their very survival. As if on cue, a repetitive, high-pitched chime interrupted his thoughts as the scanners detected a new therleon signature. The Captain sat bolt upright in his chair, searching the viewport for the source of the disturbance.

"More enemy vessels have appeared," Feyt relayed urgently.

Through the window, Xorin saw two ships rocketing out of the cave at breakneck speed. The one in front had sent his sensors haywire, a considerable therleon source contained within. He smiled malevolently when he recognized the sleek black craft. It was the same ship that had escaped the cryostation, and he knew this must be the Interloper's final desperate bid for freedom. Xorin wouldn't allow himself to fail again. If he couldn't recover the machine, then he would do the next best thing. The device would be destroyed, and the thief along with it. The High Council would be angry, their condition of retrieval unmet, but the threat the human creature posed would be neutralized. In the end, that was all that mattered.

"Target that ship!" he roared, his eyes bulging wildly.

"And the station?" Feyt asked, awaiting the Captain's orders.

"Destroy what is left of it."

# CHAPTER 22
# A TERRIBLE LOSS

RHYS COWERED in the cramped space next to Sekami and Conrad, hoping with bated breath the grül wouldn't discover their hiding place. They'd sprinted as hard as they could, trying desperately to put as much distance between themselves and the towering aliens as possible. He had lagged behind his companions, however, desperately sucking air into his six-hundred-year-old lungs and turned a corner to find the passageway empty.

Panic flooded him, then he heard a soft whistle and felt a hand reach out of nowhere to grab his ankle. Startled, he'd jumped away, realizing a moment later it was Sekami beckoning to him from beneath a nearby deck plate. Scrambling down, he'd squeezed in among a tangle of thick pipes and slid the access cover closed just moments before the grül appeared. Now, they listened, not daring to breathe as menacing footfalls echoed overhead. After what felt like an eternity, the creatures moved off, and Rhys let out a long, low sigh of relief.

"We have to find another way," Sekami whispered shakily. "The others–"

"No, dammit! My ship is our only ticket out of here. If your friends are smart, they'll have already gotten off this rock," Conrad hissed, cutting her short. As if to drive home his point, he tapped his ear, listened, then shook his head. "The CIM network is down, and BAIN ain't responding. Getting to the *Kestrel* might be a long shot, but it's better than trying whatever the hell you're suggesting!"

Rhys had to admit the pilot's words made sense. Going back to the lab now was probably the worst idea he could think of. If the grül were here to recover the machine, then the lab was exactly where they'd be headed. Sekami looked unhappy about the decision but didn't argue. She must have reached the same conclusion as well. Still, she looked so miserable about abandoning her friends, Rhys wished he could tell her they'd be alright. He couldn't, though, not for sure, and uttering such a falsehood seemed like an affront to her intelligence.

At Conrad's behest, Rhys lifted the deck plate a hairsbreadth and peeked around to make sure the corridor was empty. He waited until he was sure they were alone, then slid the heavy plate open, scrambling up to help others out of the maintenance tunnel. Without delay, Conrad turned and sprinted down the passage, leading the way toward the hangar. Rhys and Sekami hurtled after him, dodging debris and the corpses of those who hadn't been lucky enough to survive the initial attack. Rounding a corner, he felt his heart sink at the sight of the passageway ahead, its once-rounded walls deformed, terminating in a transparent, emergency barrier. In the cavern beyond, there was only devastation. Several pods had broken free, their delicate structures twisted as if by some tremendous crushing weight.

Far in the distance floated the lab, and miraculously, it was still intact. As he looked on, however, an unearthly shimmer radiated from the pod's rigid outer hull. The aura intensified and without warning, the walls of the lab caved inward. For a moment, its spherical bulkheads resisted the crushing force before losing structural integrity and collapsing in a violent implosion of metal and debris. A bright orange flash illuminated the pod's twisted remains as the oxygen-rich environment ignited before being extinguished by vacuum. Abruptly, everything changed.

Gravity within the station disappeared, and sudden weightlessness, combined with several glasses of bacca, nearly got the better of Rhys's stomach. He felt a shove in the middle of his back, propelling him toward the corridor's bulkhead. Instinctively, he grabbed hold of a rail, squeezing so tight his fingernails dug painfully into his palms. Without the familiar pull of gravity, it was impossible to orient himself. Down was up, up was down, and then it flipped, sending his mind reeling once more.

"What... the hell... was that?"

"The main pod. It housed the station's gravity generator," Sekami panted, looking as shocked and disoriented as he felt. "If the others were there–"

"I'm sure they weren't," Conrad said, his tone unconvincing. "Whatever you do, don't let go of the rail."

The pilot pulled himself back up the undamaged section of corridor and down a side passage. In a third perspective shift, another wave of dizziness washed over Rhys. The unpleasant sensation intensified when a mutilated carcass floated into the corridor's containment barrier and bounced away in an unnatural tangle of limbs. Tearing his eyes away from the macabre scene, he followed the others, hand-over-hand, until the hangar finally came into view. Sekami and Conrad had already reached the entrance, and Rhys floated to a stop beside them.

"Now comes the hard part," the pilot said, attention focused on a control module next to the door. "Looks like the hangar's atmo barrier failed, which means there's vacuum beyond this hatch. If any of the station's fail-safes are still working, we'll have a helluva time getting through this door."

Peering through its thick glass window, Rhys saw the hangar was peppered with the twisted remains of heavy machinery. It was impossible to tell if the wreckage was from other ships or the automated cargo cranes he'd seen a few weeks earlier. Either way, it was a harrowing scene, and he forced himself to ignore the bodies floating nearby. The deck itself no longer resembled anything that could be walked upon. The once-flat surface was warped, sections of metal twisted into razor sharp edges that could slice through the suit of an inattentive person.

"Looks like my ship is still in one piece. That's some good news, at least," Conrad said grimly, floating up to the window and pressing a finger against the glass. Rhys looked beyond the wrecked hangar deck to where he pointed. Sure enough, anchored to the now free-floating landing platform, sat three small craft. Two were undamaged, but the third had broken free, clinging awkwardly by one of its mangled mooring feet.

"They've broken away from the rest of the hangar deck," Rhys told them. "Is that going to be a problem?"

"No. I can still maneuver off there, but unless we find some EVA suits and get through this hatch, that ain't gonna matter."

Behind them, Rhys heard grinding metal and turned to see what had caused the commotion. Sekami floated with her hand pressed against a scanner, attempting to access a room opposite the hangar door. The hatch slid open a few centimeters before grinding to a halt, filling the air with a sound like nails on a chalkboard. The noise made him cringe, and he floated forward to help wrench it open. Bracing his feet against the frame, he pulled as hard as he could, a vein bulging in the center of his forehead. The hatch was about halfway open before it refused to budge any further. Conrad glided through the cramped opening and pressed his back against the frame, pushing with his hands and knees against the edge of the door. No use.

"It's wide enough for a suit," Sekami told them.

She was first to enter the darkened room, and Rhys heard her rummage through a locker. A weak glow filled the space when she came back with a flashlight and clicked it on. The beam swung in the darkness as they searched the room. On the far wall hung four suits, smaller and more streamlined than the bulky ones in the lab. Rhys floated over and pulled one on. In null gravity, it was one of the most awkward things he'd ever done. He was about to don the helmet when Sekami stopped him.

"Take this," she said, pressing something into his hand. He

squinted down through the dim light and recognized one of the collars they'd worn during his first encounter with the grül. He fastened it around his neck before fitting the helmet to his suit.

"Why don't we always wear these?" he asked. Inside the helmet, his voice was muffled, echoing hollowly in his ears. "You know… just in case the grül happen to show up?"

"Would doctors from your time give someone chemotherapy just in case they had cancer?" Sekami asked as she affixed one to her own neck and handed a third to Conrad. She winced slightly, touching her throat where the device chafed. "The material in the collars isn't meant for prolonged exposure."

"Excuse me? What?" Rhys asked incredulously, reaching up to remove his helmet and collar.

"Trust me, they're better than weaponized therleon particles," Sekami told him. His gloved fingers still fumbled at the helmet's clasp, and she placed a hand over his. He stopped fiddling and dropped his hand. Taking his left arm, she scrolled through the suit's flexible display and activated his magnetic boots. He felt a *click* as his heels engaged the metal deck and the bizarre sensation of weightlessness paired with the confines in a tight-fitting suit. Taking a few tentative steps, he found the movement incredibly awkward, but it helped lessen some of his jarring disorientation, nonetheless.

"Will you two hurry the hell up?" Conrad urged.

The pilot had squeezed himself through the partially open door and was glaring at them with impatience. Like she'd worn mag boots every day of her life, Sekami stepped nimbly through the constriction while Rhys stomped awkwardly along behind her. He wiggled a shoulder into the gap, turned slightly to allow the suit's air pack to slide through, then stepped clear. His companions hadn't waited for him, instead moving off to inspect the hangar door's control panel. Its faceplate had been removed, and Sekami held her arm in front of Conrad's helmet, a complicated electrical schematic displayed on the screen. She glanced up when Rhys approached and pointed at three locking carabiners near his waist.

"Once we open the hatch, there'll be a violent depressurization," she explained. "Each of those is attached to two hundred meters of microfilament within the suit. Find something to attach one to. Only *one*. The first gets us through the door, and the second is for the other side of the hatch. The third… well, it's always good to have a spare."

"Is one going to be strong enough?" Rhys asked. He wasn't thrilled about drifting off into space if his lifeline snapped.

"Each filament is rated for three thousand kilos," Sekami said nodding. "Between that and your mag boots, the only danger will be fast-moving debris."

With a gloved hand, Rhys grasped one of the hooks at his waist and looked for something solid to which he could secure it. Directly across from their position was an exposed piece of the station's structural framework, and he bent down to pass the hook through one of its holes. He attached the carabiner around the microfilament, then cinched the loop tight. Taking a hurried step back toward the others, the filament locked in place and refused to pay out anymore. He was stuck, standing in the middle of the corridor, a full meter from the hatch they were supposed to get through. Less abruptly than before, he pulled gently on the wire. This time, it came out easily, floating in a messy tangle around him. *Shit*, he thought, unsure of how to feed it back in.

"How do I…" Rhys began, looking questioningly at Sekami, a length of filament held in his hands. She pointed to his left arm.

"Look for the harness controls."

Searching the interface, Rhys selected *TENSION* and the excess wire quickly spooled back into the suit. He took up position beside his companions and waited quietly while they worked to override the door's failsafe.

"Get ready," Conrad said finally.

They braced themselves, and a moment later the hatch burst

open. Outrushing air buffeted them, knocking the pilot into Sekami and nearly toppling all three. Even through his helmet, a deafening roar filled Rhys's ears, and he felt bits of debris pelting his suit. A dime-sized piece struck his faceplate, chipping the hardened surface. He felt his heart leap into his throat before realizing the glass had not been breached. Struggling to keep balance, he stepped carefully through the hatch and attached the second carabiner to a stanchion inside the hangar before releasing the first. Conrad was last through the exit. When he was on the other side, he slammed his fist into a large red button, and the hatch snapped shut behind him.

Rhys looked out over the devastation, thinking the ship seemed a lot farther away than it had through the window. His ears rang with profound silence after the thunderous roar that had filled them moments before. Now, all he heard was his own shallow breathing, amplified tenfold inside the helmet. Behind him, a hellish cry startled his attention back to the others. Turning around, he saw Sekami crouched over Conrad, the pilot on his knees, doubled over and screaming.

"It burns! Jesus, it fuckin' *burns!*"

Seeing his face, Rhys's insides churned sickeningly. Blood pooled freely from Conrad's nose, floating in bright-red globules around the inside of his helmet. His eyes bulged insanely in their sockets, the skin around his cheeks an angry red. Looking down at Sekami, Rhys noticed that she too had a small trickle of blood pooling around one of her nostrils. He became acutely aware of a faint metallic tang in his own mouth, and a sharp pain was developing behind one of his eyes. He knew what it meant.

"Help me with him," Rhys urged.

Sekami nodded, still seeming to possess most of her faculties. Reaching over, she disengaged Conrad's boots, and he began to float free. They grasped him beneath the arms, maneuvering the weightless man between them. A few steps further, however, he began to writhe uncontrollably. Even with the protective collar Sekami had given him, Conrad was suffering much worse effects than either of them. Had something made them less susceptible? Had their exposure on the cryostation or in the lab desensitized them somehow? That didn't make much sense to Rhys, but whatever the case, it would be impossible for Conrad to fly the ship in his current state. He just hoped Sekami would be able to.

With the pilot in tow, they disengaged their tethers and began to pick their way across the ravaged deck. As best he could, Rhys tried to keep at least one magnetic boot in contact with the ground. With no other means of propulsion, losing contact with the deck would leave him stranded, floating in null gravity without any means to regain positive control. Between the unconscious pilot and the risk of puncturing his suit on one of the razor-sharp blades of decking, progress was slower than he would have liked. The longer they were out here, the foggier his mind became, and the more painful the spot behind his eye. If either his or Sekami's condition progressed to the state of Conrad's, it would be a death sentence for all three. Listening to the rapid cadence of his own breathing, Rhys didn't know how much longer they could survive.

The edge of the hangar deck fell away in a distorted twist of metal where the landing pad had been ripped free. The display inside Rhys's helmet told him exactly what he had been afraid of. From their current vantage point, it was nearly two hundred thirty meters to the nearest part of the platform. Their tethers had a maximum range of two hundred meters, at least thirty fewer than they needed. Shit. He called to Sekami but received no answer, and instead reached out to grasp her shoulder.

"Hey. You alright?" he asked. At his touch, she turned her head slightly and nodded. "I don't think we have enough line to make it over."

"About thirty meters short. We'll have to jump," she replied distractedly, her assessment confirming the information on Rhys's HUD. "Together?"

"You should go first, then I'll jump with Conrad. Just don't let us go floating off into the abyss, okay?" Rhys joked feebly, butterflies in his gut. He was an engineer dammit, not a rock-hopping astronaut.

They edged along the precipice until the other side seemed free of any suit-ripping debris. Now, the distance on his HUD read two hundred forty-six meters; an even longer jump. Rhys ensured the pilot wouldn't go floating off, then held Sekami in place as she disengaged the magnetic boots. Grasping tightly to the belt around her waist, something itched in the back of his mind, something they weren't considering. If she jumped now and missed… it was just another way to guarantee all three of them would be completely screwed. He listened as she took several deep breaths, steadying herself before the untethered jump, when it hit him. The tethers.

"Sekami, wait."

She looked back, confused, but re-magnetized her boots all the same. Pulling the third carabiner from his waist, he attached it to Sekami's tether and locked them together.

"Now you've got four hundred meters."

"Okay," she said and released her boots once more. Despite the simple reply, he heard relief in her voice.

Crouching low, Sekami pushed off gently toward her intended target, the distance between them growing slowly as the linked tethers trailed in her wake. Now, if her trajectory was wrong, the consequences would be much less damning. Her body grew smaller and smaller, until finally, she reached the other side. Like she'd done it every day of her life, she grasped the landing pad easily, bringing her feet up to absorb the impact with her legs.

"Boots are locked," she said over the headset. Even with the safety tethers, Rhys realized he had been holding his breath and expelled a sigh of relief. Now it was his turn. With Conrad's tether, he lashed the pilot's unconscious form to himself and disengaged his boots.

"Okay, Sekami, reel us in," Rhys called. He looked down at his comatose payload. "I hope you don't wake up if this doesn't work."

Holding the man tightly with one arm, he felt a gentle tug as the microfilament in Sekami's suit began to retract. A moment later, they were floating free, pulled over the precipice and out across the debris-littered abyss. Rhys prayed nothing would drift into their trajectory as the distance on the HUD ticked slowly down, his target coming ever closer. It wasn't long before Sekami's lifeline had fully retracted, and it was his turn to spool in his own tether. Awkwardly, he brought his left arm around Conrad to reach the suit menu with the fingers of his right hand and tensioned the microfilament. The slowly pooling wire snapped taut, reeling them the final meters to where Sekami stood. She caught him easily, both arms wrapping around his shoulders to halt their momentum. When his boots were magnetized, Rhys rested his helmet against hers and let out a sigh of relief.

"Let's not do that again," he said.

She smiled briefly before a grimace of pain washed over her.

"We need to keep moving."

Supporting the pilot between them, they hurried toward the gangway of the undamaged ship. Even in zero gravity, moving the catatonic man was unbearably slow. Rhys found walking in the magnetic boots incredibly unnatural. Where Sekami appeared normal, he felt like a lurching, stumbling robot. Several times, he fell out of step with her, and she had to wait for him to catch up. When they finally reached the foot of the gangway, they positioned Conrad in front of the facial scanner, and the airlock hissed open. Hurrying aboard, Sekami sealed the doors behind them and fumbled to remove her helmet. As soon as it was free, she disengaged her magnetic boots and pushed off weightlessly toward the cockpit.

"Get him strapped in," she said, pulling herself forward. "I'll bring the engines online."

"Can you fly this thing?" Rhys asked, spotting a placard of the ship's layout. He needed a medical compartment or bunks... somewhere to safely secure the unconscious pilot.

"I think so but come up to the cockpit when you're done with him. I may need your eyes."

Rhys returned his attention to the diagram and found what he was looking for. Down the passage and in the third room on the starboard side was a compartment marked "SICKBAY." He would take Conrad there. Maneuvering through the hatch, he guided them away from the direction Sekami had gone and into the medical cabin. Inside was an examination table and two drop-sided gatch beds. He positioned Conrad on his side in the nearest bed and lashed him down as best he could. Removing both their helmets, he stuck his ear close to Conrad's face. He could hear the man's rhythmic breathing and feel each gentle exhalation. Unsure of what else to do for him, Rhys disengaged his boots and pulled himself through passageway to the cockpit.

Gliding swiftly to rejoin Sekami, he nearly wrenched his shoulder from its socket trying to stop his forward momentum. It surprised him how difficult navigating null-gravity could be. Grimacing in pain, he buckled into the copilot's chair and awaited Sekami's instructions. He sensed more than heard the hum of the engines and felt a clunk when the ship's mooring feet disengaged. Sekami pulled heavily on the stick, and the craft lurched upward, the sudden g-force pressing them into their seats.

"Jeeeesus," Rhys groaned unable to move his arms or legs.

Something large hit the side of the ship with a resounding bang as they cleared the pad, but she recovered and gave him a sharp glance. He knew better than to distract her further in this crucial moment. Deftly touching the controls, she nosed the ship toward the mouth of the asteroid. Here, the debris field was denser than near the station, the entire structure on the brink of collapse. Movement caught Rhys's eye. Something else was speeding through the wreckage just ahead of them. Straining to see, he could just make out another ship, small and black and agile, heading for the mouth of the asteroid. He recognized it immediately.

"Sekami, look!"

"It's the *Erebus!*" she cried. "They made it out!"

Bobbing and weaving toward the mouth of the cavern, Sekami flew through the debris leaving Rhys to white-knuckle the arms of his seat. Finally, they were clear of the base and into the asteroid field beyond. There, floating like celestial titans, were the grül, their deadly therleon energy focused on what was left of Proxima Station. Seeing the fleet's imposing presence, Rhys suddenly realized their mistake. The *Kestrel's* abrupt appearance, along with the *Erebus*, had caught the attention of the attacking vessels. Now, they were without the relative protection of the asteroid's thick walls. The pain behind his eye intensified, and stars danced across his vision. Grasping his head in both hands, Rhys cried out.

"Don't go toward them!"

He needn't have yelled. In a desperate maneuver, Sekami veered to port, increasing the vessel's speed to escape the path of destruction. Careening through the debris littering their path, Rhys caught one final glimpse of Volkerson's ship. It was enveloped in a shimmering aura, glowing white-hot before suddenly vaporizing in a blinding display of flame and shrapnel. He heard Sekami's anguished cry, felt the *Kestrel* brush violently against another rock, but a moment later, none of it mattered. In a blinding flash of blue-green light, the whole of Proxima Station evaporated behind them. When the spots in his vision faded, Sekami's pale, terrified face swam into view. Lip trembling, she reached out a shaking hand and engaged the antimatter drive.

# CHAPTER 23
# KAELLA

THE SOFT BEEPS from the *Kestrel's* control console could no longer keep him awake. Rhys yawned and rubbed his eyes. He glanced over at the empty pilot's chair and wondered when Sekami might return. As soon as they'd put enough distance between themselves and the grül, she'd hurried back to care for the injured pilot. Rhys had taken the first watch and given his assurance he would let her know if the scanner picked up any contacts. She had been gone for almost two hours before coming back, only to look more haggard than before.

Seeing her obvious exhaustion, he'd offered to stay up a little while longer, and she was grateful for the opportunity to rest. Before heading to a bunk, she'd programmed an encrypted distress call on a frequency other than the standard emergency channel. It was their contingency plan, Sekami had explained, in the event she and Dr. Volkerson were ever separated. Once contact between them was re-established, they would set a rendezvous point. Rhys couldn't bring himself to remind her that was a waste of time. They had both seen the *Erebus* vaporized into atoms, after all, but if coding a secret message helped her process the loss, then who was he to say otherwise? In the subsequent hours since Sekami activated the beacon, they'd received no response. Now, fatigue from everything that had occurred was catching up with him, and the distress call's beep, while irritating, could no longer keep him alert.

He stood and stretched his arms above his head, wincing at the stiffness in his limbs. The skin around his neck was raw where the collar had been, and touching it sent stinging pain through his back and shoulders. A lingering headache, now more of a dull throb than stabbing pain, thumped inside his skull, and there was still the faint metallic taste of blood in his mouth. All in all, though, he felt relatively unscathed and, most importantly, alive. That was all that mattered. Somehow, they had slipped through, evading the grül for a second time. The thought didn't make him feel better. He'd been racking his brain the last several hours wondering how they'd found Proxima Station. What, after all those years, had alerted the grül to its location? Was the machine acting like some kind of homing device every time he turned it on? That didn't make sense, though. They'd been careful to keep the device shielded whenever it was activated. That was the whole point of the containment fields... he stopped, forcing his mind through the hazy memories of his first day on Proxima Station. Both inner fields had failed... he'd thrown some switches... there was a countdown until the tertiary shield went down, but had it actually failed? Nothing outside the lab was damaged, so it couldn't have been down for very long... but how long was long enough? Was that how the grül detected them?

Behind him, Rhys heard the cockpit door open and, expecting Sekami's return, was startled to see Conrad silhouetted in the open hatch, a blanket wrapped loosely around his shoulders. His face was puffy and bruised, dark rings encircling his eyes. Nevertheless, he smiled toothily and moved forward to sit in one of the unoccupied chairs. Rhys looked him up and down, noticing just how near-death the pilot appeared. It was unsettling.

"Said it before, and I'll say it again... someone's beat you with the ugly stick," Conrad needled.

"Look who's talking," Rhys retorted, giving the man a

sweeping wave of his hand. "I might be ugly, but you've already got a foot in the grave."

Conrad chuckled at this. Despite his battered appearance, he seemed to be in good spirits. Nevertheless, his moment of joviality must've been painful because his laughter cut short with an uncomfortable grimace. Wincing, he adjusted the blanket, pulling it tighter around his body.

"Hell. I'm just glad it ain't both feet. The Doc told me what you did. How you got us across the gap to the landing pad. I've never been good at expressin' gratitude, but for what it's worth, thanks."

"You don't need to thank me. Truth be told, I just didn't trust myself enough to stick the landing if I'd gone first," Rhys replied, waving away the words. "I figured she'd be stronger and faster if something went wrong."

"Well, either way, I'm grateful. I'd be floating somewhere out there in billions of vaporized little particles if the two of you had just left me for dead."

Struggling to his feet, he hobbled over to the navigation computer and began to type one-handed on the display.

"Speaking of the Doc, she asked me to find a place to lay low for a while, but honestly, that's harder than it sounds. Things are pretty fucked out here," Conrad explained. He paused a moment, seeming to contemplate where an acceptable hiding place might be before his battered eyes came alight with a sudden epiphany. "How do sandy beaches and drinks with little umbrellas sound to you?"

"Great, actually."

"Well, this place'll have all the bacca you care to drink. Only producer in the known universe!"

"Seriously? That's the best you can come up with? Your secret watering hole?" Rhys asked, dumbfounded by the thought of spending an indeterminate amount of time where Conrad's gut-burning grog was made. "What makes you think we'll be safe there?"

"Told you, those trips were totally off-books. Nothing about my little detours was left in the flight log. That jerkweed Volkerson, may he rest in peace, would've been pissed knowing I risked his supply runs like that," the pilot replied, shaking his head. "And if you're worried about the grül, they'll have a helluva time figuring out which drive signature to track. When the *Kestrel* detects enemy engagement, she's programmed to drop a bunch of decoy drones. No way they're gonna find us."

"I sure hope you're right."

Conrad returned to his chair and buckled in, then pressed a button on the flight console.

"Hey Doc, strap in for our burn to Kaella," the pilot announced. He turned to Rhys, his eyes bright. "Four days to the Proxima link station, then an easy eight-day run to paradise. You're gonna love this place."

------

RHYS BRACED in his seat as Kaella's turbulent atmosphere buffeted the ship, threatening to shake the vessel to pieces around them. He glanced at Conrad, who grinned back and looked as if he thoroughly enjoyed the bucking descent. Sekami was strapped in a third seat, seemingly unfazed while she monitored the ship's approach vector. Rhys didn't know how she did it but wished he possessed an iota of the woman's stoicism. His heart pounded as he held the arms of his chair in a death grip, feeling as though it might burst from his chest at any moment.

Until now, he hadn't minded flying, enjoyed it in fact, but this was beyond anything he'd define as 'flying.' It felt more like being strapped inside a steel coffin that was plummeting at terminal velocity through a violent tempest. *Everything's going to be fine*, he told himself as a fastener worked itself loose from the bulkhead and skittered away across the shaking deck.

When the turbulence finally subsided, he looked through the cockpit window to the ground below. It was a desolate planet whose surface resembled a Martian landscape. Grimy red dust swirled through the air, obscuring the star that cast a dim pall over the alien world. In the distance, huge mesas of crumbling rock stabbed upward, their tops shrouded in the dirty sky. As the ship banked starboard, a massive dome-covered pit materialized out of the gloom.

"I don't see any sandy beaches," he announced, shooting an accusatory look in Conrad's direction. All he got in return was a shrug and sheepish grin. What a shithead. Directing his attention back to the ground, Rhys pointed toward the yawning crater. "What's all that?"

"Byrinium quarry. Largest deposit ever discovered," Conrad replied. "The turandians have gone through a helluva lot to keep Kaella's location a secret. Get pretty militant about it too, so if the ore extraction don't kill you, the locals might."

"Any danger for us?" Sekami asked.

She had leaned forward in her seat, the scene below drawing even her focused gaze from the screen she'd been poring over.

"Not so much anymore. Not like when they first started this place. Kaella used to look a lot like Earth, but its time as an open pit mine poisoned the whole damn planet. Radiation and toxic runoff killed plants and animals in the first decade, and the colonists spent some serious cash making sure the same thing didn't happen to them."

"So, that's a no?" Rhys clarified, baffled by what had motivated the pilot to choose a radioactive hellscape of all places to hide.

"Mostly a 'no.' The quarry's containment systems have redundancies, but it'll never operate at zero risk. Just don't work that way," Conrad explained. The mine was closer now, and Rhys could see thousands of lights winking at him from beneath the transparent dome. Huge, aerial vehicles shuttled payloads of dirt and rock to the planet's surface as countless excavators chipped away at the red crust in search of dangerous ore.

"What's all the byrinium for?"

"Lines the Penning traps in a beam-core drive."

"Penning trap?"

"Storage device for antimatter. Guy named Penning inspired the idea centuries ago. Not to get into too much of the science, but it uses high-powered magnets and electrostatic fields to keep charged antiparticles in suspension," Conrad explained. He glanced down to momentarily consult the navigation console before returning he gaze to the surface. "Concept ain't too different these days; magnets, electricity, laser cooling…"

"Sounds complicated," Rhys replied.

"Was a helluva a lot more complicated 'til the turandians found this place," the pilot agreed with a nod. "Used to be no good way to keep antimatter from self-annihilating against its own container, but byrinium changed that. Once the ore's synthesized to a stable isotope, its properties enhance the strength of the trap's E.M. characteristics. Keeps everything nice and cozy pretty much indefinitely… long as the backups for your cooling system are working."

"I thought antimatter was almost impossible to manufacture."

"Somebody smarter than the three of us solved that problem a while ago. Not too long after you went and froze yourself if I recall… even once it could be mass-produced, though, there still wasn't a reliable way to store it. Not 'til Kaella's byrinium was discovered. The turandians have been stockpiling it for years and maintain a tight hold over the supply. Keeps the shielding material expensive but not prohibitively so," Conrad explained. Rhys felt the *Kestrel* bank once again, and the domed quarry dropped from view. The pilot motioned for him to sit back. "We're coming up on our LZ."

The ship descended through blowing red grime and touched down softly on the pad. Unbuckling their restraints, Rhys and Sekami followed Conrad from the cockpit to a storage compartment adjacent the airlock. From its depths, he pulled three rubbery suits, a recognizable yellow and black trefoil emblazoned on each. Radiation protection, Rhys realized, taking the protective garments in his hands. The pilot handed him an overcoat and pants, both made from some indeterminant animal hide. The coat was tattered, its fur lining matted and stinking. Gloves of the same putrid animal skin were attached to each sleeve by a lanyard. Lastly, he was given a pair of goggles and respirator.

"Here. These'll keep the dust out," Conrad said. "Sorry about the coats, but we'll blend in better if our suits are covered up. Plus, it's damn cold out there, and they'll at least keep you warm."

By the time he was dressed, Rhys looked like the demented inhabitant of some frozen wasteland. The mask and goggles concealed his face, the bulky overcoat hanging down around his knees. The pilot picked up a bag and slung it over his shoulders before opening the airlock door and exposing them to the world outside. Red dust engulfed the interior compartment, and bitter cold permeated the rubber covering Rhys's hands. Gritting his teeth against the icy wind, he fought to don the gloves attached to his overcoat. In the short time they had been exposed, his hands had become so numb that movement proved difficult.

"It's got to be minus forty out there," he exclaimed through chattering teeth, pulling the overcoat's hood snug around the respirator.

"Yup, ain't even winter. Production shuts down about a hundred days every cycle. Gets so cold, even the drones can't keep from freezing," Conrad explained over the roaring wind. The man had tucked his hands beneath his armpits and was stamping his feet for warmth. "Trust me, you don't want to get caught out here without the right gear."

Not delaying any longer, he turned and marched toward a small building next to the landing pad. After pressing the call button for what seemed like an eternity, the outer door opened, and they hurried inside. A short decontamination process later, the strangely dressed trio stepped through the inner hatch and into a cramped room. Rhys shook off the cold and lifted the goggles to his forehead to survey their dimly lit surroundings.

The room was more like a storage closet, an unsightly array of junk piled into the corners and heaped on every horizontal surface. Shoved to one side was a rectangular desk, one leg broken off, its corner supported by a rickety stack of cylindrical metal cans. Glancing around the cluttered room, there were only two things that caught Rhys's eye. The first sat atop the untidy desk. It was piece of silver-gray ore encased in a transparent container, floating unsupported inside. As the material slowly turned, it seemed to emit a faint iridescent glow. Bending over, he could feel heat radiating from the object and leaned forward to read its tag: "Byrinium – 213.2 grams."

The second thing that drew his attention was the aberration now staggering awkwardly toward them. Suddenly guarded, Rhys felt himself recoil from the creature's disturbing appearance. Its skin was splotchy and pockmarked, making the alien appear as if on the brink of death. Twisted legs bowed unnaturally at the knees, accounting for the strange, lurching gait. It paused for a moment, taking stock of the three newcomers, when its overlarge eyes fell on Conrad. Something akin to recognition played over its swollen face, and the creature straightened, forcing its deformed spine into a somewhat less-hunched position.

"I wasn't expecting you again so soon, Conrad Silas."

"Hello, Salek. Nice to see you."

Rhys heard the lie in Conrad's words, and so too, it seemed, did the creature Salek. It snorted humorlessly, pointed ears quivering as it directed its attention toward Rhys. The alien gave him nothing more than a dismissive glance before turning toward Sekami. Seeing her, its large eyes widened hungrily.

"A baukken female!" Salek exclaimed, something in his voice making the hairs on Rhys's neck stand up. He felt his stomach tighten. "She would fetch a fine price on Kaella. Have you brought her to trade?"

The creature hadn't taken its eyes off Sekami, and her face darkened with anger, fists balled at her side. Realizing the insinuation, Rhys felt himself bristle, but before he could take a step forward, Conrad intervened.

"They're what's left of my crew," he said hurriedly. "We ran into some trouble and need a place to lie low for a while."

"What sort of trouble? I seem to remember some of the enemies you've made," it said, eyes still fixed on Sekami. It licked its slavering, bloated lips, and a grotesque smile creased the corners of its mouth. "Nothing is free on Kaella, but, perhaps, you could make it worth my while."

"Per our usual agreement–"

"I'm not interested in 'usual,' Mr. Silas. Your impromptu appearance with these unfamiliar companions suggests the very *unusual*. Crew or not, this delicious-looking specimen would more than remunerate the price of my hospitality."

This time, there was no stopping Sekami. She lunged past Conrad, attempting to collar the alien and drive her balled fist into its paunchy features. Salek shrieked in surprise and pulled away just as the pilot inserted himself between them. Conrad took the brunt of the blow as the creature fell to the ground and clambered to safety on all fours. It stood up, boiling with rage and pointed toward the door.

"Good luck to you, Conrad Silas! Find somewhere else to avoid your troubles," it snarled, spit flying from its lips. "The next time any of you step foot on Kaella, I will see to it you remain here *permanently*, and I don't mean as my guests!"

"Look, I'm sure we can come to some other arrangement," Conrad said, trying to reason with their incensed host.

"You have only one thing I want," it spat, "but even now I am beginning to find her demeanor unpalatable. Get out before–"

"What about these?" Sekami interrupted and held out her hand. There, Rhys saw the three collars they had used to escape the grül. Salek eyed them skeptically.

"I have no use for such trinkets."

"Sekami, don't–" Rhys began, but she gave him a sharp look. He fell silent, understanding that if he didn't keep his mouth shut, there'd be hell to pay. Despite this brief exchange, or perhaps because of it, the creature's interest was suddenly piqued.

"Can I assume by this man's reaction these items are more than just unremarkable pieces of jewelry?" it asked with new-found curiosity. Sekami nodded, but when their host reached out to take the collars, she slipped them back into the pocket of her overcoat. This irritated the creature.

"If you wish to trade, do not waste my time with such juvenile ploys. Now, either show me what you're offering, or be gone!"

Staring daggers at the alien, Sekami fished a hand back into the coat and handed over the protective devices. Salek took them in his twisted fingers and began to inspect the collars, turning them over as his eyes crawled across every centimeter of the metallic circlets.

"While you sit mining your precious byrinium, countless lives have been lost at the hands of the grül. These collars lessen the effects of exposure to their weapons," Sekami explained in a scathing tone. "They've saved our lives more than once."

"Let me assure you, I do not partake in such proletarian efforts as mining for byrinium. I do, however, profit greatly from those who do. While I pity the unfortunate souls of which you speak, sacrifice in the name of lost causes is pointless," their host replied with a condescending smirk. "Now, if we can dispense with this inane debate over morals, what is it you want in return?"

At seeing Salek's renewed interest in trade, Conrad spoke up.

"Just some provisions and a place to hide our ship for a while… some stabilized antimatter when we're ready to leave."

"You ask much, while offering very little. I recognize the value these collars may have, if indeed they do what you claim, but I require something more."

Once again, a hungry look came into the creature's eyes, and tension returned to the room. Salek's expression, while not directed at him, made Rhys feel violated. It was like being in the presence of a salacious predator.

"I can give you a hundred thousand credits," Conrad replied quickly.

The offer was an attempt to diffuse the situation, but Rhys had no idea the value of such a sum. It must've been substantial… that, or something else had triggered the poorly veiled grimace now pasted on the pilot's face. Would it be sufficient to curb Salek's lusting, though? After pondering the terms for a moment, the alien nodded once and handed Conrad a scribbled piece of paper. Apparently, the offer had been sufficient.

"Take your ship to those coordinates," Salek said, retreating toward the back room, "and try not to find more trouble than you can handle. Kaella can be a very unforgiving place."

With that, the creature left them in the cramped room, the hatch snapping closed when it departed. Pulling up their hoods and respirators, they stepped back through the decontamination chamber and forced their way through the blowing wind. When they arrived at the *Kestrel*, Rhys removed his mask and goggles and shrugged out of the foul-smelling coat.

"I hope it was worth giving up those collars," he protested unhappily. "What're we supposed to do next time we run into the grül?"

"Sekami was right to give them to him," Conrad replied, pulling off his gear and stowing it in the locker. "Short of selling her off, there's no way a *shaain kah* turandian like Salek would've accepted anything less."

"Wait a minute. Salek is turandian?"

Rhys was surprised. Marasa had been half-turandian and pretty in an exotic sort of way, but the creature to whom they had just sold their only means of protection could be described as anything but. Remembering the penned turandians in Volkerson's IHR, he found the relationship even more implausible.

"Salek Ryym naal isn't what you'd call a 'healthy' turandian. He spent most of his childhood exposed to unrefined byrinium. His parents were colonists of the first mining operation on Kaella, back before most of the safety systems had been installed. Hell, they were the ones *designing* the safeties," Conrad explained, leading the way to the cockpit. He dropped into the pilot's chair and flipped several switches, bringing the engines back online. "Two years into their work here, his mother became pregnant but didn't opt for termination. Salek suffered a lot of developmental complications, and his time on Kaella has just compounded those issues. I'm sure whatever drug concoction he takes just to manage it all pays several someone's salaries... but don't make the mistake of underestimating him. What he lacks physically, he makes up for with vicious cunning."

"Great. Pleased to be in his debt," Rhys replied, unable to keep the sarcasm out of his voice. He sat down and strapped himself into one of the chairs. "Was he serious about stranding us here?"

Conrad hesitated, uncomfortable or unwilling to explain further. Both Rhys and Sekami looked at him expectantly, but still the pilot did not offer an explanation. Instead, he feigned intense concentration while maneuvering the ship off the landing pad and toward the coordinates Salek had given them. *He knows. He just doesn't want to tell us*, Rhys thought, refusing to buy into this exaggerated display.

"Technically, Kaella's part of the Commonwealth, but the G.C. bureaucrats in charge here do whatever the turandians tell them. Unfortunately, our friend Salek has dirt on all of them," Conrad explained, finally dropping the charade. "He's allowed to conduct whatever business he likes without anyone nosing into his affairs, and in return, he practices discretion over the information he possesses. If crossed, though, all he needs to do is pull a few strings to get the offender thrown into internment... down in the mines. Hardly anybody who ends up there gets released, and the ones who do are so broken and screwed up they die anyway. So, please, from now on, try not to piss him off."

"Would've been good information to know ahead of time," Rhys muttered. He felt a gentle bump as the ship touched down amidst a clustered sprawl of dirty buildings.

"Look, I ain't tryin' to blow things out of proportion," Conrad said, securing the engines and turning to look at them. "Just be careful is all. I don't think any of us want to end up hammering rocks for the rest of our lives. We'd have been better off just getting melted by the grül."

"Speaking of the grül, no one's told me what happens the next time we meet them without those collars. I mean, we didn't even *try* to bargain with him for something else."

"I think it's clear what he was after. Next time a sleazy turandian offers to buy *you*, talk to me about bargaining," Sekami snapped. "The collars were probably worthless by now, anyway. Once the material's been exposed to enough therleon particles, the absorption reaction is expended. Chances are, those wouldn't protect us against another attack like the one on Proxima Station."

Rhys felt foolish for questioning Sekami's decision. In the moment, it was the best choice to have been made, the only choice really. He hadn't thought about it at the time, but he knew why Salek's advances made him so angry. Since first being rescued from the cryostation, Rhys had come to rely on Sekami for nearly everything. Without her, he'd have died countless times, but that wasn't all. After seeing how vulnerable she'd become over the memory of her father, they'd shared the first intimate moment he'd experienced since Anne's death. So much had happened since that single, passionate kiss that his growing feelings for her had been swept to the back of his mind. Now, though, he knew he'd do anything to spare her from the turandian's perversions. He would gladly sacrifice the collars, depleted or not, if that's what it took.

"Sekami, I didn't mean..." he began apologetically, not really knowing what more to say. It wasn't easy to express, but she had to know how he was beginning to feel about her.

An awkward silence filled the cockpit while her ire was still palpable, but Rhys saw more than anger in her eyes. There was sadness too, along with hurt, frustration, and loneliness. He realized Salek wasn't the only thing bothering her. Everyone who'd ever meant anything to her was now gone. The sudden insight made him feel worse, knowing how hurtful his protestations must have seemed, but he hadn't meant anything by them, not in the way she seemed to have interpreted them. He hoped she wouldn't hold it against– a loud cough interrupted his thoughts, and he looked toward the sound to see Conrad shifting in his chair, clearly uncomfortable.

"We're almost out of food and water," the pilot announced, a little too loudly. "I know Salek is bringing supplies, but there're a few things I need to pick up before then. I could use some help."

"I'll go," Rhys volunteered. "Need to stretch my legs for a bit."

In truth, that was only part of the reason he wanted off the ship. He felt ashamed of his thoughtlessness and had the distinct impression Sekami wanted to be left alone. If he were stuck onboard with no one to talk to, his mind would inevitably turn toward the events of the past few weeks, and that would only serve to make things worse. Now they were safely hidden from the grül, the realization he was on an alien planet had begun to sink in. It would be the perfect distraction.

"Someone should stay with the ship. I don't trust Salek enough to leave it unguarded."

"I'll stay," Sekami offered, still not looking at either of them. "I want to boost the signal for our distress message."

"Sekami," Rhys began gently, "we both saw what happened. Dr. Volkerson isn't going to–"

"Please. Just… don't."

She busied herself at the communications console and didn't spare them another glance. Rhys wanted to say something, anything that might comfort her but instead turned and followed Conrad out of the cockpit. They slipped back into their rubber suits and fur-lined clothes before cycling the airlock and stepping out onto the frigid red surface. It was colder here than their first landing site on Kaella. *Windier anyway*, Rhys thought shivering. He pulled the heavy jacket tightly around him and ducked his head against the gale. Dirt and sand pelted his clothes and would have been painful if not for the protective layers. They trudged toward the nearest building, and the pilot pulled a hand from beneath the warmth of his armpit to swing the lever on the door.

As soon as it started to move, the front edge caught the wind and swung violently open. Conrad jumped away not a moment too soon as it clanged against the wall of the dirt-covered building. Rhys hurried in behind him and grabbed the handle. Grunting and heaving, they struggled to close it against the gale. Both were breathless with cold when the latch finally fell into place. Ears ringing in the sudden silence, Rhys looked through the dusty air at another series of decontamination locks. He stepped through, one after the other, then lifted the goggles to let his eyes adjust to their dim surroundings.

Ahead sat a large metal cage, a small gate built into the waist-high railing. Conrad pulled it open and gestured for him to board the lift. An illuminated display showed there were only five levels. Their current level, SURFACE, was the uppermost floor. The next one down, PLAZA, was rimmed in green, the touch key next to it worn and cracked. The bottom three levels, simply marked MA1, MA2, MA3, were emblazoned with the words *AUTHORIZATION REQUIRED* next to each button. Conrad selected PLAZA, and Rhys heard a *clunk* as the cage began to move. They descended for a full minute before bumping unceremoniously to a stop. Disembarking the lift, Rhys stared wide-eyed at the scene around them.

The underground street bustled with activity, noise assaulting them from every direction. The high walls and ceiling had been cut from reddish-brown bedrock, the downward grade of the floor gently drawing them forward. Interspersed every few meters, rickety stanchions supported the shaft's roof, some of which were rusted and buckling. In many places, something that looked like concrete had been applied as a sort of glue to fortify weaker material. Just seeing the crumbling rock was enough to give Rhys a twinge of uncertainty. His unease only grew as more of the street came into view.

Shop doors lined both sides of the narrow tunnel, each cut

laterally into the rock. Most of them seemed to be selling supplies, some peddling food and water, others trinkets, dusty bottles of bacca, and various unfamiliar items, but Conrad never stopped. *Where is he going,* Rhys wondered? The farther they went, the more dubious their surroundings became. Now, shops lining the street seemed darker, more disreputable, the kinds of places his barely remembered shipmates might frequent. Outside one such establishment, a baukken woman flaunted the curves of her naked body. Conrad caught him looking and nudged him in the ribs.

"I'm guessing it's been while," he goaded, a filthy grin creasing the corners of his mouth. He nodded at the prostitute. "Go ahead. I can manage on my own. That one'll give you the ride of your life."

Rhys cleared his throat uncomfortably when his brain suddenly pictured Sekami's face on the naked woman. The green-skinned prostitute approached them and slung an arm around his neck, caressing his face and pressing her body against him. Gazing seductively into his eyes, her hand moved down his chest and found his groin. Rhys felt himself tense and became painfully aware that he had begun to sweat. The woman smiled.

"Thanks, but I'd rather not," he replied, extricating himself from the courtesan's grasp. Conrad chuckled happily.

"Smart. More than one of these places has given me... well, never mind. I'll spare you the details," he guffawed. "Either way, I think we need somethin' to take the edge off."

"I thought we were coming down here for supplies. What about Sekami? Won't she–"

Conrad waved the words away, a look of exasperation crossing his still-bruised face.

"Both of those things can wait. Now, just shut up, and follow me."

# CHAPTER 24
# A SLIGHT DETOUR

CONRAD POINTED toward one of the shops lining the shaft. A simple inscription, *MINER'S REST,* adorned the transom, and several bright neon holograms flickered across the tinted windows. Ducking their heads beneath the low door, they let their eyes adjust to the dimly lit establishment. It was quiet inside except for soft, unearthly music playing in the background. The bar was mostly empty, only a handful of patrons brooding over their drinks. Conrad led the way to a seat at the end and flagged down the bartender. Another turandian, the creature held only the faintest resemblance to Salek, looking much nearer the ones Rhys remembered from the IHR.

"Some of the local stuff. Bacca," Conrad ordered, holding up two fingers. The alien nodded wordlessly and reached under the counter for a bottle. Carelessly, it filled the cups, dark liquid spilling over the bar. The familiar pungency triggered Rhys's olfactory receptors, and he wrinkled his nose.

"I'm not sure I'm up for this right now," he murmured peering into the murky depths of his glass. Its putrid odor summoned recent memories of the last time they'd drank, but that wasn't the only thing bothering him. There was a moroseness about the place, its subdued atmosphere exceedingly depressing. He was about to suggest they find somewhere else when Conrad replied in a low voice.

"We didn't come for the drinks."

He beckoned again at the barkeep, and the alien skulked back over. Leaning forward, the pilot began to whisper in its ear, the turandian's glowering expression melting into curiosity, then one of amenability. Rhys couldn't hear what had been said, but the alien nodded its head up and down, then hurried off through a door in the back. The abrupt departure made him wonder… what was Conrad up to?

"Listen, whatever you're scheming, I'm not interested," Rhys said.

The bar felt claustrophobic. When he'd volunteered to leave the ship, he thought they'd be off getting supplies, seeing the inner workings of an alien planet, interacting with the locals… those things would have been good distractions. Instead, they were sitting in a dingy bar, drinking the same godawful shit as when the grül attacked, and he was left replaying the worst moments in his head. So much for taking the edge off.

"Just wait and see, alright?"

Rhys tipped back his glass and swallowed the last of the bacca. The alien returned and signaled for them to follow. They passed through a small vestibule and were ushered into a private room, empty except for two beds and a collection of scattered cushions. A pair of pretty turandian females sat cross-legged on the floor but stood when they entered. The women sauntered over, a seductive wiggle in their hips, and grasped each man gently by the arm. Conrad allowed himself to be steered forward, but Rhys stood his ground, a mixture of anger and repressed sexual tension filling him.

"I thought I told you I wasn't up for this?"

"Look," the pilot began, annoyance edging into his voice, "I almost got melted from the inside out, so I need to unwind. Come along for the ride or go back to the ship. I don't care either way."

"If you think I'm going to stick my–"

"We ain't here for them."

"What?"

Rhys didn't understand. If the girls weren't part of whatever debauchery Conrad had planned, what were they doing there? He tried to gauge his expression, to see what the man's intentions were, but his face was implacable. Still unsure of what he was being drawn into, he allowed himself to be led toward one of the beds. The turandian motioned for him to lie down and stretched out next to him, her hand on his chest. Thoroughly uncomfortable, Rhys turned his head to see what was happening.

The woman next to Conrad had removed a glass vial from somewhere and held the dropper over his face. From it, she squeezed four drops of clear liquid into one of his eyes. He clenched it shut and a moment later let out a long, low sigh. Ah. Now, Rhys understood why they'd come. His heart began to beat quickly in anticipation at this unexpected turn of events. It was all happening so fast, and he wasn't entirely sure he wanted this. What was this woman about to give him? He'd tried his fair share of recreational drugs, but he'd known exactly what and how much it was then. Was he really prepared to take some unknown alien substance? And what about Sekami? If they were gone too long, she would start to worry.

Rhys sensed he was babbling, and the woman climbed on top to straddle him. She pressed a finger to his lips, and he noticed a faraway look in her eyes, the pupils glassy and dilated. So, she was high as well... she leaned forward, and for a moment, he thought she was about to kiss him. Her lips only brushed the side of his cheek, and he felt her soft breath on his ear.

"Let go," she whispered and uncorked the vial. He felt the stinging drops, one after the other, and reflexively squeezed his eyes shut. When the pain subsided, he blinked and looked around the room. The women had gone, and Conrad lay motionless on the other bed, his chest rising and falling in rhythmic breaths. His eyes were open, staring vacant and unfocused.

Shifting his gaze, Rhys experienced a strange delay between

his optic nerve and the processing center of his brain. It was like watching everything in slow motion. Where the chamber had been drab and featureless, everything now seemed more vibrant. The dull red walls seemed to glow, flickering like a warm fire in the depths of winter. He ran his hand along the grimy floor, feeling the red powder that covered everything on Kaella. Dusting his palms, dirt fell to the floor, sparkling as it caught the light inside the room.

He had a sudden, innate desire to leave and climbed to his feet. The door was just ahead. Grabbing the handle, he pulled it open. Outside, the rest of the bar had disappeared. In fact, *everything* had disappeared. In front of him, the doorway opened into a vast galaxy. His galaxy. He wasn't surprised. Somehow, he'd known it would lead here. Balancing on the balls of his feet, Rhys looked between the cramped little room behind him and the awe-inspiring vistas beyond. Stars twinkled as far as he could see, the rich orange and blue of a far-off nebula beckoning to him. Peering down, he edged the toes of his boots over the precipice and teetered for a moment, before allowing himself to fall forward.

The cosmos flashed by at a dizzying rate. Faster and faster he fell, until the galaxy was nothing more than a colorful blur. Rhys marveled at the stunning display, hoping he might be forever lost in this beautiful limbo. He knew the grül would never find him here. Somehow, speeding through this strange and wonderful galaxy would keep him safe. As the colors around him became more vivid, something else appeared at the furthest point of his vision, and it was growing. His trajectory was leading him straight into it.

As the object drew closer, Rhys began to lose his sense of euphoria. He knew what the object was now, and he didn't want to go any nearer. An anomaly. *The* anomaly; the same one that had set Marcus Volkerson and Jenco Ryele along their fateful path. Putting out his arms, Rhys tried to slow the headlong tilt, but it seemed only to hasten his approach. Unable to stop, he was suddenly inside the yawning mouth, a black sparking void enveloping him, and he cried out.

The blur of nebulous gas was swallowed by darkness, along with his scream. Now, Rhys was looking through a cockpit window at a planet. He recognized its blue-green oceans and puffy white clouds: Earth. There it was, as real as if he were truly standing before it. Glancing around, his surroundings seemed familiar, but he couldn't remember why. In his strange, ethereal state, he noticed someone standing next to him. A man. He was shouting, but Rhys heard only a whispering echo.

"Jenco-o-o-o-o... where are you-ou-ou-ou?"

Dread forced its way through the haze clouding his mind. He recognized this moment, knew the ghostly figure and the cockpit in which he stood. The last thing he wanted to relive in his drug-addled state was the attack on Earth. With all his might, Rhys fought to control the vision, to stop it before the inevitable conclusion, but the nightmare continued. It was worse than before... slowed down and vivid, every excruciating detail forced into his brain. Rhys called out helplessly, hysterical from the drugs and the traumatic scene he knew was about to unfold.

"Please, make it stop!" he cried. "I can't... can't..."

There was no one to hear his plea. He clenched his eyes shut, forcing himself not to watch, but the vision was inside his head, the cataclysm no less clear. As if in slow motion, a point on the planet's surface began to undulate with a massive surge of energy before igniting into a fiery conflagration. The shockwave crawled outward, burning everything in its path, before finally enveloping him in a blinding red inferno. When his eyes adjusted to the brilliance, there was nothing except a huge, disembodied face of Volkerson floating over him.

"THE PRICE OF FAILURE!" it screamed, the words resounding in his ears, over and over.

Rhys let out a cry of despair and fell to his knees, face buried in his palms. He felt a hand on his shoulder. Then two. Then ten, all touching his neck and back and arms. Soon, there were too many to count. When he opened his eyes, he nearly died of shock. He was overlooking a bottomless abyss atop the very mountain where he and Anne had exchanged their vows. Anne. Thinking of her made his stomach tighten with guilt. And now, she was there, standing clear as day in front of him. More alarmingly, there were *dozens* of her, all touching him, naked and helpless and crying. One of them stroked his hair, tears streaming down her strangely indistinct face.

"You've forgotten me," she said in the same, echoing voice. "You've forgotten everything."

"I haven't!" Rhys urged, distraught by his inability to recognize any of her distinguishing features. "I've mourned you! I wanted to die after I found out. I *wished* I'd died!"

Their sobs grew louder, a resounding din upon his ears, and the Annes began to disappear. Soon, there was only one. She let go of his shoulder and turned toward the edge.

"No! Don't!" he cried out, grabbing the woman's arm. His hand found her wrist, and he pulled her back, their bodies falling away from the edge. He closed his eyes, holding her in his arms as sadness welled up inside him. When he finally opened them, it was no longer Anne wrapped in his embrace. Instead, Rhys saw the arched form and bare breasts of Sekami, her body trembling with passion. With each thrust of her pelvis, she moaned in pleasure. Her gaze locked with his, and Rhys felt himself tense in alarm. Sekami's eyes were no longer the striking violet color he remembered. Instead, they had changed to pits of black so deep and dark he was sure they would devour his soul. A snarl twisted her mouth before her long fingers raked his chest, leaving bloody claw marks in his skin. He yelped in pain and tried to push her off, but she held on, continuing to tear at his flesh like a wild animal.

With a great heave, he dislodged her and flopped onto his belly. He clawed at the dirt, scrambling forward on all fours as he tried to escape. A steely-gripped hand clasped his ankle and began dragging him backwards. Rolling onto his back, he wound up to deliver a kick to the crazed woman but faltered. It wasn't Sekami dragging him backward, but a towering, gray-skinned alien. The corded muscles of the creature's forearms bulged as it pulled him closer. Fear gripped Rhys when he recognized the six-fingered hands, the burning eyes, the red-streaked skin... one of the grül. A surge of adrenaline fueled his instinct to flee, and he began to kick with all his might, but the beast held him fast. It was over top of him now, about to drive a pointed spike into his chest, when a huge stone smashed onto the creature's head. It dropped to the ground, twitching, and the ghostly form of Marcus Volkerson stepped forward holding the rock. He advanced on Rhys, then raised the boulder high.

"The price of failure," the man echoed and brought the rock crashing down.

"Wake up. C'mon, buddy, snap out of it!"

Rhys felt a sharp, repetitive stinging on the side of his face, the discomfort slowly dragging him back from some indeterminate plane of existence. It confused him. He'd prepared for a crushing blow, a violent and bloody end to his life, but it never came. Instead, he felt this. The sensation was wrong. In some abstract part of his mind, he realized someone was smacking him. He wanted it to stop. Sluggishly, his eyes fluttered open but were slow to focus on anything around him. If nothing else, the repetitive stinging had finally ceased.

"Fuckin' hell, I thought I'd put you in a coma!"

A tanned, crinkle-eyed face full of alarm swam into view, and Rhys realized it was Conrad who'd been slapping him. The pilot helped him sit up, and he noticed that someone had removed his boots. He didn't remember taking them off, but if truth be told, there was a lot he couldn't recall at the moment. Reaching over for them, he grasped the tabs of the first boot and tried to pull it over his foot. It wouldn't go. Something wasn't right. Rhys turned his head to look at his companion but found he suddenly lacked the strength to hold it up. Slowly, despite every effort he could muster, his chin sank to his chest.

"Mm cmn't rifft mm ed," he said. The words were muddled and unintelligible.

"Sorry, what?" Conrad asked, and a look of concern creased his brow. Rhys tried again, forcing every word out with great effort.

"I... can't... lift... my head," he repeated. The five simple words left him breathless. "Something wrong... hands."

He tried a second time to pull on his boots. There was no strength in his fingers, and both arms spasmed uncontrollably. Conrad bent to help, taking the boot from Rhys's hands. Kneeling beside him, the pilot tried to pull the boot onto Rhys's foot, but with each attempt, his knee folded uselessly.

"Keep your leg straight dammit."

"Can't."

Conrad swore in frustration and squatted over top of Rhys's leg, stabilizing it against the floor. He gave one more, forceful tug, and the boot slipped on. Pulling the second boot over Rhys's other foot, the pilot stood up and rummaged in the pockets of his coat in search of something. A few seconds later, he held up a small bottle and gave it a shake.

"Here. These should make you feel better," he said and dropped three pills into Rhys's mouth. "Chew 'em. They'll kick in faster."

Rhys got one of the pills half-chewed before his jaw started to ache. Even the act of chewing proved difficult. Dry swallowing the rest, he felt one lodge halfway down, an uncomfortable lump sticking in his throat. Nothing he could do about that. He'd just have to wait for some water. Conrad draped Rhys's arm over his shoulders and grunted at the effort to pull him to his feet. Staggering awkwardly toward the door, Rhys tried to walk on his own, but his legs wobbled uncontrollably, the effort to control them futile.

"How did... find... me?" The pilot gave him a quizzical look, and he tried to clarify. "After I left? Where... find?"

"You didn't go anywhere. I found you twitching in the same spot that turandian girl left you," Conrad explained, shaking his head. "I shouldn't have done that. It was stupid taking you there. I thought it would help us unwind but... how much did she give you? How many drops?"

Rhys tried to recall what had happened. The woman had said something. Something like... let go? He remembered her soft caress, the sting in his eye...

"Three... maybe four. Not sure."

"Three or four?! For chrissake, I *told* her you don't get more than two. No wonder you're so fucked up. Nobody can take that much raska the first time without really bad results!"

They stumbled their way out of the tavern and down the crowded street. Rhys heard laughter and jeers, and the pilot swore under his breath as he tried to hurry along. Someone jostled them, and Rhys found himself falling face first into the dirt. The laughter grew louder. Swearing evermore colorfully, the pilot hauled him to his feet and pushed through the growing throng. After what seemed like ages, the lift materialized through the press of people in the passageway, and they stepped on. At the top of the shaft, Rhys felt himself gently lowered to the ground and propped against the wall. Conrad's face appeared in front of him, bending low to secure his respirator, but Rhys stopped him.

"Let me do it," he said. He raised his hands and flexed them before positioning the respirator over his mouth. "Better, I think."

He tried to stand on his own. With one foot planted and a knee on the floor, Rhys struggled to straighten but lurched sideways into the wall. Conrad caught him.

"Easy. Easy," the man cautioned. "It's gonna take a while to get your feet back under you. Lemme help."

Rhys steadied himself against Conrad's shoulder as they passed through the airlock, then braced for the buffeting wind outside. When they opened the door, however, he was surprised.

It was still very cold, but the wind had died to nothing more than a light breeze. *Good*, he thought. Much stronger and it would have knocked him over in his current state.

By the time they reached the ship's airlock, he was exhausted. The effort to control his muscles enough to walk, even aided, had drained him. Conrad sealed the airlock and helped strip off the protective gear. Rhys sat down heavily on one of the benches, unable to stand any longer. He heard the inner door open and looked up to see Sekami. One look at her face, and he felt his heart plummet.

"I was about to come looking for you," she said, her voice filled with relief. "I thought something had hap– where're the supplies?"

"We, um, got held up," Conrad replied sheepishly, his tone unconvincing. "Rhys had a bad reaction to some local fare."

"Okay… and you ignored my connection requests for *five hours*?" Her eyes narrowed suspiciously. "You remember I'm medically trained?"

"Had to get him some help, you know? Couldn't waste time coming back here."

Sekami walked up to Rhys and knelt in front of him. She pulled a device from her pocket like the one she'd used in the station lab and clicked it on, shining it into his still-dilated eyes. It made them ache even worse. After a moment, she stood up to face Conrad.

"You can stop lying to me, right now."

"Hold on a minute. I ain't lyin'. He's got some sort of food poisoning." The pilot's feigned indignity was thoroughly unconvincing though, and Rhys knew they were busted.

"Do you think I'm an imbecile? I know an overdose looks like. Damn you!" she fumed. "What did you give him? Cocanesh? Kaellium? Raska? It better not have been raska!"

When he didn't reply, Sekami had her answer. She gave Conrad a disgusted look then turned to face Rhys, her back to the pilot.

"Can you make it to the med bay?" she asked. There was still a bite of anger in her voice. Rhys just nodded weakly and stood up. Steadying him, Sekami helped him forward a few steps, but when Conrad moved to assist, she brushed him off.

"You've done enough for the moment," she snapped. He backed off, holding up his hands.

Sekami guided Rhys down the passageway, neither of them speaking. He didn't mind. He was still having a hard time forming coherent sentences and hearing his garbled speech would probably just upset her further. When they reached the medical bay, she helped him onto the examination table.

"Do you know what he gave you?" she asked with a heavy sigh. Her voice had lost its harsh edge. Now, she just sounded tired. "I can't counteract the effects unless I know which drug is in your system. It'll be faster than testing for it."

"Last one you said. Raska," he replied. His tongue felt thick, like he'd gone days without water. "Three pills of something else about an hour ago. Not sure what but feeling a little better."

Sekami nodded and pulled an autoinjector from one of the drawers near the table. Loading a cartridge, she pushed it against his arm, and Rhys felt a familiar pinch when she pressed the button on top. Mere moments passed before the serum began to take effect. Some of his scrambled motor skills began to normalize, and he was finally able to look her in the face.

"God," he said, voice trembling as the visions resurfaced in his mind. "It was terrible. I wanted to die."

He recounted what he had seen during the drug-induced coma. As he spoke, remorse overwhelmed him. Not just for Anne, though that certainly weighed heavily on him. Seeing her there, her face indistinct and accusing him of forgetting so easily... it had all been multiplied dozens of times over by the ghostly tearful copies that surrounded him. It wasn't only thoughts of her unnecessary death that burned up his insides with guilt.

Despite his best efforts, Rhys's mind kept returning to Earth. Its devastation had blinked billions of people out of existence, people that likely had much to live for, yet here *he* was... a man who had ultimately given up on life hundreds of years before, one of the few surviving members of humanity. Sekami must have sensed his turmoil, because she took his head in her hands and ran her fingers through his hair. It was the first time they'd touched since Proxima Station. Feeling her tenderness, Rhys felt the last of his walls melt away, and he held her to him, taking comfort in the woman's embrace.

"I can't imagine how hard this has been for you," she said softly. "I'm sorry if I've seemed distant the past few weeks. I wasn't ready to admit some hard truths, and I've been in denial about... about what I lost on Proxima."

"Sekami... I'm sorry. I know what Marcus meant to you."

"Not just him. All of them. They were the closest thing I've had to family since my father died. Now, the grül have taken everything from me."

All of it circled back to the same thing: the destruction of Earth. That single act had shattered far more lives than just his. Sekami had lived a terrifying reality for years, struggling since her youth to stay one step ahead of the grül. Somehow though, after all the loss, she still managed to keep going, never surrendering to a seemingly invincible enemy. All Rhys had done since waking up was drink and abuse drugs. His few weeks of sacrifice paled in comparison to what Sekami had been through. He felt ashamed.

"Not everything," he replied softly and took her hand. Their eyes met, and once again, Rhys felt as though he'd known her for a very long time. She'd been there by his side, the first person he'd met since waking to this frightening new existence. Whether she knew it or not, Sekami was the rock to which he clung.

"I hate them, Rhys. All I can think about is revenge." There was cold fury in her voice. He didn't know how to respond, and a sense of helplessness filled him.

"How? Even if we had the machine, I can't use it. Everyone saw I don't have what it takes," he said. "And if I did, we wouldn't know where to find them."

"The grül will come to us. They only found the station after the machine was energized. I think that when the containment fields fell, enough therleon particles escaped to leave a traceable signature. We've seen enough to assume that much. If we had one of their devices, all we'd need to do is activate it."

"Then what? Turning it on and making it do what I want are two completely different things," Rhys reminded her, "and we still don't have a machine."

"No. We don't," she conceded, "but I think I might know where to find another one."

"WHILE IT IS unfortunate you could not recover the machine or the Interloper, you have fulfilled the most basic requirements of your mission. Now, your time of defiance is at its end," the High Councilmember declared. His sneering features filled the holo-screen as Captain Xorin looked on. "From the start, your methods have gone against the Enlightenment's every doctrine. Your misguided actions, while perhaps motivated by some twisted service to the grülbarvoc, have set events in motion that may ulti-mately threaten our existence. For this, you are ordered back to Vyreon. You and your crew will return at once to face judgement."

The glow of the talking head snapped off, leaving Xorin in darkness. *Was it true*, he wondered? Had the Exalted Leader finally succumbed to the Sickness? If so, the last person who'd held sway over the Council had been allowed to die, wallowing in decay until perishing from neglect. He imagined what it must have been like for the once-great warrior; to feel strength fade from his body, to experience the weakening of bones, to watch the world disappear as both sight and hearing slowly dwindled… anger boiled inside him at the thought. Such a death could have easily been prevented. Sacred rituals like the Rhonath had kept the Sickness at bay for eons… had made their kind strong.

It was why the Old Ways were so necessary. If there were no

longer enough resources within their own galaxy to sustain the grülbarvoc, then expansion into another was the logical progression. He'd never understood the High Council's aversion to such things. Greater species had preyed upon lesser ones since the dawn of time. Somehow, though, through the distortion of mind and tradition, extending life through use of the Rhonath had been deemed unnatural and unsustainable by the High Council. It was a declaration that had set their species down a road to self-annihilation, a fate that awaited them all if the Küddish Teachings were allowed to die.

Now, Xorin was faced with a choice: Return to Vyreon and heed the will of the High Council or take his faithful warriors and keep the Old Ways alive... keep *them* alive. The latter would condemn his crew to imprisonment and death if apprehended, he knew that. The High Council would send their loyal dogs after him, but the thought of dooming himself to the same end as the Exalted Leader was like a wound festering in his mind. There was something else too, something more immediate. It had nagged at him in the weeks following the destruction of Proxima Station. A single ship had slipped through his fingers, and although he was sure both the machine and the Interloper had been destroyed, he still couldn't help but wonder. If there was even a chance Volkerson was still alive, Xorin's mission remained incomplete.

*No*, he thought, making up his mind. *We will not return to Vyreon. There is still work to be done.* He slid his fingers into the shimmering interface near his chair and summoned Commander Feyt. When the Executive Officer arrived, he stood rigidly at attention while the Captain paced, a plan forming in his mind.

"I have delivered my report to the High Council, and we have been ordered back to Vyreon."

"Shall I inform the fleet?"

The Captain measured his next words carefully, watching the young warrior closely for any reaction.

"The Exalted Leader is dead, taken by the Sickness. It is the same fate that awaits us all if we return to Vyreon."

A look of surprise passed over the Commander's face before hardening into steely determination.

"The fleet's loyalty to you is unwavering, Captain," Feyt replied, raising his right fist across his chest in salute. "As is mine."

"I wonder, do you truly understand where this path leads?" Xorin probed. "When the High Council learns of our disobedience, they will send our own brethren to dispatch us."

"If that is what we must face, then so be it."

This pleased Xorin greatly, knowing without a doubt his choice for second-in-command had been the right one. Feyt knew what loyalty to him would mean. How many others would have so readily thrown away the comforts of home to protect a way of life now considered barbaric? Barbarous or not, the Old Ways alone would ensure the grülbarvoc's survival, not the mewling High Council, not their scientists' failed attempts to prevent the Sickness. The sacrifice he and his loyal band of warriors were about to make would secure them in the annals of history as the ones who stood their ground in the face of dangerous progressivism.

"Our fleet, while mighty, is by no means a match for the resources wielded by the Council. We will be but a few standing against many, and I do not wish to see our warriors fall needlessly when so much is at stake. If you truly understand the ramifications of our rebellion, then there is something you must do. You will task our fleet's science officers with developing weapons that can be used against the Vyreon assassins."

Disbelief appeared on the Commander's face.

"But Captain, our teachings forbid it! Even the Old Ways—"

"The Old Ways are about to be lost, Commander. If this is what it takes to ensure their survival, I will gladly seek weapons that function against another grülbarvoc. More is at stake than our personal honor."

Feyt did not reply, and Xorin watched silently while an internal struggle raged within the Commander. The Captain knew what he was asking the young warrior wouldn't be easy. It went against everything the Küddish teachings stood for: honor, strength, fearlessness. To vanquish a brother outside of hand-to-hand combat, there was no greater sin. Developing therleon weapons that functioned against a fellow grülbarvoc had been banned eons ago... even the progressive-minded High Council honored that founding principle. These were desperate times, however, and desperate times called for radical action. In the end, it would all be for the greater good, for the very salvation of their species.

"I will do as you ask," Feyt said finally, "but the fleet will not understand."

"Make them understand," Xorin replied.

He gave a dismissive wave, and the young warrior snapped a salute. It lacked Feyt's usual crispness, however, and a heavy weight settled in the Captain's chest as the Commander disappeared through the hatch. Xorin knew Feyt was unhappy with these new orders and sensed something had changed in the Executive Officer's resolve... perhaps the beginnings of a loss of faith. Much was at stake now. The Exalted Leader's death had solidified the Council's hold on Vyreon, and Xorin had never felt more alone. He truly was the last vestige of the Küddarian Brotherhood, his fleet the only thing that stood against the inevitable fall of their species.

It gave him little comfort. If he failed to halt the Council's march of progress, to shift the sands of time back toward Rhonath and the other Küddish teachings, the Sickness would bring about their end. He could not let that happen. Too long had he hidden his true allegiance. Too long had he allowed the High Council to manipulate the grülbarvoc for their own needs. No longer. He would take his fleet and bring new glory to the Old Ways, and he would start by running down the Interloper's lost ship.

# CHAPTER 26

# WORST LAID PLANS

"HAVE you both lost your goddamn minds?" Conrad's expression left little doubt as to what he thought about Sekami's proposal. "If you think you're going anywhere with my ship... not just no, but *hell* no!"

"At least let her finish–"

"You. Shut up," he said, poking Rhys in the sternum before turning his attention back to Sekami. "We narrowly escape the last grül attack, likely as the only survivors, find a suitable place to remain undetected, and now you want to go *looking* for them? Which of us is on drugs again? Christ!"

"You know we can't hide here forever, right?"

"Why not? Far as I can tell, they've squashed the resistance your pal Volkerson was trying to cook up," Conrad demanded, agitated by Sekami's defiance. "Whatever little science experiment you people were workin' on seems to have gone tits-up."

"And who's to say no one else is out there doing the same things we were on Proxima Station?" she fired back. "Are you so naïve to think the grül will just pack up and leave, or is it more likely they'll make sure nothing like this happens again?"

"I understand what you're getting at, but why come looking for *us* of all people?"

"Because thirty-four years ago, my father and Dr. Volkerson

took one of their machines, and they've been trying to get it back ever since," she explained, frustration permeating her voice. "They must know our ship slipped through their blockade, but they couldn't know Dr. Volkerson wasn't with us. The grül aren't going to waste all those years dogging his steps on the off chance he got away. It may not be tomorrow, or next week, or next cycle, but they'll find us. They always find us."

Conrad's shoulders slumped, and he lowered himself into a chair. Rhys knew her words had touched a nerve. She'd certainly driven home the point for him. Nowhere was safe. Not for long, anyway. They had escaped Proxima Station, but if her concerns were more than just baseless anxiety, they were living on borrowed time. Would a single lost ship be enough to keep the grül looking, even if they'd already destroyed the machine and the man who'd stolen it? There was no way to know for sure, but the conviction in her voice was enough to make him question how safe they truly were on Kaella.

"There's more... something you both need to understand before we go any further," she continued. Her demeanor changed, uncomfortably cracking each knuckle the same way she had when trying to convince him Marasa's brother wasn't in danger. "My father and Dr. Volkerson recognized the value of what they possessed. They saw the machine as the Commonwealth's only chance of survival but had no means of protecting it from the grül. Twenty-five years ago, they built a device that mimicked a therleon signature, then deceived a crew into smuggling it. In doing so, they escaped with the machine, but their actions resulted in a string of massacres that led to Vandervol Outpost... to all this, really."

Stunned silence followed these words, tension so thick in the air Rhys could almost taste it. He was shocked by the revelation that Marcus Volkerson and Jenco Ryele owned the blame for such an incalculable loss of life. He'd understood they were indirectly responsible for at least part of the tragedy that had occurred. That was one thing, but Sekami's admission that they'd willingly sacrificed thousands, maybe even hundreds of thousands, of lives to protect their own was something entirely different.

A growing sense of unease filled him the more he learned what the scientists had done. Was he on the right side of this thing? Did a right side even exist? The grül were unquestionably monsters, willing to murder entire planets to recover their property, but it was emphatically clear that what these men had done was unforgivable. Sekami's own father had tricked some unsuspecting fools into acting as bait, knowing full well it would result in horrific deaths. And for what? Some self-righteous belief they were the saviors of the Commonwealth? What if, all those years ago, Volkerson had just waited for the grül to leave, instead of killing one and stealing its machine? Would things be different now?

"So, you're telling me," the pilot began, his voice full of ice-cold fury, "the countless that've been killed… the colonies that've been destroyed… it's all because of Volkerson? And your father? Why the *fuck* have I been helping you people?"

"Did Marasa know?" Rhys demanded. Sekami's confession had reminded him of the scientist's story of where her mother died… someplace called Vandervol. It must have been the same outpost.

Sekami shook her head, eyes downcast, and Rhys felt a stab of anger, feeling once again that he'd been deceived. His anger wasn't toward Sekami. She wasn't to blame, not really. She'd been thrust into this nightmare just like him, only hers had begun from the moment of her birth. No, Rhys felt anger toward the two dead men that had gotten them all into this mess in the first place. Jenco, as much as his partner, had committed them to a conflict that should never have happened, likely wouldn't have happened if only they'd left well enough alone. Worse still, Volkerson had played on Earth's destruction to convince Rhys to join his cause without ever revealing the true reason behind the cataclysm.

"I can't undo what they've done or the lives they've ruined, but I might be able to atone for their sins. I at least have to try."

Conrad snorted derisively.

"I should throw you both to what's left of the G.C.," he fumed, staring hard at the pair of them. "Then, trade off the *Kestrel* and get as far from this place as I can…"

A battle played out over Conrad's face, clearly weighing whether to cut and run. The way things were unfolding, Rhys felt he'd be well within his rights to leave them right here on Kaella, stranded or worse. If he did, Rhys couldn't blame him. He might curse the pilot's name until the day he died, along with Volkerson's and Jenco's, but he wouldn't interfere. After all, if they pursued the grül or were left to rot in the byrinium mines, the day they died might come sooner than expected.

"… but I owe you idiots for saving my neck, and, unfortunately for me, I ain't one to welch," Conrad finished grudgingly. "So, let's hear this stupid-ass plan of yours."

Sekami, still looking guilty and ashamed, walked to the navigation computer and began to scan through various star maps. When her search was complete, Rhys saw a ball of light floating in the center of the room, projected outward by the holographic display. A moment later, countless glowing orbs filled the cockpit as a mapped representation of the Commonwealth's territory within the galaxy unfolded around them. She raised her hands, a triangle formed between her thumbs and index fingers, then moved them apart to enlarge a tiny section of the chart. A yellow light caught Rhys's attention, and he moved closer. 'Kaella' was displayed in minuscule text next to the orb.

"Our current position is approximately six-point-six light years from where Proxima Station… from where it used to be," Sekami explained, her voice tight. "After my father died, Dr. Volkerson proposed going back to the terraforming colony where they'd first discovered the machine."

"I don't know much about what y'all have been doing, but that seems like a pretty thin lead," Conrad mused. He still sounded angry. "Didn't you say this started some thirty-odd years ago? If there was anything else worth finding, it's probably long gone by now."

"You haven't heard the rest," Sekami replied. She shifted the chart, spanning a gap dozens of light years across. Now, there was a distinct blank spot where the map seemed devoid of even a single star. "The grül didn't just appear out of nowhere. We had a suspicion there might be something beyond the terraforming colony, outside the Commonwealth's boundary of charted space."

"Sekami, there's something I don't understand," Rhys said, trying to keep the lingering sense of betrayal out of his voice. "Even if we got our hands on another device, we wouldn't be able to develop the technology Volkerson hoped for. All the equipment from the lab was destroyed, and the research along with it."

"It's too late for any of that," she replied somberly. "From now on, everything hinges on your ability to control one of their machines."

Rhys was silent, a sense of dread filling him. Deep down, he hoped they never found another device and that he wouldn't have to face the grül a third time. Memories of the weeks before the station's destruction came floating to the forefront of his thoughts. The sense of self-loathing... the uulgar's terrified squeaking... bright, spurting blood... Volkerson had been right about the price of failure, but this time, it would come at a much higher cost.

"I didn't think your plan could get any thinner," Conrad said shaking his head, "but it's goddamn transparent now. How can you justify going all that way without some sort of guarantee? There could be nothing out there. Worse still, we might actually find the fuckin' grül!"

"That brings me to the next part. Do they have an IDN here?"

"What the hell good is that gonna do us?"

"What's an IDN?" Rhys asked, confused.

"An integrated data network. It's an archive that's linked back to a central hub. In this case, I'm hoping the turandian home world," she replied. Hearing this, Rhys's puzzled look deepened, and Conrad blinked several times. Sekami shifted her gaze back to the chart in front of them and continued to explain. "Kaella's a turandian mining colony, right? Well, it was the turandians who were terraforming at the edge of charted space before being wiped out by two bloodthirsty grül. If there's an IDN here, we might be able to see if there's survey data from that sector."

Though still unsure of Sekami's end goal, Rhys began to understand where she was going with this line of reasoning. Kaella and the terraforming colony had something in common; they were both established by the turandians. If the colonists on Kaella were linked to their home world, they might be able to access that data from here. The old terraforming project would probably have some useful information, which might provide clues to the surrounding area. It was good thinking on her part. Although grudgingly, Conrad seemed to agree.

"They do have an IDN here," the pilot replied, rubbing the stubble on his face. He swiped away Sekami's chart and brought up a map of Kaella's mining project, highlighting one of the buildings amongst the disorderly sprawl. "But you'll have a hard time getting' in. The turandians keep a tight hold on who's allowed access."

"What about your contact? Salek. Can he do something?"

"It ain't wise to keep asking him for favors," Conrad said warily. "Owing Salek is a dangerous position to be in. If he ever found out those collars are almost expended, we'd have all kinds of trouble on our hands."

"I know it's risky, but it's worth a shot," she urged. "We may not have access to a resource like this again."

Rhys had a bad feeling about where this plan was headed. After their last encounter with the twisted little creature, he'd been happy to be rid of him. They had given Salek their only tradable goods in exchange for a place to hide, but this new request was something different. It would require the turandian to exercise his clout with those in control of the planet, which might put him at personal risk. To get Sekami into the data archive, Salek would demand a steep price in return. What else could they offer him to make this new provision worthwhile?

"Sorry, just ain't worth it," Conrad finally told her. "You don't know Salek like I do. He wouldn't do something like this for charity, and I don't have enough credits for him to stick his neck out. You already got a taste for what he really wants."

"Then we access their network remotely."

"No can do," the pilot said, shaking his head. "Someone tried a couple cycles ago and got caught… ended up in the mines, but that ain't the point. Afterwards, they overhauled the IDN security protocols. You need to be in the building. Encrypted hardline connections only."

"That complicates things."

"Not impossible, but hard as shit. I still don't think it's worth the chance of getting caught."

"If we do this, the timing has to be right," Sekami continued, frowning in concentration. "Whatever supplies we need from Salek should be onboard so we're ready to leave at a moment's notice."

"Hang on a sec," Rhys protested. "This is a totally unnecessary risk we're considering. If you get caught, we aren't talking about a slap on the wrist… we're talking about spending the rest of our lives in the mines!"

"I know it seems like we have a choice, but we don't. Without some clue as to where we can find another machine, I don't see a path forward."

Rhys couldn't think of any good alternatives. Did there have to be a path forward? Couldn't they just stay on Kaella, or if not here, then somewhere that wasn't so dangerous? Deep down, he knew Sekami would never agree to that. She was too invested, too burdened with the things her father and his partner had done. They had trapped her in a seemingly un-winnable fight, but she wouldn't quit. Not now. Not ever. As he considered the challenges ahead, Rhys wondered if even he could turn away from the conflict he'd been thrust into. The grül had killed his planet, and despite everything he'd learned, would he really allow that to pass unanswered?

Shaking his head in resignation, he sat back in his chair, any further argument dying in his throat. Seeing his decision, Conrad swiveled around to face the comms station. He typed quickly, silently forming the words with his mouth. Rhys shifted uncomfortably, still unable to fathom the consequences of the events they were about to set in motion. He glanced sideways at Sekami, but her expression was unreadable. When his message was complete, Conrad turned back toward them.

"I asked Salek to bring us the fuel and provisions from our original agreement. He's already been transferred the credits," he said. "If you're sure about this..."

"Send it. We need the supplies either way."

Conrad pushed the button, and a single chime told them the message had been transported into the airwaves. An awkward silence fell over the cockpit while they awaited the reply. When it arrived a few minutes later, it was short and to the point. *Received. Expect delivery of supplies and A.M. traps at dawn.* Sekami reread the message, a look of resigned determination on her face.

"When the time comes, one of us will attract less attention than all three," she said. "If you send me the location of the IDN, I'll find what we're looking for."

"If you don't, you'll have endangered us for nothing," Conrad replied brusquely and pushed himself up from the chair. "Ain't got time to sit around. One of the scrubbers went down on my last run, and I didn't have time to fix it before the grül showed up. If we're gonna make a fast exit, I'd rather not be runnin' off without our life support systems fully operational."

"Need a hand?" Rhys asked. "I don't know anything about scrubbers, but I can swing a wrench."

Under normal circumstances, he would've been keen to see what his old job looked like a few hundred years in the future. At the moment, however, he didn't care about that one bit. Dozens of scenarios kept playing out in his head, each worse than the last;

Sekami had gotten caught and had been forced to labor in the mines. Or rather, she hadn't been thrown into the mines, she'd been pressed into service as one of the courtesans he'd seen in the plaza. Worst of all, though, was the scenario where Salek had been the one to catch her, and an uncomfortable scene between a bound Sekami and the repulsive turandian kept replaying in his head. The longer he ruminated on this, the more grotesque the imagery became. Hopefully, some manual labor would distract him from what was to occur in a little over twelve hours.

"I'd appreciate the help," Conrad said, turning to leave the cockpit. "Engine compartment's this way."

He followed the pilot all the way aft, beyond the hospital into an area of the ship he hadn't been. Compared with the huge shipboard machinery spaces he was used to, it was extremely cramped. The overhead was low, and he had to duck to keep from striking it. Where the bulkheads weren't obstructed by piping, they were lined with shelves of spare parts. There was a small tool board off to one side, mounted above a tidy work bench. Rhys breathed in deeply, the smell of lubricated machinery filling his nostrils. It gave him a sense of familiarity that had been so elusive since waking up.

"This might be the first time you ain't looked like a fish out of water," the pilot declared. "Want a tour?"

"Definitely."

Conrad continued aft and stepped around a large valve poking up from beneath the deck. Rhys followed him, glancing around the pristine space. It was easily the tidiest engine room he'd ever encountered. Vague memories of different ships he'd sailed on floated through his mind, some complete shitholes and others impeccably clean. None, however, compared to this. The bilges sparkled, not a speck of dust or drop of oil visible anywhere. It was evidence of just how much the *Kestrel* meant to Conrad, a relationship between man and machine Rhys understood only too well. He probably felt more at home on his own ship than he ever had on Proxima Station.

"Has everything you'd expect, probably even a few systems you're familiar with," the pilot explained. "Water pumps are over there. Potable's the largest onboard tank since there's no easy way to get more without resupplying from a port. Way in the back are our reclamation and sterilizer units."

"Where do you reclaim water from?"

Conrad didn't answer directly but grinned roguishly and pointed to a meter-square tank next to the unit.

"This here's our sewage collection system," he explained. "I'll let you figure that one out on your own."

"You don't just jettison the… wait a minute. Are you saying…" Rhys began, taken aback. "Reclamation comes from your own shit and piss?"

"Graywater too, which is mostly just sink drains and a little from the galley," Conrad replied with a nod and a chuckle. "Oh, don't look so damn disgusted. You were drinking the same swill back on Proxima. It all goes through a filtration system, gets heated to near-boiling, then finishes with a U.V. sterilizer. Everything's pumped to a standby tank for testing before it's mixed back into the main potable supply."

"Still though. Just the principle of the thing," Rhys said with a shudder. Conrad ignored him.

"$CO_2$ scrubbers are off to the starboard side. We've got two main units, and an auxiliary backup. Only one primary needs to be online at a time, and you can swap which one leads."

Three large cylinders sat at the back of the room, a series of ducts and tubes crisscrossing over the skid. Each cylinder housed two separate chambers, a touchscreen glowing on the front of each conduit. Of the two offline units, the first's display was black, powered down and silent. Its protective cover had been removed and sat unattended on the deck. The second scrubber was in *STANDBY,* while a third, the one humming quietly, showed *ONLINE.* The chambers on the running unit read *CABIN* and *VACUUM EXHAUST* respectively. Behind all this, Rhys noticed another hatch going farther aft. A trefoil plastered on the door warned of radiation hazard.

"What's through there?" he asked.

"The *Kestrel's* beam-core drive and a small in-port generator for when we aren't running main propulsion," Conrad told him. "Underway, the drive supplies enough power that we can shut down the generator. Ain't gonna take you back there now. Technically, we could go in without suits since all the byrinium and anti-matter's contained, but I don't like risking it. Never know what might happen."

Turning to the task at hand, they set about repairing the broken-down scrubber. The tools looked slightly different than the ones Rhys was used to, but it was reassuring to know a wrench was still a wrench. It felt good to turn one again. The work was something familiar, something that came naturally to him. Conrad answered his questions about the scrubber as best he could, but he was a pilot, above all else. He knew the systems well enough to perform basic maintenance, but some of Rhys's questions were more technical, and he was quick to pick up the extent of Conrad's knowledge.

"You're as smart as you are ugly," the pilot joked. "If we make it through this alive and you're looking for a place to call home, my crew's running a little thin these days."

Rhys considered this proposal. Truth be told, he hadn't given any thought to what he would do if they survived. Conrad was offering him some semblance of familiarity, and he wanted nothing more than to regain solid footing on the proverbial slippery slope he felt himself tumbling down. Then again, there was Sekami to consider. If she wasn't interested in staying aboard the *Kestrel*, Rhys was pretty sure whose company he would choose. He hoped he never had to. Together, they were all any of them had left. Rhys had never asked if someone was waiting for Conrad. He'd always assumed not, considering the man's chosen place of refuge was a corrupt mining world. Sekami, on the other hand, had already admitted Volkerson and the scientists were the only family she had.

"I'll seriously consider that. Got room for one more?" Rhys asked. Conrad gave him a sideways glance.

"Something going on between you two?"

"I'm not sure what you mean."

"Don't play dumb. I've seen the way you look at the Doc. You were ready to go to war with Salek over her honor."

"I don't know how much of that's reciprocated. I have a helluva time reading her," Rhys confessed with a shrug. "Anyway, I've got my own complicated shit to deal with. The only reason I'm in this mess is because I didn't know how to deal with my wife's suicide. I know she's been dead hundreds of years at this point, but it still only feels like nine or ten months."

"Sorry. Didn't mean to pry."

Rhys declined a reply, just finished tightening the last two bolts on the scrubber's protective cover. He placed the wrench in his pocket and wiped his hands with a rag. Glancing at Conrad, he made sure the man's fingers were clear and reached up to close the breaker, returning power to the machine. Its control screen flashed once and went black. For a moment, nothing happened. Rhys reached up to open the breaker, convinced more troubleshooting was needed, when the display suddenly came to life. Conrad keyed through the brightly glowing menu and initiated a diagnostic. When the program finished, no faults had been detected.

"Okay, let's spin 'er up," he said and pressed *RUN*. The machine performed its startup routine, and a soft whir filled the room as air was taken into the scrubber. Looking over Conrad's shoulder, Rhys watched attentively as the pilot checked applicable pressures, temperatures, and chemical levels of the repaired unit. After ten minutes of observation, he nodded in satisfaction.

"Looks good so far, but we'll keep an eye on it."

Another three hours passed performing system checks before

they decided to call it quits. They were tired and sweaty but satisfied. The repaired scrubber had performed seamlessly, and Conrad demonstrated how to vent reclaimed $CO_2$ into vacuum. Their inspection of the other equipment had yielded nothing more than a few minor leaks, all which Rhys eagerly tackled under minimal direction. The pilot had been surprised by how easily he seemed to learn the ship's systems. All it took was a few minutes looking over a piece of machinery, tracing out some pipes, asking one or two questions, and voila! Conrad confessed to finding his intuition slightly unnerving. Rhys smiled at this. It was always something he'd been good at and was what made him such a successful engineer. Best of all, however, the last few hours had been a more effective distraction from his current woes than any drug could ever be.

"That's enough for now," Conrad said, wiping off the last of his tools and securing them to the board above the bench. "Mechanically speaking, we're as ready for tomorrow as we're gonna be."

"I don't see this ending well if she gets caught," Rhys worried, stepping out of the engineering space. "Seems like a big risk for an unsure thing."

"Can't say I disagree, but the Doc knows what she's doing… or so she says."

"I still don't have to like it."

They walked back to the cramped galley and found Sekami asleep at the table, head resting on her forearms. Her tablet rested atop the counter, projecting a section of navigational star chart into the air around her. As noiselessly as they could, they crept past and selected items from the ship's food dispenser. Rhys winced as a loud grinding sound from the machine assaulted the otherwise quiet room. He glanced back and saw Sekami open a bleary eye, yawn, and stretch her arms toward the ceiling. Conrad also noticed they'd woken her.

"Sorry," he apologized sheepishly. "Still got one more thing to fix."

"Did you eat?" Rhys asked. Judging by the chart, he guessed not and set the dish in front of her. "Here. I'll get another one."

"Thank you." She yawned again, covering her mouth with a long-fingered hand. "I plotted a route to the old terraforming colony. If we need more fuel, where we'd get it... that sort of thing."

"I asked Salek for more than we need," Conrad said loudly over the growling dispenser. He banged his fist on top of the machine to quiet it, but the sound just grew louder. "As long as he doesn't look too closely at our drive's antimatter requirement, he won't know any different. With the amount of proton matter still onboard plus what we're getting from him, the *Kestrel* could run full-bore half a dozen cycles before we came close to running out."

"Are we really sure going back there is a good idea?" Rhys asked. "Didn't some cosmic anomaly cause them to—"

"I know what you're going to ask, but the answer is no," Sekami replied, shaking her head. "The anomaly affected their systems momentarily, but they crashed due to pilot error. By the time they left the surface, whatever it was had disappeared. Even if it hadn't, we wouldn't take any undue risks getting near it."

"You mean, any more than we already are," the pilot muttered. He pushed the plate of half-eaten food away and stood up. "I'm going to bed. This time tomorrow, we'll be on our way to some other god-forsaken hellhole and not rotting in the byrinium mines if we're lucky."

He waved goodnight and left without another word. Rhys and Sekami sat alone at the table and ate the bland nutrient rations, not saying much. He wasn't particularly hungry but forced down what little he could. Each time he thought about what the morning might bring, his stomach clenched into a tight knot. He wanted nothing more than to talk some sense into Sekami but knew she wouldn't hear a word of it. Her mind was set. Appetite gone, Rhys gathered up the dirty bowls and placed them into the sterilizer. He busied himself in the galley, tidying up the clutter to distract his over-imaginative brain.

"I'm worried about what's going to happen tomorrow," he said, unable to restrain himself any longer. "If you get caught–"

He turned to face Sekami and found she had moved close. The look in her eyes was that of longing, and she slipped a hand around the back of his neck. Caught off guard, Rhys tensed, feeling the press of her body, the softness of her skin. The kiss was light at first, and he felt the warmth of her breath on his cheek. He relaxed and kissed her again, harder this time, feeling a tingling sensation shoot through his body with each passionate caress of her hand.

"I know," she whispered. "I'll be careful."

# CHAPTER 27

# RENEGOTIATING TERMS

RHYS FELT as though he'd just run a marathon. He was still wrapped in Sekami's embrace and rested his head against her naked chest, feeling it rise and fall in time with her shuddering breaths. When he gazed into her violet eyes, she kissed him, the taste of her lips pushing away all other senses. He wished they could stay in this moment forever. Never mind the danger that lay ahead or the sorrow that lay behind... none of that mattered right now.

They unwound from each other's embrace and slipped off the galley table. Rhys gathered up his discarded garments, dressing slowly, and waited for Sekami to finish adjusting her clothes. As quietly as they could, they tiptoed back to their staterooms. He was about to enter his cabin when he felt a hand on his arm.

"Stay with me?" she asked softly. He nodded, acquiescing with a small smile, and followed her across the hall. So much for a good night's sleep.

---

THE NEXT MORNING, he awoke feeling more refreshed than anticipated. He rubbed his eyes and rolled onto his side toward Sekami. Her back was to him, and he moved closer, propping himself up on one elbow to press against her. He kissed the light green skin of her shoulder that poked out from beneath the bedsheet and felt her stir. She mumbled sleepily but turned toward him, and he kissed her passionately, the same electricity from the night before shooting through every fiber of his being. When their lips parted, he brushed a strand of hair from her face.

"If this isn't what you want..." Rhys began, then trailed off.

"If this wasn't what I want, you wouldn't be here," she retorted, rubbing the back of her hand across her eyes. Her voice was playful, but he knew better than to think she was joking. "After everything that's happened, this is the only thing that feels right."

"Be careful today," he replied, a serious note creeping into his voice. "If something feels off, just get out of there. I've already lost everyone I ever cared about once before. If I lose you too..."

An unexpected expression of guilt spread across Sekami's face, her eyes momentarily breaking with his. When her gaze returned, her eyes shone with unshed tears. She blinked them away and smiled reassuringly before giving him a silent nod. *What was that about?* Rhys wondered, before bending to kiss her one last time. She held him tight. Breaking apart, he slid from beneath the covers and climbed out of bed. He gathered up his clothes, dressed quietly, then approached the door.

"See you soon," he said, the hatch sliding closed behind him.

Walking back to the galley, Rhys contemplated the night's events. Things had escalated quickly, but it was good to know she shared the affection he felt for her. That, in itself, was a weight off his mind, even if it felt reminiscent of a grade school crush. For God's sake, the fate of the galaxy was at stake, and here he was worrying about whether a woman he barely knew liked him.

The whole thing seemed a little off. He'd been so quick to discover feelings for her and combine that with the constant sense he'd known her for a long time... it all felt like some weird form of Stockholm Syndrome. Moreover, Sekami still wasn't telling him something. She had looked so guilty when he mentioned losing everyone he cared about, but why? How could she feel that was any fault of hers? Lost in thought, he stepped through the galley hatch and found Conrad bent over, picking up the dishes that had been knocked to the deck in their passion.

"Uh, hey," Rhys ventured sheepishly, stepping forward to help. "How did those get down there?"

"Uh huh. You guys play a round of hide-the-salami last night?" Conrad asked suspiciously. Rhys put on his best look of confusion, and the pilot shook his head in disbelief. "Not gonna fess up, huh? Okay."

"Look, I'm sorry, alright? Things just sort of… happened."

"Well, next time, try not to diddle each other on my table," Conrad snapped. He picked up a steaming plate from the food dispenser and walked to the port-side bulkhead. Grabbing a lever on the wall, he gave it a tug, and a small, one-person counter folded out. The pilot dropped his plate down irritably, bits of brown paste spilling over the lip. "Until one of you cleans the ever-loving Christ out of my table, I ain't eating over there."

There was an awkward silence where Rhys stood uncomfortably, unsure if he should leave, while Conrad moodily ate his food. When the pilot cast him another glaring look, he readied himself for a second rebuke. Instead, the man winked.

"Guess you didn't need to pay for it after all," he said wryly. An impish smile turned up the corners of his mouth. "You're still cleaning my table, Casanova."

Rhys snorted in amusement and set to work. By the time he finished, Sekami had joined them and sat down with a plate of food at the freshly cleaned table. She was about to take a bite when a chime sounded in the galley. Conrad stood and walked to a holoscreen by the door. He tapped the monitor a few times and grunted.

"Message from Salek. Says our provisions should be here within the hour," he announced, scanning the page before turning toward Sekami. "Looks like it's time to go, Doc. You've got the coordinates?"

Sekami nodded, and Rhys fought the urge to argue. He knew she was tough and perfectly capable of avoiding detection, but he was still worried. If she got caught, he knew all too well what it would mean.

"It's not too late to call this off," he implored. "There's got to be another way."

"I'll be fine. Just be ready to leave as soon as I get back... and I mean *as soon as I get back.*" She laid a comforting hand on Rhys's arm and turned to Conrad. "Anything else?"

"A note saying the handlers will be takin' our expended antimatter traps back for reconditioning," Conrad finished. "I doubt they'll actually load the new ones, though, so I'll need help with that."

Apprehension pushed away the last of his hunger, and Rhys poked at the food on his plate, barely tasting the brown mush. When he was unable to stomach any more, Conrad beckoned for him to follow, and they made their way back to the engine room. Outside the drive compartment, the pilot approached a glowing display. He scrolled through a list of menu items before selecting *LOAD MODE.* Overhead, the lights blinked, plunging them into darkness for a fraction of a second, before low-level emergency lamps clicked on.

"Trap cooling is on batteries now," Conrad explained. "Generator's shut down and the A.M. injection systems are isolated from the ship. It's the only safe way to load the stuff while we're out there."

Hearing a familiar double beep, Rhys touched the embedded communicator, and Sekami's voice filled his ear.

"I'm heading to the IDN. Be careful, you two."

"And you," he said, almost in unison with Conrad. He gazed absentmindedly at the floor, a worried look etching his features. The pilot tapped him on the arm.

"We'll be loading from the outside since draggin' a bunch of antimatter traps through here is a bad idea," Conrad explained. "I'll need a second pair of hands to help swap the depleted ones.

Salek's men ain't gonna install them, think it's too risky for what they get paid. They'll just push it out here in a protective crate, and we'll be the suckers who actually handle the stuff."

"Great. How dangerous are we talking?"

"Like I said, less than a gram of byrinium can kill you, and we'll be handling several *quadrillion* particles of antimatter," Conrad told him matter-of-factly, "but don't worry. If everything goes to hell, there won't be time to get worked up about it."

They traipsed back to the airlock and donned the radiation suits and furs. Once dressed, Rhys peered through the thick window to Kaella's surface. The wind had strengthened again and was kicking up an almost impenetrable haze of red dust. Nearly an hour passed before six figures materialized out of the gloom. Each wore a bulky protective suit making their progress in the howling wind unbearably slow. They bent forward against the frigid tempest in a never-ending battle to stay upright. With them hovered two, meter-and-a-half-square crates, each guided forward by an ungainly trio.

When the caravan finally reached the ship, Conrad opened the hatch and ushered the handlers inside. The first team pushed a crate up the ramp into the protection of the airlock, while the second remained outside. Wind whipped inside the compartment, filling it with red Kaellian dust and a sound like a freight train. It was impossible to hear anything. Conrad bent toward the nearest figure, hand-signaling intermittently. The stranger gesticulated wildly at the two crates they had brought, and Rhys saw the pilot nod.

"This one's got our provisions," Conrad yelled, voice tinny through the respirator mic. He turned back to Rhys and tapped the box inside the airlock. Even over the roaring wind, the man's shouts hurt his ears. "Our antimatter traps are outside. Gotta load 'em now so they can leave with the expended canisters."

Rhys nodded and followed Conrad outside. As soon as he stepped foot through the outer hatch, the force of the wind knocked him sideways. His arms spun wildly as he fought to keep balance before the pilot grabbed his matted fur coat and hauled him backward. More carefully this time, he crept down the ramp and trudged toward the crate of antimatter traps. Conrad motioned toward the aft end of the ship, and they leaned their shoulders into the floating container. It glided easily once they got it moving.

"There are four manual locks to loosen before I can open the loading port," the pilot yelled. He pointed at two sets of releasing gear inset into the belly of the *Kestrel*. "Twist counterclockwise two turns, then give it a push. You'll feel it release. Take the starboard side, and I'll take port."

Rhys moved to the right side and positioned himself in front of the locks. Conrad spun his finger in a circle, giving the signal to loosen the gear, and Rhys turned the handles until they could go no further. With a hearty shove, he felt a thud as each one seated into its unlocked position. The pilot motioned for him to step away and slid back a protective panel integrated with the hull plating. Beneath the cover was another touchscreen, and he pushed an orange button on the display. A blast of air escaped the belly of the *Kestrel*, momentarily blowing away some of the red Kaellian dust as the loading port emerged.

Inside, Rhys saw five rows of six canisters, each of which was hooked to an umbilical disappearing into the interior of the ship. Roughly two-thirds of the containers displayed green lights around their periphery, while the final ten showed one yellow and nine red. They positioned the crate of fresh antimatter as close as they could, and Conrad leaned over to the nearest red canister and unclasped its umbilical. He grasped the mass of tubes and wires and waved his hand underneath.

"Pressurized with inert gas."

Rhys stuck his gloved hand underneath. Although he couldn't feel it on his skin, he could see where the gas made ripples in the material of his suit. Conrad pulled the expended trap out of its containment and placed it on the ground. With a grunt, he lifted the crate's lid and revealed ten identical canisters. At the pilot's behest, Rhys gingerly picked up the first one and handed it to Conrad, who slid it smoothly into the empty housing. He passed the umbilical over the top of the canister, using the gas to blow away some of the dirt that had accumulated on its surface before latching the mechanism closed.

They repeated the process nine more times until all the replacement traps had been inserted into the ship, and the expended ones were housed neatly in the crate. Conrad pushed another button on the touchscreen and slid its protective cover closed. The loading port disappeared into the vessel, and Rhys returned to the starboard side, tugging each releasing gear back into place. He turned the handles clockwise, feeling them set into the locked position with a satisfying *click*. The door secured, they pushed the crate to the waiting handlers, who promptly began their journey back the way they had come. Rhys watched them go, disappearing into the swirling dust like ghostly wraiths, before turning away. Bent against the wind, he trudged up the ramp to the open airlock and stepped inside. When the hatch snapped shut behind them, Rhys pulled off his respirator and checked the time.

"How much longer do you think Sekami will–"

Something solid connected with the back of his head, and he went down hard. Stars danced in his vision, the impact bringing him to the verge of blacking out. Muffled shouts were all around, as if reaching him through a thick wall. There was another sharp pain in his ribs, and for a moment, he was unable to gasp for air, winded by a vicious kick. Something heavy fell onto his legs, and he heard more yelling. Thankfully, he received no more blows. Lying on the cold deck, his vision swimming, Rhys could just make out Conrad's form. He'd been forced to his knees, his arms raised in submission. Behind the pilot stood one of the suited figures who'd guided the first crate onto the ship. Its features were hidden behind the mirrored surface of its helmet.

"Looks like this one's still awake," a voice said from above Rhys.

He felt a toe nudge him in the back, rolling him over like a rag doll so he was looking up into a pointed, hair-covered face. He experienced a moment of confusion, thinking the creature that leered evilly down at him was Otaan Yabar, but no. This Hanekaarian's hair was reddish-brown, its stinking breath washing over him as it towered above. In its hand was a metal rod, a smear of red covering the end. Reaching up, Rhys gingerly touched the back of his head and felt searing pain. When he pulled away his fingers, they too were covered in blood.

"You cheap-shot fucking coward," Rhys slurred. He'd wanted his words to have more venom, but the blow had rung him like a bell. For his efforts, the assailant delivered another kick to his ribs, and he doubled up once again.

"What do you want?" Conrad demanded. "This was all part of our arrangement with Salek."

The masked figure shoved him from behind, and the pilot fell forward onto his hands. Grabbing him roughly by the collar, the stranger yanked him back to a kneeling position. Conrad coughed and rubbed his throat where the shirt had choked him. His captor grabbed a handful of hair and pulled his head backward to expose his throat.

"Save your words, human," came a distorted voice through the helmet's enunciator. "Salek will soon be here to renegotiate your deal."

Conrad started to protest, but when the helmeted figure flashed a blade in front of his face, the pilot fell silent. The longer they waited, the more Rhys's head began to hurt. He was still bleeding from the gash in his skull, and he desperately needed something to stem the flow. Weakly, he raised a hand to attract Conrad's attention.

"Head… hurts."

"Let me help my friend," the pilot demanded. The helmeted figure looked over to assess Rhys's condition and gave a nod. Conrad scrambled to his feet and strode quickly to a medical kit mounted on one of the bulkheads. Ripping it from the wall, he hurried back to where Rhys lay and opened the box. Rhys heard him rummage through the kit and the sound of its contents skittering noisily across the deck. A pair of hands helped him sit in an upright position. When Conrad pulled his hair away from the congealed edges of the wound, Rhys winced in pain.

"How bad?"

"Skull doesn't seem fractured, so you're probably alright. Might have a concussion, but I ain't a doctor," the pilot replied. Rhys saw Conrad's eyes flick upward toward the Hanekaarian, hate written in every crease and line of his face. He finished dressing the wound, at which time the creature growled menacingly down at them.

"Back," it croaked and pointed to where the pilot had been kneeling before.

Now he was sitting up, Rhys noticed there was a third assailant in the room. This one, gangly and lizard-like, exchanged places with the Hanekaarian standing guard over him, who moved to stand near the airlock entrance. Every few minutes, the four-armed alien peered out the window, checking periodically for Salek's impending arrival. Some minutes later, a knock reverberated through the airlock door, and the Hanekaarian glanced up once more.

"Salek has arrived," it said and opened the outer hatch.

Three figures stepped inside. At the head of the group, hands bound in front of her, was Sekami. She was shivering, her tattered overcoat nowhere to be seen, the rubbery suit her only protection from the elements outside. That wasn't the worst of it. When the alien escorting her ripped the respirator from her face, her features hidden beneath were battered. Blood oozed from a split lower lip, and a bruise had begun to form around one of her eyes, its lid puffy and swollen. She was prodded forward, and bringing up the rear was Salek himself. The turandian surveyed the scene in front of him, and an unctuous smile creased his lips. Boiling rage coursed through Rhys at the smugness oozing from the deformed cretin.

"Thank you for receiving me on such short notice," Salek greeted, voice dripping with insincerity. "You and your companions have been so gracious in accepting my hospitality, I knew I shouldn't have worried."

"What did you do to her, you bastard?" Rhys growled. He wanted to lunge at the twisted little creature and wrap his fingers around its throat until it stopped breathing. Salek looked down at him with loathing.

"Nothing I hadn't warned you of should you cross me again," he spat, dropping the affable posturing.

Rhys tried feebly to rise, but the gangly-armed guard smacked him in the back of the head. The blow wasn't hard, but it sent lightning bolts of pain shooting through his bandaged skull all the same. His vision blurred as needle-pricks spread down his spine to the very tips of his fingers and toes. Head wobbling drunkenly, he fought to stay conscious. Seeing Rhys subdued once more, Salek continued.

"You should count yourselves lucky," he said, turning back to Conrad. "If this *whore* had been discovered by anyone else, her presence might've compromised my position on Kaella. What would the Elders think if *a guest under my protection* was caught breaking into a secure facility? Were you so naïve to think I wasn't monitoring your every move? You disappoint me, Mr. Silas. I'd always thought you more astute, but I see now that I was wrong. By your own hand, you and your blustering friend will live out the rest of your days in the byrinium mines."

The turandian walked toward Sekami and grasped her gently by the chin. When she tried to pull away, Salek drew back and slapped her across the face.

"This one, on the other hand, will make several of my less-reputable clients very happy."

"Try it, and see what happens," she seethed, spitting a mouthful of blood at his feet.

"My guards are quite adept at convincing people to do what I want. You'll be broken, in time," Salek replied, ignoring her murderous stare and waving a hand toward his cronies. "There will come a time, when even one as strong-willed as you, will realize obedience is better than the consequences of defiance."

"I'll die before that happens."

"The beauty of one in my position, is that I won't let you."

He smiled at her, an air of complete self-satisfaction emanating from the malformed creature. Throwing caution to the wind, Rhys decided to act. Mustering what was left of his strength, he rammed his elbow into the crotch of the assailant standing over him. The alien bent double, momentarily incapacitated by the surprise attack. Taking advantage of his captor's lapse, Rhys wrestled the club from its grasp and slammed the bat as hard as he could into the alien's neck. There was a loud crunch, and a blood-curdling shriek filled the room as the guard crashed to the floor. Head still swimming, Rhys swayed unsteadily on his feet and looked around.

The airlock had erupted in chaos. As soon as the others realized what was happening, each of them joined the fray. Rhys searched frantically for his friends and spotted Sekami advancing on Salek, now cowering in the corner of the airlock. Before she could reach him, however, she was jerked backward when the Hanekaarian grabbed a fistful of her black hair. She cried out in pain, and the assailant caught her by the throat, its muscled arms bulging as it squeezed. Terrible gurgling sounds began to rise from her throat as she beat her fists against its head and neck, but the Hanekaarian held her fast. Rhys let out a howl of rage and leaped forward, swinging his club in a powerful arc at her aggressor's skull.

At the last moment, his target saw the impending strike and raised an arm in defense. Though nothing more than a glancing blow, it had the desired effect. The Hanekaarian released Sekami and turned its attention toward Rhys, who only just realized how big the creature really was. Rage burned in its eyes as it advanced. He raised the club and struck again, his full weight behind the attack. To Rhys's dismay, the Hanekaarian easily caught the weapon in its hand and yanked it away, the metal rod clattering to the floor. It wrapped him in all four arms and began to squeeze, crushing the air from his lungs. Feet jerking frantically, darkness began to creep into the periphery of his vision. Behind his captor, two more guards kicked a prostrate Conrad. His sight fading quickly, Rhys knew this was going to be the end. *Well*, he thought, at least they wouldn't die at the hands of the grül.

"Tell them to stop, or I will end you!"

The threat reverberated through the airlock. Rhys felt the pressure around his chest lessen slightly, and through a laborious effort, was able to drag in a ragged breath. Out of the corner of his eye, he saw Sekami. She stood behind Salek, a blade held to the turandian's throat. His eyes bulged with fear.

"Stop! All of you!" he shrieked. The aliens pummeling Conrad paused uncertainly.

"Let my friends go," she demanded pressing the knife harder against Salek's throat. A droplet of blood ran down his neck, and he began to whine pitifully.

"Do what she says. Back away from the humans."

Rhys felt the grip on him loosen, and he dropped to his knees, hacking and gasping for each lungful of air. Pain searing his chest, he crawled to where Conrad lie. He felt the pilot stir and heard him groan, uttering a string of colorful expletives beneath his breath. When he finally sat up, Conrad glared across the room at Salek.

"Doc, put that shriveled pile of uulgar shit out of his misery."

"If you kill me, they won't stop until you're all dead," Salek warned, but fear etched his face, nonetheless.

"Maybe, but you won't be around to see it," Sekami snarled, pressing the blade even harder against his throat. "Tell them to go, and I'll release you once our safety's guaranteed."

They watched the last of Salek's resolve melt away. He motioned for his guards to leave, and Rhys felt cold wind whip through the airlock. He counted to himself as each one left the ship. When all four assailants had departed, he closed the hatch behind them.

"Rhys, help Conrad to the cockpit," she instructed, jerking her head toward the door. "I'll make sure this one doesn't try anything else."

"What about our bargain?" Salek demanded frantically. Sekami, her knife still poised at his throat, bared her teeth.

"Not until your thugs are out of sight," she snarled. Without taking her eyes off the back of the turandian's head, her next words were for Rhys. "Get us out of here."

Wordlessly, he pulled the pilot to his feet and guided him toward the cockpit. Conrad grimaced in pain and pressed a hand to his torso when Rhys deposited him in front of the flight controls. For the most part, he seemed alright. No visible signs of bleeding, though a few cracked ribs wouldn't be a surprise. He'd endured a hell of a beating, after all. Gritting his teeth, Conrad reached toward the console, giving only a cursory glance at the startup permissives before bringing the engines online. They didn't have time for a thorough run-through.

Pulling back on the throttle, Conrad lifted off, a little erratically at first but steadying up. Rhys scanned the console, looking for anything that might jump out to his less-than-trained eye. There was no telling what Salek's cronies could have done while they were fueling, but he saw green lights across the board. That, at least, was a good sign. Without warning, a blinking red light made his heart jump to his throat, and he bent forward to read the alarm.

*STBD AIRLOCK OPEN.*

The light flicked back to green as quickly as it had come. He and Conrad exchanged a worried look.

"I'll go check on her," Rhys said. He turned to leave but hadn't take two steps before the hatch opened, and Sekami stepped in. She was alone.

"Where's Salek?"

"Lying in the dirt with two broken legs, hopefully," she

muttered, glaring out the window into Kaella's swirling red dust. "I shoved him out after he unlocked my restraints."

She walked doggedly forward and collapsed into the chair beside Conrad, buckling herself in. Rhys settled into one of the empty seats and fastened his harness. Looking over, he studied Sekami's bruised face.

"Was it worth it?" he asked.

Fishing a hand into her pocket, she held up a small black data drive.

"Let's get out of here," Conrad said and pulled back hard on the stick.

Rhys felt his body press heavily into the seat as the ship sped through the turbulent atmosphere. When they finally burst through the Kaellian dust into bright sunshine, he felt utterly relieved to be alive.

# CHAPTER 28

# SEKAMI'S DISCOVERY

SEKAMI INSERTED the drive into the ship's computer and returned to the settee next to Rhys. They were in one of the unused staterooms Conrad's old crew had converted to an improvised lounge, and it was a good place to blow off steam while the *Kestrel* cruised on autopilot. Rhys and Sekami sat on a small sofa next to Conrad, who reclined in an over-sized armchair. After their narrow escape from Salek and his thugs, Sekami had plotted coordinates back to the quantum link station and spent the next two hours tending their wounds. When she was satisfied none of them had suffered any lasting injuries, they'd gathered in the lounge to hear what she'd dug up in the IDN.

"BAIN, show me the files for AZ-16781," Sekami instructed.

There was a short pause while the computer searched the drive for the requested information. A moment later, AZ-16781 appeared in large letters on the holoscreen in front of them. Embedded within the file was a collection of graphs, photos, and video feeds. She selected the first item, and a series of numbers and images Rhys did not understand appeared on the display.

"Some of this might seem unnecessary, but it should make sense in the end," she explained, indicating the data in front of them. "When the turandians discovered Kaella over a hundred years ago, they changed the course of history. Byrinium, as you both know, it's what shields the antiprotons inside Penning traps. Beam-core engines were lightyears ahead of any other prime mover, but without a stable means of antimatter storage, it wasn't considered viable technology. The turandians found that byrinium, coupled with continuous laser cooling, could be used to store antimatter indefinitely and took steps to keep Kaella's location a secret. Once their mining operation was up and running, they revealed their discovery, and advances in antimatter propulsion leaped forward."

"Took 'em a while to figure out how to convert annihilation energy to exhaust velocity, though," Conrad chimed in. "Gotta hand it to the Hanekaarians for that one."

"It's true. Kaella's byrinium deposit led to some of the most groundbreaking advancements of the twenty-seventh century," Sekami agreed, nodding.

"Wait a minute," Rhys interjected, a little confused. "That makes it sound like the entire Commonwealth knows Kaella's location. If that's true, why are the turandians so obsessed with guarding access to their network?"

"The entire G.C. doesn't know it's location, only that the turandians possess a stable source of shielding material," Conrad countered. "I worked a byrinium ore ship back when I was cuttin' my teeth as a pilot. Shittiest job I ever had. Too much risk for too little pay. Point is, we made runs to Kaella, and you wouldn't believe how careful they are keepin' its location under wraps. Among other precautions, any ship making port there has her nav recorder wiped before she's allowed to leave."

*Except us*, Rhys thought. *We didn't wipe our nav recorder.* They had left Kaella in a hurry, barely escaping with their lives, and he shuddered to think what the rest of his life would've been like if they hadn't... at the thought of the mines on that cold, dead world. Even that, however, paled in comparison to the fate that would've awaited Sekami.

"Okay, so they have the byrinium market cornered. Big whoop. How does knowing that help us?"

"Do you recognize the name AZ-16781?" she asked.

Rhys racked his brain, struggling to remember where he might have heard such a random string of numbers. It sounded familiar, but he couldn't put his finger on what it meant. He shrugged his shoulders.

"That's the planetary designation where Dr. Volkerson and my father crash landed, thirty-four years ago," she told them. "According to what I found in the IDN, AZ-16781 wasn't just another terraforming colony. It was the site of a new byrinium mine. These graphs represent seismic data brought back by a survey team before the terraforming operation had begun."

The images behind Sekami showed a series of wavy lines projected on to a three-dimensional grid. In different areas of the graph, the lines were all parallel, running together in a logarithmic arc until intersecting another set of parallel lines going in a different direction. Rhys saw random sections where sets of curving lines disappeared altogether, giving way to areas of fuzzy dots and splotches. He didn't know what any of it meant but suspected the turandians must've liked what they saw. Regardless, this all still seemed rather pointless.

"If they went through the trouble of establishing a colony, they must have expected to find more byrinium," Rhys reasoned. "Otherwise, why go in the first place?"

"Precisely."

"Hang on a minute," Conrad cut in, an accusatory note in his voice. "Didn't we already decide that going back to AZ-1639-whatever isn't worth the effort? Sorry, I just don't see why you risked our lives for any of this."

"I'm getting there," Sekami said, growing more eager by the minute. "The turandian Elders never discovered what happened to their first terraforming mission on AZ-16781. *We* know the grül were responsible, but only because Dr. Volkerson stumbled upon their raid of the terraforming colony. Shortly after losing contact, the Elders sent a second team to finish what they'd started. The new crew got the mine up and running, then continued terraforming the surface. If we went back now, their operation would probably look a lot like Kaella's."

"And they didn't think anything was wrong? Just kept plugging forward like nothing had happened?"

"Pretty much," Sekami replied. "The Kaellian mines were only expected to last eight or nine generations before they dried up, and the reserves from their new quarry would extend that mark by at least a few more. The turandians knew they'd have to make another massive discovery if they wanted to maintain control over the market, which is exactly what happened. Production on their new mine had only been underway for about ten months when the colonists discovered another world, 'BQ3,' approximately eight hundred billion kilometers from AZ-16781. Based on samples brought back by their exploratory rovers, they expected the new planet would contain large byrinium veins as well."

"BQ3?"

"I'm guessing it stands for 'Byrinium Quarry Three.'"

"Oh. Creative."

Sekami swiped away the first set of data and displayed a star chart from within her original search parameters. It was the same map they'd seen back on Kaella, and she shifted the view with her hands. Now, most of the visible area was blacked out, a dark void representing an unexplored region of space. Within this, she circled a smaller area where two dots glowed like signal fires in a sea of darkness.

"This is where the two planets are located. The nearest link station drops us around one-point-three trillion kilometers from BQ3."

"I still don't understand how this helps," Conrad pressed. "If it's more grül tech you're after, none of this seems particularly compelling."

"I haven't finished," she replied. "The colonists on AZ-16781 sent a survey team to collect more detailed information on BQ3's viability but went out of radio contact shortly after landing on the surface."

"So?" Conrad asked, still clearly unconvinced.

*'So' is right*, Rhys thought. Just because a survey team lost contact didn't mean the grül were responsible. The ship could have crashed or encountered some kind of unexpected toxin… there were any number of reasons that were just as likely as the next.

"So, the same thing happened to the second team they sent… and the third," Sekami explained. "The last team was able to get a message back to the colony before they were never heard from again. Most of it was garbled, except for this."

She swiped away the map and procured one last file. It was a video recording, broken and distorted with intermittent static. The face of a turandian woman appeared on the screen, her yellow-green eyes looking somberly into the camera.

"We've located the second survey ship sent to BQ3–"

A hiss of static filled the screen for a moment before the image resolved.

"This report is to document my autopsy findings for the crew–"

Once again, the image buzzed with interference.

"The bodies of Team Two were found mutilated. I am unable to pinpoint a cause of death at this time. Suspect some sort of attack, though no signs of blunt-force trauma. Systemic capillary rupture, and internal organs exhibiting severe desiccation–"

A crash reverberated from the holoscreen, and for a moment, Rhys wondered if it was another artifact in the recording. Something was different, though. The image never wavered, and the woman's eyes had gone wide with fear. She turned away from the camera, the image fixed on the side of her head. They could hear shouting coming from somewhere behind her, but then, the voices took on a more ominous tone. They were no longer shouting. They were screaming.

"Something's here, oh God, something's here!"

The woman turned back toward the camera.

"If you receive this, please send help! I don't know how long we'll survi–" she begged, but her words were cut short. A moment of intense pain contorted her features before the screen went black.

A subdued hush had fallen over the lounge. As much as he hated to admit it, Rhys found the evidence difficult to deny. An unidentified presence that was responsible for the disappearance of several expeditions sounded frighteningly like the grül. The description of the survey team's bodies reminded him of what he'd seen in Volkerson's IHR, and the expression on the turandian's face in her final moments held an uncanny resemblance to Conrad's during their escape from Proxima Station… the excruciating pain… the sensation of burning from the inside out… if Sekami had truly wanted to track down the grül, there was a decent chance she'd found them. Rhys's heart sank at the thought of another encounter with their terrifying foe. He glanced at Conrad, who looked as unhappy as he felt, and it was a moment before anyone spoke. When the muted trance finally ended, it was the pilot who broke the silence.

"Did they ever figure out…" his voice trailing off.

"No," Sekami replied, shaking her head. "They planned a fourth expedition, one better equipped with weapons and soldiers, but it was abandoned after the appearance of the grül fleet. You may not want to hear it, but I think BQ3 is our best chance of finding what we're looking for."

"This seems like a bad idea," Conrad objected, leaning forward, and running his hands through his hair. "Like, *really* bad. What if this mystery planet is their home world or a military base or something? Are we going to zoom in and say somethin' like 'hi, don't mind us, just here to take your shit'?"

"I don't think it's their home world."

"You have absolutely nothing to base that assessment on. It ain't too late to call this whole thing off," he protested, but Sekami raised her hands and tried to reason with him.

"The data brought back by the colony's probe didn't indicate any settlements, on the surface or otherwise. If BQ3 really is overrun with grül, don't you think they would've ransacked the colony on AZ-16781?" she asked stubbornly. "There was no guarantee we'd find anything when we agreed to break into Kaella's IDN. We were grasping at straws, but that was the best plan any of us could come up with. Now that we have tangible evidence of something beyond the terraforming colony, you want to quit? If I'm wrong about this, and there's nothing out there, I'll let it go. We'll do what you wanted in the first place. We'll go into hiding and try to stay ahead of the grül."

"Finding nothing ain't what I'm afraid of," Conrad muttered, shaking his head as if to tell Sekami she'd never understand.

Rhys sat there and tried to think of a way out of their current predicament. He didn't want to admit it, but he agreed with the pilot. Simply barreling headlong toward some unknown world where they might run into the grül did, in fact, seem like a bad idea. He'd never tell Sekami, but he'd half hoped her search of the IDN would be unproductive. Risking a confrontation without the machine, or a plan for that matter, wasn't high on his list of priorities. At this point, Rhys would happily spend the rest of his days avoiding the grül for as long as they could. He knew Sekami would never agree to that, however. The best he could hope for was that they didn't find anything on BQ3.

"The only advantage we have is that they don't know we're coming," Rhys said finally, grasping for anything that might bolster their spirits. "That has to count for something."

"That doesn't count for shit, and you know it."

"Look, we've escaped them twice already, and I doubt they'll expect us to go looking for them," he countered. "If we get there and the whole planet is infested with grül, we'll just turn our asses around and make a run for it."

Sekami raised her eyebrows and shifted her gaze to Conrad. The pilot shook his head resignedly and scowled at the pair of them.

"I swear you two are gonna be the death of me."

IN THE FINAL moments before their arrival on a potentially hostile planet, Rhys fought off a growing sense of dread. He tugged nervously at the beard covering his chin, a nest of brown hair that had grown bushy in the nearly two months since passing through the Kaellian link station. Pressed against his restraints by the ship's gradual deceleration, he craned his neck to peer out of the cockpit window at the planet below, its brightly lit surface radiant against the black void. *It looks like Earth*, he thought, taking in the brown-and-green landmasses, the blue bodies of water, and the white puffy clouds.

He tried to catch the eyes of his seated companions, but their focus was directed toward the blinking lights on the control console. Conrad, too, hadn't bothered to shave. His usual stubble had grown into a thick black beard, concealing the cuts and scrapes from their fight with Salek's men. Pink scars over his cheekbones, though no longer open wounds, were a constant reminder the grül hadn't been their only enemy. Sekami, however, looked the same as ever. Fierce. Confident. Beautiful. Any sign of the abuse she'd endured by Salek and his men had long since faded. During the months-long journey from Kaella, she and Rhys had grown close, and an intimacy he'd never expected burned inside him. It made him afraid of what they might find on this new world and what he'd do if something happened to her. Now that they had arrived, what would be waiting for them?

"No other ships on the scanner," Conrad said, disrupting Rhys's musings as he frowned at the instruments in front of him. "Seems like we're on our own. Should I take 'er down?"

"Not yet," Sekami replied. "Let's start with a few low-orbit flyovers. Surface scans will be easier up here."

Conrad nodded once and keyed the commands into the flight computer. While BAIN guided them through several revolutions of the planet, Rhys stared in awe at the earth-like world below. It looked nothing like Kaella's desolate wasteland. Lush green forests and craggy mountains reached into the sky, and the light from a faraway star gleamed off the surface of its oceans like a beacon. How long had it been since he'd seen water like that? Weeks? Months? A year? *No*, he reminded himself, *centuries*. Peering down at the unspoiled planet, his apprehension for their arrival on BQ3 had given way to a powerful sense of claustrophobia. They had been on the ship far too long, and he wanted nothing more than to be free of its confines, if only for a short while. Glancing back at Sekami, he wondered anxiously how long her scans were going to take.

SEVERAL PAINSTAKINGLY-SLOW HOURS LATER, BAIN completed its holographic rendering of the planet's surface. Sekami began poring over the model, centimeter by centimeter, studying its topography like a hawk in search of prey. Minutes passed in silence, and Rhys felt a twinge of impatience. How much longer were they going to wait? He sensed Conrad's tolerance growing thin as well, but before either he or the pilot could express their annoyance, Sekami turned back to the console. She keyed a command into the computer and gave an apologetic smile while they waited for it to process her query.

"I have the information you requested, Dr. Ryele," the

computer announced. "Seventeen sites on BQ3 match your search parameters. They are now marked on the globe."

One by one, seventeen red-orange blips appeared on the holographic model. There was no discernible pattern that Rhys could see, the location of each one completely random.

"I asked BAIN to analyze the information I took from the IDN and mark areas that could match the survey teams' landing sites," she said, shifting her eyes away from the globe to look at them. "I'm hoping one of these is close to where the video file from the third expedition was sent. If not, we'll need to expand our search."

"Wonderful," Conrad snorted in exasperation. "So, if by some miracle we don't fall into the same trap as the turandians, you'll have us wander around the planet until we do?"

"It's at least a starting point," Rhys replied, finding it more difficult with each passing minute not to let his annoyance get the better of him. He'd grown tired of their constant bickering. Sekami and Conrad hadn't shared a civil word with each other in over a week, and it was starting to piss him off. They all needed to get off the ship and soon. "We're here, like it or not, so we have to try something."

The pilot just shook his head and rolled his eyes.

"Which one first?" he asked, tone only slightly less petulant than before.

Sekami twisted the model back and forth, looking at one site then the next. Eventually, she shrugged her shoulders and made a swiping motion through the air that sent the globe freewheeling.

"I don't know," she admitted when the rotating sphere slowed to a stop. She pointed at random to one of the glowing dots. "Here, I guess. If there are only seventeen, it shouldn't take long to figure out if this whole trip was a waste of time."

Conrad took manual control of the ship and began to ease them toward the surface. When they burst through the clouds, Rhys leaned forward to see what lay below. He wasn't disappointed. For the first time since waking from cryosleep, he saw trees. *Real* trees. In the distance, wind rippled across a rolling meadow of tall grass, bending their stalks in submission. From their vantage in the sky, he could see where the tree line ended and an imposing mountain range began. The headwaters of a roaring river snaked down the mountainside before tumbling over a cliff into the valley below. Like his home of old, it was a stunning landscape, full of wild and untamed splendor.

"Keep a lookout for a good place to set down," Conrad said, guiding the ship low over rocky terrain.

They scanned the surface for a viable landing site, and it wasn't long before they spotted a relatively flat swathe of dirt and gravel. Rhys felt the ship bank to starboard as the *Kestrel* maneuvered into position and a gentle bump when they touched down. A near-imperceptible whine of machinery slowly faded from the background as the antimatter drive spooled down, the sudden silence leaving his ears ringing. With the eagerness of a shore-starved mariner, he fumbled with the restraints confining him in his seat, cursing under his breath until the clasp on the harness clicked open.

"The atmosphere is mostly nitrogen, with just over eighteen percent oxygen… a few trace elements," Sekami read out from her display. "Sensors aren't picking up any toxins, so we can leave the EVA suits. Gravity is nineteen percent over a standard g, so between that and the lower oxygen content, it'll feel like you're carrying several extra kilos while breathing through a tube. Temperature is around fifteen degrees celsius."

They strode from the cockpit, stepped through the airlock, and cycled the hatch outside. Hurrying eagerly down the gangway, Rhys stepped onto the alien world. The ground felt springy underfoot, the increased gravity pressing his boot deeper than normal into soft dirt. Almost immediately, he noticed his breathing increase, the thin air burning in his chest. It was welcome stimulation from their previous lethargy aboard the *Kestrel*. The long and uneventful voyage to BQ3 had left him feeling stifled, a perception that was now being stripped away by crisp mountain air.

Below their landing site sat a small lake fed by a gurgling fork in the river. *More of a pond, really*, Rhys thought. He walked down the sloping bank, boots squishing through increasingly muddy ground as he neared the edge. Feeling it lap against the toes of his boots, he crouched down and dipped his hands into the cool water, splashing some onto his face. It was ice cold and, God, did it feel good! If there was one thing he wanted more than anything right now, it was to wash away the lingering vitriol from everything that had happened to him; the torturous month with the machine, seeing Proxima Station blown to bits, and the brutal beating from Salek's men, to name a few. Without another moment's hesitation, he stripped and dove headfirst into the lake. He came up sputtering, the freezing-cold water sending endorphins coursing through his body. Like a wet dog, he shook free the droplets from his damp hair and basked in the utter isolation of this new, unadulterated planet. Looking back toward the ship, he saw Sekami striding down the bank toward the water's edge.

"When was the last time you went swimming?" he shouted happily, waving at her to join him.

"I'm not going in there," she objected, holding up her hands and shaking her head. "There's no telling what kind of bacteria–."

"Just for a bit. C'mon, you'll love it."

While he treaded water, Rhys felt something brush against his leg. In an instant, all his newfound assuredness vanished, and he bolted from the water, fueled by a sudden surge of adrenaline. Without bothering to stop for his clothes, he squelched through the mud and was halfway up the bank before regaining his wits. Heart beating like a jackhammer, he stopped a few paces from Sekami and saw a look of alarm creasing her face at his sudden exodus.

"Something rubbed against my leg," he stammered, pointing back toward the lake. As they watched, a tiny fish broke the surface, flipping in the air like an acrobat, before splashing back down. Sekami's concern gave way to a smile, and she snorted in amusement.

"If you're done parading your hardware, get dressed and come help us," she teased, shaking her head and hiking back up the bank.

Rhys looked toward the water and couldn't help but shiver, unsure if it was from the brisk alpine air or his brush with the alien water dweller. It couldn't have been a baitfish. Whatever creature had rubbed against his leg felt big… slimy. He craned his neck to see what lurked below, but the reflection off the lake made its surface impenetrable. Scooping up his clothes, he looked down at the thick layer of mud covering his feet. Jamming them back into his boots like that was far from ideal but returning to the lake to rinse off sounded even less appealing. Nevertheless, he gritted his teeth and dipped his feet into the water, quickly shook clean, then slipped them back into his boots.

He returned to the ship fully clothed and found Conrad standing outside, a thousand-meter stare filling the pilot's eyes. Rhys was about to ask what was wrong, when the pilot touched the skin near his left ear, and the vacant expression vanished. Even after months of having his own implant, Rhys still found it disconcerting to watch someone access the CIM. It was like looking into the eyes of a zombie… or a crazy person. Back in the physical world, a swarm of disk-like objects detached themselves from the *Kestrel's* hull, circled the ship once, then came to hover in front of them. BAIN drones, Rhys realized. Their central red eyes blinked once and shifted to green.

"Deploy to each of the sites from Dr. Ryele's search parameters," Conrad instructed the hovering cloud. "Look for anything that might resemble a crash site or alien tech."

"That will take some time," BAIN replied, its voice emanating in unison from the drone swarm.

"How long do you need?"

"Based on our initial surface scans, I estimate thirty-two hours."

"Keep us posted," the pilot replied.

———

RHYS'S BREATH came in ragged gasps as he scrambled toward a small, rocky saddle in the truncated ridgeline. Pausing for a moment, he looked back the way he'd come, surprised by how close the ship appeared. It couldn't be more than a kilometer or two from his current position. His eyes traced the steep dirt slope above him and watched as a few loose pebbles broke free, tumbling down toward the icy snowfield in dirty brown rivulets. To his left, a crumbling rock face towered above, reaching nearly three hundred meters into the bright blue sky. Just looking at it gave him vertigo, and he felt himself sway unsteadily over his precarious footholds. He continued upward and was hit by a buffeting wind when he crested the exposed ridge.

The other side of the saddle looked out over a collection of melt-washed gullies, each ending abruptly in a cliff that dropped hundreds of meters to the valley below. At the bottom, a field of rock and snow led to the base of a towering goliath, a gigantic curving blade of granite that stabbed into the sky like a tooth. Far below sat another lake, larger than the one he'd swam in, its milky blue water fed by a flowing river of glacial melt. Except for a grassy plateau on its northern bank, the shoreline consisted of blocky talus sloped steeply toward the water's edge. For perhaps the first time since waking up, overlooking unspoiled wilderness, Rhys felt truly at peace. He couldn't have said how much time passed as he gazed across the rugged landscape, before the spell was broken by a soft beep in his ear.

"Hey."

"Conrad and I just finished going through BAIN's data packages." Sekami's voice. "There's some interesting footage from Site Four."

"More grül?" Rhys asked, immediately apprehensive. A scene played out in his mind of a horde of gray-skinned warriors surrounding a cage of terrified prisoners, all crying out in despair while their organs were drained of blood and plasma. It made his skin crawl.

"I don't know. Looks like a crash site of some kind. Could be from one of the turandian survey teams."

"Anything else?"

"No. Only the drone from Site Four brought back anything promising."

"I'll head down," Rhys said, shading his eyes to gauge the length of his return journey. "Might take an hour to get back."

"Just stay put. We'll come to you."

Rhys watched the ship from his vantage point as it lifted off and flew toward him, steadily gaining altitude. When it reached the ridge, he covered his face against the abrasive cloud kicked up by its maneuvering engines. He squinted through the haze as a small hatch opened on the belly of the ship, and a ladder descended from its depths.

Hauling himself up, he gasped heavily in the thin air, arms burning with exertion. It was a tight squeeze through the small door, but he managed to wiggle through, brushing the dirt and dust from his clothes when the hatch snapped shut behind him. He felt the ship bank gently left and steadied himself against the bulkhead while he walked toward the cockpit. Stepping in to join the others, he peeked out the window to the ground below. Now, they were directly above the tooth-shaped spire of granite, and with a clear view of the summit, its pinnacle appeared no larger than the *Kestrel's* galley table. In a different time, it might've been a climb he'd have done with Anne.

"What did you find?" Rhys asked, pushing the thought away and returning his attention back inside the cockpit.

"Some unexplained variation in the local flora, but it's all pretty overgrown at this point," Sekami replied. "You'll see when we get there. Shouldn't be long now."

*Flora,* Rhys wondered? She's wound up over some dumb plants? Their bird's eye view of the mountainous landscape zoomed by as he pondered this. A few minutes later, the snow-covered peaks shortened and gave way to densely forested hills. Here, ancient trees had grown tall, nearly obscuring any view of the ground.

"We're coming up on Site Four," Conrad announced.

Almost immediately, Rhys saw what Sekami had meant. Ahead was a thick press of trees, the smallest of which towered thirty meters into the air. Directly in line with their trajectory, however, was a fifteen-meter-wide swath of land that had, at some point, been scraped clean of vegetation. Here, the trees were much shorter, barely two meters in height, growing up between hundreds of splintered logs. Trees that had once stood as tall as the rest of the forest were nothing more than rotting debris, covered in moss and ferns by the passage of time. The unsightly scar in the landscape went on for nearly a kilometer. Conrad maneuvered the ship over the mysterious gash and touched down gently in the shortest of the new growth.

"What do you think? Crash of some kind?" the pilot asked. "Any need for rad gear?"

"I doubt we'd suffer a harmful dose if it's from the turandian scouting trips," Sekami replied, shaking her head. Nevertheless, she leaned forward and pressed a button. One of the disk-shaped drones whizzed by the window and sped away from the ship. A series of beeps chimed on the console.

"There's definitely something here... it's faint, too weak to need suits," she said, frowning at the report, "but... wait a minute. It's not byrinium. How–"

She stopped speaking, and Conrad leaned forward to peer at the illuminated screen. His brow furrowed as he scanned the report. As he read, the color began to drain from his face, and he looked as though he might vomit. He placed a hand on the console to steady himself, before turning abruptly and leaving the cockpit.

"Hey, wait a minute. Where are you going?" Rhys asked. "Does someone mind telling me what's going on? What kind of–"

"Therleon," Sekami interrupted. "The drone is picking up a residual therleon signature."

He felt his stomach do a somersault, the bodily equivalent of a spiraling trapeze artist, and he understood what had alarmed the pilot. A residual therleon presence confirmed one thing: in some way, the grül did, in fact, have something to do with the missing expeditions. The thought of another encounter with the murderous aliens terrified him, and the one thing he'd hoped they wouldn't find was staring him in the face.

"I don't get it," he said, voice wavering slightly. "Does that mean a grül ship crashed here instead?"

Sekami bit her lip and shrugged but didn't answer. Her face was a mask of fear, optimism, and confusion at this unexpected discovery. Their goal had been to find evidence of the lost survey teams in hopes of picking up the next piece in their trail of crumbs. Instead, they had perhaps just stumbled upon the entire pie. If his perception was at all accurate, she was just as scared as him. It wasn't an unreasonable reaction, even despite the fact they had gone looking for this. Still though, it was terrifying to think they might actually succeed. He reached out and placed a comforting hand on her shoulder, and she seemed reassured by the gesture. They left the cockpit and found Conrad rummaging through the storeroom outside the airlock. When he straightened, he held in his hands three backpacks and one of the biggest rifles Rhys had ever seen.

"What's all this?" he asked, taking a bag from the pilot's outstretched hand.

"Insurance. You've got water, rations, headlamp, a thermal blanket... and this."

From the depths of his pack, Conrad pulled a handgun, careful to keep it pointed away from the others. The frame was sleek and black, its low-profile sights equipped with brightly colored dots. The weapon resembled the ones Rhys remembered, but there was something about it he couldn't put his finger on. Then it hit him. A slide. The pistol had no slide.

"Am I missing something?" he asked, confused by what he saw. "How does it extract casings?"

"Doesn't use cased projectiles."

Rhys frowned.

"So, what am I supposed to do? Hit a grül over the head with it?"

"I didn't say 'no projectiles,'" Conrad retorted. He pushed a button on the grip and caught the magazine as it fell out of the bottom. He handed it to Rhys. Just as the man had said, there were no bullets, only a small, sealed port at the top. "The magazines house a compound that generates high-velocity projectiles. More accurate than a rifled barrel and packs a bigger punch than one of those old-school .44's. A single clip produces upwards of five hundred rounds. Four hundred eighty-five to be precise."

"Must give quite a kick."

"Nah. Recoil absorption keeps it minimal."

Taking back the magazine, Conrad inserted in into the pistol. He flipped it over, and Rhys saw a small display he hadn't noticed before. The number on the screen read '326.'

"Rounds remaining?" he guessed.

"Yup," Conrad said. "Ever fire a weapon before?"

"Hey, I'm a six-hundred-forty-year-old Montanan, remember? It's been a while, but I can handle myself," he replied, grinning weakly.

The pilot smirked, but when Rhys tried to share the joke with Sekami, he saw only a crestfallen look on her face. She turned away, leaving him baffled as to what he'd said to upset her. She'd been relatively calm since discovering the therleon presence, but something in his words had elicited her sudden withdrawal. Things were beginning to feel off in the way she acted.

Thinking back, it seemed her guilt, or whatever this recurring emotion was supposed to be, had become more frequent of late. He'd seen it after their night together on Kaella, when he'd mentioned the loss of his wife. Before that, it had been little things, tiny clues he hadn't picked up on at the time; an ill-concealed look here… an involuntary gesture there. Now that he was aware of it, Rhys realized it had only ever happened when talking about his old life. Was that just a coincidence, or did it actually mean something? She didn't strike him as the jealous type, so what was going on? He didn't have time to ask before Sekami was opening the airlock door and striding through the hatch.

Slinging the pack over his shoulders, he followed her down the ramp and began to pick his way through the fallen trees. Here and there, Sekami would stop to turn over a moss-covered object, searching for debris that might have originated from a crash. Most of what she unearthed were just rocks or rotting pieces of wood. After thirty minutes of this, they'd barely gone half a kilometer when she finally discovered something. During one of her kick-and-flip maneuvers, she overturned a piece of metal distinctly artificial in origin. She yelled in surprise and beckoned for them to come see.

"Look at this," she cried, almost manic in her discovery of the rounded plate. "I knew there was something here!"

Without waiting for them to reply, she hitched up her pack and began to run, vaulting over rocks and logs, heading farther down the stretch of truncated vegetation. The two men exchanged a glance, then ran after her. By the time she stopped, Rhys was gasping for air. He collapsed to his knees, chest heaving as he fought for each ragged breath in the thin atmosphere. Eventually, his pounding heart began to slow, and the black edges that had crept into his vision began to fade. Sitting back on his heels, he nearly toppled over, suddenly aware of what rested in front of them.

Dug into the ground was the carcass of a ship. He hadn't seen it before, in part because of his own physiological distress, but mostly due to the ferns and other small plants that had taken root around it. The vessel was almost buried, a huge mound of dirt enveloping the craft as it ground to a halt some indeterminate number of years ago. Moss grew everywhere, making the entire structure look like some hulking greenish-brown sentinel. Walking around the mound, Rhys realized the hull wasn't just gouged open. It was split entirely in two.

"Where's the rest of it?" he inquired.

"Come again?" Conrad asked.

"Look at it. Those holes aren't just damage to the hull. That's all some kind of internal framing," he explained, pointing at the cross-section of the ship. "This is just part of a bigger vessel. So, where's the rest of it?"

Conrad looked closer and nodded his head. Now, he too seemed to notice there was a portion of the ship unaccounted for.

"None of the drones picked up anything else like this. If the rest didn't burn up on entry, it's probably at the bottom of an ocean," the pilot replied, shrugging.

They stepped carefully through the jagged opening and into the dark innards of the ship. Rhys pulled the headlamp from his bag and clicked it on. He hesitated for a moment, then removed the pistol. Just in case. Inside, the wilds had claimed the place for its own. The air felt cool and damp, the same prolific moss growing everywhere he looked. Rhys moved deeper into the vessel, swinging the beam of his headlamp into places that hadn't seen light in years. Sekami and Conrad followed behind, the luminance from their own headlamps casting long, ghostly shadows ahead of him. Creeping forward, he heard a loud snap to his right, and he instinctively leveled the pistol toward the sound. A streak of fur flashed across his path, and he barely managed to restrain himself from firing blindly into the dark.

"What the hell was that?" Conrad demanded.

"I don't think it likes the light," Rhys said, his heart pounding. "Keep an eye, just don't shoot me in the back."

They continued forward and stepped into the remains of a partially crushed cockpit. The windows were obscured by the dirt mound outside, and only pinpoints of light entered through small holes in the hull. The interior of the craft felt strangely organic, as if it had grown from the ground like some twisted, grotesque plant. Rhys tried to remember what the grül craft in Volkerson's IHR had looked like, but his surroundings were too far lost to time for any reasonable comparison.

As he moved through the cockpit, he inspected the broken equipment, most of it covered in excrement from whatever creature had decided to make the ship its home. There was so much to see in this strange, unfamiliar wreckage, but at the same time, nothing at all. Glancing around, Rhys knew they weren't likely to find anything here. Except for the bones of a few small rodents, the ship appeared empty. He turned to leave, the beam of his headlamp swinging through the darkness. A muted glint caught his eye, and he hesitated. Looking back, its source made the breath catch in his throat. There, sitting on the floor, was an ugly black sphere, its hammered surface weakly reflecting the light of his headlamp.

"Holy shit," he breathed, unable to believe what he was looking at. Sekami had been right all along. With nothing more than a fool's hope, they had discovered another machine. He felt the hairs on the back of his neck stand up, filled with sudden fear that its owner was lurking in the shadows behind them. He spun around, panicked, but there was nothing… only the backs of his companions.

"Hey, uh, guys," he called out. "Take a look at this."

They walked up to stand beside him, the beams of their lamps washing over the machine. He heard Sekami's softly indrawn breath and a confused 'the hell is that?' from Conrad. Moving forward, Rhys crouched down to get a better look. Unlike the device in the lab that floated unsupported, this one lay motionless on the floor as if it had been dumped unceremoniously in the corner. Rhys let his hands hover over the machine's surface for a moment, the memory of its disastrous effects at the forefront of his mind. He spared a questioning glance at Sekami, and she nodded her approval. Taking a deep breath, he steadied himself before grasping the orb with both hands.

Something sparked inside him, and he felt a faint vibration, then nothing. Without warning, the machine deformed within his grasp. They all watched in horror as the blackened sphere began to disintegrate, crumbling and cracking between Rhys's hands until nothing but a pile of brittle shell and dust lay at his feet. He was frozen, hands still outstretched, shocked by the abrupt turn of events. All the anticipation that had built inside him evaporated. Part of him had hoped they wouldn't find another machine, but when they had, his will to fight had been rekindled, only to be snuffed out an instant later. Unless they could defy the impossible odds of finding a third, there was nothing left to do but run and hide. Still dazed, he dusted his hands and stumbled back through darkness to the world outside.

"That's it," Sekami said angrily, stepping into the sunlight behind him. It was the first time she's spoken since finding the wreckage. "This entire trip has been for nothing!"

Her anger, though sudden, came as no surprise. From the start, both he and Conrad had been skeptical of her plan. She'd never been able to offer a guarantee of success. In the end, though, her instinct had been correct. They hadn't found the turandians. Instead, they'd stumbled upon the very thing she'd hoped the lost expeditions would lead them to. If only for a moment, he'd held another of the deadly machines in his grasp... and none of that mattered. They'd overcome all the odds to get here, to find another device, only to have it literally fall to pieces in his hands.

"It's not been for nothing," he said gently, offering words that might comfort her. "Sekami, all the evidence pointed against us finding anything here, but we trusted your gut and came anyway. There still might be something–"

"There's nothing else here," she bit back, visibly upset. "The odds of finding another one..."

"Can't we send out more drones? If we look for the other part of the ship–"

"It won't matter! Don't you see? Everyone we know is dead, and it's all been for nothing," she said again, shaking her head. Her whole body had begun to tremble uncontrollably. "God,

Rhys, the things I've done because I believed in Dr. Volkerson's cause. People have died because of him, because of *me*. I've lied to our scientists, to my friends, to you…"

"That's in the past. We've been over this," Rhys replied. He took her by the shoulders and tried to console her. "I understand why you had to–"

"You don't understand!" she cried, shaking free of his grasp. Angry tears brimmed her eyes. "I've done more to hurt you than you can possibly imagine."

"What do you mean?" Rhys demanded, a knot beginning to grow in the pit of his stomach. Considering the circumstances, her distress seemed excessive, over the top. It was beginning to freak him out. "Sekami, what are you talking about?"

Her lip trembled while she searched for the words to describe her transgressions. Looking into those strikingly violet eyes, Rhys wanted nothing more than to hold her. To tell her that, no matter what, it would all be okay. Eventually, Sekami found her voice and confessed the guilt that had consumed her.

"You aren't from the past. I've known you all my life."

RHYS CRASHED BLINDLY through the underbrush, barely noticing the branches that tore at his clothes and left angry red scratches on his skin. If anything, the pain only fueled his headlong retreat as he tried to escape the terrible revelation that had just been laid at his feet. *You aren't from the past. I've known you all my life.* Over and over, Sekami's words resounded in his brain like some sadistic drumbeat... a dirge marching him forward against his will.

The implications of what she was telling him hadn't registered at first. He'd just stood there confused, waiting for the punchline, until slowly realizing it would never come. When her words finally sank in, they'd hit him like a gut punch. The more she told him, the worse it got. Everything he thought he knew was a lie. All his memories from before waking up on that godforsaken cryostation were false. His dog, his time as a mariner, the *Denebola* going down... *Oh, Jesus,* he thought, another earth-shattering realization smacking him in the face. Anne... the wife he'd loved so dearly. The pain and guilt surrounding her memory was nothing more than a fabrication, a tool to serve some twisted plan that had been concocted by Volkerson. It all boiled down to that fucking snake, who'd somehow convinced Sekami to play along.

He felt lost, a sailor set adrift in a turbulent sea without the guiding light of a single star. His experiences, good and bad, were what defined him. With that foundation gone, Rhys felt himself spiraling toward an abyss from which there would be no return. In his haste, he stumbled on an exposed root and came crashing to the ground. He felt a white-hot stab of pain as his teeth banged closed on his tongue, and the metallic tang of blood filled his mouth. Laying in the dirt, his mind spinning uncontrollably, he screamed at the top of his lungs until his throat was raw. It was a sound full of rage and sorrow and confusion, all mixed together in a growing storm of anguish.

The meaning of time ceased. He couldn't have said how much passed before he picked himself up off the ground. It could have been minutes... hours... days... it didn't matter. Nothing mattered. Slogging forward, his shoulders heavy with despair, Rhys stumbled toward a break in the trees and found himself overlooking a cliff to the valley below. Where the ground abruptly ended, a few trees leaned precariously over the edge. He trudged forward with purpose and stopped when his toes found the crumbling precipice. Far below, jagged rocks beckoned like fingers. *It would be so easy*, he thought, a lump forming in his throat as he teetered on the edge.

"Just do it!" he screamed. It would be a fitting end, killing himself the way he had wanted when first learning of his fabricated wife's death. All he had to do was take a final step...

Once again, he hesitated a moment too long, and his resolve broke. He backed away from the edge and collapsed to the ground, his whole body racked with angry sobs. Slowly, filled with despair more profound than anything in his fabricated past, Rhys drifted off to sleep.

Dusk had arrived when he finally awoke, dragged from his fitful stupor by freezing night air. Shivering, he pulled the blanket from his pack and wrapped it around himself. His teeth began to chatter, cold nipping at his ears and nose, but nothing in the universe would compel him to return to the ship. He folded his arms across his chest, the blanket's heat-reflective material crinkling noisily around him.

Looking up, he saw the first of countless stars winking at him through a deepening blue-black sky. An orange hue glowed on the horizon as the last rays of the setting star cast eerie shadows across the alien planet. How could something so magnificent exist when all he felt was pain? It felt like a sick joke, as if the universe was making light of the transgressions that had been committed against him. Pulling the blanket tighter, he propped his back against a rock that overlooked the valley. Darkness had almost swallowed the world around him when he heard a beep in his ear.

"Rhys?" It was Sekami's voice. "Are you there?"

He reached up and touched his ear, turning off the CIM. It was too soon to face her again. He just wanted to be left alone. The things she had told him only left more unanswered questions, until her words had finally overloaded his mind.

In her crisis of doubt, she had confessed everything. Through painful tears, she had explained their childhood together… about the trauma they shared over a life on the run from the grül… about the fleeting moments of reprieve where they laughed over meals… about the unspoken love that had grown between them, and how that love had never been allowed to flourish under Volkerson's hawkish gaze. The young girl from Sekami's IHR memory, sitting on the hill with Jenco, hadn't been talking about playing with Volkerson, *she had been talking about Rhys!* But how? How did any of that make sense? If he wasn't from the past, where was he born? Who were his parents? And how had he come to be in the company of the outlaw scientists in the first place? A numbing reality began to creep icily into his veins, and Rhys realized he had no idea who he was.

When he demanded to know why they had deceived him, Sekami's answer was more devastating than he could've imagined. In a small voice, she told him how Jenco Ryele had been like a father to him, nurturing him through the pain of learning to use the grül device in a way Dr. Volkerson never could. The man had taught him about machines, about engineering, how to fly... an education that had been the source of his exceptional mechanical intuition over the past months. It didn't come from some fabricated story about marine engineering but a father figure he couldn't remember.

The seed of their deception came at the moment of Earth's desolation, nearly four years ago. Rhys had been with Dr. Volkerson on the bridge and seen the carnage firsthand, had watched Jenco blinked out of existence along with the rest of humanity. Overwhelmed with grief, his will to fight, along with his sanity, had died with the man he held so dear. Volkerson, too, had suffered great loss. Greater, in fact, than his own. Not only had his friend and partner been lost in the attack, but also Rhys. His only hope against their seemingly undefeatable enemy had become useless. As a last resort, he reshaped Rhys's memory into one that had no ties to the past... a mind that would rather forget... that might one day rejoin his fight against the grül.

Rhys felt violated. Every instinct he possessed was based on a set of experiences that weren't real. If he couldn't trust those, then what? He wondered for a moment if he would ever regain his lost identity, but another thought struck him, one even more disconcerting. Did he want to? He imagined it would be like committing suicide; a conscious decision to destroy his present awareness in the hopes of regaining some unknown past. Maybe the old memories would be better... somehow, he doubted it. At least now, there was some iota of happiness in the life he had never led. He realized suddenly that he would never go through with it, if the opportunity to retrieve his past ever presented itself. Regardless of whether they were painful, the few remaining memories he possessed were the only ones he knew. It was almost a relief, in a way, knowing the source of his pain and guilt wasn't real. Almost.

Dawn was only a few hours away by the time Rhys dozed off again. When he awoke, the stiffness in his neck was a painful reminder of the rock he'd slept against. He struggled to his feet, joints cracking loudly in the crisp morning air. There was still a faint taste of blood in his mouth from his fall the previous day. Glancing around, he searched for a familiar landmark to gauge his location but found none. It didn't matter. The last thing he wanted to do right now was return to the ship. Not yet. He didn't know if he'd be able to forgive Sekami. Maybe someday, after much atonement and a hell of a lot more explanation, but today was not that day. Volkerson on the other hand... Rhys felt a twinge of disappointment knowing the man was already dead. A picture formed in his mind of hoisting a rock high, the scientist cowering in the dirt, hand raised for mercy...

From his makeshift camp, Rhys could see trampled brush where he'd staggered out of the trees toward the cliff's edge. That direction would lead him back to the ship and back to a reality he wanted to avoid a while longer. Instead, he turned and walked along the precipice, the morning sun warming his neck while his mind churned through the things Sekami had confessed. He had covered nearly half a dozen kilometers when he came to a river, its roiling water falling in a misty curtain over the edge. One look at the turbulent surface and he knew it was impassable, the choice to turn back or follow the river his only options. He chose the latter, and the forest thickened as he traveled upstream.

The underbrush was so dense Rhys was forced out onto the large boulders lining the riverbank. He hopped from one to the next, carefully picking his way over the rocks. When the gently sloping grade steepened, he looked up and saw the mouth of a cave nestled into the hillside. He climbed higher, losing sight of the cavern when he came to a stony ledge above his head. Grunting, he caught the shelf with his hands and pulled up to see what lay beyond.

To the left of the cave was a small open glade, sunlight dotting the ground through the treetop foliage high above. It had been cleared of boulders, only dirt and pebbles covering the ground. Several pieces of disassembled machinery sat near the edge, a pile of discarded parts rusting in the center. The trash heap was reminiscent of the wreckage they'd discovered the previous day, but it was the thing least worthy of his attention. There, at the mouth of the cave, its back to the river, sat a solitary figure. The creature was hunched over something on the ground, a carcass of some kind. Tufts of fur drifted over the dirt clearing, and a patch of blood-soaked earth lay at the stranger's feet. Surprised by another presence, Rhys dropped out of sight, sure the glade's occupant could hear his heart's thunderous beating.

He hadn't expected to come across anyone up here. Careful not to make a sound, he braced one foot against a large boulder and grabbed the ledge a second time. Pulling up to his chin, Rhys peeked over the edge. The figure, still facing away from him, was covered in a tattered cloak, its features hidden from sight. Even hunched, he could tell the stranger stood over two meters tall. Poking out from beneath the cloak, Rhys saw a weapon of some kind carried in a thick leathery holster. He craned his neck to see more, placing most of his weight onto the foot pressing against the boulder. To his dismay, the rock shifted, and resounding crunch filled the air. The figure turned toward the sound, giving Rhys his first good look at its face. He recognized the gray mottling, the red-streaked skin, and ducked his head out of sight. Fear froze his insides, and his hands began to tremble.

*Shit, shit, shit,* he thought on the verge of panic. It was one of *them,* a grül! Adrenaline coursed through his veins, the instinct to flee kicking into high gear as he hurried his way back down the slippery rocks. Without warning, both feet shot out from under him, and he went tumbling down the boulders. Landing hard on a wide flat rock, he couldn't suppress the cry of pain that escaped his lips. He clapped a hand over his mouth and strained his ears, listening hard to hear if he was being followed. Not daring to breathe, he waited for what felt like an eternity, but nothing could be heard over the roaring river. A minute passed. Then two, and he felt his nerves begin to settle. Maybe it hadn't noticed him…

As if out of thin air, a six-fingered hand the size of a dinner plate wrenched him off the rock and tossed him like a rag doll. He skidded to a halt in the dirt a dozen paces from where he'd been a moment before and scrambled to his feet to face the oncoming threat. The warrior advanced with surprising speed, the ragged cloak slipping from its shoulders as it came. Thin, sinewy muscles rippled beneath the grül's leathery skin, and the snarl on its face left no doubt as to its intent. Rhys slung the pack from his shoulders, fumbling with the buckles and searching frantically inside. Where the hell was his fucking pistol?! When his fingers touched cool metal, he leveled the weapon and fired. Shot after shot grazed off the alien's tough hide. Unfazed, it reached for its own weapon and drew it calmly out of the holster. The creature had barely slowed its forward momentum from the onslaught Rhys rained down. In a moment of cold realization, he knew he was going to die at the hands of the grül after all.

Out of nowhere, Conrad burst through the trees, tackling Rhys out of the way just as the warrior opened fire. The muzzle glowed white-hot as a burst of energy rocketed out of the barrel, striking the pilot in the shoulder, and sending a spray of red across the forest floor. He shrieked in pain as they fell to the ground in a tangle of limbs. Rhys scrambled to his feet and began dragging the wounded man, but Conrad shook him off.

"Help her!" he screamed, pointing at the grül with his uninjured arm.

Sekami had arrived to join the fray and launched herself onto the alien's back, swinging wildly as it tried to throw her off. Rhys scooped up the pistol and rushed toward them. He was still several paces away when Sekami could no longer maintain her grip and fell to the ground in a cloud of dust. The grül raised its weapon toward her but before it could fire, Rhys unloaded another barrage from his pistol. He knew it wouldn't kill the beast, but it had the desired effect all the same.

Distracted by this fresh attack, the grül turned its weapon on him and pulled the trigger. A flash of white light flickered weakly at the muzzle, sputtered for a moment, and then went out. Confusion passed over the alien's face as the gun malfunctioned in its hand. In its moment of hesitation, Sekami jumped to her feet and kicked the weapon away. A second kick to one of its legs brought the creature down on one knee, and Rhys rushed forward to smash his pistol into its head. Snarling, it caught his arm and threw him back before slamming a large fist into Sekami's chest. She landed hard on the dusty ground and rolled away in a fit of coughing.

"Just die, you bastard!" Conrad screamed from behind them.

The pilot hefted his huge rifle and fired. The projectile blew a fist-sized hole in the creature's shoulder, but still it continued to fight. He shot three more times before the warrior finally collapsed, blood pooling around its corpse. Drained of the strength to keep the weapon raised, the rifle slipped from the pilot's hand and thudded in the dirt. He grasped his injured arm, teetered for a moment in shock, then sat down heavily on the nearest boulder. Rhys crawled to his feet and slowly approached their fallen enemy. He nudged the corpse with the toe of his boot.

"Is it dead?"

"I can plug him with another round if you'd like," Conrad replied unsteadily, "but from the looks of him, I'd guess he only had another few days before he was worm food."

Rhys frowned while he inspected the body. Unlike the grül who'd invaded Proxima Station, this one's physical characteristics showed the telling effects of disease. The tufted hair around its ears was white, the long fingers twisted and knobby. Raw sores covered its hide, and yellow, jaundiced eyes peered up at him in a lifeless stare. Milky cataracts dulled the fierce intelligence that had once burned there. If this was what it took to bring down a single ailing warrior, he shuddered to think of the outcome if he'd stumbled across a horde of healthy ones.

"Don't touch it," he replied, beginning to tremble with relief and leftover adrenaline. "Looks sick."

He sensed movement from the corner of his eye and noticed Sekami had come to stand beside the mutilated body. An awkward silence hung between them, neither finding the words nor the courage to speak. He knew he should say something... 'thanks for saving me' for starters, but the words kept sticking in his throat. He was still angry, almost hating the fact that, once again, she had to come to his aid. Had he done something so terrible in a past life that the universe felt he deserved such unrelenting punishment? The question filled him with a disquieting sense of uncertainty. It had been meant to be rhetorical, but Rhys did indeed have a past life... one he had no memory of. He'd never really believed in Karma but was willing to revisit that stance considering everything that had happened. Before he could wallow in any further self-pity, however, the dead grül's hand shot out and grasped him by the ankle. Yelling in surprise and terror, he tried to scramble back, but the alien held a crushing grip on his leg. Rhys looked down into the creature's milky eyes, and its mouth opened in a snarl.

"You... should... be... dead," it croaked.

With a howl, Sekami brought her boot down on its head, all her hate and anger toward the grülbarvoc boiling over as she stomped again and again, continuing well after the old warrior stopped moving. Rhys kicked his leg free of its lifeless grasp and pulled her away from the bloodied corpse. Slowly, the anger faded from her shoulders, and a look of guilt and sadness he'd come to recognize lined her face.

"Rhys, I... I'm so sorry," she stammered.

He stood there awkwardly, torn between anger, betrayal, and his own maddening desire to comfort the woman who'd saved his life yet again. He wanted to yell at her, to tell her how pissed and hurt and betrayed he felt. Standing over their fallen enemy, Rhys struggled to define the emotional tumult inside him. Was he still angry? Certainly. Did he want answers? Without question. Would he forgive the woman with a shared past he couldn't remember? He didn't know. More than ever, he just felt lost.

"You should check on Conrad," he said, changing the subject to avoid acknowledging her apology.

Her lip made an involuntary twitch as if she was about to burst into tears, but they never came. Digging wordlessly into her pack, she pulled out a med kit and took Conrad's arm to inspect his injury. He let out a sharp intake of breath and reflexively pulled away. Rhys watched from a distance as she dressed the wound. The attack, one meant for him, had left a hideous gash in Conrad's shoulder. The edges were charred black, cauterized by the therleon energy harnessed within the grülbarvoc weapon. White bone poked out from where his flesh had burned away. Through the pilot's colorful swearing, Sekami cleaned away dirt and grime before applying a sterile bandage. When she was finished, she helped him to his feet.

Rhys walked back to where the dead grül lay, searching the area for the weapon Sekami had kicked from its grasp. He found it wedged between two boulders near the river and fished it out. It felt heavy in his hand as he turned it over, inspecting it. The gun was old, countless tiny chips and scratches etched into the worn surface. It too, looked as if there weren't much life left in the aged weapon. Luckily for him, it had misfired. Gripping the handle, a tingling sensation like the one he'd experienced with the stolen therleon generator crept up his arm. Pointing it at their conquered foe, he squeezed the trigger. There was no white-hot burst of energy, no weak flickering light. Nothing. Rhys squeezed it half a dozen times with the same result.

"Piece of shit," he said, about to toss the gun away but changed his mind. Even if the thing didn't work, they still might be able to learn something from it. Thinking better of his decision to discard their only artifact, he stuck it into his pack and zipped the bag close. He heard Sekami call his name and looked up to see her standing at the cave entrance, waiting. Pushing his personal feelings aside for a moment, he climbed back to the ledge where he'd first seen the grül and pulled himself up. Conrad nestled himself against some rocks, the large grül-killing rifle in his lap. Rhys pulled the headlamp from his pack, clicked it on, and followed Sekami inside.

They crept through the dark, uncomfortably aware of how loudly their feet crunched over the rock-strewn ground. Eventually, the tunnel opened into a larger chamber, and the beams from their headlamps illuminated the dead grül's lair. The sparse surroundings offered little of interest; a few filthy blankets, a cracked pot, a makeshift cup, and not much else. Looking around, Rhys knew they would find even fewer answers here than they had at the crash site. It was one more stop in a long list of dead ends, another proverbial middle finger from the universe at large. Dejectedly, he shook his head and turned away. Sekami followed behind, and they stepped back out into the bright midday sun.

"What do you think it was doing here?" Rhys asked, squinting as his eyes adjusted from the dark.

"I don't know," she replied with a shrug, "but it's been here awhile… based on all the junk laying around. Why it came to this planet in the first place, I have no idea. At least we know what happened to the turandian expeditions. How that helps us…"

Rhys gazed absentmindedly at the mouth of the cave and scuffed his boot in the dirt, kicking distractedly at a partially buried rock. What were they supposed to do now? They had found a machine that was beyond repair and a grül warrior on the brink of death… exactly what they'd been looking for, only to have those very things be as little use to them as if they'd found nothing at all. If there was no clear path forward, why go anywhere? Maybe they should just stay here, hidden on the Earth-like world of BQ3…

"HEY-Y-Y-Y!"

Conrad's voice floated up to them, echoing through the trees. He frowned questioningly at Sekami and hurried over to the rocky ledge to see what their companion was shouting about. Looking down to where the alien's mangled body still lay, he saw the pilot jumping up and down. Something was in his hand, and he waved it through the air with his uninjured arm. Rhys shook his head and cupped his ears to let the pilot know they couldn't hear him. Conrad stuck whatever he was holding into his pocket and tapped his ear.

"BAIN just picked up a distress call coming in over the emergency frequency," he announced, words tumbling out in his excitement. "The scientists from Proxima Station are alive!"

# CHAPTER 31

# PICKING UP THE TRAIL

DOUBT HAD BEGUN to fill Fleet Captain Xorin's mind, worming its way into his brain like a parasite. There had been no trace of the lost ship since leaving Proxima Station. He sensed a palpable tension in the air as he scanned the bridge, could see the crew's sideways looks, and hear their muttered comments. Uncertainty had spread like a virus until it threatened to infect even his resolute nature. Too much time had passed without any sign of where their quarry had gone. Now, he feared the trail was cold once again.

The lost ship's disappearance wasn't the only thing hanging like a black cloud over the crew. His directive to develop grülbarvoc-killing weapons hadn't been well received. Three of his warriors refused, even after being subjected to a particularly vicious Duoranath. Xorin had ordered Feyt to make examples of them, and the Commander had begrudgingly obeyed. Now, he felt the beginnings of discontent. The crew would embrace the Küddish teachings, he knew, but their loyalty to him had been tested by the prospect of dishonoring themselves. To kill a fellow grülbarvoc outside the use of hand-to-hand combat was forbidden, in the Old Ways and the New. Had he asked too much? Was abandoning that sacred doctrine to ensure the survival of their species too high a price?

Anger flashed inside him at the doubt poisoning his thoughts. Doubt was a sign of weakness. It was a symptom that preceded the fall of every great leader. Never in his life had he questioned the decisions he'd made. He was a *Fleet Captain*, born of blood and battle, and the last of those who might once again make the grül-barvoc strong. If his crew would not follow him willingly, he would just need to–

An unexpected interruption from one of his warriors invaded his thoughts.

"Captain, we have intercepted a distress call!"

"Where is it coming from?" he asked, pushing aside his smoldering anger, and leaning forward in anticipation.

"A small survival craft," the warrior replied. "Not far from our current position."

Xorin sat back, annoyed. If it wasn't their missing ship, he didn't care to be bothered with it. He was about to deliver a blistering rebuke when the oblivious soldier turned to face him. Glaring down, Xorin opened his mouth in a snarl but faltered. Something had set the warrior's eyes burning with excitement, and he clenched his jaw shut to wait for the rest of the report.

"The call was received by at least one other ship."

"And?"

"Sir, the drive signature of the responding vessel matches the one we are looking for."

A thrill of optimism filled Xorin at this news. In a stroke of dumb luck, the final loose end in their long campaign was once again within his grasp. He slipped his hands into the shimmering control interface to inform the fleet of their discovery. *We have located the missing ship. Upon gaining a shooting solution, disable engines with the intent to capture. Our defiance of the High Council will not be in vain. The last of the Interloper's confederates will become the first sacrificed in our revival of the Küddarian Brotherhood. A new dawn of grülbarvoc supremacy is at hand, where all our people shall be spared the horrors of the Sickness. Do not despair, brothers, and prepare yourselves for glory!*

He removed his hands from the console but found the young sergeant still staring up at him expectantly.

"Something else?"

"The survival craft," the warrior said, nodding, "the one issuing the distress call... you will not believe what they have onboard."

# CHAPTER 32
# THE DISTRESS CALL

SEKAMI SCRAMBLED down from their perch, and Rhys hurried after her. She set a blistering pace, and one misstep would send them tumbling down the riverbank with a broken ankle or worse. She barely seemed to land on one boulder, before bounding recklessly to the next. By the time they reached the spot where Conrad waited, Rhys was thoroughly winded, beads of sweat trickling down his brow.

"When?" Sekami demanded through her own ragged gasps.

"Not two minutes ago," the pilot replied, pulling the thing he'd been waving out of his pocket and handing it to her. The device was small, about the size of a matchbox. "Once the ship picked up the transmission, BAIN relayed the distress call here."

Supported in Sekami's hand, he pressed his thumb against its surface and the device sprung to life. A hologram materialized in front of them, showing the distinct hair-covered features of Otaan Yabar. Rhys's heart leapt at seeing the familiar face. At least one of the team was still alive! When the message began to play, Sekami held it up so they could hear.

"Mayday, mayday. This is Otaan Yabar of the S/V Hermes. Our survival craft has lost propulsion, and support systems are failing. We have two souls onboard. Broadcasting on all emergency frequencies. Anyone, please respond. Mayday, mayday. This is Otaan Yabar…"

The message looped back and began to replay.

"Two onboard… I wonder who else made it," Sekami mused, gazing at the device in her hand, before handing it back with a renewed air of urgency. "We need to get back to the *Kestrel*."

She set out toward the ship, vanishing into the trees without waiting for a reply. Rhys slung the pack over his shoulders and grasped Conrad by the hand, pulling him to his feet. The pilot hefted the grül-killing rifle in his good arm, grimacing in pain whenever it slid awkwardly out of position. Seeing his discomfort, Rhys plucked the weapon from his grasp, and Conrad nodded his thanks, grateful to pass the burden to someone with two uninjured arms. Hurrying along as best they could, it wasn't long before Sekami's grueling pace had them all laboring for breath.

As they picked their way through the dense underbrush, Rhys was astounded by how far he'd gone in his blind charge through the forest. Sweat and dirt stung his eyes as he worked his way forward, wincing when brambles left bright red tracks down his already scratched arms. When he stepped over the last rotting log into the clearing of the grül crash site, his knees nearly buckled in exhaustion. He sat down heavily on a mossy trunk and watched Sekami soldier her way up the ramp to the airlock. Conrad, huffing along behind, sat down next to him to catch his breath.

"You know, I keep thinkin'," the pilot wheezed, gazing intently at him. "You're a pretty lucky guy."

Rhys snorted humorlessly. "How's that?"

"Well, the way I figure, it's lucky we found you when we did."

"Uh huh."

"And it was lucky there was only one dyin' grül…"

"This going anywhere?"

"… then to top it all off, I'd say it was pretty goddamn lucky that thing didn't go off and turn your head into a spaghetti dinner," Conrad finished, gesturing toward the pack where the grül weapon was stowed. "You mind explainin' any of that to me?"

Rhys didn't know how to respond. There was a note in Conrad's voice he couldn't place. It wasn't accusatory, per se, but for some reason, it still made him defensive. How could he tell Conrad what he wanted to know when he didn't even know himself? So much new information had been dropped on him in the last twenty-four hours, he was still processing what it all meant. The only thing that kept him from drawing some very dark conclusions, conclusions his mind couldn't handle, was to avoid thinking about it as much as possible. Like that would ever work. He wasn't just obsessed with what Sekami had told him; he was consumed by it.

"I can't. At this point, you know as much about me as I do," he finally replied. If Sekami had truly told him everything she knew, then the only person who could have given him more information was already dead. Unless... his thoughts darkened as they turned toward Volkerson. If that sonofabitch was still among the living, there was going to be hell to pay. "Let's go see who else is alive."

They dragged their tired bodies up the gangway and found Sekami in the cockpit, hunched over the navigation console. She didn't acknowledge them when they entered but instead remained focused on her task. When she finally glanced up, her face was alight with a glimmer of hope.

"Otaan Yabar and Marasa Bok naal are both still alive," she said, pointing toward the star chart in front of her. "Their call originated from here, about fifty hours away at max burn rate."

"How are we just now finding out about this? We've been broadcasting our own call for months," Conrad exclaimed. "Wouldn't they know to monitor your super-secret frequency?"

"I would've thought so... it doesn't make sense to me either," Sekami answered with a frown. "And what would they be doing all the way out here, of all places?"

"That'll be the first of about a thousand questions I'll have when we pick them up."

Conrad positioned himself at the controls and brought the engines to life, Rhys and Sekami strapping into their seats. The vessel steadily gained altitude until bursting through the clouds in a flurry of swirling white. Looking down at BQ3's unfettered wilderness, Rhys felt a pang of regret as they departed the Earth-like planet. It felt like home... the one he remembered. He may never have actually been to Montana, but it would always hold a special place in his heart. As he stared pensively through the cockpit window, he thought he might like to come back some-day... if they survived.

Sitting back, he closed his eyes and felt his body press gently into the seat as the ship accelerated to cruising speed. He had been fearful of this moment, the point at which there would be nothing to distract him from the terrible knowledge he'd been given. Now, his mind was left to wander down whatever path it chose, and there would be nothing he could do to stop it. The sound of footsteps and the cockpit door snapping shut compelled him to crack open an eye, and he saw Sekami sitting next to him. She was looking at him with a mixture of sadness and relief, as if a great weight had been lifted from her shoulders. He didn't share her sentiment. If anything, he felt more conflicted than ever.

"You can't imagine how hard it's been," she began. "Having lived my entire life beside you, laughing with you, loving you, and seeing you look at me without recognition, without any memory of the things we've shared."

"I'm sure it's been awful," he replied. There was more bite to his voice than he'd intended, and she looked ashamed. *It was probably true, though*, he admitted to himself. It would indeed be terrible to have someone he held so dear not know who he was... but if she truly cared about him, how could she have allowed something so awful to happen? "Why did you go along with it? The mind wipe. I seem to recall hearing you tell Marasa that Volkerson would never do such a thing."

Sekami didn't say anything at first, and he could tell she must have asked herself that same question hundreds of times. He didn't know if that made it any better.

"I wasn't there when the grül attacked Earth," she began tentatively, choosing each word carefully, as if the wrong ones might be the difference between life and death. "When I first heard what happened, Marcus told me you'd died with my father."

This caught Rhys off guard. When he'd thought Volkerson's actions could sink no lower, some new piece of information was added to the scientist's growing list of offenses. Why would he tell Sekami that Rhys had died? So she would be more obedient? More determined? He drew a blank, unable to imagine any good reason to deceive Sekami of all people. To her benefit, he felt some of his anger toward her begin to ease.

"I was heartbroken. I hated the grül, hated myself even more for being the one who'd survived. Marcus urged me to use that hate. He was sure we could still discover a way to use the machine to avenge you, my father, everyone. I tried to keep going, but it was so much harder without you," Sekami explained, trailing off as she was forced to relive the harrowing memories. "For almost three years, I thought you were dead. When I found evidence you'd been abandoned on a remote cryostation, I confronted Dr. Volkerson and demanded to know why. He admitted to what he'd done and told me what I wanted to know... the reason he'd discarded you and lied to me."

"Because I watched your father die," Rhys said, a lump in his throat making it difficult to speak. She nodded.

"Seeing it crippled your mind with grief. After it happened, you... you tried to blow yourself out an airlock! Dr. Volkerson only wanted to spare me the pain of watching you spiral into madness. He imagined thinking you'd died with my father would be an easier burden to bear."

"That's great for you, but what about my memories?" Rhys demanded. He was torn between a growing sense of pity for Sekami and smoldering rage toward Volkerson. "If he'd already screwed with them, why give me so many fucking terrible ones?"

"He tried to help you, to find some other way to lessen the pain of my father's passing, but nothing worked. No matter what he tried, your real memories always broke through. He couldn't just make it all go away. He tried, but the trauma was too severe. It had to be attached to something real for you, something tangible. If you'd just felt this terrible sense of loss, the cognitive reconstruction would never have stuck. That's the reason your new memories contain so much pain, the reason for Anne... for all of it."

It was a depressing prospect, knowing nothing in his identity was real. He felt an empty spot, a hole that had, until recently, been occupied by the memory of a fake, suicidal wife. Very badly, he wanted that void to be filled by something, memories of Sekami before he'd been frozen perhaps, but there was nothing... just the empty, gaping chasm of sorrow Volkerson had been afraid of. Jenco, despite everything he'd done, must've been a great man. Rhys couldn't imagine killing himself over the death of a surrogate father figure, but maybe that was a good thing. The cards were on the table now, and Rhys didn't feel himself slipping into madness. That, at least, was good news.

"It took countless attempts, but I persuaded Marcus we'd never succeed without you. He let me return to the cryostation on condition I wouldn't reveal your past. He was convinced it would disrupt the reconstruction if you found out. I disagreed but promised to keep my end of the bargain since it was the only way I'd ever see you again."

Her words weren't sugarcoated but offered a little comfort all the same. Everything she'd done had been to get him back, to honor the memory of her father, and not out of some blind loyalty to Volkerson. Correct or not, Sekami had followed her heart and had tried to do the right thing. Even though he had no memory of the man, Rhys felt an emptiness when she spoke of her father. He wished he could remember Jenco Ryele, to offer her comforting words that didn't feel hollow, as if from a stranger.

"The only thing I've felt since learning the truth is hate," he confessed, not knowing what else to say. "For Volkerson. I wish I could've been the one to hurt him, to *kill* him, and I don't know how to let that go. He feels as much responsible for what's happened to me as the grül. When we received the distress call, I hoped he was one of the survivors."

"What he did– what *we* did– was unforgivable," she admitted, her eyes cast downward with growing shame. "I won't ask you to continue helping me. If we're able to fix the *Hermes* survival craft, I'll stay with Marasa and Otaan Yabar. You and Conrad will be free to go your separate way."

Hearing her voice this proposition, Rhys realized that was the one thing he didn't want to happen. The last of his anger toward her melted away, and he took her hand in his grasp. At his touch, she lifted her eyes to meet his gaze.

"You and Conrad are the only two people left in this galaxy who mean anything to me," he said quietly. "I'm not going anywhere without you."

# CHAPTER 33
# THE TRAP

WHEN THE *KESTREL* reached her destination two days later, her occupants looked out into a sea of infinite darkness. The nearest planet was the one they'd departed, its life-giving star just one more point of light in the dotted expanse. Conrad reached for the controls and pushed a button to scan for the survival craft's homing beacon. They all waited with bated breath, listening to the soft pinging, until a dot appeared on the display, glowing like a signal fire. Excitedly, Sekami leaned forward and pointed at the screen.

"There they are! Thirty thousand kilometers and closing," she announced and spun around to face the communications console. She flipped a switch, and a small blue status light came on. "*Hermes* survival craft, this is Sekami Ryele aboard the *S/V Kestrel*. Do you read?"

There was a moment of silence, just a few clicks of radio interference, before a woman's voice responded.

"Sekami? Oh my god! Sekami, is that really you?"

"It's me, Marasa," she replied, a real smile spreading across her face for the first time in weeks. "Rhys is here, too, and a pilot named Conrad. Is everyone over there okay?"

"Our life support systems went down a few days ago. The

scrubbers are overloaded, and we've only got a few hours of air left," the woman answered, her voice tight. "Where are you?"

"Not far. We're coming up on your position."

Rhys looked through the cockpit window, straining his eyes for a glimpse of the survival craft he knew to be out there. Slowly, a white speck appeared against the void, growing larger as they neared the scientists' transmitted location. With ten kilometers to go, Conrad gave another burst of counter-thrust and crept forward at what felt like a snail's pace, until he had maneuvered the *Kestrel* alongside the damaged craft. Even with only one good arm, the man possessed a deft touch. He typed a command into the computer, and a gentle thump reverberated through the hull.

"Umbilical connected," BAIN announced.

"Match pressures."

A yellow light blinked on the display, before changing to steady green. Rhys felt an uncomfortable sensation in his ears and made chewing motions to get them to pop.

"The *Kestrel* now matches the survival craft's internal pressure," the computer informed them.

They unbuckled their restraints and hurried toward the airlock. Sekami released the hatch, and the smiling face of Marasa Bok naal beamed back at them from the other side. The two women greeted in the turandian fashion then embraced, joyous tears glistening in Marasa's eyes. When they broke apart, Rhys nodded hello, careful not to repeat the same mistakes he'd made the first time they met. Marasa ignored this and threw her arms around his neck in a surprising show of affection. Otaan Yabar moved into the *Kestrel's* airlock and acknowledged them with his own cultural equivalent of gratitude. A sling supported the Hanekaarian's left arm where a recent injury left a dark red stain on the dressing.

"I don't understand how this is possible. Rhys and I... we saw the *Erebus* vaporized," Sekami exclaimed once all the greetings had been passed around. "How did you survive the attack?"

"The *Erebus* was broadcasting a false therleon signature,"

Marasa explained. "As soon as the grül noticed the decoy, they went after it, which was how the *Hermes* slipped through undetected."

The smile slowly faded from Sekami's face, and a dark look filled her eyes.

"The grül... what did you use to trick their sensors?"

"We don't know exactly. Some sort of signal transmitter," Otaan Yabar replied. "It generated a substantial amount of heat. There was a large, skid-mounted cooling system attached to an XCT field antenna. Very inefficient."

"I know what it was. We used something just like it to escape the grül twenty-five years ago after Rhys..." Sekami began but faltered. "After Rhys first activated the machine."

Her words were met with a confused look between the two rescued scientists.

"What do you mean, 'after Rhys first activated the machine?' Are you telling us he's from *our* time?" Marasa demanded. She'd become uncharacteristically heated, but Otaan Yabar looked on with intense curiosity. "Was Kieron right all along? Did Volkerson exile him for no reason?"

"I'm not defending Dr. Volkerson's actions. Rhys witnessed the death of my father, and for a long time, I'd been led to believe he died as well. When I found out he was alive, frozen and wiped of his memories, I went to get him," Sekami explained. "I'm telling you this now because its secrecy no longer matters. After Rhys first activated the machine, my father used that data to build a device like the one you described, but because his invention resulted in a string of massacres, he refused to build another. I don't know where or how you got it, but that doesn't matter. I'm just glad you're safe."

Hearing her describe the first time he'd used the machine, Rhys did some mental math. *Six*, he realized. He was six years old the first time they'd made him turn it on. What had that been like for his prepubescent self? Had they made him murder his pet gerbil too? The idea made him shudder. From everything he'd learned about Jenco, he hoped his apparent father figure wouldn't subject a child to such a traumatic experience... on the other hand, the man had, inadvertently or not, doomed billions of people to their deaths. Forcing him to use the machine paled in comparison to what he'd done in leading the grül to Vandervol, a transgression Sekami had conveniently neglected to tell the scientists.

He tried to push the unpleasant thought from his head. What good would it do, telling Marasa she'd been helping the man responsible for her own mother's death? Besides, there was something else troubling him. Marasa and Otaan Yabar had left Proxima Station on the *Hermes*... their message from a few days ago confirmed that. If they'd used the *Erebus* as a decoy and had access to another ship, what were they doing out here on a survival craft? Where the hell was the *Hermes*?

"We weren't the only ones who escaped. Dr. Volkerson was onboard as well," Marasa explained, still visibly angry by what Sekami had revealed. "After the station was destroyed, he became very withdrawn and refused to tell us where we were going. For most of last several weeks, he's been locked up with that infernal machine."

"Then, where is he?" Rhys demanded. His voice hardened at the mention of Volkerson's name. The promise he'd made to himself should he ever again come face-to-face with that bastard was fresh in his mind. "I thought you said it was just the two of you."

"It *is* just the two of us," she replied, shifting her gaze back to him. "About ten days ago, he seemed, I don't know... *unhinged*. Nothing he told us made sense. He kept babbling about a key, or locks... something about changing the locks. When he tried to force us off the *Hermes*, he said it was for our own protection, that he would be back soon. Otaan Yabar resisted, and that's when Dr. Volkerson shot him."

"He *shot* you?" Sekami exclaimed, glancing questioningly at the sling supporting the Hanekaarian's arm. He nodded, and a low growl escaped his throat.

"There's something else," Marasa said, hesitantly. She exchanged another look with Otaan Yabar, and the Hanekaarian gave her a little nod. "Before disappearing with the *Hermes*, he told us the machine couldn't fall into the wrong hands and placed it onboard the survival craft with us."

Silence filled the airlock as they all gaped at her, mouths hanging open in disbelief. Their long, dangerous journey in search of another machine had finally come to an end. Here, at the edge of charted space, the very device they sought to replace had come back into their possession. Rhys feared what it meant. Would Sekami remain hellbent on exacting retribution from the grül, or would she let it all go, just be happy they had found more survivors, and allow them to get as far away from here as possible? The hush was punctuated when Conrad let out a long, low whistle.

"Coulda led with that," he muttered.

"Volkerson left the machine?" Rhys asked. The news was shocking. After all the man had done, all the people he'd let die to keep the grül from recovering their technology, it seemed inconceivable he would abandon it… to just leave it floating around in space.

"That's not the half of it. Two days ago, the machine suddenly energized, and we don't know why," Marasa explained. "That's when we sent out the distress call. We'd given up thinking Dr. Volkerson was coming back."

More bad news. Once again, it was beginning to pile up.

"Listen, I'm happy you're alright, but this changes things. If that machine is over there cranking out whatever crap almost melted our insides, then the fleet we saw at Proxima is probably on its way here right now," Conrad urged, unnerved. He turned toward Rhys. "Can you turn it off?"

"Maybe… but if not, I'm not up for dragging a grül-magnet around with us," he replied. "There's something I don't understand, though. If it's been running the last two days, how the hell aren't you both already dead?"

"We've had a lot of time to study the data from Proxima Station," Otaan Yabar explained, uncharacteristically animated given the circumstances. "It's not so much the presence of therleon particles that's deadly, but how they're used. Remember the uulgar? It was subjected to multiple doses of concentrated particles with no adverse effects–"

"Your dissertation can wait," Sekami interrupted. "If we can't deactivate the machine, then we leave without it. Take Rhys to the survival craft and see what you can do."

Rhys nodded and followed the Hanekaarian back through the *Kestrel's* flexible umbilical. When they entered the craft, he glanced around at the cramped space. It was a single room, a few benches built into the bulkheads behind the pilot and copilot chairs. *Ten days in here would be enough to drive anyone mad*, Rhys thought, remembering his own experience on the *Denebola's* life raft. He paused, forcing himself to accept the fact those memories weren't real. He'd never even been in a life raft for all he knew. Still, though, the claustrophobic vessel made his skin itch with perceived trauma. Shaking his head for clarity, he tried to focus on why they were there.

In the center of the compartment, hovering in place, was the machine. Seeing it made the hairs on the back of his neck stand up. Light shimmered from its fluid-like core, sending ghostly shadows dancing over the bulkheads. He sensed a slight hum emanating from the device, as if the air itself were vibrating. Taking a deep breath, he reached out and touched its rough surface. The familiar sensation shot up his arm and across his chest, filling him from head to toe with an unwelcome sense of fracture. For a moment, he endured the tumult, holding his fear at bay for a little while longer.

When he finally took his hand away, the device fell silent, transforming into nothing more than an ugly, black sphere. He turned toward Otaan Yabar, a triumphant smile plastered on his face, when suddenly, the room was once again bathed in shimmering light. An instant later, the *Kestrel's* alarm began to ring, and the Hanekaarian looked at Rhys with foreboding.

"I don't understand. Why didn't it–"

"Get that thing over here!"

A shout reverberated from inside the tunnel. Conrad had appeared at the other end of the umbilical and was waving furiously at them to hurry. Fear was etched in deep lines across his face.

"We've got company!"

Working fast, they guided the device through the passage until they were inside the *Kestrel's* airlock. As soon as they were onboard, the pilot closed the hatch and slammed his fist into a red button marked *EMERGENCY RELEASE*. In a puff of vapor, the umbilical detached from the ship's hull and coiled away like the skin of a gigantic white snake. There was no time to waste, the machine left unsecured as they sprinted for the cockpit. Rhys heard the drive's telltale whine against his pounding ears, the pitch of its engines climbing beyond his range of hearing. When they burst into the cockpit, what he saw nearly made his heart stop.

Seven massive ships of the grül armada were bearing down on their position. Conrad pushed by to assist Sekami, who had already brought the engines online. At the back, Marasa sat in one of the jump seats, her skin ashen and eyes unfocused, seemingly petrified in the face of imminent danger. With the maneuvering thrusters already powered up, Rhys threw himself in a seat next to Otaan Yabar and hurried to buckle his harness.

"Hold on!"

The pilot pulled hard on the stick, trying to swing them out of the line of fire, but it was too late. A powerful blast rocked the *Kestrel*, and Rhys was thrown outward, his right arm wrenched painfully backwards as it caught in the unfastened restraints. The ship spun wildly, shrieking alarms and countless blinking lights bombarding the inside of the cockpit. Conrad was distraught.

"The thrusters are gone! Drive's dead too!"

They were sitting ducks, adrift in space, and the grül were advancing quickly.

"Fire at them!" Rhys urged in his panic. "Do something!"

"This ain't a combat ship, you idiot!" the pilot cried. Outside, the flagship had separated from the rest of the fleet and was now gliding toward their position. "What are they waiting for? They could finish us off with another shot."

"They intend to board us," Sekami murmured, her face ashen at the realization of what was to come. "They've disabled our propulsion, and now they're sending a boarding party."

Rhys's hands shook uncontrollably. The last of their luck had run out during the encounter with the old, dying grül. Now, with the *Kestrel's* engines offline, he knew there could be no escape. The leviathan was right on top of them, and a knot tightened in his stomach when he felt the *Kestrel* begin to move… *upward*. Passing through a transparent forcefield, the other ships disappeared from view, and he understood. They were being drawn into the belly of the beast. Any lingering glimmer of hope he still clung to evaporated. If only they'd gotten to the scientists sooner, they might have escaped. A little more time, and they could've deactivated the machine… a lightbulb clicked on in Rhys's head. The machine! Without wasting another second, he climbed to his feet and sprinted from the cockpit.

Kicking himself, he wondered why it hadn't occurred to him earlier. Deep in his heart, he sensed this would be the moment of clarity he'd needed all along. Now, faced with imminent death, Rhys knew he would finally succeed in controlling the machine. He just needed to get there ahead of the grül. Hearing a beep from his CIM, he touched his ear.

"Where are you going? They're outside the airlock!" Sekami's voice was full of panicked urgency.

"The machine! I'm going for the machine! I can control it, Sekami. I know I can!"

"I don't understand." There was confusion in her voice. "Rhys, don't do this! We need to hide!"

There wasn't time to explain. He ignored her and kept running, careening into the airlock where the machine still churned out its invisible particles. Ominous clunks from outside the ship reverberated through the hull, and he locked the inner door behind him. Placing his hands atop the sphere, Rhys tried to focus his mind. Two familiar holes appeared in front of him, and he plunged his arms inside. With everything he'd learned in the past few days, the stuttering synaptic overload imparted by the machine was worse than ever. He closed his eyes, feeling himself sink into the recesses of his own psyche, when a shout escaped his lips.

"NO!"

He couldn't afford to be lulled into complacency, not in this moment. He forced himself to concentrate, and his eyes snapped open, mind suddenly laser-focused to repel their attackers. Ahead of him, the outer door began to shimmer, deforming first at the center then spreading to the very edges of the hatch. Suddenly, the undulating surface exploded in a surge of energy. Rhys ducked behind the machine, protecting himself from flying shrapnel, as it pelted every surface inside the airlock. When he looked back, a ragged hole had replaced the outer door, and on the other side stood ten menacing warriors.

They rushed forward, and he focused every fiber of his being into the machine. He imagined the aliens ripped apart, vaporized in the same fashion as the airlock door, but they kept coming. Nothing was happening, and a nagging doubt began to fill his mind. *Please*, Rhys thought. The first warrior was only a meter away. *FOCUS!* he shouted in his head, but it was too late. The creature stuck out its arm, hooking it around his chest and slamming him to the floor. Ripped from the machine's depths, Rhys saw the dancing shadows fade to nothing as it fell dormant once more. The sphere remained that way for only an instant before the airlock was again bathed in ghostly light. He experienced a moment of inane incredulity, baffled as to why the device kept reactivating, but then a second warrior was on top of him, binding his hands together and pinning him to the deck as he struggled to break free.

"Find the others," the first growled.

With lightning-fast speed, the soldiers breached the inner door and flooded into the ship. Rhys struggled on the floor, swearing and cursing, but nothing he did fazed his captor. Screams floated out from inside the *Kestrel*, and a report from Conrad's grül-killing rifle reverberated down the passage. Burning hate filled him as he prayed the pilot had killed at least one. A minute later, though, the soldiers all returned uninjured. The same could not be said for the people in their custody. Led at gunpoint, hands bound in front of them, were his friends. Each of them looked more battered than the last as they were forced to the deck beside him.

"Commander Feyt, the other human had this," one warrior said, handing the first alien Conrad's huge rifle. The creature, who Rhys could only assume was their leader, took the weapon in its hands and swung it in a powerful arc, smashing it against the bulkhead.

"Get them up," it said, gesturing at the prisoners.

Roughly, they were jerked to their feet and pushed through the hole in the *Kestrel's* hull. Rhys struggled against his restraints and felt something pressed to the back of his head. It was enough to make him stop. Glancing around, he took in the strange, alien qualities of the gigantic vessel. Its construction seemed to defy the laws of physics. Like the crash on BQ3, it was as if the ship had been grown, not built. Its hull looked like one continuous piece, devoid of any welds or rivets, each curving line melting seam-lessly into the next structural member. Pale light illuminated their path, reminding Rhys of the machine's shimmering core and creating the illusion they were walking underwater. Looking up at the strange lights, he didn't see any wires, and something Sekami had said during his first day on Proxima Station floated into his mind. If what she'd said was true, then all of this was powered by the grül's mysterious therleon particles.

Their captors led them toward an ovoidal pod and forced

them inside. The aperture melted closed around them, encasing the prisoners and their captors inside the seed-like structure. It began to rise, slowly at first, then picked up speed. When they finally slid to a halt and the strange doors melted open, they were pulled into another room where huge membranous windows overlooked the rest of the grül fleet. The prisoners were yanked toward a particularly large grül, and in a moment of recognition, Rhys knew he'd stood face-to-face with this alien once before. It was the same one who'd led the boarding party on Proxima Station. With a brutal kick, they were forced to their knees in front of the massive creature.

"Fleet Captain Xorin, we discovered this one attempting to use the stolen property," the grül commander croaked.

The one called Xorin drew close, and it was only then Rhys realized how menacing the beast truly was. It was a head taller than the others and bulging with gray-skinned muscles. A jagged scar creased the left side of its face, accentuating the deadly ferocity that burned in its black eyes. The creature peered intently at Rhys, then shifted its gaze toward the machine.

"Find out what they have done. I want to know how a human could activate our technology," it growled.

Obediently, one of Xorin's warriors moved away from the rest of the group. Rhys watched in apprehension as the soldier positioned the machine on a raised platform at the back of the room, then placed itself behind a strange, tube-like umbilical. Guiding it smoothly down from the ceiling, the warrior slid the umbilical over the exposed core, and the sphere's dancing light was obscured once more. Xorin stalked down the line of prisoners and paused in front of Marasa. The creature peered down at her in disgust, and she began to shake uncontrollably.

"This one first," it said, pointing at her.

She was pulled roughly to her feet and shoved toward a rounded console in the center of the room. Seeing it filled Rhys with dread. Like everything else onboard, the device looked as if it had sprung from the ship itself. Its rough, black surface gave the console the appearance of nothing more than a ball of hammered iron, devoid of extraordinary features, but he knew what was hidden beneath the seemingly innocuous shell.

Xorin stepped behind the device and slid his arms inside. Marasa was suddenly lifted into the air by an invisible force, and a look of sheer terror etched itself onto her face. A single weeping sob was cut short when her body stiffened, eyes rolling to the back of her head as if in the grips of some demonic possession. Trembling violently, her spine arched grotesquely as the machine held her suspended above the floor. Her foot jerked wildly in an involuntary spasm. Whatever the creature was doing, she no longer had control of her body. Abruptly, in a voice that was harsh and choppy, Marasa spoke.

"I... don't... know... where... he... is..."

Rhys was confused. Where *who* is? No one had said anything. Was Xorin speaking to her somehow? Through the machine? Out of the corner of his eye, he saw Sekami struggling with her captor, pleading that grül Captain stop whatever he was doing. The creature ignored her protestations, and the guard struck her violently. Anger flared inside Rhys, but before he could open his mouth, a bellow reverberated through the bridge.

"WHERE IS MARCUS VOLKERSON?" Xorin roared in a furious eruption, spit flying from its snarling mouth.

With an ear-splitting shriek of pain, Marasa's trance was broken. Rivers of tears and mucus began to stream down her face, turning slowly from clear to bright red. They watched, horrified, as blood poured freely from the woman's ears and nose, scarlet flecks dotting the corners of her mouth with each gurgling cough. Before their eyes, Xorin appeared to rejuvenate, the crimson streaks in his skin radiating heat as if a fire burned inside him, until only a shriveled, mutilated husk remained of the scientist's body.

Sekami cried out, her face a visage of anguish as she struggled against her bonds. Seeing Marasa's lifeless eyes, a lump rose in Rhys's throat, and he felt the room spin. *This isn't happening*, he thought, fighting the urge to pass out. It couldn't end like this. The killing had been abrupt, senseless... he knew what the grül were capable of, had seen the IHR footage of the slaughtered turandians, but somehow, seeing it in person made it all much, much worse.

The creature stood straighter than before, a crazed look in its eyes as it stepped menacingly toward its next victim. Grabbing Conrad by the throat, it dragged him toward the machine, but the pilot fought wildly, punching and biting like a cornered animal. In a desperate attempt for freedom, he kicked backward, connecting with Xorin's knee. The Captain stumbled, released his quarry, and roared in anger. Turning back, he ripped a familiar-looking pistol from its holster. Conrad crawled frantically away, but the incensed grül bore down on him. When it rammed its foot into the small of his back, pinning him to the floor, he cried out. Xorin pointed its weapon at the back of Conrad's head, and a look of defeat filled the pilot's eyes. He glanced toward Rhys, and for one final time, their gaze met.

"Been a helluva ride, Amigo. I'll see you on the other side–"

A flash of bright light illuminated the bridge when the shot rang out. Conrad's corpse fell to the deck with a sickening slap, a cauterized hole in the center of what remained of his face. Stunned, Rhys felt cold detachment creep through his veins as he looked at the bodies in front of him. *This is a nightmare*, he thought numbly. *This is a nightmare, and I'm going to wake up on the Kestrel, or BQ3, or fucking anywhere but here.* As much as he willed it to be true, his denial didn't last long. Xorin moved down the line toward Otaan Yabar, kicking Conrad's body unceremoniously out of the way. The flippant, callous act was Rhys's final breaking point, and something inside him snapped. Mustering all his strength, he broke free of his captor's grasp and knocked the pistol from the Captain's huge hand. The weapon skidded away on the floor, and Rhys dove after it. Grasping it in both hands, he spun around to face the creature, leveling the gun at its head.

"This is for my friends!" he screamed.

An anticlimactic *click* filled the room. He squeezed again. *Click.* What the hell? He cycled the trigger, again and again, but nothing happened. Xorin began to laugh, the humorless sound deep and guttural. Like a pack of hyenas, it was taken up by the other warriors on the bridge. Xorin stalked over and yanked the pistol away from a stupefied-looking Rhys.

"Our weapons do not function against the grülbarvoc," it snarled, no longer laughing.

It raised a sinewy fist and backhanded Rhys across the face. The powerful blow knocked him to the ground, filling his vision with stars and threatening to send him spiraling into unconsciousness. Lying on the alien bridge, his head throbbing, Rhys knew he was beaten. Heavy footfalls reverberated through the deck as the creature advanced, and he looked up into the muzzle of the gun. Like an animal taken to slaughter, he clenched his eyes shut and waited for the inevitable end.

# CHAPTER 34
# THE HARBINGER

*CLICK*. His stomach lurched. There was a momentous pause where everything seemed to hang in the balance, and then... *click*. Not daring to believe he wasn't already dead, Rhys cracked open an eye. The weapon was still pointed at his head, but with each pull of its trigger, only a weak flicker and a muted *click* came out. Confusion twisted Xorin's face before he jammed the weapon back into its holster. Storming toward Feyt, he ripped the gun from the Commander's belt and fired a test-shot at one of the limp bodies lying on the deck. The energy pulse left a singed hole in Conrad's chest. With a functional weapon, the Captain returned once more to his position in front of Rhys and fired. *Click*.

A frustrated roar escaped the creature's lips as it reached back and slammed the gun into the side of Rhys's face. The tooth-rattling blow sent a spray of blood flying from his mouth, and he felt the embedded CIM shatter as he crashed to the floor. Spots filled his vision as the incensed alien grabbed Sekami by the hair. *No, please, not her*, he thought defeatedly, lacking the strength to push himself off the deck. Garbling some indistinct protest through a mouthful of blood, he watched in horror as the beast raised its weapon to her face and fired. *Click*. Rhys was too beaten, too broken to understand what it meant.

"What is this devilry?" Xorin bellowed, hurling Sekami back down next to Rhys. "Cast them into the void!"

Rhys felt a pair of hands begin dragging him away, while two more soldiers shoved forward Otaan Yabar and a struggling, kicking Sekami. She was a rock… an unyielding force pushing back against their captors. He wanted to fight, to aid her effort, but what good would it do? Nothing would change their fate now. Resistance was just one more futile gesture. They had tried their hardest to defeat the grül, but in the end, their efforts hadn't even come close. The grül were stronger, smarter, and more ruthless than they could have imagined. It wasn't self-pity he felt. It was more like acceptance. If these creatures were meant to conquer the galaxy, then he didn't want to be around to witness the aftermath anyway.

"Battle stations!"

The warrior dragging him hesitated, then dropped him hard on the deck only a few meters from where he'd been lying. Pounding feet were all around as the grül rushed to assume their positions. Through the haze of his concussed brain, Rhys heard a high-pitched warbling throughout the bridge. Hands still tightly bound, he pushed himself to his knees to see what had sparked the sudden alert. Through the window, another vessel floated in front of the fleet, dwarfed by the massive grül ships. He felt a hand grip his arm.

"The *Hermes*," Sekami whispered, squeezing him so tightly it hurt. "Dr. Volkerson came back! He might be able to–"

She cut her words short and gazed fearfully up at Xorin. Where before the creature had been focused on the new arrival, now it peered intently down at them, leaving no doubt as to what the evil curl in its lip meant. Sekami had just told the Captain exactly what he'd tortured Marasa to discover.

"Target that ship!" he commanded, jabbing a finger toward the tiny spacecraft.

A growing rumble resonated from deep within the vessel as its fearsome weaponry powered up. The fleet began to spread out, forming an arc in front of their insignificant adversary. A glow emanated from the central aperture of each spacecraft as they prepared to fire. Rhys saw Xorin raise a hand, about to give the command, when the creature faltered. Two of his ships were still moving, pivoting slowly toward each other until they were almost nose-to-nose. Confusion rippled through the bridge at this unexpected turn of events. For a moment, nothing happened. Then, with undulating blasts of therleon energy, both ships fired.

A collective roar went up from the bridge as the vessels blew apart in violent atomization. Fragments that hadn't been instantly vaporized flew in all directions, peppering the hull with a sound like blowing sand. Stunned by what had just occurred, Rhys blinked away the spots in his vision, a faint blue-green aura the only remaining evidence of each ship's prior existence. Now, four more vessels turned to face each other, and with stupefied wonder, he shielded his eyes against the brilliant flashes of light until only one ship, Xorin's ship, remained.

"Fire, you fools! Destroy that ship!" the Captain bellowed, but the vibrations building from within the vessel had died. Now, an eeriness fell over the bridge, its utter silence a stark contrast to the torturous screams from moments ago.

"Sir, something has corrupted our network," Commander Feyt announced. "All systems have been forced offline."

Xorin rounded on him, rage twisting his scarred face, but paused when a sudden glow bathed the bridge in artificial light. There, materialized on a shimmering, fluid-like viewscreen, was the face of Marcus Volkerson. The missing scientist looked down on them like some omnipotent being. Slowly, Xorin turned toward the intruder, and they studied each other for a time, sizing one another up in a test of wills. It was the grül Captain who spoke first.

"At last, after all this time, the Interloper shows his face," the creature growled, "not before allowing countless others to die in his stead."

Volkerson did not respond but continued to regard Xorin

quietly.

"Tell me, how have you destroyed my fleet? Never in grül-barvoc history has our technology been undermined in such a way."

Still, the scientist refused to speak. His appearance was startling. Disheveled hair and several weeks growth on his normally clean-shaven jaw gave Rhys the impression of... madness was too strong a word. Shrewd intelligence still burned in his eyes, but there was something else there too, behind the aloof demeanor and the calculating gaze... a wildness. Volkerson looked like a man on the brink.

"You must forgive my rudeness," he said finally. "As reluctant as I am to admit it, the inhabitants of the Commonwealth have failed to decipher grülbarvoc language."

At this, Rhys glanced questioningly at Sekami, but the look on her face showed she was as confused as him. Was this some kind of ploy? A diversion tactic? What was the purpose of feigning incomprehension? As far as he knew, the grül had been speaking some dialect his CIM could– he paused, mid-thought, and remembered... the CIM. Xorin had smashed it. He felt the broken pieces crunch beneath his jaw and knew it had been rendered useless. So how was he still able to understand Volkerson? It made sense once he thought about it. He'd been from the twenty-seventh century all along, so of course he could understand the language used by Sekami and the others. Perhaps the CIM had never been a translator at all, just a convenient lie to explain away his comprehension.

"Then perhaps, I will use your Common Tongue," Xorin replied. He said the words slowly, over-enunciating each one like someone still learning proper syntax. Now, Rhys was thoroughly confused. If they hadn't been speaking a shared language, how had he understood everything the grül were saying in the first place? He didn't have time to consider this before a malicious sneer spread across Volkerson's lips, filling him with a sense of foreboding.

"Since I have your attention, I suppose I should thank you," he said. "I would never have achieved this victory without your assistance."

A look of pure hatred flashed across Xorin's face, the creature bristling at the insinuation.

"I would never help—" but Volkerson cut him off.

"From the start, I've known what you are," he continued, forging through the Captain's venomous protestations. He was no longer smiling, and a ruthless glint shone in the scientist's eyes. "The grül are a disease. A deadly pandemic that, left unchecked, would destroy a galaxy living in tenuous coexistence. When I found two of your kind slaughtering defenseless colonists, I knew our governments possessed nothing that could stand against such weaponry. The G.C. was too blind, too *stupid*, to foresee something like this... but perhaps, with a piece of that technology, I could find a way for us to survive."

Xorin was deathly quiet, holding the man's gaze with a look of murderous loathing. The rest of his warriors, however, had become agitated by the scientist's inflammatory proclamation. Rhys felt something tighten in his gut as he watched Commander Feyt attempt to control the crew. He wished Volkerson would shut up. Every word the scientist spoke only added to the steaming pile of shit he, Sekami, and Otaan Yabar were in. If these monsters couldn't have the man who'd murdered their brethren, they were going to settle for the next best thing.

From the far side the bridge, a solitary warrior stood up from its station and stalked purposefully toward them. Something in its eyes set an alarm blaring inside Rhys's head. Slowly, it slid an ornate-looking blade from beneath its protective garments, before rushing purposefully toward Sekami. The beast was only a meter away when Feyt took notice and delivered a stinging blow to the warrior's arm, the weapon clattering to the ground. Two more soldiers leaped forward to subdue the assailant, dragging the snarling creature away from the prisoners. Volkerson's face, looking down from above, was alight with malice.

"Do you feel it, Captain? The doubt, the fear, the *hopelessness* we've lived with for so long. Embrace this moment. It will be the least of your suffering. I have so much more to tell you," the scientist exclaimed, seeming to take cruel pleasure in the chaos he'd created. His words began to tumble out, faster and faster, as if the last thirty-four years would be wasted if he delayed much longer. "The first and most important question was how to use your machine. It became quickly apparent that only a precise DNA sequence could activate it. If we discovered a way around this, however, we could develop weapons without such constraints. Neither my partner nor I had the requisite genes to operate the machine, and the odds of capturing a grül to coerce were nonexistent. So, with no real options, we were forced to improvise. Unfortunately, a failed, decades-long experiment left us no closer to achieving our goal than when we'd started. After you destroyed Proxima Station, I knew I couldn't stay ahead of you forever. Once again, I was forced to rethink my strategy."

With an irrational flash of anger, Rhys realized that *he* was the 'failed experiment' the scientist referred to. Even as their last hope of rescue, the sonofabitch had managed to fill him with resentment. He'd had enough of the man's lies, his deceits, his claims of righteousness… all Rhys wanted was to take Sekami and Otaan Yabar and get as far from this place as possible. Let Volkerson and the grül kill each other. He couldn't stand to hear anymore. Neither, it seemed, could Xorin.

"I have endured the ravings of a madman for long enough. There is nothing left to discuss," Xorin snarled, turning away from the screen. He stepped over Marasa's shriveled corpse and hastened toward the central interface. When the creature placed its huge hands on the rough, black skin, however, no shimmering holes appeared on its surface. The console was as cold and lifeless as a ball of metal.

"Don't you understand? The ship no longer belongs to you. I stopped searching for the keys to your technology and changed the locks instead. I had all the data I needed to develop a virus, a trojan horse of sorts, for the stolen machine... I just needed a way to infect your systems," Volkerson sneered, reveling in his quarry's utter helplessness. "Logically, you must've tracked the device during times of unshielded operation. So, I deposited the infected machine in a survival craft and triggered it remotely. I wish I could say it was difficult, condemning the last of my scientists to that fate, but I knew you'd be wary of simply finding the machine adrift in space. When you integrated the device with your system, you allowed my code to quietly infect your vessel, reprogramming itself to my DNA. In truth, I'd only expected to infect your ship. Imagine my delight when the virus spread to your entire fleet."

Stunned, Rhys turned toward Sekami and knew by the look on her face, she was just as horrified as him. Volkerson had used the others as bait, knowing full well they'd probably be killed by the grül. Marasa had been right. The man had become unhinged. Suddenly, before any of them could protest, they were yanked to their feet and dragged directly in front of Volkerson's disembodied head. Xorin picked up the knife that had been dropped on the deck and pulled Sekami to him. Placing the blade at her throat, he snarled at the scientist.

"Release my ship or watch the last of your friends die."

A look of cold detachment hardened Volkerson's face, and he set his jaw.

"Do with them what you will. They're nothing more than engineered specimens of an experiment to combine grül DNA with that of a baukken and that of a human," he replied with contempt.

An icy hand gripped Rhys's spine at these words. What the scientist said couldn't be true... it couldn't! It didn't make sense. Volkerson was lying... lying because he was crazy, or because Rhys had failed him, or to distract the grül, or... or... or... or... this entire catastrophe was nothing more than a nightmare... Marasa... Conrad... soon, he would wake up. He *had* to wake up. Turning his gaze to meet Sekami's, her look of horror confirmed his worst fears. This was indeed a nightmare, but he wasn't going to wake up... their nightmare had become reality.

"I don't understand," Sekami stammered up at Volkerson. "My father–"

"YOUR FATHER," the man shouted, suddenly enraged by the mention of Jenco, "LOST FAITH IN OUR CAUSE!"

For a moment, a true madman stared down at them. His eyes bulged, his nostrils flared, and he looked truly insane. Volkerson breathed heavily, glaring wide-eyed at them, before hiding his derangement behind a mask of disdain.

"Jenco Ryele knew as well as I, we couldn't control the machine ourselves. Your precious 'father' lied to you from the start! It was he who suggested we combine our own DNA with the two grül we'd found," Volkerson spat, lashing out with an acid tongue. "We created two specimens, one from each of us. I first sensed his loss of faith when he began referring to you as his daughter. He went out of his way to prove your incompatibility with the machine, so he could spare you from the toll we suspected it might take. I tolerated this only because he agreed, grudgingly I will admit, to allow me to use the human-grül amalgamation as I saw fit. When his conscience began to outweigh his reason, and he demanded we tell Rhys the truth, I could no longer stand by and let him jeopardize our work."

"W-what're you saying?" Sekami asked. Tears had begun to leak silently down her cheeks at learning the horrible truth of their existence. "What did you do?"

"Only what was necessary," Volkerson said, becoming distant. "Jenco Ryele died at my hands, as will the son and daughter that were never truly his."

It was too much. A storm of rage, confusion, and despair burst forth from Rhys's chest in a rising tempest. Spit flew from his mouth as he cursed the scientist's name, and for a moment, he was as deranged as Volkerson. The man cast his cold eyes on them for one final loathing-filled moment before ending the transmission.

No longer having anywhere to direct his fury, Rhys sank to his knees, hopelessness and hate and fear filling him. He didn't know what to do anymore. How? How could he be one of *them*? Yet again, he'd been fed a lie to hide a terrible truth. The machine didn't respond to Rhys because he possessed some lost piece of the human genome. All along, it had been because he was half-grül... an unholy creation of science... an abomination.

With downcast eyes, he heard approaching footsteps and saw the toes of Captain Xorin's boots in front of him. He tensed, expecting to receive a final killing blow, but instead of inflicting pain, the creature released the bonds around his hands. They fell limply into his lap as he stared numbly at the floor. He felt Sekami's long fingers slip between his own and raised his eyes to meet her tear-streaked face.

"I'm so sorry. For everything. I wouldn't have done the things I have if I'd known."

He wanted to take comfort in her words, but they couldn't erase the knowledge of what lived inside him. Shifting his gaze, he saw Xorin watching them, an expression of newfound curiosity on the creature's face. It didn't matter. It was all going to end when Volkerson destroyed the last ship in the grülbarvoc fleet.

"You understand our language."

It wasn't a question. It was a declaration, a statement acknowledging them as something more than senseless beasts, but only them. Rhys knew the sentiment did not extend to Otaan Yabar... or Marasa... or Conrad. He glared up at the Captain, hate filling every fiber of his being. At least he would die knowing the ones who had slaughtered his friends, the ones responsible for scorching the Earth, had also met their end. Once again, a warbling alarm was broadcast throughout the bridge, intermixed with the sound of a countdown.

*Therleon containment disabled. Five minutes until core overload.*

Volkerson's trap had been sprung. Panic infected the bridge as the grül tried frantically to avert their impending doom. Kneeling on the deck beside Sekami and Otaan Yabar, Rhys searched for some semblance of inner calm. His last moments with them shouldn't be so filled with rage, but it was difficult to force his thoughts away from Volkerson. Sekami didn't deserve this. She'd done everything she'd been asked by the man watching over her, a man who was supposed to be her friend... her father's friend. Rhys no longer cared what happened to himself, but the woman beside him had sacrificed too much for too long. That she should die at the hands of the man to whom she'd been so loyal was sickening. Anger and disgust crept back into his mind at the thought of Volkerson's blood, of grül blood, running through his veins. Through his veins... *through his veins*... the realization washed over him like ice water.

He embraced Sekami tightly, then sprang to his feet. Running toward the Captain, he skidded to a halt as Commander Feyt rushed forward to block him. Interpreting this as a final, misplaced attempt for revenge, Xorin roared like a cornered animal and raised his blade high.

"I share Volkerson's DNA!" Rhys shouted not a moment too soon. The Captain's hand paused mid-stroke, knife poised only centimeters from his face. "Your ship. Volkerson said it only responds to his DNA... DNA he used to create *me*. You already know I can activate the machine. If I can stop the overload, swear you'll let us go."

Their fates hung in the balance as the creature considered his offer. Rhys had neglected to explain that although he may be able to activate grül technology, he'd never successfully controlled it... he wasn't about to let that slip. They were dead anyway. It couldn't hurt to try one last time. When the Captain lowered the knife, his decision was clear. He gave Feyt a sharp nod, who turned on his heel and motioned for Rhys to follow.

*Three minutes until core overload.*

He ran hard to catch up to his guide, whose long legs carried the Commander at a much faster pace. Feyt had already reached the lift by the time Rhys was still several meters from the door. His lungs burned when he finally stumbled through the hatch, and he felt a sudden drop as the pod began to plummet. The journey downward was longer than the one to the bridge, and he realized they must be descending to the very depths of the grül ship. When the pod slid to a halt, they stepped out into a huge, spherical room. The walls were bare, and like everything else he'd seen, devoid of a single telltale weld. Directly in the center was a gigantic, glowing mass of energy. The silvery, fluid-like form pulsated as it swelled then shrank, back and forth in constant undulation. The way it kept shifting, tongues of white-hot energy blooming outward, made the substance appear extremely unstable. Feyt led him toward an interface, its rough black surface all too familiar.

*One minute until core overload.*

Stepping in front of the console, Rhys felt a droplet of sweat trickle down his neck. There wasn't time to wonder if it was from the room's extreme heat or his own terror. *Give me something*, he thought, praying that luck might at last be on his side. He touched the black skin and two holes appeared in front of him; a promising start. Closing his eyes, he tried to focus, to prevent the core from overloading, to reactivate the containment field, to do anything that might keep them and the ship alive.

*Fifteen seconds until core overload.*

A familiar uncertainty gnawed at the edge of his mind. He tried to fight against it, but it kept growing. In a moment of cold realization, Rhys knew this had been a mistake. They should've tried to escape on the *Kestrel*, tried anything besides what had failed so many times before. He had no idea what he was doing. After countless failures with Volkerson's machine, why had he suddenly thought he'd be able to control something even bigger? Now, it was too late, and he could feel the electricity in the room as the reactor began to exceed its limits.

*Three, two, one...*

When the countdown reached zero, a brilliant flash exploded outward from the center of the room.

THERE WAS ONLY RED... scorching, fiery red that burned like the light of a dying star. Rhys's eyes were clamped shut, and slowly, tentatively, he opened them. Blinding white light was everywhere, replacing the crimson glow that had shone through his eyelids. Squinting, he tried to identify something else, but only endless, radiant white glared back at him. *Am I dead?* he wondered, a twinge of disappointment beginning to tug at him. He could feel his arms, his legs, his feet... there were his toes... he wiggled them. Eventually, his eyes began to adjust, and when his surroundings materialized out of white-washed obscurity, his jaw dropped in disbelief.

He was still standing in front of the ship's core, up to his elbows in the ugly, black console. Blinding light filled the reactor compartment, radiating from a storm of explosive therleon energy, but it was no longer rushing toward them in a destructive wave. Something held the storm at bay, its devastating force churning and bubbling like the Eye of Jupiter. Off to one side, Feyt crouched immobile, arms raised defensively against the blast and gaping up at him in awe. Disbelief filled the creature's eyes, mirroring the curiosity he'd seen in Xorin's face just minutes before... but that could only mean one thing, and that one thing didn't seem possible.

Only then did Rhys sense the electric tingling that filled his body, flooding into the console through his fingertips. His eyes went wide with shock. The invisible barrier, the one holding the destructive therleon force at bay, had been created by *him*. Now, disbelief welled up inside his chest. This couldn't be possible. Maybe he really was dead. Perhaps he'd become stuck in some bizarre purgatory where he'd be forced to relive his final moments, over and over. He flexed his hands to compress the storm of energy, its bright light intensifying the smaller he made it, dimming when he allowed it to grow.

"It worked. Holy shit, it actually worked!" Rhys whispered, relief and incredulity flooding through him.

When it had mattered most, he'd achieved what Volkerson couldn't draw out of him with force and coercion. A euphoric sense of calm filled him, stripping away the pain and loss he'd felt since BQ3. It was a far cry from the disjointed chaos the machine reaped on him each time before. For a moment, he allowed the tranquility to fill him, washing clean the pestilence that clung to his soul. But what next? Now that he had contained it, what was he supposed to do with this shimmering ball of destruction? If his concentration started to slip, would he be able to regain control in time? He pushed the thought away. He alone was preventing their demise, and even daring to entertain such an idea could be deadly. There had to be a way to dispose of the overloaded core.

"Rhys."

Hearing his name, he tensed, suddenly on edge. That voice! He knew the man to whom it belonged.

"You can't stop me... even if you've learned to control their technology."

Volkerson's words were clear, but where were they coming from? Rhys moved his jaw, felt the shattered, broken pieces of the CIM crunch uncomfortably beneath his skin, and knew the scientist wasn't using the communicator. Somehow, he must've gotten onboard.

"Where are you?!" Rhys screamed in fury, eyes darting around the room. How had Volkerson boarded the ship, and why risk life and limb to be here? For an instant, he had the fleeting desire to release the destructive energy within his grasp if it meant killing the man who'd ruined his life, but something didn't add up. There was nowhere in the room to hide, and by the expression on the Commander's face, he seemed oblivious to the presence of the scientist's disembodied voice.

"Are you so desperate for revenge you'd kill the last of your friends just to see me dead?" Volkerson asked. Rhys twisted around to see where he was hiding, but paused when the words sank in. How could the man have known that's what he'd been thinking?

"You always were a slow learner. I'm not onboard, Rhys. If you release the core now, you'd only be murdering Sekami and Otaan Yabar. The second you interfaced with the grül ship, it formed a bridge between our minds… a network, so to speak. It's what allowed my virus to infect their fleet."

Volkerson was in his head, Rhys realized, boring into his brain like a flesh-eating parasite. It made his skin crawl. He wanted to rip his arms out of the console, to end the invasion into his mind, but if he did that, the barrier around the core would fail. If that happened, they'd all be vaporized. Sekami's death would be on his hands. Despite finally learning to control the machine, he was still locked within the bastard's grasp, and there was nothing he could do about it.

"I've underestimated you. I never expected you to survive all this time. Even if I had, I wouldn't have believed you'd learn to use their technology, to unlock your true potential." Rhys felt the voice change, sensed a maniacal resoluteness creep into its tone. "It's not too late. The grül are still the true enemy. Think about what they've done. Their kind can't be allowed to survive. We alone can stop them."

"They're only here because you killed one and stole their machine!" Rhys shouted. He had heard enough. Volkerson's presumption was sickening, that after all the man had done,

Rhys would still help in his unspeakable quest for genocide. "You murdered our friends... your own partner. The grül destroyed Earth because of you! I hope you burn in hell, monster!"

"MONSTER?" Volkerson roared, his voice consuming the very essence of Rhys's consciousness. "I'll show you a monster, Rhys Kelly!"

Vivid images were forced into Rhys's mind, and he found himself staring through a window at a distant blue-green world, wisps of white cloud streaking its upper atmosphere. Earth... before its desolation. An aching sorrow tugged at his heart seeing the doomed planet. He wanted to reach out, to press his hands longingly against the glass, but seemed unable to move them. Something was wrong. In the window, reflected back at him, was a face. Not his face, but the sharp features and intense gray eyes of Marcus Volkerson. When the face blinked, Rhys blinked, and he understood. This was a memory, and he was watching everything through the scientist's eyes.

As if he were a marionette, his gaze was forced away from the window. He found himself in a cramped room, only slightly bigger than the airlock of Conrad's ship. It was filled with monitoring devices, each one emitting a cacophony of electronic beeps. Rhys recognized some of the equipment. He'd seen it in the lab on Proxima Station. There, hunched over a holoscreen, was Jenco Ryele. His back was turned, and the baukken typed with feverish intensity, utterly focused on the display in front of him. A transparent, pulsating barrier divided the room, and behind it sat... Rhys.

It was strange seeing himself, like some out-of-body experience. His arms were inside the familiar grül machine, grimacing and sweating from the toll his efforts must be exacting. With mounting awe, he watched as a shimmering ball of energy began to take shape in front of the open core. It was beautiful and terrible at the same time, seeing himself use the machine in a way he'd never thought possible.

"Marcus, if he loses control, the *Erebus's* containment won't hold," Jenco reported, his voice tense. "This needs to stop."

"Not yet. We've never come this far." Rhys heard the brusque words escape his own lips but knew they'd been Volkerson's. "If we purge the containment now, the grül will know exactly where to find us. Give him time to disperse it."

"Please," memory-Rhys begged. "Make it stop!"

"Concentrate. You created it. You alone can dissipate its energy," Volkerson urged. "Remember what's at stake. Remember the price of failure!"

"I c-can't... can't hol-hol-hold... can't... *can't... CAN'T!*"

The ball of light grew unstable, and an involuntary expletive escaped Volkerson's lips. Rhys's view swung away from the containment, and fingers that were not his own typed rapidly over a console. A moment later, the words CONTAINMENT PURGE blinked back at him from the screen. Through the window, he saw the glowing sphere hurtle safely out into space... or so he thought. With mounting horror, he watched as its path slowly began to deflect, bending toward the planet in a steepening arc until disappearing behind the horizon. A moment later, in a brilliant flash of reddish light, fire burned through Earth's atmosphere.

Indescribable anguish filled Rhys as he watched it spread, the conflagration growing rapidly until it had engulfed the entire planet. What had he done? He imagined the screams of billions of people as they were blinked out existence, vaporized by an alien technology he'd tried and failed to control. His insides twisted with shame, not wanting to believe the truth about Earth's destruction but knowing in his heart it must be so. He couldn't bear to watch any more, but Volkerson wasn't through with him yet, his consciousness still trapped inside the scientist's memory.

A terrible scream filled his ears, and his view was once again forced away to see Jenco wrestling to subdue a squirming, kicking body. His body. Memory-Rhys had been pulled from the machine and was screaming, fighting tooth and nail against the man trying to keep him under control. Volkerson rushed forward and pulled open a nearby cabinet to retrieve an autoinjector, before jamming it against one of the flailing legs. Their gaze met for a moment, and Rhys saw emptiness in his own eyes, a harrowing shell that had been left by a departure from sanity. Slowly, with dwindling strength in his movements, memory-Rhys's body stilled.

"What have we done?" Jenco asked quietly, still grasping the limp form. His voice trembled. "Marcus, why did we ever think we could control this?"

The man's hands were shaking when he finally let go of Rhys's arms. As if in a daze, he stood up, seemed to hesitate, then walked purposefully toward the door.

"Where are you going?" Rhys heard Volkerson call. He was still kneeling next to his own sedated body.

"To the cockpit. We need to tell someone, Marcus. The G.C. We need to turn the grül machine over to them."

With a few quick strides, Volkerson moved to block the door.

"Jenco, let's think about this. We're closer to our goal than we've ever been. We only need a little more ti–"

Looking through the eyes of his surrogate, Rhys saw sudden anger twist the baukken's face. He tried to push past, but Volkerson wouldn't budge, standing squarely in the way of the man's intended path. Hands came up to gently grip Jenco's shoulders, but he brushed them roughly away.

"We just committed genocide! Against an entire planet... *your* planet! How can you still think what we're doing is justified?" he demanded, trying once again to leave the room. This time when Volkerson's hands came up, they shoved Jenco forcefully backward. Caught off guard, the baukken staggered, tripped over Rhys's prone body, and toppled to the floor. A look of surprise plastered his face.

"What the hell is wrong with you?" he asked, incredulous.

Getting up, he charged toward Volkerson, toward Rhys, but the bigger man was ready. He deflected Jenco's blow and jammed the autoinjector into the side of the baukken's neck. A look of surprise passed over Jenco's face, and a few seconds later, he sank to his knees, the contents of the serum quickly taking hold. Crouching down, Volkerson grasped his partner by the throat and began to squeeze. Rhys wanted to yell, to release his grip, to do anything but watch helplessly as the light faded from Jenco's eyes.

When the baukken's lifeless body stopped spasming, he heard Volkerson's breath, his own breath, coming in short, quaking gasps. He felt nauseous, as if he himself had coldly listened to Jenco's final choking gasps for air. Powerless to end Volkerson's horrific invasion into his mind, Rhys watched as their collective consciousness moved toward the prone form of his memory-self. They stumbled to their knees next to the body and pulled back a single eyelid. Only a weak moan escaped the lips of his sedated form.

"Don't worry," he heard Volkerson say. "When this is over, you won't remember a thing."

The scene dissolved around him, and Rhys found himself back inside the grül reactor room. Light danced off the walls, and he felt two hands shaking him roughly by the shoulders. Commander Feyt's stricken face swam into view.

"The containment is going to breach!" the creature bellowed, pointing urgently toward the rippling sphere of energy. "You must open the firing aperture!"

"I... can't..."

Everything Rhys had just seen weighed on him like a mountain. Earth... his own origins... what he'd done... it all overloaded his mind the same way Volkerson had overloaded the ship's core. Stripped of the focus he so desperately needed, he watched tongues of blue-white flame break through the barrier restraining the reactor's destructive force. It was only a matter of time before the invisible confines failed, and the fiery, billowing contents inside spilled out to consume the helpless lifeforms onboard. As they had been nearly four years ago, needless deaths would once again be the price of his failure.

Through the haze of his torment, Rhys still sensed Volkerson's consciousness. He could feel the man's triumph, his elation, his sanctimonious belief in his own righteousness as the therleon network bridged the gap between their minds. It sickened him. He wanted it to end, but the only way he knew how spelled certain death for him, for Otaan Yabar, and for Sekami. With his will to fight dwindling, Rhys realized he'd only delayed the inevitable.

Helplessness filled him as he sensed the final act of Volkerson's plan carried out; the bridge doors locked closed, and the infected machine freed from whatever shielding its umbilical provided. It was a killing stroke. Everyone on the bridge, grül or baukken or Hanekaarian alike, was about to be massacred.

"SEKAMI!"

The howl burst from his chest in a thundering roar. Desperate to save his friends, Rhys forced every fiber of his being to concentrate, animal instinct focusing his mind. The churning cloud of therleon particles shrank to the size of a fist, white-hot light radiating from the densely compacted core. *You must open the firing aperture.* Feyt's words resonated in his ears, and in a moment of clarity, he understood the Commander's instruction. This wasn't just the reactor room. It was the very heart of the ship, the place where deadly, planet-killing energy originated. He willed the mechanism to open, and like a giant iris, a hole began to form in the far bulkhead of the massive room. It twisted open, growing larger and larger, until nothing seemed to separate them from the vacuum of space. A star-dotted expanse stretched out in all directions, empty except for one thing. There, floating directly ahead of them and glinting in the light of a billion stars, was the *Hermes*. With great effort, Rhys forced the glowing core through the open aperture.

He held his breath as the shimmering ball of energy flew soundlessly toward the scientist's ship, and in a blinding display of blue-green light, the *Hermes* and its deranged occupant were vaporized. There was no resounding boom. No inescapable shockwave. Nothing but a faint, dwindling aura remained. Once more, Rhys was alone, the presence in his head vanished without a trace. Volkerson, the man responsible for a galaxy in shambles, was dead.

Numbly, Rhys pulled his arms from the interface and stared disbelievingly at the back of his hands. He'd done it. Somehow, against insurmountable odds, he'd survived. He wouldn't have guessed it was possible, not with the information he possessed. It felt surreal, knowing his success was what had allowed him to live long enough to see this moment. The thought made something tug at the back of his mind, and he remembered. Sekami. Without delay, Rhys hurried back to the pod with Commander Feyt. *Please don't be dead*, he prayed, dread mounting ever higher the nearer their destination they came. Reaching the bridge, they found the doors still locked and struggled to force them open. Behind the hatch, a truly gruesome scene met their eyes.

The bodies of Xorin's soldiers lay everywhere, blood pooling around their lifeless corpses. A few were still alive, moaning piteously from the effects of Volkerson's hijacked machine. Rhys didn't care. How many billions had died at the hands of these monsters, he didn't know, but a taste of their own horrific weaponry seemed like just retribution. Frantically, he searched everywhere for Sekami, hoping against hope that somehow, she and the Hanekaarian had survived the onslaught of deadly therleon energy.

When he found her, she was concealed beneath Otaan Yabar's broken form. They were hidden behind a thick bulkhead, as far from the machine as possible. Racing over, Rhys pulled the lifeless corpse off her and gently eased the Hanekaarian to the ground. Sekami was covered in blood, much of it belonging to the Otaan Yabar, but she was far from unharmed. Dark green rivulets dripped from her ears and nose, and a trickle ran down her chin from the corner of her mouth. He cradled her unresponsive body in his arms.

"Sekami," he whispered, heart pounding in his chest. *Don't be dead. Please, don't be dead*, he prayed. "It's over. You have to wake up."

Her eyes were closed, and she didn't move. Rhys placed his fingers against her neck feeling for a pulse but couldn't locate the telltale *thump-thump, thump-thump*. Slowly, the realization of his utter isolation began to sink in. Despair washed over him, and he buried his face in the woman's shoulder. Everyone he cared about had been murdered. Conrad, Marasa, Otaan Yabar... and now, Sekami. Hot, angry tears poured from his eyes and mixed with the red and green blood soaking the woman's shirt. A muffled cry escaped his lips, the effort to contain it making his body shake. Kneeling there, holding her in arms, he felt something soft on his cheek. A hand. His sobs caught in his throat, and he raised his head, not daring to believe. Sekami's eyes were cracked open, and her fingers gently caressed his face.

"Otaan Yabar," she whispered, "he tried to shield me."

Tears ran into Rhys's beard, his voice too strangled to reply, and he embraced her tightly. A weak cough escaped her lips, and he loosened his grip. Dropping her hand from his cheek, she pointed back toward the center of the room, at one of the lifeless bodies littering the deck.

"Their captain."

As gently as he could, Rhys slid out from under Sekami and propped her against the wall. He walked to where she had pointed, slipping across the bloody deck to look for himself. There, in a puddle of his own sanguineous fluids, was Xorin, the powerful warrior reduced to nothing more than a mutilated carcass. Feyt stepped toward him, and he looked up into the Commander's weathered face.

"I've kept my end of the bargain," Rhys said, refusing to break eye contact with the towering alien. "Will you let us leave?"

Feyt regarded him for a long time before speaking.

"Fleet Captain Xorin was the most fearsome warrior the grül-barvoc have ever known. His efforts were only to keep our people from traveling down a path to oblivion..." the Commander began. Rhys bit back the urge to scream at Feyt, to tell him the Captain was nothing more than a blood-thirsty animal, "… but I have come to believe his methods were misguided. Those of us who survived the Interloper's attack owe you a life debt."

Feyt crossed an arm over his chest in a kind of salute.

"Whatever else you might be, a part of you will always be grülbarvoc," the creature continued, looking between him and Sekami.

"Then, that's the part we'll try to forget," Rhys replied tersely, revulsed by the reminder of what lived inside him. He fell silent for a moment, wondering what came next. The *Kestrel's* drive had been destroyed, not to mention the gaping hole in the side where the grül had breached the starboard airlock… and what about the last of the grül? He'd just reduced their ship to nothing more than a floating piece of space junk when he ejected the core. "What now?"

He watched Feyt glance around the bridge, taking in the mutilated bodies, the moans of the few surviving warriors, and the deadly machine that had wreaked so much havoc.

"Captain Xorin was born of a time before the Enlightenment. His actions, *our* actions, have gone against everything in this new era of grülbarvoc ideology. There will be consequences. I will take the remainder of his crew and return to Vyreon to face judgement from the High Council," the Commander explained, his voice solemn. He took another look around the room. "Our warship is no longer capable of making the journey home. The vessel we used to board the Interloper's refuge will not have been infected. It can accommodate the few of us who remain."

"What about the machine?" Rhys asked, skeptical of the sincerity of Feyt's words. "And us? You destroyed our engines."

"No, only stalled their matter-antimatter reactions. I trust you will be able to reboot your system without lasting effect," the Commander replied. "As for the machine, I cannot allow it to remain in your possession. It will return to Vyreon with me, isolated within a containment, so the Interloper's virus can be studied."

As far as Rhys was concerned, that was fine by him. He wanted nothing more to do with the goddamn machine anyway. Without another word to Feyt, he turned his back and walked to where Sekami rested, breathing softly, her eyes closed. Gently, he helped her to her feet and guided them past the few grül that remained alive. Struggling their way toward the lift, they stepped inside, never bothering to look back.

Rhys hurried them toward the *Kestrel*, a sense of unreality filling him at the stark difference between their departure from the grül ship and the manner in which they'd arrived. Everything seemed surreal. He climbed through the ragged hole in the airlock and felt Sekami hesitate when he tried to lead her toward the cockpit. Turning, he saw her reach out for an illuminated control panel just inside the inner hatch and helped her toward it, watching her fingers move slowly over its glowing surface. With the final press of a button, a protective field snapped across the outer airlock door, sealing the breached hull.

Back in the cockpit, he deposited Sekami into the pilot's chair, and she began rebooting the propulsion system. As promised, the engines came online, and before long, the drive's telltale whine imparted them with a comforting sense of familiarity. Looking around, though, he felt intense sorrow. Here they were on Conrad's ship, without him… without the others.

That Rhys should survive only because of what he was pained him beyond words. Guilt like he'd felt at Anne's suicide, merely a fabrication in a madman's desperate crusade, gnawed at him while Sekami maneuvered the *Kestrel* through the transparent barrier and away from the gigantic warship.

It wasn't long before a small boarding craft, carrying the last survivors from Volkerson's attack, exited the mothership like a wasp from its hive. A black, shapeless anomaly formed in front of the departing vessel, bending the light of distant stars around it.

In a moment, the tiny craft flew toward the wormhole and was gone.

"Do you trust them?" Rhys asked uneasily, still gazing out the cockpit window.

"I don't know who to trust anymore," Sekami replied in a somber voice. Turning, he knelt in front of her and took the woman's hands in his.

"You can trust me."

Sekami smiled.

# EPILOGUE

A SOFT HISS of vapor escaped the chamber's periphery as Commander Feyt pushed open the lid of his sleeping pod. He felt groggy, a state of being he was typically unafflicted with. The return journey from the Interloper's distant galaxy had been uneventful and had allowed him too much time to brood over the events of the past several months; how they had detected a mysterious surge of therleon particles, how it had led them to the Interloper's hidden station, and how his final trap had been sprung on their unsuspecting fleet… it all weighed heavily on Feyt in a way he'd never thought possible.

Most troubling, he'd almost allowed himself to be led astray by Captain Xorin's teachings of the Old Ways. Privately, Feyt still saw credence in some of the fallen warrior's beliefs, but too much was at stake to entertain such dangerous ideals. He knew the High Council was watching his every move, analyzing every word he spoke and those of the crew's few surviving members. Their salvation, *his* salvation, the Commander reminded himself, had come from one of the very creatures the Captain had proclaimed was nothing more than a simple-minded beast, of no more use than fodder for the Rhonath.

Feyt had already begun to doubt Xorin's fitness for leadership, even before the strange human-grülbarvoc amalgamation, the one called Rhys Kelly, saved their lives. He'd seen the madness growing, the unhinged obsession in the Captain's eyes after nearly thirty-three cycles in pursuit of the Interloper... and he'd nearly been convinced the Old Ways were the only means by which the grülbarvoc might be led back from oblivion. He realized much of what had driven the Küddarian Brotherhood was fear, though they would never have admitted it. Perhaps, they never knew it was there, marching them forward and driving them to stave off the Sickness at all costs. He imagined it would be terrible when its symptoms began to afflict him... his strength and vision fading... his bones weakening... his own body eating itself from the inside... it would come for them all, in the end.

Stepping out of his sleeping pod, the Commander stretched, his back stiff from the previous night's restlessness, and pulled worn leather garments over his muscled form. He had another debriefing with the High Council, and anything other than punctuality would not be tolerated. When he and his crew had first returned to Vyreon, they'd been whisked off to give an exhaustive report. Feyt had endured their impotent rage at Xorin's final acts of defiance, had explained how the Interloper hadn't died on Proxima Station, and that the machine was still at large. He told them everything they wanted to hear, over and over, until it seemed as though no matter how many times he said it, the Council would never be satisfied with his answers. Nearly a full cycle later, he would once again be required to endure their incomprehension. He straightened the last of his garments and left his chambers.

When he arrived at the meeting place, the young warrior standing guard snapped a salute, then ushered him inside. The room was empty. Feyt waited, patiently looking up toward the raised dais on which the High Council would sit, until the scheduled appointment time came and went. *Captain Xorin was right to detest these fools*, he thought, becoming more annoyed with each passing minute.

The Council demanded his punctuality but would never hold

themselves to the same standard. None, as far as he knew, had ever been in battle. These were career politicians, the formative members of the Enlightenment, who had been allowed to avoid the life of a grülbarvoc warrior. They had shunned indoctrination of military discipline, and it showed. Not that Feyt was bitter about that. He understood, especially considering recent events, the need for diplomacy, understood why these politicians were a necessary inconvenience.

If the grülbarvoc had continued along the path of manifest destiny taught by the Küddarian Brotherhood, it would only have been a matter of time before some faraway race stood against them... someone who might prove a formidable adversary... someone like the Interloper. Yet, the High Council's buffoonery had allowed three zealots faithful to the Küddish Teachings to escape, a mistake that had set off a chain of events lasting nearly thirty-three cycles.

Eventually, a hatch on the far wall slid open and in walked the eleven doddering members of the High Council. Lacking the restorative effects of the Rhonath, each was in various states of decay from the Sickness. Their sallow faces were unreadable as they took up positions on the dais. None of them spoke, only looked down at Feyt like wizened vultures over a fresh carcass. The Commander stared back, unfazed by their lack of decorum. He'd been kept waiting this long. What did a little more lost time matter now? A Councilmember named Gyvan cleared his throat.

"Commander, we have come to a troubling conclusion." Feyt waited as a mutter of agreement ran through the Council's ranks, its members trading furtive glances. "The High Council believes the actions of the late Exalted Leader and his pawn, Fleet Captain Xorin, have put the grülbarvoc at risk."

"At risk from whom?" Feyt asked, a frown creasing his leathery brow. "The Interloper is dead, and we have recovered the stolen machine. I do not believe Rhys Kelly and Sekami Ryele have the means, nor the desire, to seek vengeance against us.

When we parted ways, I felt they understood Xorin's actions were his own, not the will of the grülbarvoc High Coun–"

"We will address their continued existence shortly," Gyvan interrupted, "but the more pressing matter is the transmission we have intercepted from within the Interloper's galaxy. It seems the sudden disappearance of Xorin's fleet has prompted its inhabitants to come out of hiding. Their government has partially reformed. Those left are picking up the pieces of the destruction wrought by the Exalted Leader's misguided attempt to keep us hidden from view. His efforts have served only to do the exact opposite. There have been rumblings, based on the messages our surveillance analysts picked up, that the Galactic Commonwealth seeks retribution for what was done to it."

Feyt considered this a moment. The thought didn't scare him. He'd seen firsthand how ineffectual their armaments had been against the grülbarvoc. With such rudimentary weapons, the entire G.C. could mount an assault and be repelled by a single grülbarvoc flotilla. A thought itched the back of his mind, and an image of Xorin's mutilated corpse laying on the deck of his own bridge came floating to the front. Feyt caught himself. That was the same dangerous complacency that had doomed the Captain to his horrific fate. He couldn't allow himself to fall victim to the same mistakes.

"Then, we must take every precaution. Even if the G.C. possessed weapons to rival our own, which I know personally they do not, their armies would not know where to find us," the Commander replied. "Isolation from their galaxy will prevent further confrontation–"

"You are missing the larger picture, Commander." It was the second time Gyvan had interrupted him, the second time today he shared Xorin's dislike of the Council. "Your own report has shown them to be more than just mindless animals, as Exalted Leader Küddar believed. The Interloper vanquished one of our most highly trained fleets, and he was just one man... a harbinger of what may come. If such a mind exists in a galaxy believed to lack intelligent life, then there must be others."

"The Interloper possessed a piece of our technology," Feyt reminded the Council, an edge to his voice. "Without that, he would not have been able to infect our fleet, would not have had the means to murder our brethren. Our people were desperate in the face of vanishing resources, a desperation that led most of them to accept your promise of science over ancient rituals like the Rhonath. Yet, it was your own short-sightedness that allowed the machine to fall into enemy hands. Instead of finding a way to bridge the gap between the grülbarvoc who clung to the Old Ways and those embracing the New, you turned to incarceration and summary execution! You preach the importance of your own progressive ideals, without any meaningful result, yet doom those who hold to the practices our kind have followed for thousands of generations."

At his words, an indignant rabble broke out between the members of the Council, some yelling down at him, pointing their fingers or pounding their fists on the dais. Feyt was angry. He was stuck between two sides, the Old and the New, each as intolerant as the other. How had he gotten here? Only a cycle ago, everything had made sense. He'd had a purpose, a mission. Now, he felt conflicted. With the Captain gone, he recognized Xorin's teachings for what they were… dangerous radicalism, a belief that the grülbarvoc were superior to all others and that their survival was ordained by destiny. The Küddarian Brotherhood had allowed their species to consume every available resource, every weaker lifeform, until nothing was left to sustain their way of life.

It was the same self-righteous mindset he saw embedded in the High Council but on the opposite end of the political spectrum; a wanton refusal to accept or believe anything that hadn't originated from within their own ideological echo chamber. Gyvan, however, seemed unfazed and held up a hand to silence the uproar.

"Be careful, Commander. Such declarations could have

weighty repercussions," he said lightly. The threat hung in the air, pressure building inside the room as Feyt held Gyvan's gaze. When the Councilmember finally blinked, the uncomfortable tension dissipated. "Squabbling will get us nowhere. This meeting has been called to inform you of our decisions."

"What decisions?"

"With the looming threat of retaliation, we believe the best course of action would be to make contact with the G.C., to explain that Xorin acted as a rogue agent, that his actions were not condoned by the grülbarvoc High Council," Gyvan explained. "For their own good, they must abandon their quest for vengeance against our people. As you yourself have said, their weaponry is no match for ours."

Feyt couldn't believe what he was hearing. Was Gyvan serious? The Council wanted to contact an alien government, one he himself had helped terrorize for many cycles, and try to explain why countless of their people had been murdered? It was insane... idiotic. Not only would the G.C. not care who was responsible, it would probably incense them further, drive them to do something stupid... like search out Vyreon and mount an attack. Then, the grülbarvoc would have no choice but to respond... or was that the Council's plan all along? *No*, Feyt thought, shaking his head. The High Council would do everything in its power to run away from a fight, and in this case, that would be the right decision.

"I must strongly object," Feyt replied. "Any attempt to curb their bloodlust would serve only to strengthen their resolve... and in case you have already forgotten, they cannot understand our language."

"That brings us to our second decision," the Councilmember said, ignoring Feyt's protestations. "As the ranking member of Xorin's surviving crew, you possess valuable knowledge of the events leading up to and resulting in, his death. If the G.C. is hell-bent on exacting revenge, as you say, they will investigate any means by which to gain an advantage. We cannot allow a single piece of our technology or member of our species to remain in their galaxy."

"Of course not," Feyt replied, confused as to why Gyvan was bringing this up. What did the Council think Xorin's fleet had been doing the last thirty-three cycles? "We have already recovered the machine and all the escaped grülbarvoc exiles have been accounted for."

"I am speaking of the Interloper's creations... Rhys Kelly and Sekami Ryele, as you call them."

Feyt was dumbstruck. The Interloper's companions were the last things he expected to come up. What purpose would there be to bring them here? Their existence, while interesting, was far from pivotal, strategically speaking. He opened his mouth to reply but couldn't think of anything to say and closed it again.

"They are born of grülbarvoc genetics, and so, they too must be brought back into the sphere of our control. They cannot be allowed to fall into enemy hands," the Councilmember said. "If the G.C. discovers such a pair exists, they may try to exploit them... or perhaps, these creatures are not as forgiving as you think and volunteer to help the G.C."

"Again, I must protest," Feyt replied. He'd found his voice once more. "Whatever else Rhys Kelly and his companion might be, they are the reason I am still alive. Those few of us who survived the Interloper's attack owe them a life debt. I cannot repay that sacred obligation with abduction and captivity."

"This is not imprisonment, Commander. They would be free to live among us. You claim they inherited the same genetic imprint of our language as do all grülbarvoc. If that is true, these creatures could act as a bridge between our people and those of the G.C.," Gyvan clarified, sharing a cautious glance with the other members of the Council. "If their government decides it wants retribution against the grülbarvoc, and mount some asinine assault, they may force our hand. The Council does not wish to destroy what is left of their civilization because they harbor some misplaced yearning for revenge. If he is made to understand our position, Rhys Kelly may well be the key to preventing a war."

Feyt was silent as he mulled over the Council's request. It was true that if the Interloper had found a way to kill the grülbarvoc, what prevented someone else from doing the same? He thought of Xorin's vessel, floating broken and abandoned in a far-off galaxy, and the wealth of knowledge that might be gleaned from its remains. With only a boarding craft left at his disposal, he hadn't possessed the means to destroy it. If the G.C. found the warship, found Rhys, would they be able to learn enough to become a formidable enemy? From what he'd seen, the alien races residing in that distant galaxy were nothing if not resourceful... and the Council was right. The G.C. wouldn't just sit by and let the injustices done to them go unanswered. *Would Rhys Kelly aid in his government's efforts?* Feyt wondered. Unlikely. Not after learning what the Interloper had done... but would he care if the entire grülbarvoc race was wiped from existence? Again, probably not, and Feyt couldn't blame him.

"There is something else. Xorin's warship, while effectively disabled, is still intact. With only a boarding craft left uninfected, I possessed no weaponry capable of destroying it," he reported. "From what I have learned during my tenure as Captain Xorin's Executive Officer, I agree with your assessment of the alien government. They will not simply forget. I do not, however, believe Rhys Kelly nor Sekami Ryele will help the grülbarvoc."

"This mission is not about helping us, Commander Feyt. We have proven our might is far superior to theirs. This is about preventing their government from doing something that might instigate a war... from using our technology and those who share our genetic superiority to become a legitimate threat," Gyvan replied. The Councilmember's voice was hard. Determined. "You must bring them back so we can make them understand it is not only our existence that is threatened... if the G.C. continues along this path, it may spell annihilation for us all."

Something in Gyvan's tone had triggered an alarm inside Feyt, and he sensed a plot hidden beneath the High Council's secretive glances. Was using Rhys Kelly to broker peace between their governments truly the reason for this idiotic mission? He doubted it, somehow, but Gyvan's face betrayed nothing as to the Council's ulterior motives. As much as he disagreed with their stated reasoning, he would indeed seek out Rhys Kelly and his baukken companion. If he didn't, the Council would just send someone else... someone who didn't owe the human a life debt... someone the human wouldn't trust... someone who might kill or harm the human if he resisted. This was the only way Feyt could stay in the game and the only way he might ensure Rhys Kelly's survival.

"I will do as you ask," the Commander replied, keeping his voice level.

"We are glad to hear it. First and foremost, Xorin's ship must be destroyed. The Galactic Commonwealth cannot be allowed access to another shred of grülbarvoc technology. Then, you will track down the last of the Interloper's companions and bring them back to Vyreon. We have prepared a stealth ship for you and a crew of our most-trusted warriors. You will leave at once," Gyvan told him. For a moment, he gazed down from the dais, and the Commander saw a strange glint in the Councilmember's yellowing eyes. "Do not make the same mistakes as your predecessor... *Captain*."

Feyt heard the new title attached to his name, but instead of the pride he'd imagined at earning his own command, he felt only foreboding. He'd been given a captainship because Xorin died a madman, he was being sent on a mission he didn't agree with, and his crew, loyal only to the Council, would be watching his every move as if he were a criminal awaiting judgement... but there was nothing he could do about it. Snapping a salute, Captain Feyt turned on his heel and walked from the council chambers.

WHEN HE REACHED the designated hangar, he climbed aboard the stealth ship to find the crew already waiting for him, positioned in front of their consoles and ready for departure. He felt their eyes on him, each of the eight stony faces unfamiliar. Feyt understood. They didn't know him, and in their minds, he hadn't earned the right to lead them. These warriors had never seen him fight, knew only that he had returned to Vyreon, beaten and shamed, after a seemingly endless campaign in search of an elusive prey that had nearly killed him. Better to die in battle than returned dishonored. With a heavy weight pressing down on him, Feyt sat in the cockpit's only empty chair and felt the restraints' organic tendrils crawl over his shoulders, securing him in his seat.

"Ready for departure… *Captain*," one of the warriors said. He heard disdain in her voice but ignored it and gave the command to lift off.

Feeling a gentle hum beneath him, Feyt watched the yellowish atmosphere of Vyreon fall away, replaced by a black veil dotted with countless pinpoints of light. Far in the distance, the twin stars that gave life to his home world burned brightly against the void. *How long?* he wondered pensively. How long before he felt their warmth on his face again? Thirty-three cycles pursuing the Interloper had left him yearning for a near-forgotten home, and now that he'd returned, destiny would once again take him elsewhere.

Feyt did not understand the concept of fair and unfair. Orders were orders, and he'd agreed to this mission of his own volition. Nevertheless, he hoped only a fraction of the time he'd spent away from Vyreon would pass before he could return. Staring into the infinite distance ahead of them, Captain Feyt conveyed the coordinates of Xorin's ship to the navigational computer and turned his thoughts toward their objective. As if force of will could provide an answer to the path that lay ahead, his mind reached out. *Where are you, Rhys Kelly?*

*The End*

# ACKNOWLEDGMENTS

This book would not have been possible without the unyielding love and support from my friends and family. First and foremost, I would like to thank my wife Kelsey for the countless hours and frequent bleary-eyed predawn conversations listening to me agonize over the minutiae of *The Harbinger*. Her patience in allowing me to bounce off her every idea passing through my gray matter has been invaluable these last years.

To my friend John, who helped shape my writing into something coherent, always motivating me through the dull and often lonely trips aboard the *USNS Sisler*. The ship's lounge will never again see so much raw, creative failings as the hours whittled away over our own respective labors of love.

My mother-in-law, Sheryl, who has read every version, minute change, and often abandoned rewrites of entire chapters, perspectives, and, in effect, the whole book, was patient through each painstaking amendment. With each change, her support and feedback was always thoughtful, timely, and most importantly, honest.

Countless others supported me through this journey. Their feedback helped hone my writing from the cringe-worthy ramblings of a modestly educated mariner to something (hopefully) enjoyable to read. I won't be able to thank everyone who deserves it, mostly due to my own deficient memory banks, but I will try nonetheless. My parents and siblings, Kayla D., Alex S., Matt L., Nick R., Ken M., Bobby H., Brad B., and Tyler M. For everyone else, thank you a thousand times over.

# ABOUT THE AUTHOR

H.K. Farrell is an emerging author of speculative science fiction. He is a systems engineer by trade, having worked in the U.S. Merchant Marine for nearly a decade before hanging up his coveralls in 2019. When not sparring with his toddler or wandering the Montana wilderness, he toils at his computer conjuring fantastical worlds of technology, mayhem, and extraterrestrials.

www.hkfarrell.com

facebook.com/h.k.farrell.official

instagram.com/h.k.farrell

tiktok.com/@h.k.farrell